LOOK BEHIND YOU

LOOK BEHIND YOU

A Suspense Novel

Sarah Haley Head

[Handwritten inscription: 1.27-04 To Dan Doughty Thanks for your interest in my book. Hope you enjoy Sarah Haley Head]

iUniverse, Inc.
New York Lincoln Shanghai

Look Behind You

A Suspense Novel

iUniverse, Inc.

For information address:
iUniverse, Inc.
2021 Pine Lake Road, Suite 100
Lincoln, NE 68512
www.iuniverse.com

ISBN: 0-595-28370-5 (pbk)
ISBN: 0-595-65775-3 (cloth)

Printed in the United States of America

ACKNOWLEDGMENTS

This book has been so long in the making that there have been many people involved in getting it to its final form. There were, however, some who worked with me to the point of tedium, proving many times over their patience and commitment to see the job to its end.

My youngest son, Paul, played a major role in keeping the computer, the printer, and his mother working. His encouragement as well as the hours of troubleshooting were invaluable. Kudos to you, Paul.

Thanks also to Annabob Parker, a retired English teacher, who searched out my grammatical errors. If any remain, it is my fault. Thanks to Kathy Trower, a special writing friend, who also edited and encouraged. A special thanks to Kim Howell. She gave freely of her computer expertise to do things with the text that I could not. Bless you, Kim.

Others to whom thanks belong are: Sarah Herman, Anne Johnston, Bettye Kyle, Donna Jones, Lois Milner, the members of the Cleburne County Writers' Guild, especially Georgie McIrvin, and to all the others who offered their encouragement for what was at times a discouraging process.

A special thanks to Ned, my beloved, who put up with the scorched meals, the writers' dementia that accompanies deadlines, and the general preoccupation with imaginary people who took so much of my attention from him.

Last, but not least, my thanks to Josh Cook who guided me through the publication readiness process, and to the publishers who worked so hard to get *Look Behind You* from manuscript to book form.

Thanks everyone!

PROLOGUE

▼

Chicago, 1972

Laura Bordeaux carried a bag of groceries in one arm and her twenty-six month old daughter, Binkie, in the other. Careful not to slip on the ice and snow that covered the sidewalk, Laura walked up their front porch steps and put down the paper bag. She dug a key out of her coat pocket and managed to unlock the door. "Here we are, Sweetheart," she told the baby. "We'll be warm in no time."

It had started snowing before daylight, and it had come down steadily all day. In just the past several minutes, the flakes had gotten much thicker, making a white curtain which was difficult to see through. Driving home had been a challenge. Not only had the visibility been poor, but the streets were already slicking over. The temperature had dropped several degrees in the last hour, and the north wind was blowing harder by the minute. The blizzard which was forecast for the Chicago area had arrived.

Laura wasn't worried. There was plenty to eat and only yesterday she had the fuel tank in the cellar filled. With the Lord's help, she and Binkie would manage just fine. They would be safely sheltered from the storm.

She put the groceries on the kitchen table, then released Binkie from her heavy snowsuit. The child immediately headed for her toy box which was kept conveniently in one corner of the room. She pulled out her old Pooh Bear. "Pooh Bear want chockit," she said.

"And I'll bet you want some too," Laura said, smiling at the sweet picture her daughter made dressed in her pink corduroy jumper with her black curls all a-tumble around her face. "Let me put up these things, then all three of us will have hot chocolate."

Even though it was only four o' clock, it was dark as night by the time Laura got their steaming cups of cocoa on the table. The heavy snow storm had blotted out the remaining daylight. Laura lifted Binkie onto the thick catalogs she had placed in one of the chairs then sat down next to her. From her position at the table, she saw for the first time that the door to the cellar was cracked open.

"I thought I felt a draft," she said. "No wonder it's not warm in here."

Binkie nodded her head, as she watched her mother leave the table, continuing her monologue. "I know I closed it after I checked the fuel oil gauge, but I guess I didn't push hard enough. These old doors don't fit like they should, anyway." She bumped the door with her shoulder, as she turned the knob to make sure the latch clicked. "That's got it!" Laura resumed her seat at the table.

The house had been built in the fifties, and she'd traded conveniences, such as smoothly fitting doors, for the more important advantages of being close to her job at Hives Elementary School and the child care center where she'd enrolled Binkie.

Her husband, David, had been killed in the Vietnam War when Laura was five months pregnant. They had met in their Senior year at Chicago's Loyola University, where they were enrolled in education courses. David was working on a secondary teaching degree, and Laura on a elementary degree. Drawn to each other from the moment they met, David and Laura had been inseparable. They were married a few months after they'd both graduated.

The war hung like a black cloud on the horizon of their future. At first, they believed that it would be over before it posed a serious threat to their lives. But the military "action" only became more deadly as the months passed. Then David was called into service. They were allowed six months of marriage, conducted on his leaves of absence, before he was shipped overseas. Laura discovered she was pregnant two weeks after he left, and received the notice of his death four-and-a-half months later.

For a brief time, Laura wanted to die, too. But when she felt the little one kicking inside her, so alive and vulnerable, she began to look forward to holding in her arms the product of her and David's intense love for each other. Since Binkie's birth, Laura resented every moment that kept her away from her precious child.

The wind had grown even stronger. It howled as it passed under the eaves of the house, rattling windows and threatening to whisk away the weak warmth of the furnace.

"I'll give you your bathe," she said, "then we'll have a soup picnic in the bedroom where it's warmer." She got up to rinse the cups out at the sink.

Binkie clapped her hands, smiling with delight. "Ohhh, pic-pic!"

The small child watched as Laura heated soup from a can and poured it into a wide-mouthed thermos, then gathered apples, crackers, and cheese on a tray. "I'll get you into the crib first." She carried Binkie up the stairs to their bedroom. After placing the child in her crib, she said, "I'll be right back, Sweetheart." Binkie leaned against the top rail, apparently content to wait.

Laura was halfway down the stairs before she noticed that the kitchen light was off. She looked back up the stairs where the light shone brightly from the bedroom door. The electricity was obviously still on. Had the kitchen bulb burned out, or had she automatically turned off the light? Laura walked to the bottom of the stairs and across to the kitchen door. Before she could check the switch, she heard a bumping sound behind her. Swinging around, she saw that a man stood across from her in the living room door, his bulk filling its frame. For a second, Laura froze, her mind not fully comprehending the man's presence. He took a step toward her, allowing the light from upstairs to reveal his face. She recognized him.

"What are you doing here?" Laura demanded, fear making her voice sharp. She began to move backwards toward the foot of the stairs. There was a telephone in her bedroom.

With a grunt he moved toward her, allowing her to see a large knife in his left hand. Total panic sent Laura flying up the stairs to her bedroom. She reached the door and flung it shut, but he was too fast for her to get it locked. He knocked the door open with such force, that Laura flew backwards, cracking her head on the footboard of her bed before landing on the floor.

Her vision darkened, but she struggled to remain conscious.

Laura managed to get back on her feet. She wanted to get between him and her baby, but again, he was too quick. The man pushed her back down onto the floor. He knelt beside her and, as he raised his arm high into the air, the knife she'd seen downstairs glinted coldly before it plunged into her stomach. The pain took Laura's breath away, but the instinct to survive and to protect her child gave her the strength to wrench herself from the man's hold. Momentarily startled at finding this thin slip of a woman free of his grasp, he didn't immediately grab her again.

O Lord, please help me! She cried out silently as, in a surge of desperation, she grabbed her dresser bench and heaved it through the nearby window, screaming for help. It faced her neighbor's house and maybe, just maybe, they could hear her.

Laura heard the glass shatter and felt the cold wind pour into the bedroom like liquid ice. Then the man grabbed her by a handful of her long hair and again pushed her to the floor. This time he straddled her body with the massive weight of his, making certain she wouldn't get away a second time.

She could hear Binkie screaming and knew that her daughter was as terrified as she. *I don't know why you're allowing this to happen, Lord,* she prayed, *but please keep my baby safe. Please, Lord, keep my baby safe.*

The repeating sting of the knife drained her of all her strength, so Laura could only look at her baby's tear-drenched face and little reaching hands. Then Laura felt a warmth spread over her. She no longer felt the pain or the cold. As she sank into a soft and comforting place, she heard David's voice say, "It's okay, Sweetheart. Our baby won't be harmed." Laura's lovely smile spread across her face, as she looked for the last time at her baby's sweet face

The man, who had raised the knife for another strike, drew back in surprise. What made this woman smile while he was literally butchering her? What kind of person was she, that she robbed him of the surge of pleasure which was supposed to be his at this very moment of her death? He stood up and backed toward the door, his intention to also kill the baby forgotten. It was as if another presence had entered the room. Looking nervously behind him, he turned, then ran quickly down the stairs and out of the house, leaving the door open behind him. After a moment, the door slammed shut behind him.

*   *   *   *

"I'm telling you, Jake, I heard a woman screaming." Gloria Manchetti pushed the mute button on the television set and leaned forward in her chair to listen.

"Aw, it's just the wind." Her husband lay fully reclined in his matching chair, his beer belly mounded under his white tee shirt like that of a pregnant woman. "You're always hearing something when the wind blows like this. 'Jake, go see if someone's at the door,' 'Jake, I heard someone upstairs," he mimicked her. But he couldn't deny the crash of glass they both heard just then. "That sounds like it's coming from Mrs. Bordeaux's house," he said, pulling his chair upright. "You don't suppose she'd got some man over there she's fighting with, do you?"

"That sweet thing ain't got no boyfriend, and you know it." Gloria was up from her chair and on her way to look out the window. "Lord, look at that. I believe her window's broken. I can see the curtains flapping."

Jake crowded in next to his wife to get a look. He could see the jagged glass that remained in the lit upstairs window of the Bordeaux house. He didn't stop to argue with his wife when she said, "Call the police, Jake. Something bad's happened over there."

The police were quick to respond in spite of the snowstorm. At a pounding on their front door, Jake opened it to a burley uniformed policeman, who introduced himself as Officer Mangrove. He asked a few terse questions, as he scribbled on a note pad, he said, "We've got men at the Bordeaux house now. I want you to stay right here in case there's something else I need to ask."

"We're not likely to go anywhere in this storm, Officer," Jake said as Mangrove quickly disappeared into the thick curtain of snow.

The other officers had found Laura's blood-soaked body on the floor of the upstairs bedroom and her small child lying in her crib. The baby was hoarse from screaming and could only whisper over and over again, "I want my mommy."

The investigators all felt that if the baby didn't die of pneumonia it would be a miracle. Officer Ellen Bentlow made it her duty to ride with the child in the ambulance. She later told her fellow officers that the child remained as cold as a chunk of ice in spite of the warmth of the ambulance and the blanket in which they wrapped her.

Later, Ellen said, "I'm just glad she'd too young to remember her mother being killed." The horror of the young woman's death weighed heavily on Ellen's mind. She had seen violent death before, but nothing like the obscene butchery performed on that young woman's body. They would be looking for a monster, and she, for one, wanted to help bring him in.

The next of kin, the victim's sister-in-law, Leigh Bordeaux Nelson, had taken the baby home with her. The following year the man who murdered Laura, the fuel delivery man, was arrested. His own wife turned him in. She told police that he had come home on the night of the Bordeaux murder with a bloody butcher knife. He had thrown it into the kitchen sink and demanded that she wash it. He was so certain she would obey him, she said, that he walked away without seeing what she did.

She had wrapped the knife with newspaper and hid it behind the potato bin. It stayed there until he put her in the hospital with the worst beating yet. He had asked where she had put the knife, and she told him she threw it away. She sustained a broken jaw, a broken rib, a serious concussion, and cuts and contusions all over her body. When she was dismissed from the hospital, she went home, got the knife, and took it to the police station. The blood on the knife matched the samples of Laura's blood.

Two years later, John Macon Rider was convicted, not only of Laura's murder, but also that of two other young mothers. After his conviction and death sentence, Rider claimed that he had killed eleven other women. All of them had been young and each had a small child. The police began searching files from several states to verify his claims, hoping to close on unsolved cases in states where Rider had said he committed his evil acts. Six years later, Rider was executed.

By that time, Leigh and Binkie, who was now called by her real name, Amy, had moved to Ashley Springs, Arkansas. Leigh, who had lost her husband to cancer just a year before Laura's death, had chosen the town because Laura had talked so much about the Ozark Mountain area where she and David had gone on their honeymoon. Leigh thought it would be a safe place in which to rear her brother's child.

CHAPTER 1

▼

June, 2004

On the last evening of his life, Walter Thurmond sought the relative coolness of the white latticed gazebo on his back lawn. Corbin Creek, which lay at the foot of his lawn some hundred and fifty feet downhill from where he sat, ran through his property and divided the lawn from his pasture lands. Frogs gathered in the cool water, croaking in alternating stanzas, providing a curtain of white noise that shut out other sounds of the dying day.

Walter sat in the bench swing seat that was suspended on two chains from the center of the gazebo ceiling. He arranged his newspaper to better catch the last rays of the setting sun. Donald Mercer, Walter's closest friend, had made both the front page and the obituary column in the weekly issue of the Ashley Springs Gazette.

Six days earlier, Don was found outside his house in the back yard. He was lying on the ground beneath the open door of the fuse box. The newspaper article described huge splashes of blood on the wall of his white brick house, and how the ground around the body was soaked in more blood. Walter grimaced as he read the specifics of the crime scene. Evidently, the news people had gotten there before the sheriff secured the area.

Don had bought a large, cattle ranch a few years back. It was his ranch manager who found Don's body when he stopped by for the day's orders. The man had placed a call to the sheriff's office on his truck phone. Somehow, the news media had picked up that call, and Walter wondered how many clues had been destroyed by the carelessness of the eager beaver reporters. He meant to speak to Sheriff Morgan about his methods of security.

Walter rattled the paper in his agitation, and continued to read the rest of the story. A police source speculated that the killer approached Don from behind and slashed his throat so deeply that his head was almost severed from his body. He would speak to the police chief, too. To Walter's mind, they were mighty casual about describing the whole damn thing and didn't seem respectful of Don's place in the community.

Sheriff Morgan was quoted as saying that he had no idea as to why Mercer had met his death in such a grisly manner, but that his department and the entire police force would be working around the clock.

Walter turned the pages back to the obituary which he'd briefly skimmed before reading the front page article. In the column it stated that Donald Mercer, sixty-six, was predeceased by his wife, Edna Poe Mercer. The survivors included two brothers who live in California, an assortment of nieces and nephews, and one older sister who suffers from Alzheimer's disease and resides in a nursing home in El Dorado. Walter had witnessed the fact that only one brother and two nephews attended the funeral.

A piss poor showing, as far as he was concerned. Don and Edna had no children to grieve for them or to recall memories of their times together.

"What the hell!" Don had said, back when every couple they knew were re-producing like a hutch full of rabbits, "Who needs the snotty-nosed little rug rats anyway? All they do is keep you up all night and cost you a boat load of money."

But Walter knew that Don regretted not having a son to take over his prosperous law firm. Not like him and Grace. Neither one of them had wanted kids, especially after Grace's lying to him about her supposed pregnancy. Selfishness was probably the only trait the two of them shared. While Walter had always acknowledged his childlessness for what it was, a desire to fill his life with making money and having fun; Grace hid behind her pathetic attempts to convince her friends that she was sacrificing motherhood for the good of an already over-crowded planet. But then, Walter thought Grace was pathetic, period.

He rolled the newspaper up and absentmindedly whacked it against the seat of the swing. He didn't notice how rapidly the night was settling in around him. Grace had gone to one of her charity dinners, so even the house up the steep, sloped lawn behind him was dark. Walter also failed to notice that the frogs momentarily stopped their singing, as they marked the passage of a dark figure across the creek's foot bridge.

"Damn," Walter muttered, a sorrow filling him as it had not since he'd first heard of Don's horrible death. "We had some great times together, back when we were young," he spoke silently to his friend. "We had the world by the tail, didn't we?"

After high school, Walter had enlisted in the Navy and Don in the Marines. They both went to Korea, managed to survive, and came back to Ashley Springs. Don then enrolled at the University of Arkansas at Fayetteville to earn his law degree. Walter became his father's partner, both on the cattle ranch and in the chain of twenty Sun Belle Grocery Stores.

Walter settled easily into being a wealthy landowner and businessman. He married Grace, the daughter of a poor dirt farmer. A mistake on Walter's part, as most of the town saw it. But back then, Grace had been built, as his old man had been fond of saying, like a brick shit house.

Walter chased her hot and heavy, then after they had dated for almost three months, Grace told him she was pregnant. Addled by Grace's good looks and her insatiable appetite for sex, Walter didn't ask questions. They were married in a ceremony completely lacking any romantic, let alone spiritual, trappings. Judge Malcolm, a friend of the Thurmonds, conducted the brief ritual. About a month later, Grace said she lost the baby. In those days, Walter was ignorant in such matters and didn't want a child anyway, so he accepted her story.

But after only a few more months of marriage, life became pretty routine. Grace wasn't nearly as ready to accommodate him sexually as she'd first been. She began to come up with excuses as to why they shouldn't do it. Walter quickly tired of her games and began to ignore Grace for weeks at a time. After he had his first affair, she didn't seem very sexy to him anymore, so he went on to another affair. Also, his special sexual needs began to come to the forefront again. They could only be satisfied on his jaunts to New Orleans or Chicago, or other cities with places that pandered to his special appetite.

It wasn't long until one of Grace's friends spilled the beans about the women he dated. When Grace faced him with it, Walter half-heartedly denied his unfaithfulness, not really caring that she knew. In a fit of spitefulness, Grace told him she hadn't been pregnant when they got married. Walter told Grace to file for divorce and that he wouldn't contest it.

Unwilling to give up her social position, as well as having unlimited money to spend, Grace ran to his old man, who then told his son that it wouldn't be good for business to have a messy divorce in the family. Knowing that his father was right, Walter dropped the subject. By the time his father died, Grace knew too much about his business, such as a second set of books he kept on some of his stores. Also, thanks again to his father, she was listed as a partner on the ranch. She could wreak legal and financial havoc in his life.

Grace's number one priority continued to be to impress the social-climbers who constituted high society in Ashley Springs. Her haughty bossiness had not endeared her to the circle of women who followed her lead. Walter felt certain that the other women remembered that Grace came from a family that didn't have a pot to pee in until Walter bought it for them. He was also certain that they wouldn't mention it to her.

Walter roused from his reverie to realize that it was almost pitch black inside the gazebo. Outside, he could make only a faint distinction between the night sky and the deeper darkness of the trees. There was no moon tonight. In fact, while Walter had wandered back through time, the clouds had gathered overhead so that not even the stars relieved the darkness. Distant tongues of lightning flickered above the horizon, etching zigzag patterns of violence without the promise of rain.

He thought of the crops that lay limp in the fields under the daily onslaught of a burning sun. The relentless parching of the earth seemed to create an atmosphere conducive to violence. He knew there had been a number of break-ins, wife beatings, and general mayhem in the county lately that seemed to increase as the temperature rose.

The uneasiness which Walter had felt since he'd first heard of Don's murder came back so strongly that he felt the hairs on the back of his neck stir. He wondered if Don had known his killer. Was it a crazy person who happened to kill him, or was he deliberately chosen to die? What if it was someone he and Don knew?

A scuffling sound at the steps that led into the gazebo interrupted Walter's thoughts.

A tall figure, darker than the night, stepped into the building.

"Who is it?" Walter said, his voice sharp with alarm.

"It's just me," a familiar voice spoke softly.

"Man!" Walter said, laughing with relief. "You had me going there for a minute. My nerves are like most folks around here right now, a little on edge. Well, come on, have a seat." Walter moved over to one end of the swing. "What, might I ask, brings you around this time of the evening?"

He sensed, as much as saw, his visitor moving toward the back of the swing. It seemed more than a little odd that someone would come way back here, especially a person he knew no better than he did this one. Why not knock on the front door of the house, then leave when there was no answer?

As Walter turned to follow the movement behind him, he felt a stir of air near his ear, before he heard a coarse whisper, "Once long ago, Walter, you had the power, but not now, old boy. Now it's your turn!"

The last three words were said in a singsong chant, like that of a child at play.

"What the…!" Walter could make no sense of what his visitor was saying. As he moved to get up from the swing, he felt the pinching grasp of a hand in his hair. At the same time, he was yanked forcefully against the back of the swing, hitting his head hard enough that he saw stars.

He felt the hot breath against his ear again, as he heard the voice whisper, "Have fun in hell, Walter."

Before he could pull away from the clutching hand, a scalding pain began on the right side of his neck and crossed swiftly to the opposite ear. A thick choking liquid cut off his breath and sprayed onto his hands and legs. Walter's dying brain lifted him to his feet before the sucking, swirling blackness drained the last spark of consciousness from him.

The killer worked swiftly for several minutes, then walked up to the house and onto the screened porch. The object was still where it had been on the last visit. Putting the souvenir into the satchel with the tools, the killer moved silently back down the lawn. Moments later, the frogs again hushed as the dark figure quickly re-crossed the foot bridge. After a few seconds of silence, they resumed their mating serenades.

On the hill above the gazebo, lights came on in Walter's house, marking Grace's progression as she made her way from the front hall to the kitchen. After making herself a peanut butter and jelly sandwich and pouring a glass of milk, she put her snack on a tray, then flipped out the lights as she made her way upstairs. She hummed a tuneless ditty, feeling very pleased with herself. As the president of the state chapter of the *Save the Hungry of the World*, she had just chaired a very successful dinner for procuring funds to feed the poor children of a third-world country. Their goal of fifty-thousand dollars had been met and then some.

Quite a feather in my cap, Grace thought, with satisfaction.

After she finished her sandwich, Grace went about the nightly ritual of cleansing her face, rolling her hair on sponge rollers, and putting her false teeth in a soaking solution, all without once thinking of Walter. It never occurred to her to check to see if he were in his room. The earlier years of waiting for him to come home at night, had ended one evening when he told her just how much he detested her. If Grace's memory served her correctly, that was the same time she'd told him that she'd lied to him about being pregnant.

They'd had very little to do with each other since then. She only went to him when she needed more money, or required his considerable influence to help her accomplish some goal. She never asked him where he was going, or when he would be home. It didn't matter anymore.

Right now, Grace's mind was pleasantly filled with the trip she planned for early tomorrow morning. After she kept her appointment with her orthodontist in Little Rock, she and Nadine Benson would do some serious shopping.

The phone rang, which was common for this time of night. The women who knew her well and wanted to talk to her about some project or share a bit of gossip, also knew they could usually find her at home late in the evening.

But it wasn't one of her society friends. Instead, she heard the voice of Amy Bordeaux, owner of a beautiful antiques and gift shop in downtown Ashley Springs. Grace liked Amy, who seemed to have no social ambitions and was always friendly. She was considering asking the young woman to join her bridge club group.

"We've completed the refinishing job on your sewing cabinet," Amy said. "Would it be all right if I delivered it to your house in the morning?"

"Yes, of course it will," Grace said. It wasn't until they'd hung up, that she remembered her shopping trip. But she knew Walter would be there. He told her that morning he planned to stay home and do some paper work tomorrow.

CHAPTER 2

▼

The morning sun slanted into the back of the shop as Amy Bordeaux pushed open the double doors and propped them with wedges of wood. "Hey! You guys made it, huh?" She walked over to the GMC pick-up parked in the alley. Her dark eyes and long black hair, inherited from her French grandmother, emphasized the beauty of her smooth, slightly tan complexion. The pale coral shirt only accented her natural beauty, while the jeans she wore emphasized her long legs and slim figure.

"Yes, Ma'am, we made it." Barney Scott, her business partner and surrogate father, frowned at her as he got out of the cab. "Our backs are ruined for life," he complained, "and we're about to put ourselves into the hospital getting this monstrosity into the shop. Right, boys?"

Despite his sixty-odd years, Barney jumped nimbly onto the back of the truck, as the two men sitting on each side of the tailgate grinned at each other. They had heard similar arguments before. In the center of the truck bed sat a solid oak roll-top desk. Amy knew that it was a very heavy piece of furniture, but nothing that the men couldn't handle. She'd seen the three men move larger pieces than the desk.

"Well, if you live through this," she said, "I'll be glad to treat all of you to breakfast. That is if I don't have to call an ambulance first."

When he smiled, as he did now, Barney's darkly tanned face contrasted nicely with his white teeth. Even at his age, his skin was smooth and his body lean and muscular. Amy thought, for the fiftieth time at least, that it was a shame he had never married. She smiled at thinking that Barney shouldn't be single. Here she was thirty-two years old and not married herself; at least not anymore, she wasn't. Once was enough for her.

"Okay, fellows, let's get this thing unloaded." Barney gripped one end of the desk while Miguel did the same. They pulled it up several inches. The other helper, Samuel, slid the dolly underneath the lifted edge and balanced the load on the two back wheels. Then Barney quickly jumped down to hook two metal ramps onto the tailgate of the truck. With the ease of long practice, the men lowered the desk down the ramp, then rolled it into the back of the shop. In a matter of seconds, the men had the desk off the dolly and standing in the spot Amy wanted it.

"I believe you owe us the price of three breakfasts, Ma'am," Barney said, as he and Amy followed the men back outside.

"Cheaper than an ambulance run," Amy retorted, as she dug into her jeans pocket for the roll of bills she'd put there for this purpose. "That desk is a beauty, isn't it? Nadine will be ecstatic when I tell her I have it. She wants to give it to Mr. Benson for their fortieth anniversary which is two weeks from now."

"After we get through refinishing it, perhaps Mr. Benson wouldn't mind loading it up and taking it to his house," Barney said, a smile tugging at the corners of his mouth.

William Benson was a short man and probably didn't weigh more than a hundred and fifty pounds soaking wet. He was a hopeless hypochondriac, forever complaining about one ailment or another. The people who knew him, which was almost everyone in the county, had learned to not ask him how he felt. Amy believed he probably sought sympathy because of his henpecked status at home. The community felt Nadine Benson's iron will whenever a project included her volunteer expertise. She bossed her husband relentlessly on such occasions.

"Aren't you having breakfast with us?" Barney asked, after Amy had handed him two twenty-dollar bills. The money was for the two helpers. Barney would pay for their meal.

"No, I'm going to deliver the sewing cabinet this morning. I'm a little late getting that done. Besides, we need more room back here." She waved her arm toward the work space crammed with both antiques and "junktiques," all of them precious to their owners. "Later today I'll deliver that gooseneck rocker."

"You're right about needing the space," Barney agreed. "I plan to rearrange some of this stuff so we can at least get to the front without squeezing through. Let me help you get those two pieces loaded for you, then we'll be on our way."

Barney made quick work of getting the furniture into the back of her Suburban. "Take it easy, Boss. See you later." The three men drove off as Amy turned back to the shop. She needed to make out the invoices for the two pieces.

As Amy sat down at her computer, she thought about her life now and the one she had led only three years ago. Comparing her past teaching position at the university to the ownership of a very successful antique and gift business, she found the latter to be far more satisfying. Her BA and MA degrees in business administration, the subject she taught at the university, provided a helpful background for her present management duties.

Her Aunt Leigh originally owned the shop. Three years ago, Leigh signed it over to Amy, for the sum of one dollar, including the original building and its contents. Leigh wanted to devote her full time to her writing. She had sold two novels and was anxious to add to her list. In the past three years, Leigh had three best sellers to her credit, proving that she, too, had made the right choice. Amy had then asked Barney to become her business partner. He had been there since Amy was three years old and the first year of Leigh's business endeavor. Barney was more family than he was a partner.

She checked her watch and saw that it was over an hour before time to open the shop. In the event she didn't make it back by nine o' clock, her reliable clerk, Mary Griffin, would do that.

The day was already warming up, but the air was still cool enough for Amy to leave the Burb's windows down. As she passed the pink stucco front of Sadie's Café, only two doors down from her own shop, Amy could see that it was packed with the usual morning coffee crowd. The customers were mostly men who gathered daily to share the latest gossip. She knew the subject for today and for the next month of days, would be poor Donald Mercer. The cause of his murder would be endlessly discussed and analyzed by the local sages.

To squelch her distressing thoughts, she turned her attention to the beautiful scenery around her. She had turned off Main Street onto Old Post Road which rose steeply and, in only a few hundred feet, provided a panoramic view of the valley and Perry Lake.

The Ozark foothills surrounded the town of Ashley Springs, which was a tourist town each year from late April until the middle of October. Harmony River, famous for its trout fishing, and Perry Lake, known for its deep water bass, provided fun for thousands of tourists from every state in the Union.

Most of the natives of the area were very tolerant of the friendly crowds of outsiders and did all they could to encourage their return. The community as a whole wanted to see their hometown continue to thrive through tourism, but some of the old-timers grumbled about strangers taking over their space. However, Amy knew that if they were forced to choose, those same men would not want the area to revert to the conditions that existed in the years before the dam was built on the river.

Amy's mind drifted back to the present as she got closer to her destination. She remembered that Don Mercer had been a very close friend of the Thurmonds, the people to whom she was delivering the antique sewing machine. There was something about Mercer's death that seemed to pose a threat to everyone who lived in the Ashley Springs area. Everyone knew that Don's throat had been cut so deeply that he was almost decapitated. That tidbit of horror was told to Barney by one of the deputies who'd been at the scene. Since the police apparently didn't have a clue as to the motive behind his murder, no one knew who else might fall victim to such a vicious anger.

It had left most people, including Amy, with an uneasy feeling. She hoped fervently that Sheriff Morgan and the other law enforcement officers would very soon make an arrest. "The killer is probably long gone from here," she said.

Feeling slightly better for her verbalized self-assurance, Amy pulled the Suburban over into the slow lane for the steeper climb up Bitterweed Mountain. From here she could look out across the valley to Bountiful Mountain. Her Aunt Leigh's house, Eagle's Nest, sat at the very top. She had been invited there for dinner tonight. It was always a treat to visit her aunt, but what was even more special, Leigh usually invited Amy up when she needed a final critique of her latest novel. Amy loved being the first one to read the finished product. Leigh Nelson's name was a familiar one, even in the international neighborhoods of mystery book fans.

Amy slowed down to turn right onto a narrow paved road. Another road to the left led up the side of Bitterweed Mountain to an old, abandoned country club building. That road was pitted with holes and overgrown by weeds, seldom used by anyone except the occasional hunter. This was a stark contrast to the road Amy now took which led her to the first delivery site. The pavement curved smooth and long between enormous pines to the residence of Grace and Walter Thurmond.

The enormous two-story white house was reminiscent of Twelve Oaks in *Gone With the Wind*. The Thurmond's lawn was also eye-catching thanks to Grace's Japanese gardener, Moto Kabuki. He knew how to plan and execute the botanical feast for the eyes which Amy was now enjoying.

She stopped her vehicle in the circular drive in front of the huge house and ran up the shallow brick steps to the front door to press the doorbell. She could hear the deep chimes beyond the heavy oak door. Except for the vigorous chorus of bird song, all else was quiet. Grace apparently was not at home. If Amy remembered correctly from past visits here, today was the maid's day off, and Grace was probably on one of her shopping trips.

Amy tried not to disturb the bees on the overhanging rose bushes as she made her way on a stone path to the rear of the house. If the back screen porch was unlocked, she could leave the sewing cabinet there safely enough. There was no one in sight. Amy ducked the overhead limbs and reached the screened area. Even Moto was absent from his rounds of watering, weeding, and mowing.

She swiftly covered the short distance to the door and found, to her relief, that the door was unlatched. Amy immediately retraced her steps, got back into the Suburban, and drove on the paved driveway around the opposite end of the house. She parked in the broad area provided for deliveries. Propping the screen door open, Amy carefully lifted the cabinet from the truck bed and carried it onto the porch, placing it in a corner at the end of a rattan sofa.

She left the cabinet wrapped in its protective covering so that anyone looking at it would see only a disreputable looking lump of khaki-colored quilting. She would call later and let Grace know where she had left the antique piece. Out of curiosity, Amy walked over to the end table where she'd seen Grace lay the wooden darning egg that had been in the drawer of the cabinet. Amy had asked Grace to keep it, since it could get lost in the shuffle at the shop. It wasn't on the end table, so Grace had probably put it in a safe place.

As Amy returned to her vehicle, she glanced down the sloping lawn to where the gazebo stood. Its beautiful spool-carved roof supports reflected the morning sunlight. Amy thought the gazebo was one of the best finds she'd ever made. That thought was validated each time she saw it. The octagon-shaped building had stood behind the old Carville home for at least forty years.

When the last surviving Carville, Amos Hatley Carville, decided to have his old home torn down and to sell the land which had been in his family since before the Civil War, Amy asked his permission to salvage the gazebo.

"I'll find it a good home," she'd promised.

As soon as she told Grace about the beautiful old gazebo, it was sold. Amy and Barney had overseen the little building's transportation to the Thurmond lawn, then had fussed over its restoration like a pair of mother hens. Now, with Moto's skilled ministrations, the gazebo shone like a jewel inside the fringe of red and pink impatiens, and against the Irish-green blanket of grass. Beyond that, at the foot of the lawn, Corbin Creek sparkled with reflecting sunlight.

Amy turned to get into the truck, then stopped with one foot on the running board. Something was wrong. She looked back at the small building. Large dark patterns stained the light grey of the flooring. Amy walked a few feet down the wide flagstone path that led to the gazebo, trying to determine if the shadows created the illusion of discolored blotches. From there she could see a man's foot protruding from behind the railing near the steps.

Amy, thinking that Moto had fallen and hurt himself, moved swiftly down the path As she neared the gazebo, she called out, "Hello, this is Amy Bordeaux. Are you hurt?"

CHAPTER 3

▼

The foot did not move. For just a second, she slowed her approach, some instinct making her wish to turn back, to wait for someone else to discover who laid beyond the latticed railing. But then, common sense reasserted itself. Whoever it was needed help, and she was the only person around.

She was almost to the steps when she heard and then saw, hundreds of flies swarming near the large dark areas that covered most of the floor nearest her. She saw more dark spots on the railings. Flies rose in clouds as she put her foot on the first step. They came at her, hitting her in the face, in her hair, and on her arms. Amy closed her eyes and frantically batted at them. Then, covering her face with her hands, she peeped through the cracks between her fingers and saw the figure lying on the floor. It was Walter Thurmond.

For a split second, Amy froze, unable to make sense of what she was seeing. Then reality hit her, and she fell backwards down the steps, and onto the lawn. She crawled for a few feet before she managed to get to her feet and stumble back uphill toward the Suburban. Amy felt a cloud of cold air fold about her while her mind flashed pictures of what she had just seen. The images of pools of black blood seemed to intermix with pools of fresh red blood. Her mind was too filled with the horror of what she had just seen to analyze the strange phenomena.

Not quite to her vehicle, Amy leaned over and lost her morning coffee onto the flagstone path. The image of the gaping wound beneath Thurmond's chin made her stomach boil in protest. She fought to wipe that gruesome picture from her mind.

After the heaving finally stopped, she struggled up the last several feet to her vehicle.

Clawing at the door, she managed to find the handle and get inside. Amy became aware of the eerie quiet that enveloped the house and yard. Even the birds were silent. The dried, darkened blood, and the number of flies covering the body, made it obvious that Thurmond had been dead for a while, maybe for several hours.

Fear rippled down her back. She looked around for any signs that the killer was still there. Nothing stirred. Amy locked the doors and picked up her cell phone. It took Amy three tries before she could dial the courthouse number she wanted. By now her whole body jerked in hard spasms, which tightened the muscles in her chest and made it hard for her to breathe.

"Sheriff's Department. How may I help you?"

"Marlene, this is Amy." Marlene Phann, the sheriff's only female deputy, was also a good friend of hers.

"Hey, girl, how ya doing? What's going on?"

For a split second, Amy found it impossible to articulate what she'd just seen. Tears of shock and fear rolled down her cheeks. "I'm at Grace Thurmond's house, Marlene," she managed. "Mr. Thurmond is dead."

Marlene's voice altered to take on a professional tone. "Where is the body?"

"In the gazebo at the back of the house."

"Have you touched anything?"

"Nothing except the back screen door."

"Is there anyone else there?"

"No one that I can see."

"Can you tell me how he died?"

"I think his throat is cut. There's a lot of blood, and there's something wrong with his mouth." Amy almost gagged at the last words.

"Where is your car, Amy?"

"I'm sitting in it near the back door."

"I think you should drive back down to the road. The sheriff is on his way. If he asks you why you moved that vehicle, tell him I told you to. We don't know who may still be around there, so lock your doors. Hang in there, Girl. Help is on the way."

Her nerves crawled with the desperate need to get as far away from her ghastly discovery as possible, Amy immediately followed Deputy Phann's orders. She drove quickly around the house and down the driveway to the highway. Parking in a grassy area across from the gate, Amy turned off the motor.

Walter Thurmond had been savagely murdered, and she had a clear mental picture of his condition. His pants had been pulled down to below his knees, and there was a bloody hole where his genitals should have been. His mouth, grossly swollen, had been stitched shut with what appeared to be black thread, his cheeks puffed out as if he had taken a huge mouthful of food. Suddenly, it hit her what must be in there.

"Oh, no!" Amy wailed, breaking the silence of the surrounding woods around her.

Someone was insane beyond anything she could ever imagine. That same someone was loose in the county, free to strike again. Anxious for the sheriff to get there, Amy checked to be sure her doors were locked. From where she sat, the road curved to disappear around the looming bulk of Bitterweed Mountain which lay between her and the town. The trees that grew along the road and up the sides of the mountain seemed dense and alien.

In less than five minutes, although it seemed like an hour to her, Amy heard the wail of approaching sirens. In seconds, Archie Ledbetter's unit bounced recklessly around the curve. With a screeching of tires, he pulled up next to her. Amy, happy to see his homely face, lowered her window.

"Ms. Amy, you want to ride up there with me?"

"Thanks, Archie, but I can follow you."

She heard another siren getting very near and waited where she was. A wreck at this point would be more than she could take. Sheriff Morgan only slowed enough to call out, "Follow me, please." Behind the sheriff's car, a state trooper swung his car in a wide arc and parked lengthwise across the road, making an effective road block.

Amy fell into the procession of vehicles going up to the house. They all parked, one behind the other, in the large circular driveway. The sheriff hoisted his generous six foot-three frame out of the county's tan Suburban with its star and shield logo on its doors and walked back to where Amy sat.

"Hello, Ms. Bordeaux." Sheriff Morgan leaned down to her window. Spider veins on his nose and cheeks were tell-tale evidence of his alcohol habit. She thought his crooked, ex-boxer's nose and rough complexion were at odds with his expressive grey eyes and long lashes. "You've had a bad experience today," he said, sounding sympathetic.

"Yes, you could say that." She paled at the image that rose in her mind.

"Easy, easy." The sheriff barely touched her arm. "I'm not asking you to go back around there right now. You stay here until we can look the situation over.

I'll need your statement about how you came to be here, and how you discovered the body."

A black Bronco pulled up beside the sheriff. Its driver lowered the window next to Amy's vehicle. "Hi, Frank. I heard the call on my radio and thought I'd better come on out." The man behind the wheel looked to be in his early thirties. He had a squarish, pleasant face framed by thick brown hair. He looked over at Amy, smiled and nodded before he gave his attention back the sheriff. Amy didn't care who he was, she only wanted away from this place.

"We've not been back there yet, Ben, but I'm afraid I already know what we'll find," Sheriff Morgan said, as he stepped back from Amy's window. "Ben, meet Ms. Amy Bordeaux," he said. "She's the one who found the body. Ms. Amy, this is Detective Ben Edwards, our investigative officer."

Without waiting for either of them to acknowledge the introduction, the sheriff told Amy, "You wait right here while we get on back there." He touched the brim of his Stetson, and took long strides back to where Archie Ledbetter waited. Edwards backed his vehicle into a space behind Amy's, then the three men disappeared around the house by the same route she had taken earlier. It was very quiet, creating the spooky atmosphere Amy had experienced right after her discovery.

She listened to the tick of her cooling engine and the burst of song from the resident mockingbird. At least he hadn't been intimidated to silence, she thought. To keep her mind off the scene at the gazebo, Amy deliberately thought about Grace, who would soon learn of her husband's death. It was commonly known around town that Grace and Walter were more business partners than marriage partners. Walter's years of unfaithfulness were also common knowledge. The men at Sadie's Café would laugh and say that Walter was off on 'business' in New Orleans again. Amy's sympathy was with Grace, since she personally knew the hurt that came from knowing your husband slept with other women. Grace had probably gone through much the same painful process that she had, but with a different ending.

Amy had ended her marriage of one year to the unfaithful Stephen Abramson and with Leigh and Barney's help, made a new life for herself. But Grace, with many more years invested into her marriage, had chosen to ignore Walter's duplicity and to live her life as Ashley Springs' leading social influence. Walter's wealth, which he shared generously with his wife, probably weighed heavily toward Grace's decision to remain in her beautiful house. However, the hurt and shame of Walter's infidelity must still have been a source of agony for Grace.

Amy wondered what her reaction to her husband's death would be. She was the sole heir to his millions. That should provide some degree of comfort to the widow. But regardless of monetary gain, Amy knew she wouldn't want to experience the ordeal that was ahead of Grace. One thought kept returning. How did Grace really feel about her husband?

"Ms. Bordeaux?" Amy jumped so violently, that she whacked her elbow on the frame of the truck door. Her heart was stuttering around in her chest even when she saw who was at her window. "Sorry, I didn't mean to startle you." Sheriff Morgan was again leaning down to speak to her. She had not heard him approach and fleetingly thought how quietly he moved for such a large man.

"Please, Sheriff, would you just call me Amy? I haven't heard Ms. Bordeaux since I last taught school." Amy wanted to deal with social niceties instead of what she'd seen.

"It's a terrible sight back there, even for us," he said. "Do you feel like talking?"

Amy shrugged knowing that he was really saying that he needed to hear her story. He opened her door, "Would you come with me, please?"

He walked ahead of her and pointed to one of the lacy ironwork chairs on the veranda. She sat, while he remained standing. "Just tell me how you came to be here, and how you discovered the body," he said, leaning back against the wall and folding his arms across his chest.

Amy told him how she had completed the work on the cabinet and decided to deliver it this morning. She described how she had driven to the back, after getting no answer at the front door, and decided to put the piece of furniture on the porch. "That's when I looked down at the gazebo and saw a discoloration on the floor. I walked down several yards, trying to decide if the dark splotches were just shadows or something else. When I got closer, I saw someone's foot and thought maybe Moto had fallen and injured himself. But when I got closer I saw…"

Amy jumped up and ran to the edge of the veranda, but did no more than gag. The sheriff waited quietly until her nausea passed.

"You don't have to describe anymore," he said, "but I'll need you to wait here a little longer until we get a chance to survey the scene. You'll have to drive your vehicle to the back of the house to the spot where you had parked it, so we can determine the angle of your viewpoint. Okay?"

He disappeared around the corner of the house for a second time. Amy started across the drive to her truck and heard someone call her name. She turned to see Detective Edwards bending over to avoid the prickly rose bush limbs that crowded the stone path.

"If you don't mind," he said. "I have a few questions to ask you." Amy reluctantly retraced her steps and sat down in the same chair she'd just vacated. "I would like you to tell me about your arrival here, you know, when you got here, what you did first, then your succeeding actions."

"I just got through telling Sheriff Morgan all that." Amy interrupted him as she rose from the chair, prepared to go back to her vehicle.

Edwards effectively blocked her from leaving by stepping in front of her. "I know you did, Ms. Bordeaux, and I'm sorry for putting you through an unpleasant chore again, but there's the possibility that some detail you didn't think of in the first telling, will be recalled in the second. Now if you would have patience just a little longer, I'd be very grateful."

Amy saw that beneath the detective's polite exterior there was a decidedly business-like attitude. If she didn't talk now, he'd be after her later. Reluctantly, she began.

CHAPTER 4

▼

Barney walked to the long table at the back of Sadie's Café. He had fed his helpers the promised breakfast and then had taken them by Marchesi's Liquor store for them to buy their weekly six-packs. After delivering them to their respective mobile homes, he was now ready to catch up on the latest news of the Mercer murder.

"Hello, fellows," he greeted the seven men lounging behind their thick stoneware cups of black coffee. He pulled out one of the chrome-framed and nauseous yellow plastic chairs. It went well with the gloomy brown of the cheap paneling on the walls and the dirt gray tile floor. The original owner had obviously possessed little concern for creating a pleasant ambiance of comfort and light for her customers. Sadie, long since retired, had been replaced by Vera Haynes who evidently shared the same decorating philosophy. She had changed nothing.

"Hi, Hon." Vera plunked down a clone of the other men's cups and poured coffee to its rim, splashing some on the table. "Here let me wipe that up for you. I don't want your clothes all mussed," she said, as she smeared the coffee into an even greater area of wetness. "You ready for one of my delicious doughnuts? Made them fresh this morning." The men laughed because they knew the bakery delivered them each day.

"Woman, those clunkers would break a tiger's tooth." Barney was grinning.

Like the rest of the regular customers, he enjoyed teasing Vera. She had a good sense of humor and a generous heart. Many a person down on his or her luck, were fed here free of charge for as long as it took them to find a job.

"Aw, shut your mouth, Barney Scott," Vera said, smiling back at him. "You know they're soft as a down pillow. I'll heat one up for you." She hurried over to the cash register where a customer was waiting to pay his bill.

"Hey, Barn, have you heard about the latest suspect in the Mercer case?" Bob Mayson, the town crier, always had information no one else possessed. Usually it was only rumor and that, often as not, started by Bob himself. Barney shook his head as he dumped a heaping teaspoon of sugar into his cup.

Needing no encouragement, Bob said, "Well, I was just telling the boys here what Archie Ledbetter told me. He thinks the murderer was probably a hobo who dropped off a train. You know the back of Don's house ain't but a coupla' hundred yards from the railroad tracks."

Barney shared the skepticism he saw reflected on the other men's faces.

"I told you, Bob," Cliff Herman, another of the regulars, spoke. "You ought not go around saying Archie told you that. It could cause him some trouble."

"Speak of the devil, that was his car just went by faster than he supposed to," said Jim Arnold, who sat facing the large front windows. He put his chair down on all four legs with a thump. "His lights were flashing. Listen! He's hit his siren." Some of Vera's customers were already outside on the sidewalk by that time.

"Wonder what that's all about?" Cliff said.

"From the sound of the siren," Vera said, "I'd say he's headed out on Old Post Road and up Bitterweed Mountain."

"There's not much up that way but a few rent houses and the Thurmond's place."

"Yeah, I got outside just in time to see him take a left on Post." Billy Joe Smith, a relative newcomer to the town, sat back down at his table. Billy was working for Dr. Rice, the veterinarian. "Something bad's done happened, I bet." He sounded as if he hoped it had, and the grin on his thin face reminded Barney of a ferret.

Barney thought of Amy. She was making deliveries, and if he remembered correctly, one of the pieces belonged to Grace Thurmond.

"Could be a wreck," Vera said, "There's a couple of them steep curves out there where the weeds and such are so grown up, you couldn't see an eighteen-wheeler around them. Only last week Otto Chance was telling how he almost went into the ditch trying to miss that Purefoy kid in that red truck of his. Otto said it was the Lord's wonder he didn't turn over. It made him so mad, he said he followed the kid home and blessed him out right there in his own yard. Turned out not to be such a good idea, though."

"Yeah," Bob Mayson said, taking up the tale, "old Elmer Purefoy came tearing out into the yard and 'tole Otto he'd better not hear him saying nothing to his kid any more, or he'd regret it. Otto said wasn't nothing left for him to do but leave, and he did."

General laughter filled the room. Everyone in Ashley Springs knew that both Bud Purefoy and his old man were as tough as wood haulers' butts. Several of the men sitting around the table had, on one occasion or another, wished the Purefoys lived in another county. It was a general belief that Bud, with his wild ways, was bound for the state pen.

Barney wasn't paying attention to the gossip and speculation being bantered about. He had a growing feeling that whatever it was that took Archie Ledbetter recklessly down Main Street was somehow connected to Amy. Tossing a couple of dollar bills on the table, he rose to leave.

"I'd better get back to the store," he said. "See if the boss has anything she needs me to do. We've got enough work at the shop to keep me busy for a month."

The men knew Barney's term for Amy was affectionate. They also knew that if anyone even hinted at disrespect toward her, they would have a quickly dangerous Barney to placate. A few of the men remembered when Barney had come to Ashley Springs. He'd just shown up one day, a stranger who came and stayed. He went to work for Leigh as a cleaner and refinisher of old furniture and became an indispensable part of her life.

In small town fashion there was the usual gossip for a while. But nothing interesting seemed to develop between Barney and Leigh, and no one caught them sneaking into each other's living quarters. So the townspeople turned their attention to more current and scandalous events.

Barney pressed down on the accelerator of his '89 GMC truck and the powerful 454 motor roared as he recklessly sped up the steep incline of Bitterweed Mountain. As he drove around the last curve, he put on his brakes so hard that the bed of the truck fish tailed toward the ditch. He barely missed Trooper Slade Angstrom, who was waving him down.

"Are you crazy?" Slade walked to where Barney sat in his truck. "Where do you think you're going, anyway?"

"I heard there's trouble up here. Amy Bordeaux came up this way not long ago. Is she all right? She's not hurt, is she?"

Slade shook his head. "No, she's not hurt, and you can't go where she is. The sheriff ordered that no one be let past here and that includes you."

"No problem," Barney said, as he restarted the motor and put the truck in reverse. When he had backed about twenty feet away from where Slade stood, he put his brakes on, shifted into drive, then stomped the accelerator. Before the trooper knew what Barney was up to, he drove his truck down into the ditch and around the state car. He watched Barney's truck disappear up the Thurmond's road, then shrugged his shoulders. The sheriff would take care of him soon enough.

Barney only put the brakes on when he got to the Thurmond house. There was barely room for him to park in the crowded driveway without getting into one of Moto's flower beds. He cut his motor and hit the ground running.

Amy was still on the veranda. She was pale, and he could see she'd been crying. A young man was talking to her, notepad in hand, and a camera looped around his neck.

When she saw Barney, Amy rose to meet him.

"Oh, Barney, it was horrible!" she said, as he put his arms around her. "Who can be so sick?"

"You're fine now," he soothed her. "Sit down and tell old Barn what's happened."

"Mr. Thurmond is dead, Barney. Killed by whoever killed Mr. Mercer!"

"We don't know that the same person committed both murders, Ms. Bordeaux." The man with the notepad spoke. "There are some similarities, but we can't be positive at this point that both men were killed by the same perp."

Amy stiffened in Barney's arms, then pushed him back to look up at Edwards. She swiped at the tears on her face with her forearm. "Are you suggesting that we have *two* insane killers running around loose?" Her voice rose to a combative shriek. "If you think that's true, why aren't you looking behind every tree and every bush? Why are you standing here asking me questions that I've already answered?"

The detective had the grace to look uncomfortable. Barney almost felt sorry for him.

"This is all necessary, I'm afraid," Edwards said. "Without information that's even slightly connected to what's happened here, our chances of finding the perpetrator could be delayed." Only then did he look at Barney. "And who are you?"

"I'm Ms. Bordeaux's business partner, Barney Scott. Who are you?" Barney was instantly contentious. Amy sat up, ready to intervene if necessary.

"I'm Detective Ben Edwards." The lawman's face wore the detached expression of the professional cop. "Will you excuse us while I finish getting the information I need? Ms. Bordeaux will be ready to leave before much longer."

"I don't think you should be asking her questions right now," Barney said.

Amy broke in before Barney could make a really rash statement. "It's okay, Barn. Let me get this over with, okay?"

Barney stared at the detective for a moment, then relaxed somewhat. "I'll be by my truck," he said, as he gave Amy's shoulder a squeeze.

Leaning against the fender of his vehicle, Barney pulled out a crumpled pack of cigarettes and put one between his lips. He had quit smoking six months ago, but in times of stress, Amy knew he still liked the feel of one in his mouth.

She could see he was watching Edwards as the detective continued talking to her. Barney probably remembered seeing the man around town, if he hadn't placed him as the new man at the sheriff's office. Archie Ledbetter walked around the end of the house to say something to the detective. Amy got up and went over to Barney.

Her voice trembled with stress as she said, "Archie said Sheriff Morgan wants me to drive to the back of the house and park where I did before." Amy pointed her thumb back at the detective. "He said you could go with me, after I told him I wouldn't go back there unless he let you back there, too."

Edwards unfastened one end of the yellow plastic tape that was stretched across both ends of the house. He let it fall to the driveway as Amy steered her vehicle to the back of the house and slowly drove to the exact spot where she had stopped to unload the sewing cabinet. She was careful not to look down the lawn where the gazebo stood.

Sheriff Morgan walked to the side where Barney sat, effectively blocking his view of the crime scene. "We need a couple of pictures of your truck, Ms. Bordeaux," he said. "Then I want you to walk with me down the path to where you stopped before." He saw Amy's horrified look, and quickly added, "Everything's been covered, so you won't see as much as you did before. It won't take a minute, and then you can leave. If the two of you will climb out on the other side of the truck, you can stand inside the porch while we get the snapshots we need."

While Edwards flashed his bulbs from different angles toward the Suburban, Sheriff Morgan spoke to Amy. "I'm sorry you've been put through all this, but I need your promise that you will not say a word to anyone about what you've seen here." The sheriff's expression was hard as he looked at Barney. "We want to keep details of the death quiet. Such details can trip up a killer, and we're going to need all the advantages we can get on this one."

Amy could see why everyone respected the sheriff. Café gossip occasionally spread the results of someone foolishly taking him on. They always lost. She willingly gave him her promise. What she'd seen, she would be more than happy to forget.

"You know I haven't seen anything, Sheriff," Barney said. "All I want to do is to get Amy back home."

Sheriff Morgan nodded. When he was satisfied that Barney could see nothing from his position on the other side of the vehicle, he ignored the two of them while he directed one of his deputies to begin a ground search around the gazebo, then he walked over to Ben. "Be sure you've gotten everything down in black and white before we start this next bit of business." he said. "I don't want anything coming back to haunt us."

I've got it covered, Sheriff," Edwards said.

Frank looked around for a minute, checking over in his mind the routines they had followed. Satisfied that everything was in order, Frank walked back and took Amy gently by the arm. As he led her away from the truck, he said, "Keep your eyes down and tell me when you get to the spot where you saw the body."

When Amy neared the gazebo steps, she found it hard not to stare at the covered lump she knew were the remains of Thurmond. Flies were still hovering around the dried blood, frustrated that their main course was denied them. She stepped up onto the first step and said, "I was right here. May I leave now?"

When the sheriff nodded his head, she literally ran back up the hill to the truck. Barney was already behind the wheel with the motor started. When they were once again in the front driveway, he said, "Are you sure you feel like driving? I can come back later to get my truck."

"No, Barn, that's not necessary." Amy was already scooting over to get under the wheel.

"You're going home, right?"

"No, I'm going to work. I can't just sit around and wonder who this maniac will kill next."

Barney nodded. "Okay. I'll meet you at the shop."

As he turned to go to his truck, Amy heard him mutter, "Bad stuff!"

CHAPTER 5

▼

As Sheriff Morgan watched Amy and Barney drive off, he pushed his Stetson to the back of his head and wiped the sweat from his forehead with the red bandana he used as a handkerchief. The heat seemed even more stifling than earlier in the day. What little breeze there had been, died. Not even a leaf moved in the trees surrounding the gazebo. The humidity nullified any cooling effect the shade might have.

"I'm getting too old for this crap," he announced to no one in particular. Frank walked around to the back of the house. Back at the gazebo, he stepped gingerly around the huge splotches of sticky black blood, stirring up yet another flight of flies. In spite of his years of dealing with the seamier side of human nature and developing hardened sensitivities, he felt his own stomach stir uncomfortably. "Be sure to get a close up of that note in his hand," he said, as he walked away from the cloud of insects.

James Canterly, a freelance photographer who had just arrived, late as usual, nodded his head and stepped in close to click off several pictures of the wad of paper in the body's left hand. Jim worked occasionally for Edward Wimberton, who was both coroner and funeral home owner.

But on a case like this one, James wished he'd had a legitimate excuse to not come. "Anything else, Sheriff?" he said, as he backed away from the blood and the expanding odor.

Frank looked over at Edwards, who was standing in the gazebo's back entrance, facing Corbin Creek below. "You need anything else, Ben?"

"I have everything I need except for the creek area. Jim, you might take a couple of shots from up here down toward the creek, then take some around the footbridge. I figure the killer probably came from that direction." Ben returned his attention to the pad of paper on which he was making rough sketches of the scene, and the proximity of objects to the body. "Give me a call when those films are developed, Jim."

After Canterly had moved away, Frank leaned over the body and with a pair of tweezers, transferred the bloody note into a plastic bag. He turned to Wimberton, who had finished his visual survey of the body and was patiently waiting with his helper a few feet away, a stretcher on wheels between them.

"I guess we can finish up the rest of our business without the body, Ed, so you fellas can have it now. Be careful of that outline when you pick him up, I don't want that paint smeared about." Ben had carefully placed plastic strips around the body, then sprayed its outline on the floor. "Also, Ed," Frank added, "be sure to stay on the stone path going back up. We don't want any evidence mashed into oblivion."

Frank watched with an eagle eye as the coroner and his helper loaded the body and pushed it up the hill to where the ambulance was parked in the driveway. When they had gotten past the critical area surrounding the gazebo, Frank joined two of his deputies, Pete and Archie. The two of them were walking very slowly through the grass in circles, gradually working their way out into larger and larger orbits. Occasionally they bent and retrieved objects with a gloved hand to place in plastic bags like the one Frank had put the note into.

Frank had told them before their first involvement in a crime scene, "If you keep your hands in your pocket at a crime scene, then you aren't so quick to touch something you shouldn't. He had probably repeated that statement a hundred times in the past several years. But he knew that more evidence is contaminated or lost by incompetent professionals than by any other method. He would also add, "And it ain't happening on my watch."

Ben walked near Frank, as he joined the three men in the widening search for clues. "My thinking is," he said in a low voice, "that our search will be just as unproductive as the one at the Mercer scene. We're not going to catch him making a careless mistake, I don't think."

"And my thinking is this son-of-a-bitch is human like the rest of us. He's bound to mess up some way, and I'm going to be in his face when he does."

"So you think he'll kill again?"

"That's my worst nightmare," Frank admitted.

He resented the hell out of the killer for choosing Hickorytree County in which to practice his grotesque homicidal talents. He especially resented the psycho for not delaying his deadly practices for just six more months. Frank wasn't running for another term. He had a cabin on the other side of Perry Lake where he planned to live, with nothing more to worry about than where he'd catch his next bass or trout. He no longer had the energy for the exhausting demands of pursuing felons, let alone for performing the mental gymnastics required to out-think a psychotic killer. A case like this one could kill a man. Especially a man who was worn down and in poor health like himself.

Most of the murders that occurred during Frank's career were honky-tonk shootings and knifings, usually with witnesses, or the occasional domestic killing which was always easy to solve. All he had to do was run down the husband, once it was the wife, and put his or her butt in jail until trial. There had been nothing too difficult to handle, with maybe one exception.

There was this one case, a double murder, which happened about twenty-two years ago that still haunted Frank. The killer remained unknown to this day, and the circumstances surrounding the case were as much a mystery today as when it occurred. Back then, Sheriff Maurice Riley claimed he knew who the killer was, but nothing had ever come of it.

Maurice had claimed he didn't have enough proof to take to the district attorney. He never told anyone else who he thought it was, so when Riley was killed in a one-car crash, whatever he knew died with him. Frank, being a new deputy at the time, had no authority to proceed with an investigation, but it had always bothered him that no final conclusion was reached.

It was still an open file, but no one seemed interested enough to dig up old bones, so to speak. He wondered why it had come to his mind so clearly at this particular moment. Frank shook his head impatiently. No need worrying his mind about an ancient case when he had the present murders to work on.

Ed Wimberton had placed the approximate time of Walter's death between seven p.m. and two a.m. this morning. The heat and humidity had remained high during the night and that made it impossible for Ed to be any more exact at the time. The body would go to the State Medical Examiner's Laboratory in Little Rock which handled all sudden and/or suspicious deaths in Arkansas. Frank would have to be present to witness the autopsy. He hated that, but would never admit to any of his men how squeamish it made him.

He looked down at the plastic bag which held the bloody note. It looked just like the one found in Mercer's hand. It carried the same cryptic message in block letters, "WHAT GOES AROUND...." The hand printed words were distorted with messy blots and scratches of black ink. After fingerprinting tests and paper analysis, the note would go to handwriting experts, as did the first note. He had yet to hear anything on that one.

"Okay, boys, listen up." Frank moved closer to the men whose attention he now had. "Keep everything you've seen or heard here under wraps. I don't want any details, no matter how small, talked about outside of those persons you see here now. No girl friend and no wife will spread gossip to terrorize and outrage our community any more than it is right now. The piece of garbage doing this filthy work would love nothing better than to see everyone in a panic. He'd also like to see his handiwork in print, and although we can't prevent the news media from saying what they want to about these murders, nothing of what they say will come from us.

"This perp wants to know he's worrying the crap out of us and we're not going to give him the satisfaction of knowing he's right. You understand what I'm saying?" Frank looked around at the men, who were standing very still and looking back at him. To a man, they nodded their understanding. Getting on Frank's bad side was a major headache.

"What needs saying about this case," Frank finished, "I'll say myself. Right?" Like bobbing automatons, the men once more nodded their agreement.

Satisfied that they would keep their mouths shut, he said, "Archie, you locate Mrs. Thurmond. I heard she's shopping somewhere in Little Rock with Nadine Benson. Check with William and see if he knows which stores they planned to hit. Pete, you go round up the gardener and the maid. Ben can take their statements."

Pete and Archie all but ran to their units, happy to escape the odor of death that with the day's increasing heat, hung like a foul layer of smog over the bright green lawn.

CHAPTER 6

▼

As Amy drove back to town, she had trouble keeping a steady pressure on the gas pedal. Her knees had not stopped trembling for the past hour. She gripped the steering wheel and shook her head violently, as if that would fling the putrid pictures from her mind.

"Think of something else," she told herself loudly. "Think about tonight with Leigh and how we'll talk about…" Her voice trailed away, then she said, "We'll talk about what happened to Mr. Thurmond, of course."

By the time Amy reached the shop she felt herself slipping from the edgy high of nerves and tension, into a weary, depressed state. It was easy to believe that someone had gotten so angry with Mercer that he had, in the rage of the moment, hacked the man to death. But two people brutally murdered in less than a week certainly weren't crimes of the moment. This was no accidental meeting between a homicidal maniac and the two men who died at his hands. Amy believed that Thurmond's death lent credence to the probability that the killer knew his victims well, and had a specific reason for wanting them dead.

Although the sheriff had not said so, Amy also felt certain that Don Mercer's body had been mutilated just as had Walter Thurmond's. There was a deadly purpose being played out in this, until now, safe and peaceful area that Amy loved. She wondered if there would be others.

As Amy pulled her Suburban into the alley behind the shop, Barney parked directly behind her. He was opening her door before she could pull the keys from the ignition. "Are you sure you don't want to go home and rest a little while,

Amy?" His face mirrored his concern for her. "Pinkie, Mary, and I can handle everything here."

"I'm sure you can, Barn, but I need to get back into my real life. Anyway, I forgot to tell you earlier that Pinkie called before I left this morning to say Tim wasn't feeling well, and she wanted to do a few things for him before she comes in. So I need to be here."

Mrs. Althea Spencer, better known to her friends as Pinkie, lived with her husband at Simmons House Inn, which was located six blocks east of Amy's shop. The inn was actually a retirement home for senior citizens who could afford to live comfortably without the worry of yard upkeep and other such responsibilities. It was a real help for Amy to have the older woman as a part-time clerk.

Amy reached inside the storage closet door and took her teal blue smock off its hook. "A lot of orders for flowers will be coming in," she continued. "The news of Mr. Thurmond's death will spread like wild fire. He's well known all over the state, you know."

"Yes, I do know." Barney hesitated a moment, then said, "I'm moving into your garage apartment. There's no way you're going to stay out there by yourself."

Amy lived almost five miles east of the city limits in a tri-level house on the river. It was a beautiful spot, but somewhat isolated. Her nearest neighbor lived at least a half mile away.

She opened her mouth to protest, but Barney shook his head, "I'm doing it, Boss, like it or not. You are not staying out there by yourself."

After a moment, she relaxed and smiled. "Sure, Barn. To tell the truth, I like the idea of having you there."

"That's my girl." Barney put his arms around her and gave her a hard squeeze before disappearing into the workshop area.

"Is something wrong, Amy?" Mary Griffith, one of Amy's full-time workers, was standing in the doorway. Amy wondered how much of her conversation the woman had heard. "Mr. Thurmond was killed," she said.

Mary stopped in her tracks, a shocked expression on her face. "Killed!" Mary lowered her voice to ask, "When did it happen?"

"Some time last night would be my guess," Amy said, as they parted ways. "We'll talk later, okay?"

Customers began to talk about Thurmond's death as the hours passed and the news spread over town. Amy decided she would call Aunt Leigh before the noon news came on. She knew someone would call the Little Rock television stations.

Two such violent deaths would make interesting fodder for the media, especially since both men were so well known.

Amy hoped that the fact that she found the second body would remain a secret. She had no desire to be interviewed by news reporters. She let Leigh's phone ring several times, but there was no answer. She wondered where her aunt had gone so early in the day.

"Good morning," Pinkie Spencer hurried into the shop. She went directly back to the storage closet. "Sorry I'm so late," she apologized breathlessly, as she put on her smock. Brushing back a strand of almost pure white hair with a hand laced with thin blue veins, she said, "Tim was feeling poorly and I needed to see that he ate his breakfast and took his medicine."

Pinkie shook her head. "Of course you've heard about Walter Thurmond." Mary and Amy both nodded as Pinkie continued, "It upset Tim quite a bit, and the other boarders are in something of a tizzy since we all knew him so well. Poor Grace, I feel so sorry for her."

"We know what you mean," Amy said. "Wouldn't you rather stay home with Mr. Tim today? I'm going to call Nancy Waggoner to come in anyway."

"Thank you, but that won't be necessary," Pinkie said quickly. "He doesn't like for me to hover over him, and if he starts to feel worse, someone will call me."

Satisfied that Pinkie was okay with working, Amy called Nancy, who agreed to come in as soon as she could get ready. Amy had no sooner put down the phone, than it began ringing with customers' orders for flowers. News of the second murder was spreading swiftly into wider and wider circles. People for miles around wanted to get their orders into the flower shops early.

Nancy was there in less than thirty minutes. Amy put her on phone duty to write down the orders, and Mary, who wrote a beautiful script, to write names and requested messages on the donor cards. Amy asked Pinkie to handle any walk-in customers. Amy stayed in the workroom, putting together the arrangements of both live and silk flowers.

At noon there was a break in business. Amy ordered in pizza and drinks for the four of them. Nancy took her food to the storage room. Almost immediately the others heard the thumping beat of rock music on the radio Amy kept in there. They had settled down to eat when Barney came in. He'd been to Sadie's to get some "real" food, as he put it.

He hardly got inside the door before he started giving them the news he had picked up at the café. "Archie Ledbetter found Grace and Nadine," he announced.

Amy glanced at the other two women. She hadn't told them about making the delivery that morning, so they wouldn't know that she hadn't found Grace at home.

"Where were they?" she asked.

Barney frowned, wondering if he'd made a slip, but Mary had gotten up to wait on another a customer, and Pinkie was cutting off another piece of pizza. Neither of them were paying any special attention to him, so he went on with his news.

"He met them on their way back up from Little Rock on Highway Five. Archie recognized Grace's red Cadillac. He took them to Sheriff Morgan so he could break the news to Grace. Frank was thoughtful enough to have Molly Greerson and Anna Ellison there." Barney had named two of Grace's closest friends. "Jim Arnold was in the sheriff's office on some business when they came in, and he told us that Grace took the news pretty well, but old Nadine had a fit. Said she squawked and carried on like it'd been her own husband who was dead. Luckily, the other two women stayed calm."

Amy listened to Barney with astonishment. He very seldom repeated the gossip he heard at the café, or any other place for that matter.

"I hope Mrs. Thurmond has family to help her through this," Mary said, back from waiting on her customer.

"Grace has a nephew in Russellville." Pinky offered. "I don't think they're very close.'

There was a brief silence as they each had their own thoughts on the plight Grace was now in. The violent demise of her husband changed things for her.

Amy folded the circle of cardboard her pizza had been on, and pushed it into a plastic trash bag. "There's something I need to tell you, Mary and Pinkie." Amy gathered her courage and continued to the two attentive women. "I was the one who found Mr. Thurmond."

The shock of her statement held her friends mute for the moment, so she hurried on. "I don't want to talk about it, and I want you both to promise that you won't say anything about this, not even to Nancy. However, this being a small town, it's bound to get out before too much longer, and I wanted you to hear it from me first, okay?"

"Of course, Amy," Pinkie reached over and squeezed her hand. "Mary and I understand perfectly, don't we?"

"Yes, certainly," Mary said, as she stood up. "I'd better get more cards out of the workroom."

After telling Amy that he would deliver the rocker left in the Suburban to its owner, Barney went back to the workshop. The four women were very busy until after four o' clock when there was a lull that lasted long enough to convince them the rush was over for the day.

"I've made a wreath for the Thurmond's front door," Amy announced. "I'm going to take it out there, and I'll tell Grace about her sewing cabinet before things get too crazy for her. I think you can do without me now." Amy turned back at the workroom door. "That reminds me, Nancy, can you come back tomorrow?"

"I could use the spending money," Nancy said, "so it works for me."

Barney had come up front in time to hear Amy say she was going to the Thurmond house. He watched as Amy wrapped the white wreath with its dark blue flowers and black ribbon in tissue paper. "Are you sure you want to go back to that house?" Wrinkles of concern marred his normally smooth forehead. "I'm not busy, so let me take it out there for you."

"I'm sure that I *don't* want to go back." Amy finished wrapping the wreath and motioned for Barney to open the back door for her. "But I'm also sure that if I don't go back now, it will just get harder and harder to return. Grace is, after all, a friend and a faithful customer. Besides I'm not going anywhere near that back lawn."

"Are you going to tell her you found Walter?"

"Not unless she says something first."

"You've got guts, Boss, you know that?" He smiled as he turned from placing the wreath in her car and gave her a brief hug. "You're also a pretty darn nice person."

"I don't know what I'd do without you, Barn," she said, as she got into her car.

For the second time that day, Amy drove up Bitterweed Mountain, then followed the course of the circular driveway at the Thurmond's house, only this time to park her car near the front door. The yellow police tape was still draped across the driveway that led to the back of the house. Anna McNear, the Thurmond's maid, answered Amy's ring. Her smile was a mere ghost of the cheerful grin she usually had for Amy. Her eyes and nose were red from crying.

"Please come in," she said softly. "Just a minute and I'll get Mrs. Thurmond."

"No, no," Amy said quickly. "I don't want to disturb her. I brought a wreath for the front door. I'll just hang it on this hook I put there for the Christmas wreath last year. Just tell Mrs. Thurmond that I'll talk to her later."

Before she could go on to tell Anna about the sewing cabinet on the back porch, Grace came to the door. "Oh, Amy, it's you. I thought maybe James and Hattie had gotten here. But I'm glad you're here, come on in."

Reluctantly, Amy followed Grace into the living room. The last thing she wanted right now was to talk about what happened to Mr. Thurmond. She sat at the other end of the sofa where Grace now sat. Tears were pouring down Grace's cheeks. She wiped at them with a soggy linen handkerchief she held balled up in one hand.

"I can't bear to think of Walter dying the way he did, Amy. Who would do such a terrible thing? Everybody liked him, you know." Fresh tears followed the others.

Amy couldn't think of anything to say that might bring even an atom of comfort to Grace. She decided to get to her reason for being there. "Your sewing cabinet is on the back porch. I wanted you to know so you could have someone move it into the house." After mentioning the cabinet, Amy cringed inside. She was probably going to ask her when she put it there.

But Grace just stared off into space, as she said, "Yes, of course."

Quickly, just in case she thought of a question to ask, Amy rose to her feet. "I made a wreath for your front door, so I'll hang it and be on my way. She paused a moment then said, "I am so very sorry about your husband. If there is anything I can do, please let me know."

The grieving woman seemed too preoccupied with her own thoughts to fully absorb what Amy had said. Anna was nowhere in sight when Amy got back to the door. As she pulled the door open, she saw a man standing there with his hand raised, prepared to ring the doorbell.

The man spoke first. "I'm James Lendall, Mrs. Thurmond's nephew. Would you please tell her that my wife and I are here." Lendall apparently thought that Amy was the maid, though she certainly wasn't dressed for the part.

He wore the supercilious expression of a person who thinks well of himself and pays little attention to others. Amy thought the man probably didn't pay attention to his wife's apparel either. She was dressed more for a party than for a visit with a grieving relative. She wore a bright pink suit, stiletto-heeled patent pumps, and so much make-up that it was difficult to tell what the woman really looked like. Bracelets clanked when she moved her arms. The woman wore a bored expression that went well with Lendall's self-satisfied one.

Amy stood back to let the pair into the foyer. Before she closed the door, she heard Mrs. Lendall raise her voice to a volume suitable for the near deaf to say, "You poor darling!"

Amy retrieved the wreath from the back seat of her car and quickly placed it on the door. *If those two are all the family Grace has,* she thought, *then I really feel sorry for her.*

CHAPTER 7

▼

It was after five o'clock when she got back to the shop. Mary had already gone home. Earlier in the day she had told Amy she was working on an oil painting and was anxious to get back to it.

Amy thanked Nancy again for coming in on such short notice, then turned to Pinkie. "If you are the least concerned for Mr. Tim tomorrow, don't even think about coming in."

"I'm certain it's just an allergy causing his hoarseness," Pinkie said. "I called Dr. Thompson and got some cough syrup. That should help. I'll see you in the morning."

Amy locked the door behind Pinkie and Nancy, then cleared the register, putting the day's receipts into a bank bag. Then she called Leigh. Her aunt answered so quickly that she knew Leigh was sitting at her computer. "Hi," Amy said. "Is dinner still on?"

"Of course it is and don't you dare tell me you won't be here."

"No way," Amy assured her. "I had called earlier, and you didn't answer. I just wanted to be sure I still have the invitation."

"Indeed you do, Chickadee. We're having your aunt's famous lasagna, with key lime pie for dessert. Both of your favorites, right?"

"You know it is." Amy hesitated a moment. "You heard about Walter Thurmond?"

"I've been at the Little Rock library all day, doing research. Why? Is there something I should hear about him?"

"He was murdered last night."

After a second of shocked silence, Leigh said, "What on earth is going on in this town, anyway? First Don and now Walter. Why would anyone want to kill them?"

"And I'll tell you something else," Amy continued. "Your niece was the one who found the body." Unexpectedly, tears came to Amy's eyes and to her disgust, she began to cry. 'I'm sorry, I didn't mean to do this." She grabbed a tissue from a box on the counter and wiped her eyes.

"Come to Eagle's Nest immediately," Leigh demanded. "Or should I come down and get you? I can be there in minutes."

Amy took a deep breath and said, "No, I'm all right. Really." She wiped her eyes on the back of her arm. "I haven't really had time to deal with it yet. Hearing your voice set me off, I guess. I've got to run home for a quick shower and change, then I'll be there."

"If you're sure. We'll talk over a good stiff drink. How's that?"

Amy could hear the worry in Leigh's voice. "That sounds good to me," she said.

She no sooner put the phone down than it rang. Thinking that it was probably another customer, Amy hesitated to answer, but habit overcame her reluctance.

"Bordeaux Antiques and Gifts. May I help you?"

"I'd like to speak to Amy Bordeaux, please."

Her heart skipped a beat before thudding so thickly that Amy felt she couldn't breathe. Anger boiled up, making her blood pressure rise. She swallowed hard to gain some control before she said cooly, "This is she."

"Amy!" The baritone voice she remembered too well, even after all these years, still had its characteristic smoothness. "Sorry I didn't recognize your voice."

It was so typical of Stephen to not recognize a voice that supposedly had meant a lot to him at one time, while Amy knew his instantly. That pretty much described their former relationship, but she'd been too enamored the first several months of marriage to see that.

"It's been a long time," he repeated himself. "How are you?"

A dozen nasty remarks crowded her mind, as Amy fought to keep her cool.

"Are you still there?" he said.

"Yes, I'm still here, Stephen," she said calmly. "But I'm closing the shop. I have a date this evening." She was pleased with how disinterested she sounded.

"I'm sure you have. But it's a date, right? You're not married?"

"No, but you are." Amy's voice had an edge to it. "And how is your wonderful Jane these days. Is she as devoted to you as ever?"

"She was fine the last time I saw her." Stephen's voice remained unruffled. "As a matter of fact, we've been separated for a couple of months. Look," he said quickly, before she could comment on his marital status. "I expect to be in your area next week, and I was wondering if I might stop by and take you out to dinner. We could talk for a while and see how things go."

Amy wondered what on earth he meant by, "see how things go." She wasn't the least interested in seeing him, let alone seeing how things went. "We have nothing to talk about, Stephen," she said firmly. "Anything we had was finished a long time ago. When you dumped me for Jane and her father's money, you ended any need for us to ever talk again. Good-bye."

She sat still, her hand on the phone. Bittersweet memories rushed through her mind, forming a remembered collage of joy and despair. Stephen had once lifted her to heights of happiness. But he had also plunged her into depths of rejection and hurt that had ripped her very soul apart. It had taken her a very long time to reach her present state of objectivity after that careless destruction of her ego.

Amy stood and stretched, a smile brightening her face. "Well, Stephen," she said. "So Jane kicked you out. Maybe she found you in bed with another bimbo like herself. But what do I care? I'm off to keep my date."

She laughed aloud, suddenly feeling carefree and happy. Stephen had done her a wonderful favor when he left her. Amy just hadn't known it at the time. She hurried out of the shop and drove swiftly home.

Once there, she rushed through her shower, anxious to reach Leigh and the relief of unloading the day's experiences to someone she trusted. After she'd dressed, Amy brushed her thick black hair into a pony tail, then twisted it into a French roll. She clipped on square amber earrings and slipped her feet into gold-colored *Magdesian* thongs, then with a quick spray of *Lagerfeld*, Amy picked up a small leather handbag and hurried down the stairs.

The drive up Bountiful Mountain was on a narrow paved road that meandered up the steep incline. In places it traced the outer edges of cliffs, providing a breathtaking view of the valley below. Amy found it less challenging to keep her eyes on the road. She was a little nervous of heights, even though she appreciated the area's panoramic scenery those same heights provided.

Being on a mountain top with a road that did not encourage traffic, added to the exclusiveness of Leigh's home. There were times during the winter months when icy conditions cut her off from the world below. "It takes away all excuses to not write," she admitted to Amy, after a long spell of involuntary seclusion. However, since most of Leigh's winter months were spent in sunnier climes like Bermuda or Spain, bad weather at Eagle's Nest was rarely a problem for her.

Amy's Camry easily climbed the last steep slope, which led into her aunt's driveway and provided a view of the house. Leigh discovered the old building on one of her wandering drives that she liked to take when trying to plot out a new story. She had a decorator's flair for bringing out the best features of a house. The white and scaly outside walls were now resplendent in forest green with sky blue trim.

The hydrangea bushes, with their heavy clusters of flowers, added the perfect touch. A flagstone path led to the front steps of the porch. Amy much preferred the casual beauty of Leigh's home to the formal elegance of Grace Thurmond's.

She parked beside a red Miata, which seemed vaguely familiar to her. Leigh hadn't said anything about inviting someone else. Feeling a little disappointed, Amy punched the doorbell and waited.

"Why are you standing out here ringing the door bell? Come in, come in!" Leigh's arms went around Amy, and the warmth conveyed by her firm hug was both welcome and stabilizing. Hannibal, Leigh's huge golden retriever, insisted on being included in the greeting. Amy patted his head, then scratched him behind his velvety ears.

"Hello, Hannibal," she said. "You haven't seen me for a while, have you, boy? Your mistress is slacking off there."

"If the two of you will come inside, I'll close this door," Leigh said, in mock exasperation.

Amy and Hannibal followed Leigh's tall, slim figure across the thick, ecru carpeting that covered all of the downstairs except for the kitchen and eating area. Leigh's tan bare feet, sporting bright red toenails, winked in and out beneath her Egyptian-print caftan. Pewter ankle bracelets clinked softly with each step. A drift of exotic perfume left a pleasant backwash for them to move through.

"We have company, darling," Leigh said, as she and Amy entered the glass enclosed porch Leigh called her sitting room. Amy saw a lovely young woman, about her own age, seated in one of the wicker chairs covered in flowered chintz that matched the wicker sofa.

"I'm sorry," the woman said, as she rose to her feet. "I didn't mean to intrude on your family dinner." Her husky voice was pleasant and friendly.

"Nonsense, Gayle," Leigh said. "I planned to have you and Amy meet soon anyway. Amy, this is Gayle Armbruster, another writer. Gayle, this is my niece, Amy. You may have noticed her shop in town, Bordeaux's Antiques and Gift Shop? Amy is the owner."

"I'm a novice merely hoping to be a writer, and yes, I have seen your shop." Gayle said, as she smiled in a friendly way. "I've wanted to stop in, but am always busy with something else when I think of it."

Amy was struck by how beautiful this stranger was, and hoped her own smile disguised her reluctance to share Leigh for the evening.

Out of character for him, Hannibal moved to place himself between Gayle and Amy.

"Hannibal, don't be rude," Leigh scolded. He completely ignored his mistress and sat himself firmly on both of Amy's feet.

"It's nice to meet you, Gayle." Amy reached over the big dog to offer her hand.

Gayle's brown eyes sparkled with good humor as she stretched out her own hand to take Amy's. "He must be jealous of you, which is a fine attitude for a dog to have toward family members." Then added, "I'm not staying. I just brought Leigh the chapters she so kindly offered to proofread for me."

Amy wondered guiltily if the woman had picked up on her thoughts.

Gayle moved past Amy and Hannibal toward the entrance hallway. "Leigh, thanks a million. I'll call you in a few days."

Amy and Leigh followed her to the front door, Hannibal plodding between them. "I hope we meet again soon, Amy." Gayle said, as she stepped out onto the porch.

"Thank you, and so do I," Amy said sincerely.

They both stood at the door until Gayle had backed her car out of the driveway and turned it down the mountain road. "What do you think?" Leigh said.

"About Gayle? She's beautiful, and has good manners to boot. I've seen her a few times, driving around town, and wondered who she was. How do you happen to know her?

"I met her at the country club a couple of weeks ago when I gave a talk to the local writer's group. We spoke briefly after the meeting and she told me she had started a novel. We met again in the post office last week, and she asked if I'd read some of what she'd written, and I said yes. So, tonight she called to ask if she could bring it up to me, and again I said yes. I'll try to read her manuscript in the next couple of days." Changing her line of thought, Leigh said, "You'll never guess where she lives."

"How many guesses do I get?"

"You'd never get it right. She lives in the old Anderson home." Leigh waited expectantly.

"So, there's something I'm supposed to know about the old Anderson home?" Amy raised her eyebrows, inquiringly. "I know it's very old and belongs to someone in Alabama."

"Right, but that's not what I'm talking about. Of course, you were only eight years old when it happened," Leigh admitted. "Dr. and Mrs. Anderson were found in their beds, dead from multiple blows from a knife and a hammer. The killer, or killers, were never caught. The son, only about eleven years old at the time, was never found. It was assumed the perpetrators had kidnaped him although that was never proven."

"I don't remember the actual murders," Amy said. "But I do remember people talking about it, even years after it had happened." She screwed up her face as if in sudden pain. "Then brutal murders are not a new thing in Ashley Springs, are they?"

Leigh reached over to pat Amy's hand. "First, let me fix us a drink. Brandy?"

Her wet bar was cleverly concealed in a large roll-top desk almost identical to the one Amy had found for Nadine Benson. Only Leigh would dare to restyle an antique and get such interesting results. As she raised the roll top, lines of bottles were revealed standing where cubby holes once had been. A beveled mirror covered the back wall of the desk and reflected the sparkle of the bottles and glasses. Leigh opened a door on the bottom left side of the desk and removed two brandy snifters. She splashed a generous amount of cognac in both, then sat back down on the sofa.

After handing Amy her drink, Leigh extended her arm along the back, touching her niece's shoulder with her fingertips. "I'm listening," she said quietly.

CHAPTER 8

▼

Amy took a sip of her brandy, then began talking. She left out nothing, knowing that Leigh would never repeat any of the gruesome details. When Amy described the fly-covered genital area, and the black stitches that held Thurmond's mouth shut, Leigh gasped and said, "Oh, my dear child!"

After Amy finished the description of her nightmarish experience, Leigh was silent for a few moments. Then she reached over to take Amy's hand in hers and said, "I'm so sorry, darling, that you were the one to find Walter. You may not know this, but I dated Walter occasionally many years ago. That was right after you and I came here to live. I found him to be a boorish, vain young man, and I don't know that age improved him any."

Her ploy to distract Amy worked. "You're full of surprises, Leigh. I would have thought Mr. Thurmond was too old to catch your interest."

"Exactly the reason I was interested in him. I had been a widow long enough for men to intrigue me again. Walter, being older, seemed such a sophisticated person, compared to the few other men I had dated. Actually, he was arrogant and self-centered, and I finally had the good sense to admit to that. He married Grace only a few months after our fling had ended. I remember thinking that his wife would have her work cut out for her if she managed to hang on to him. Grace did very well, but I never envied her position."

Amy smiled at her aunt, as she said, "You could have been the social maven of Ashley Springs. Just think, all the women in this town following your lead like they do Grace's."

"That's enough out of you." Leigh playfully punched Amy on the shoulder, then her smile faded. "I want to try something. This may seem heartless to you, but I want you to retell your experience this morning as nearly verbatim as you can make it. And then tell it again."

Amy began to protest, but Leigh interrupted. "I promise you, Amy, the retelling will dilute the strength of the horror that you saw. So do this for me, okay?"

With Leigh prompting her, Amy told and retold the story. A half-hour later, she could repeat the details without nausea rolling in her stomach. The vivid colors, and the awful overpowering smell of the murder scene retreated to a distance that Amy thought she could bear. Although she could never accept the cruelty of the mutilation and death of Thurmond, Amy at least felt more comfortable inside herself.

"Now," said Leigh, after the last telling. "We will adjourn to the kitchen. Do you think you can eat now? I've gone to a great deal of trouble, so don't you dare say no."

Amy laughed. "Would you believe I'm famished? I thought that I would never eat again. But that wonderful smell filling the house has changed my mind. Lead on."

Hannibal got up from his position on the floor at Leigh's feet. He waved his tail expectantly. "Follow me, troops," Leigh said, as she led the way down the hall to the kitchen.

Leigh was a great cook and enjoyed preparing meals for guests. Her labor-efficient kitchen was also her favorite room in the house. The cabinets were of yellow oak and the counters were topped with pale yellow ceramic tiles. The appliances were black with copper trim. A large oak table was the center piece, and a matching sideboard stood against one wall. On the terra cotta tile floor, Leigh had placed several pale yellow scatter rugs. Hannibal chose to lie on the one nearest the table.

"Such a heavenly smell," Amy said, as she breathed in the fragrant air. "What may I do to help hurry things along?"

"Set the table, please. Another five minutes and the lasagna will be perfect."

Leigh tossed a salad while Amy took the poppy-patterned dishes from the sideboard. She also got out the glasses, silver, and napkins, then placed the cruets of oil and vinegar on the marble lazy Susan. Leigh added the wooden bowl of salad greens and a crispy hot loaf of French bread. From the oven, she took out the pan of bubbling lasagne and put it on a large copper trivet that Amy had placed near the center of the table.

"Shall we eat?" Leigh asked. Hannibal, who had quietly watched his two favorite humans make the preparations for their food, whined pitifully and thumped his tail on the floor.

"Right," Leigh said, as she got up from her place at the table and went to the pantry.

She poured him a generous helping of Choice Bits, then the three of them focused on their meal.

"Uhmm, this is pure heaven." Amy ladled another helping of lasagna onto her plate. "You're the best, Auntie."

"It's always a pleasure to cook for you." Leigh smiled at her niece. "You eat like a truck driver and look like a model."

"With broad hips," Amy amended. "I don't remember your ever refusing good food either, and you've always been thin. Good family genes, huh?"

Leigh poured more wine into their glasses. "Speaking of genes, could it be that our killer has a gene-related psychosis, or do you think his rage comes entirely from his environment? Something that happened to him when he was young? Or maybe both? In some cases, such deadly violence is a combination of trauma and inheritance."

"You mean child abuse." Amy frowned. "There's an argument for each side, of course. I think that an evil environment can twist a perfectly normal child into a total mess."

"Specifically, I was thinking of sexual abuse," Leigh said. "According to the research I did for my book, *Lethal Intent*, the mutilation of the genitals indicates that the psychosis of the killer is sex related. Not a passion for the sex act, understand, but a twisted view of what the sex act is, as applied to the killer's own experiences and notions of revenge. Something has smoldered inside this person, perhaps for a very long time, and is exploding in this deadly expression of rage."

"I certainly don't have the answers," said Amy, But what you said makes perfect sense."

She paused a moment, then said. "But why was Thurmond's mouth sewn shut? I asked the sheriff that question this morning, and he said he had no idea. However, I had the feeling that he did. I also asked him if Mr. Mercer's body had been in the same condition, and he nearly bit my head off. He said it was none of my business, and that if I knew what was healthy for me, I would say nothing to anyone about what I saw. He was actually threatening about it."

"I can imagine he feels very threatened himself, what with two murders he must try to solve. I'm sure, at this point, Frank Morgan has no idea who committed them." Leigh leaned across to put her hand on Amy's. "Take his advice,

Chickadee, and don't tell another soul what you told me tonight. You could say something to the wrong person and invite the killer's attention to yourself. I imagine that by now he already knows that you found Walter's body."

"Are you saying I'm in danger?" Amy felt a small thrill of alarm.

"I'm saying that you don't want the killer to think you're particularly interested in knowing who he is. Just go about your business as usual."

"Almost word for word what Sheriff Morgan said to me," Amy admitted. "Do you think the killer may be someone here in town that we know?" Amy felt even more alarm at that thought.

"He seemed to know Mercer and Thurmond pretty well, didn't he?" Leigh raised her eye brows. "I mean, he knew where Don's fuse box was, in order to turn out the lights and make Don open his back door. He also seemed to know that Walter spent time in the evenings in that gazebo. When you consider those things, you have to believe that it's someone both men knew, ergo, there's the possibility that we could know him too."

Until this moment, Amy realized that she thought of the killer as some evil stranger who just happened to kill Mercer and Thurmond. Not very reasonable, she knew, but better than facing the reality that the madman was someone they knew.

"That really scares me," she said.

"I'd rather have you scared and cautious, than lulled into a false sense of security," Leigh said. "Just because you find it hard to accept that someone you know, or have a passing acquaintance with, has a Mr. Hyde tucked away in his soul, doesn't mean you should ignore your own vulnerability. The old bromide, 'better safe than sorry', has a lot of meaning here, Dear One. That's good advice, even if it is old as the hills."

"I have no intention of getting mixed up in this insane mess," Amy said. "What I saw today makes me want to hide until the killer is caught. Whoever he is, he is definitely totally insane."

Leigh gave Amy a knowing look. "I know all about your innate nosiness, as well as your talent for instinctively knowing things no one else picks up on. You will keep your antenna turned off, right? Otherwise, Barney and I will have to put you under lock and key."

Again, Amy assured Leigh she was happy to stick to her own business. She had already decided against mentioning the strange pictures that flashed through her mind when she saw Mr. Thurmond's body. Leigh was so protective of her that Amy wasn't about to worry her with something she didn't understand herself. At least, not yet.

She helped Leigh clean up the kitchen and, as she was putting the leftover lasagna into a covered bowl for Barney, Amy remembered the telephone call she'd gotten before leaving the shop. "I have something of interest to tell you. It has nothing to do with this evening's subject," Amy said, as she dumped the spoon she'd used into the hot sudsy water. "It would take you a million years to guess who called me this afternoon."

"In which case, I'll pass," Leigh said with a smile. "That means you have about five seconds to tell me."

"Stephen."

Leigh's mouth dropped open. "You mean, Stephen the Snake?"

"The one and only," Amy said, laughing at Leigh's expression. "Think how I felt when I heard that voice from my past."

Leigh lost all interest in the pan she'd been scrubbing. "Why on earth was he calling you after all this time? Isn't he still married? His watchdog wife would never give him permission to call you. Had he snuck out, or what?"

"It seems that he and his Royal Jane have been separated for a couple of months. He said he would be in this area next week and wanted to take me out to dinner."

"And you said?"

"And I said to the effect of, 'Sorry, I'm not interested,' and hung up in his ear."

Leigh clapped her hands. "Good for you, Chickadee! I hope that gives him the tiniest idea of how you felt when he rejected you."

"I doubt that it was too much of a blow to him. A little dampening to his ego, maybe. But you know something? After the shock of hearing his voice, I didn't feel a thing except extreme relief. Isn't that great?"

The two of them talked about what could have prompted Stephen to call, both of them giggling and making up silly circumstances. They were happy to be laughing about something that at one time caused Amy intense pain. His call had placed him irrevocably into the dusty past.

As they repeated their good nights on the front porch, Leigh again cautioned Amy to be alert to her surroundings, and silent on the subject of the murder. Hannibal woofed his farewell, as Amy got into her car.

All through that night, Amy tossed restlessly, her sleep troubled with a dream of two people fighting. She heard screams and felt a bone-chilling cold that seeped into the middle of her being, making her ache with violent shivers. In the dream, Amy looked down from a height at red pools of blood spreading out below her. She heard the words, "I love you, Binkie. Mommy loves you." She felt as if she were in a snow blizzard, the cold like liquid ice seeping into the very center of her body. Amy woke herself crying out, "Mommy!"

It was a long time before she felt warm again.

CHAPTER 9

▼

The pen moved rapidly across the page, documenting the latest execution. Dim lamplight created a weak barrier against the dark shadows that filled the room and spread beyond it to the empty rooms of the two-story house. Occasionally the hand stopped in its race across the page as the author listened to the settling creaks of the old building as it adjusted to the cooler air of the night. Sometimes the sounds became stealthy footsteps, creeping down the staircase, or the bump of a door closing in the upper hallway. But then, only silence would follow, and the pen would again resume its flight across the page.

Words, thick and black, spread across the paper, as the narrative of anger and hurt took form. A narrative that recorded the judgement, sentencing, and execution of Walter Thurmond. Details of Thurmond's crimes, even to conversations held in the distant past, enforced both a feeling of justification and a strong sense of satisfaction for a job well done.

The collusion of the police, the sheriff, and their friends, as well as the participation of the judge in freeing the culprits, had already been documented. Games that were played by the "good old boys," and a law that served to protect the criminals and allow despicable atrocities to continue. At that point in time, only the victims had paid.

But that was now changed, for the once-powerful were now the helpless playthings of a justice more deadly than any they might imagine. When the final execution was completed, the sordid history of their sadistic arrogance would stand revealed. The precise application of punishment would be recognized by all who read this record. Common sense inspired by genius, they would think. These acts would exonerate forever those who were forced to operate outside the law, and might even inspire some to take up the cause of stamping out such atrocious behavior.

The hand paused in its rush to complete this particular chapter in history. In each case, every precaution had been taken to prevent harm to innocent bystanders. However, there had been two such deaths that were necessary in order to maintain secrecy. Their murders wouldn't be connected to the executions, and were not recorded here. A separate journal was kept on them. There was a deep satisfaction in knowing that when killing was the only answer, the strength was there to complete the job. To wield the power of deciding a person's destiny, leaving them alive or condemning them to death, gave one an emotional high unsurpassed by any pharmaceutical concoction.

The name of the next person slated for removal had already been drawn. He was keeping company with a very nice woman and by so doing, placed her life in jeopardy. Prevailing circumstances would decide her fate when the time came.

Finished, the black clad figure closed the journal and rose to place it into the wall safe with the others. The tall, narrow bookcase swung back into place and became a part of the wall again. Six dead, four others yet to meet their destiny. No need to hurry. Yet, impatience ran along nerve endings like a hot liquid. Just the thought of the knife slicing, blood spurting, and the victims' abject terror just before death, was an aphrodisiac more powerful than any mating urge that lesser beings sought. So why be so cautious? The police could never guess who was slaughtering the pigs.

The front door closed softly and the sound of footsteps neared the dark room. "Is it recorded?" *A beloved voice spoke at the door.*

"I just finished. Did you miss me today?"

"I always miss you when we're apart."

Hand in hand, they climbed the stairs together. They shared everything, the past, the present, and the future. When all the pigs were dead, they would still be together.

CHAPTER 10

▼

The next morning, Amy looked up from Nadine Benton's roll-top desk to which she was applying the last strokes of varnish to see Gayle Armbruster making her way through the clutter that seemed to proliferate in the workshop area. Glancing through the large double doors she had left open to help disperse the varnish fumes, Amy could see Gayle's red car parked in the alley.

"Good morning!" Gayle called out.

"Hi." Amy stood up, wincing as her back protested at being stooped over so long. "Come on in! That is, if you can get through the junk." She dropped the paintbrush into a can of cleaning liquid, and began pulling off her work gloves.

"Please don't stop what you're doing," Gayle protested. "I won't take but a minute of your time, and I can talk while you work."

"No problem," Amy said. "I was at a stopping point, anyhow."

She thought Gayle looked great for this early in the day. The crisp white shirt, denim shorts, and red thongs accented her slim figure. The white yachting cap with its navy insignia was a nice touch. Amy was conscious of her own paint-splattered work shirt and baggy shorts. She brushed her hair back from her face, then motioned toward an old side chair near the desk. As she pulled up a nearby stool for herself, she said "Have a seat. This coat of varnish has to dry first before I can sand it. What's happening?"

"I came to ask a tremendous favor." Gayle's lilting laugh made Amy smile. "I know it's pretty forward of me, considering that we only met last evening."

"I'll do what I can. What did you have in mind?"

"Well," Gayle explained, "every once in a while, when I'm stuck on some writing project, or I'm just plain tired of looking at words, I get in my car and drive around."

Just as Leigh says she likes to do, thought Amy.

Gayle continued, "The other day I was driving out on Highway 124 east of here, and I saw some iron beds propped against an old barn. Grass had grown up all around them, so they've probably been there for some time. I'm hoping the owner will sell them. The name on the mailbox was Mary Griffith. Do you know her?"

"Yes," Amy said. "As a matter of fact, Mary works for me here in the shop."

"What a wonderful coincidence." Gayle clapped her hands in delight. "Then would you ride out with me to look at them? They're rusty, but otherwise I think they're in pretty good shape. After meeting you last night, I thought you would be the very one to know whether or not they are good buys."

The hopeful expression on Gayle's face made Amy smile again. She glanced at her watch. "I've got almost an hour and a half before I open the shop, and Mary doesn't come in until nine o' clock, so we can probably catch her at home. If I think they're a good bargain, will you want to pick them up?"

"I don't think so." Gayle twisted her face into a frown, and Amy noticed even that looked good on her. "That is, my car wouldn't accommodate them. I do, however, want you to refinish them, or whatever it is that needs doing to them, if you could. Do you have a way of getting them here?"

"We can stop by my house, since it's on the way to Mary's place, and pick up the Suburban. Let me give her a ring to see if it's okay for us to go out there now."

Amy could tell from Mary's voice that she was reluctant to have someone disrupt her time at home. However, she agreed to let them look at the beds. While at the phone, Amy also called Barney at Sadie's Café to let him know where she would be.

It was another clear morning, promising heat and discomfort later in the day. But for now the air retained some of the freshness of the night's cooling. Amy had her car windows down.

"Too much wind for you?"

"No, it feels great." Gayle took her hat off and pushed a strand of her sun-streaked, blonde hair out of her face. "You know, my driving around serves a purpose other than helping me to relax. I am familiarizing myself with the area. Like the locations of both the populated sections along the river and lake, and the areas that are left to nature. The mountains are beautiful and I'm sure there are still plenty of unpeopled spaces here."

"They are becoming more difficult to find with each passing year," Amy said. "Our lake and river draw thousands of tourists each year. Many of them come back to either build a vacation home, or to move here permanently."

"If you don't mind my asking, how do you happen to live here? Were you born here?"

"No, that blessed event happened in Chicago." Amy hesitated a moment before going on. "My mother died when I was very young, and my dad was killed in the Vietnam War before I was born. Aunt Leigh, who is my dad's sister, adopted me soon after my mother died. That's when we moved here." Amy wondered at herself for revealing so much.

"Leigh adopted you? How wonderful! But being only a baby at the time, wouldn't you naturally call her 'mother'?"

Feeling she was giving far too much personal information, Amy nevertheless felt compelled to finish what she'd started. "Leigh taught me to call her 'Aunt.' Then when I was old enough to carry on a conversation, she explained that my real mother was the only one deserving that title. Leigh said she was happy just to have me with her."

Amy could hear the sincerity in Gayle's voice when she said, "You're blessed to have someone like Leigh to love you so unselfishly."

"I know."

"So, you're satisfied living the small town life, huh?" Gayle smiled at her.

"As, apparently, are you." Amy smiled in return. "Why are you here?" This business of asking questions could go both ways, she had decided.

"I come from a small town too. Then a girlfriend and I moved to the Big Apple to make our fortune. We decided to go into business for ourselves, rather than work for someone else. There were no fast food stores in the neighborhood we looked at, so we decided a coffee shop would do well.

"It just happened to be a neighborhood that Yuppies were moving into, and our business took off. We made buckets of money. I cooked enough doughnuts to feed China before our first real pay day and our first real cook." Gayle's infectious laugh pealed out.

"So, then what happened?" Gayle had no second thoughts about sharing her life with a near stranger. *Maybe I hold back too much sometimes*, Amy thought, as she listened to Gayle continue her tale.

"Marion liked the donut business more than I did, and eventually bought me out. I invested the money that I got from the business in stocks and bonds, then went to work at Carnsworth Department Store as a model in the bridal department. Can you believe that? It was pretty good money and a lot of fun, so I stayed with that for five years.

"But eventually the big city life got on my nerves. Sections of the town, once prosperous and popular, began to turn into abandoned buildings covered with gang graffiti. Store robberies became common, and the better stores began moving out of the downtown area, and into huge malls.

"I moved to Mobile, Alabama, where I had some kinfolks, but that proved to be unsatisfactory, so I decided to find a small, peaceful town where I felt safe. A friend of mine had been to Arkansas and convinced me that the Ozark Mountains would be the perfect place to live. I was just lucky to find a place here." Gayle smiled. "That's my story, and here I am."

"There's definitely something to be said for feeling safe here." Then Amy frowned. "That is until recently."

"You mean the murders?" Gayle said.

"Exactly. It gives me the creeps to know that someone totally nuts is running loose in our community. Until it's established that there's a specific motive for the two killings, I guess we'll all feel a bit vulnerable."

"I don't think we have anything to be worried about."

Amy looked over at Gayle, surprised by the certainty behind her words. "How can you be so sure?"

Gayle laughed again. "I only meant that both victims were male and well past middle-age, the exact opposite from us. I should think that any other victims probably would be of a similar description."

"Good heavens! You sound like a certain detective I know." Amy instantly realized she shouldn't have mentioned the detective, but to her relief, Gayle didn't seem to notice.

"No, no," Gayle protested. "That's just the way it happens in the murder mysteries I've read, which I'll immediately admit makes me a novice in such matters."

"Sometimes truth really is stranger than fiction," Amy said, as she swung the Camry into her driveway. "And in this case, I'd rather not get too relaxed about anything,"

A low wall of red brick lined each side of the paved drive, which curved in front of the house and up to the enclosed garage. Amy had pushed the electronic door opener and now drove in to park next to the Suburban.

Leigh had the house built after the two of them moved to Arkansas. She wanted to make a real home for her little girl and bought this river lot located a few miles outside of town. At that time most of the river property was undeveloped, with no city water supply or sewer system. There was electricity and Leigh chose to heat with propane gas, so they had all the comforts of city living without the hassle of traffic and noisy neighbors.

Leigh had the deed put in Amy's name on her eighteenth birthday. A few years later, after Amy's divorce, she returned to Ashley Springs to live. Leigh bought Eagles Nest and moved out.

At Amy's protests, Leigh had said, "You don't need me around on a daily basis, and frankly, I would enjoy some independence myself. It's best for both of us." Leigh was right.

"I love it," Gayle said, as they walked across the tree-shaded yard which sloped at the back to the blue-green water of the flowing river. Flower beds, lined with rocks and loaded with blossoms of every color, covered a large area of the yard. Big, flat stones made up the path that led down the river bank to a rock patio at the edge of the water.

"Come on in," Amy invited after she unlocked the front door.

The house was built on three levels. Steps descended from the small foyer into the living room. The entire back wall, which faced the river, was glass. There was a deck outside the living room that provided shade for a second deck on the lower floor. Along one wall two sets of stairs were divided by a broad landing area. One ascended to the bedroom area on the top floor. The other descended to the lower floor where the kitchen, dining room, den and a guest bedroom and bath were located. The cathedral ceiling created the illusion of spaciousness.

After a quick tour of the house, Gayle said, "You've got so much room! I've never seen space used so efficiently."

"Now you sound like a real estate agent," Amy teased.

"Oh, no. I just like seeing different interiors, especially one as interesting as this. It gives me ideas for description in my stories. Where did Leigh find her house plans?"

"She designed the house herself, then had the blueprints made by an architectural firm in Little Rock."

"She's a very talented lady," Gayle said admiringly.

Amy led the way back to the kitchen and picked up a set of keys from a basket near the stove. She took off one key and left it on a shelf in the garage. "Barney said he'd mow the yard today," Amy explained. "He'll need the key to the storage house."

Several minutes later, Amy turned onto the dusty road that led to Mary Griffith's house. Mary had renovated the house just enough to suit her needs. She had converted the attic into a studio, but left the bottom floor structurally unchanged. New paint and paper lightened the rooms, and Amy, who had helped Mary do the painting, thought it looked very nice. The outside of the house was a pale yellow and the shutters and trim were white. A huge improvement over the original unpainted cedar exterior.

Amy gave the horn a brief bleat to let her know they had arrived, then she and Gayle got out of the Suburban and walked toward the house. Mary raised the large attic window, and for a fraction of a second, Amy saw her freeze. She could have sworn that Mary looked angry, but the expression was fleeting.

"I'll be down as soon as I clean my hands," she said, as she closed the window.

I hope we didn't upset her too much by coming out now, Amy thought. *And I hope Gayle didn't see the same thing I did.*

"So, this Mary is an artist?" Gayle asked, after she and Amy had settled on a bench under one of the huge oak trees that surrounded the house.

"A very good one, too," Amy said, relieved that Gayle apparently hadn't noticed Mary's frown. "I have several of her paintings in my shop. You'll have to come in to see them."

After about five minutes, Mary, dressed in a long-sleeved denim shirt and jeans, came out on the porch, wiping her hands on a white towel. Amy walked over near the steps.

"I'm sorry to interrupt your work," she said, smiling, "but I'd like you to meet Gayle Armbruster. Gayle, this is Mary Griffith."

Amy could sense Mary's drawing back even though she hadn't moved. She knew Mary was shy, although strangely enough, she didn't seem to have a problem with the customers at the shop. Gayle, who certainly wasn't bashful at all, walked up to the porch's edge where Mary stood, holding out her hand. "It's very nice to meet you Ms. Griffith. And I, too, am sorry we've caused you to stop your work. I promise we'll be quick."

"No problem," Mary said abruptly. She ignored Gayle's outstretched hand and quickly led them out to the barn.

Amy turned to see how her new acquaintance handled the snub and was surprised to see a strange expression on her face. Had she not known better, Amy would have thought that Gayle was badly frightened for some reason.

CHAPTER 11

▼

"Not very friendly," Gayle whispered. Amy chose not to respond, as the two of them followed Mary to the barn.

The three of them waded through the tall weeds that had grown unattended. Amy saw that the iron bedsteads were in good shape, considering that they had been outside in the weather for several months. The pair had exceptionally tall headboards which were made with graceful curls and swirls of iron. Amy thought they were quite beautiful really. She wondered why Mary had not mentioned the beds to her, since that was the business they were in. Amy knew they could have sold them very quickly.

"What do you think, Amy?" Gayle said. "They are pretty, aren't they?

"Yes, I think they could be beautiful when they're refinished. I wouldn't mind having them for myself."

"How much do you want for them?" Gayle asked Mary.

"I think they're worth every penny of four hundred dollars," Mary said, looking at the ground instead of at Gayle.

Gayle quickly said, "That's fine. I think they're worth every penny too, Mary."

Amy knew Mary was more upset at their visit than she'd first thought. The price was double what it should have been. However, Gayle wasn't the least daunted. She dug a roll of bills out of her shorts pocket and eagerly counted out four hundreds. It was as if she were anxious to pacify this unfriendly person for having bothered her.

Mary stuffed the bills in her jeans pocket without a word, then walked away to open the large gate so Amy could drive the Suburban in next to the beds. Amy and Gayle lifted the heavy pieces together, while Mary heaved others in all by herself.

When they had the last piece placed in the back of the Suburban, Amy got behind the wheel and said, "Thanks so much. Again, I'm sorry we intruded on your painting time."

Mary just said, "I'll see you at the shop." She did not speak to Gayle.

"She doesn't look like an artist, know what I mean?" Gayle said as they drove away.

"No. I didn't know artists had to look any particular way," Amy said. "Mary is an independent spirit who doesn't worry about what people think of her. I wish I could be more that way."

"Sorry, I didn't mean to be critical of your friend." Gayle apparently realized she had over-stepped her bounds with Amy.

"Mary lived on that farm for most of her life. From what I've been told by those who knew her back then, she had to work in the fields just as a man would."

"Must have been a very tough life," Gayle said softly.

Back at the shop, Amy parked near the large double doors. Barney came to their aid, and she introduced Gayle to him. "It's mighty nice to meet you," he said, in his best down-home way. Amy wondered what he was thinking.

"It may take us a while to get to them," Amy said, as the two women watched Barney prop the pieces against the workshop wall. "You can see how far behind we are." She waved her hand around the crowded area. "Some of the customers have been waiting weeks for us to get theirs pieces done." She could hear the telephone ringing up front and the buzz of people's voices. "Who opened the shop, Barney?"

"Pinky got here a few minutes ago," he said.

"If you'll excuse me," she said to Gayle, "I'd better change into my other clothes and get up there to do my job."

"Of course," Gayle said, smiling. "I've taken up enough of your time. Thank you for helping me. I'll call you later."

Pinkie waved at Amy from across the shop where she was helping two customers. Three other women were at the cash register, looking unhappy. Amy apologized for keeping them waiting, as she took their money and rang up the sales. She was relieved to see Mary, and then Nancy come in. Amy turned her attention to the growing number of customers.

A steady stream of tourists, and a constantly ringing phone made yesterday's business seem light by comparison. Amy sold a gate-leg table to a lady from Pine

Bluff. Another customer wanted a round oak table that had glass balls clutched in lions' feet, but didn't want to pay the price. It sold almost immediately to another lady who barely waited for the first woman to walk off. At the rate these items were being sold, Amy knew she would need to make a tour of antique wholesale houses to find replacements very soon. The flower orders for the Thurmond funeral kept pouring in as well.

At noon, Barney took orders for food again. This time they all decided on plate lunches from Sadie's. Another noon time lull, and they were busy again. During one of their most hectic times, Amy saw Bud Purefoy come in, a young man that she only knew by sight and reputation. He stood at the front door looking around, and she wondered what on earth he could want in a gift shop. Nancy looked up and saw him too. She waved to get his attention, and Bud walked over to where she stood.

They had a whispered conversation Amy thought looked pretty intense, with Nancy shaking her head, and Bud bending over her as if to bully her into something. Nancy glanced her way and saw Amy watching them. When the telephone rang again, she raised her voice enough for Amy to hear. "I can't talk now, Bud. You can see I'm busy." She seemed embarrassed to have the other women looking at her. "I'll talk to you later."

Bud, managing to look both furtive and disgusted, slumped his way out of the front door without acknowledging Amy or any of the other women. What a contrast in types the two young people were, Amy was thinking as she went back to the flower cooler to check supplies. Bud, tall and thin, had an acne-scarred face that apparently wore only one expression, and that was sullen.

Nancy had a friendly, outgoing personality, as well as the kind of looks and figure that naturally draws male attention. Amy felt Nancy could do much better than Bud, but knew there was no accounting for a teenager's taste in anything, especially in boys.

Late that afternoon, the influx of customers finally slowed down until there were only occasional browsers who drifted through, answering to the inquiry, "May I help you?" with, "No, I'm just looking, thank you." Amy, Mary, and Nancy had time now to clean up some of the clutter they'd had to neglect while busy.

The bell over the front door jingled again to announce Leigh's arrival. She had an armload of packages and managed to put them on the counter top without dropping any of them.

"Whew," she said, as she sat down on one of the stools behind the counter. "That sun is hot out there! I heard rumbles of thunder north of here just now, so maybe we'll get a good shower and cool things off."

"I certainly hope so," Pinkie said. "It's been too dry for too long. I heard the men talking yesterday about how everyone should be careful with burning trash, and such. They said the timber is so dry, it's ready to burst into flames all on its own. That's a scary thought, isn't it?"

"Let's pray no one gets careless." Leigh shook her head. "There are too many houses built in the wooded areas all around here, including mine. Rain would certainly be a blessing."

"So," said Amy, changing the subject. "Where are you off to, Auntie, mine?"

"And why do you think I'm 'off to' somewhere?" Leigh smiled at her niece. "Your ESP at work again? Well, you're right. I came by to tell you I've got to go to New York. I'm flying out of Little Rock on the six-twenty. Julia Kettelbaum called after you left last night and said they're talking a movie deal for my book, *Turned Around*. She wants me to meet with the Hollywood people in the morning."

"How wonderful," Pinkie said. "Congratulations!"

"Thank you kindly." Leigh turned to Amy. "You have all your troops here. I take it you've been busy?"

"That's for sure. I don't know what I'd do without these ladies. I also had an unexpected customer early this morning. You'll never guess who," Amy challenged Leigh.

"Let's don't play that game because I never win. Who was it?"

"Gayle Armbruster."

Amy went on to explain that Gayle had asked her help with the bedsteads which, as it happened, belonged to Mary. "Barney and I will refinish them for her, but I warned her it may take a while for us to get to them."

"That's wonderful, darling." Leigh looked pleased. "You need friends of your own age too, doesn't she, Pinkie? And you too, Mary." Leigh smiled at her. "You stay much too much alone in your lovely farmhouse."

While Pinkie nodded her vigorous agreement, Amy saw that Mary was embarrassed by the unwanted attention. She went to her rescue. "My wonderful Aunt Fix-Body should leave other people's business to them, shouldn't she, Mary?" Amy turned the attention away from Mary and back to Leigh. "When do you think you'll get back from the glamourous city?"

"Not for a few days, at least. I need you to do me a couple of favors, if you will. I've tried to call Gayle and haven't gotten her. Would you call her later today and tell her that I'm taking the manuscript with me to read during one of those times when you hurry up and wait."

"I'll call her this evening," Amy promised.

Barney came in from the back. "Hello, one of my favorite persons." He hugged Leigh warmly. "Thanks for the lasagna. I'll have it for supper this evening."

"You're entirely welcome." After she told Barney about her trip, Leigh turned to Amy "There's another favor I had on my mind. Hannibal watched me packing this morning and has figured out he'll not be staying at home. He thinks he's headed for the vet, and you know how much he hates that. I'd like for you to keep him if you don't mind."

"I would be extremely irate if you put him in that holding tank again. Hannibal and I get along famously. I'm his best buddy, next to you."

"You've got that right," Leigh agreed. "Barney, would you have time to pick him up later? I've got his things packed." Hannibal's things included his sleeping pad, a large chew bone, and a dilapidated old teddy bear he slept with.

The telephone rang. Pinkie, being the closest to it, answered. She hung up almost immediately. "That was Bob Merriweather at the house." She reached under the counter to get her purse. "He said Tim started feeling much worse a few minutes ago. I'll need to take him to the doctor."

"I'll pick you up at the front curb," Barney said, as he hurried toward the back of the building where his truck was parked in the alley.

"Would you like me to go with you, Pinkie?" Amy said.

"No, but thanks anyway. I'm sure he'll be all right. He's been having a few spells lately and this time he will go to see Dr. Thompson," Pinkie said, as she walked toward the front door. "You know how stubborn men can be about their own health."

Amy walked with her to the door. Barney was pulling up to the curb.

She hugged her friend. "I'll call you tonight," she said.

"Poor dear," Leigh said, looking sad, as she watched Pinkie leave. "Cancer is such a horrid disease, and a very difficult one for a spouse to deal with." Amy knew her aunt was thinking of her own husband's untimely death.

The telephone rang again. This time it was Marlene at the courthouse saying that Amy needed to come over and sign her written statement. To keep Mary and Nancy from being reminded of her role in the discovery of Thurmond's death, she pretended Marlene was a customer. "Yes," she said. "I can take care of that," and hung up.

"I must leave if I'm to make my flight out of Little Rock," Leigh said, reaching out to hug Amy. She gathered up her packages from the counter top and looked Amy in the eye. "You must be very careful. I'll call you from my hotel every night."

After Leigh left, Amy turned to Mary and Nancy. "I'm pooped," she declared. "And I know you are as well. I'm glad it's time to close. You've both been wonderful help and there'll be a bonus in your paychecks this week. Nancy, do you think you can work in Ms. Pinkie's place if she can't come back? I have a feeling she'll need to be with Mr. Tim."

Nancy said she could.

Before Amy was through with the closing up chores, the phone rang once more. It was Pinkie. Dr. Thompson was sending Tim to Little Rock for tests. Bob Merriweather was driving them down. After Amy offered to go with them, and Pinkie had adamantly refused, Amy said, "I'll check on you the first thing in the morning."

She located Gayle's number on the note pad where she'd written it earlier. Gayle answered after three rings, and Amy told her what Leigh had said about her manuscript.

After thanking her for the message, Gayle said, "I ran into Nadine Benson yesterday. I asked her if she knew of any really good places to eat in this area. She says the Sheep Pen has wonderful food. I wondered if you'd go with me some evening soon to see if it's as good as Mrs. Benson claims it is."

"I've been there, and Nadine is right, it is good."

"I know you're having a busy time of it in your shop right now, so we'll go whenever you think you can. I just wanted to see if you'd be interested."

"I appreciate your thoughtfulness," Amy said. "Please call me later because I'd love to go with you."

After Amy had replaced the phone, she finished totaling the day's receipts and added a few items to the shelves. Barney came in just as she finished. "Where have you been?" Amy said. "It's been awfully quiet in back."

"I went to Eagle's Nest and brought your star boarder back."

Hannibal walked over to where Amy sat and laid his broad head on her knees, his feathery tail waved his pleasure at seeing her, or perhaps it was the head scratching she was giving him. "I'm happy you're going to be staying with me, boy." She stood up and stretched. "I have had it," she told Barney, "I'm going to the courthouse to sign my statement, then we are going home."

"I'll take care of everything in back, then I'll be out there too."

As Amy got into her car, thunder rumbled distantly and she prayed that it would rain. But the thunderstorms were fated to move north of Ashley Springs that night and again brought no relief from the dangerously dry heat.

CHAPTER 12

▼

The day of Walter Thurmond's funeral, cars passed Amy's shop slowly, reminding her of a cortege. No voices were raised in greeting or conversation, as people met on the sidewalks, instead, they spoke in subdued tones. The approaching funeral service, and the cause of its taking place, had put a damper on the community spirit, stifling the normal buzz and bustle of ordinary life. Most of the businesses in town, like Amy's, would close for the funeral, so even the day's schedule was out of kilter.

A call came for Nancy, and Amy listened to the happy lift in the young woman's voice as she talked. Young people had a way of ignoring unhappy events and focusing on their more lighthearted pursuits. Amy thought there was something to be said for their sometimes myopic view of life.

After hanging up, Nancy approached Amy where she still stood at the front window.

"Ms. Amy, that was Alicia. You know, Alicia Morgan? Her mom is letting her have the car this afternoon, and we want to go shopping in Place City. I wondered if it would be okay if I got off earlier than you'd planned for me to. We have to be back by five o' clock, and it's a forty-five minute drive over there." Nancy stopped, eyebrows raised questioningly and hope in her eyes.

Amy knew, considering the mood of the town, that there probably wouldn't be much business after the funeral. She, herself, was leaving immediately after the funeral to visit with Tim and Pinkie at the hospital in Little Rock. Even with both of them gone, Amy knew that Barney and Mary would be able to handle things.

"Have you checked with your mother on this?" Amy wasn't about to take the responsibility for Nancy's leaving town, in case she 'forgot' to tell her mother. She knew from her years of teaching that with teenagers even the semblance of permission worked for them.

"I'll call Mom now, if it's okay with you."

As she watched Nancy make her call, Amy wondered if boys were included in the 'shopping' trip. If so, she hoped Bud Purefoy wouldn't be one of them.

"Ms. Amy, Mom wants to talk to you."

She took the phone and said, "Good morning, Mrs. Waggoner."

"I hate to be a bother, Ms. Bordeaux," Anita said, "but I wanted to be certain it was all right with you for Nancy to take off early. Sometimes Nancy states things the way she wants them to be. I wouldn't want her causing you any inconvenience."

Amy knew Anita Waggoner only as Nancy's mother, she had not been around the woman socially. Right now she was thinking that Anita sounded a little too meek by today's standards. Nice, but maybe a little soft? "It's fine with me, Mrs. Waggoner, as long as it's okay with you. We aren't likely to be busy this afternoon, so it certainly won't be inconvenient."

She handed the phone back to Nancy, who promised her mother again that she and Alicia would be back before five o' clock. Before Nancy could gather up her things, Alicia was already parked in front, tooting her horn.

Amy shook her head, as she watched the two girls drive off. Nancy had told her friend that she could go before she had asked anyone. So much for adults thinking that they were in charge. *Thank goodness, I don't have that worry!* Amy thought, as she walked over to the phone

She dialed St. Vincent's Infirmary and asked for Tim Spencer's room. A nurse answered and asked her to wait while she called Mrs. Spencer.

"Good morning, Amy," Pinkie's firm voice spoke in her ear.

"Did I take you away from something?" Amy asked.

"No. I was talking with the patient across the hall while the nurse was with Tim."

"Have you heard from the doctors yet?"

"They ran some tests this morning, but we won't have all the results until later today." Pinkie's voice quavered slightly, as she went on, "However, the doctor thinks the liver may be involved. He's having a biopsy done."

"Is Mr. Tim comfortable?" Amy hated pain in any form.

"Yes. He's asleep most of the time."

"I'll be down this afternoon," Amy said. "I'm leaving right after the Thurmond funeral."

"I wish you wouldn't bother," Pinkie fussed, but then added, "though I'll admit I would be happy to have your company."

After saying goodbye, Amy whistled for Hannibal. He would keep her company while she ate lunch, then got ready for the service.

But once at home, Amy found she couldn't eat lunch, even though she hadn't had breakfast. She filled her time with weeding some of the flower beds. At one-fifteen, Amy dropped Hannibal off at the shop, then drove across town to the United Methodist Church. Even though she arrived at the church thirty minutes before the service was to begin, she still had to park almost two blocks away.

She was hot and sweaty by the time she reached the front steps. Strobe-like flash bulbs blinded her as a gaggle of newsmen pointed their cameras at any and all who approached the front door. Thankfully, none of them seemed to recognize Amy as being the one who found the body. She had heard they were relegated to the outside of the church at Grace's specific request.

In spite of its enormous seating capacity, the church was filled to overflowing with both the caring and the curious. Amy found herself seated between two very large ladies, both of whom stared at her as if she had intruded into their personal spaces. She smiled at them apologetically and wiggled back against the hard wooden seat.

The cooling system proved insufficient for its task as the air in the crowded church became warm and stale long before the lengthy eulogies were finished. Everyone of importance was there and most of them, it seemed, had something wonderful to say about Mr. Thurmond. Except for the mayor, Lester Harvey Lumley. His bombastic delivery seemed to be slanted more toward proving his own importance by claiming a close friendship with the deceased than for doing honor to Thurmond. But finally, all that could be said was said, and the crowd shuffled outside into the hotter, but fresher air.

Most of the people were heading home, or back to work. Less than half the attendees drove to the cemetery. The Reverend Raddings must have felt the heat also, because the grave side service was blessedly brief, with only a few Bible readings and some hastily said prayers. In honor of Walter's service in Korea, there was a twenty-one gun salute, then Grace was presented with the triangularly-folded flag.

Amy found this a particularly sad moment. The flag represented so much more than Walter Thurmond. It spoke eloquently of all the men who had served their country, some who died in battle and others who came home changed forever from the people they once were.

After the presentation of the flag, the minister went to Grace first, then to the nephew and wife to offer his final words of condolence. A babble of low-voiced conversations broke out, as the crowd began scattering in different directions. Knots of people formed here and there, as they shook hands and talked for a few minutes, their expressions less solemn.

The sound of muffled laughter sounded among the groups farthest from the grave site. Probably friends who had not seen each other for a while, reviving a few common memories. Amy thought the lighter mood was partly due to a sense of relief at being among the lucky ones who were walking away from the grim business of death. All of them free to re-enter their normal lives once again.

Grace had looked lonely underneath the tent, with no children or grandchildren to fill the seats around her. Except for her nephew and his wife, she had no one to truly grieve with her, to hold her close and comfort her, since Grace's immediate family members were all dead.

Anxious to be away from the repressive atmosphere that seemed to hover over the cemetery, Amy decided to not wait for the crowd around Grace to thin out enough to approach her. She circled around the tent and struck out in the direction of the cemetery gate.

Off to one side, Amy noticed two people standing near a large clump of bushes some distance away from the grave site. The woman was mostly hidden from view by the greenery, so Amy could see only her hand on the man's arm. Something on the woman's wrist, a bracelet or watch, caught the sunlight and sent tiny jags of light sparking.

She glanced back at the couple, as she reached the cemetery gate. Amy still couldn't see the woman, but the man was Billy Joe Smith, better known as B.J., who worked for Dr. Lee Rash, the veterinarian. Amy was surprised to see B.J. here because Smith publicly expressed his dislike for Walter Thurmond. She had heard the man make derogatory remarks about Thurmond when they both were in Sadie's at the same time.

It was common knowledge that Mr. Thurmond had fired Smith as Moto's yard helper a few months ago. Talk had it that Smith had stolen some items from the Thurmond house. As she thought about it now, the whole affair seemed strange. Smith was not arrested and apparently had no problem getting a job with Dr. Rash.

Dismissing that line of thought, Amy began the hot walk back to her car. As she hurried through the humid, sticky heat, she was again haunted by the recurring picture of Walter's body. The funeral had brought back that day all too plainly. The feeling of nausea and disgust no longer accompanied the memories, but there was another emotion that had formed. It was especially keen today. Surprisingly, it was fear.

She told herself there was nothing to fear, yet the feeling grew. Amy thought perhaps it came from a subconscious dread of the killer becoming interested in her. Then she knew with certainty that the fear was not for herself, but for his next victim. It was her absolute knowing that there would be another victim that fed the root of her fear. A cold shudder brought goose bumps to her arms in spite of the cloying heat of this dreadful summer.

CHAPTER 13

━━━━━━━━━━ ▼ ━━━━━━━━━━

Amy opened the door to Tim's room and saw that he was asleep.

Pinkie walked over to the other side of the bed. She put her arm around Amy and motioned to her to go into the hall. The two of them walked down the hall a few feet to a small waiting room. They hugged each other and cried, then hugged again.

"My goodness," Amy said, wiping her eyes on a tissue Pinkie handed her. "I came to give you what support I could, and here you are comforting me."

"We'll do just fine," the older woman said firmly. "Having friends who share our hard times helps to make the burden lighter."

"Oh, Pinkie," Amy laughed through her tears. "You sound so…so Pinkie!"

"Well, I hope so," she said, smiling. "I asked my cousin, Ellen, to come down and sit with Tim for a while. I'd like to get out of the building for a short time. Have you had lunch yet? I think I may be able to eat something."

"As a matter of fact, I haven't even had breakfast," Amy admitted.

"Then lunch will be our first priority. But let's wait for Ellen in the room."

She led the way back to Tim's room. He was still asleep, so they sat on opposite sides of the bed, foregoing further conversation.

A few minutes later, Ellen Cantrell came in. When Pinkie introduced her cousin to Amy, Ellen said, in a near whisper, "Pinkie talks a lot about you."

After the three of them moved back out into the hallway, Ellen added, "You're every bit as lovely as she said you are." Then she turned to Pinkie. "Don't you worry, Hon, I'll be right here should Tim need anything. You go somewhere and relax for a while. You've about worn yourself out."

Ellen's appearance was solid and comforting, in her cotton shirtwaist dress and low-heeled walking shoes. Her brown eyes, magnified by horn-rimmed glasses, looked kind, and her smile was sweet. Amy breathed a prayer of thanksgiving that Pinkie had someone she could rely on for help.

The two of them agreed to go to Cain's Cafeteria, which was in the mall just across from the hospital. When they had settled at a table with their dishes of food, Amy told Pinkie about meeting Grace's nephew and his wife. "I had a strong feeling that they were there for more than to express their sympathy for Grace."

"Indulging in a little gossip here," Pinkie said, smiling. For a moment her face lost its tired, worn look. "Walter let everyone know that he couldn't tolerate being around James, who was Grace's only sister's child. The sister died a few years back and James is all the family Grace has left, so she occasionally visited with them. But if he and his wife are opportunists, you can be sure that Grace will put them in their place."

She took a bite of her salmon croquette and chewed thoughtfully for a moment before speaking again. "I knew Grace when she was very young. She was a pretty thing back then and wore her clothes well. I could understand Walter's being interested in her, but frankly, we were all surprised when they got married. But then, Grace had the kind of personality that attracted men like Walter."

"You mean she flirted with most men," Amy said.

"I suppose you could say that. But she behaved herself once she and Walter became an item. I've watched her change over the years from a young woman who was out of her league, into a ruling social matriarch. She never looked back once she had Walter's money behind her. The women of the town would never dare bring up her past because most of their husbands are indebted to Walter in one way or another."

"And now that he's gone, do you think she'll hold her social position without his influence to back her?"

"She has the money, and money is power. Yes, I think Grace will continue pretty much as she always has." Pinkie frowned. "Amy, have you adjusted, for lack of a better word, to having found Walter's body?"

"I've managed to put it out of my mind at least for most of the time. As long as I don't dwell on it, I manage pretty well. Thank you for caring." Amy reached over and patted Pinkie's hand. "You said you knew Mercer and Thurmond when they were much younger. Doesn't it seem strange to you that they were both murdered within a week's time? I mean, of course it's strange, but why the two of them?"

"I don't know, Amy. I've never been included in their social or business circles to know that much about them. Tim and I moved to Ashley Springs when those two were in the tenth grade. I was only twenty years old then." Pinkie smiled, "I guess because I was married I felt so much older. They seemed like children to me."

"What kind of people were they back then?"

"Full of spit and vinegar, as my father liked to say. They thought they had the world by the tail, and I guess they did. There was a group of about ten boys who stayed together most of the time, a bunch of troublemakers, really. Certainly not like the gangs that you hear of now, but their parents were always paying fines for their speeding, drunk driving, and disturbing the peace. The adults would talk the law officers into dropping the charges, and the boys would become that much more incorrigible.

"Then when the Korean War became an issue, they began to break up. Some of them, like Walter and Don, joined the armed forces. Being from two of the wealthier families around here, this was a big surprise to most folks. Just before they enlisted, there was talk that they had gang-raped a young girl and gossip had it that this was what brought on their moment of patriotism. It was their way of getting out from under a bad situation.

"It was also said that the families paid the girl's father a good sum of money. According to Tim, the enlistments were part of the deal they made with the sheriff, so the rape was more than idle talk."

"Do you know who the girl was?"

"No one seemed to know. Her family supposedly had a farm near Buffalo Shoals, a rugged and isolated part of the county. If the girl was from there, it would be easy for her family to hide her away from the public eye."

"So, what happened to the other men?"

"Alton Greenway was killed in Korea. Marvin Schneider moved to Florida when he got out of the service, married, and stayed there. Chester Plummer is in Louisiana, I think. Two others moved away to settle in California and Utah. The other three still live in our area."

"Would you tell me who they are?"

Pinkie put down her fork and looked at Amy, not saying anything for a second or two. "I probably shouldn't have told you all I did. I don't think I'll say anymore, although I realize you can find out from other sources. Knowing you, you'd want to say something to them and that might cause more trouble than it would be help. Neither of us knows if Walter's friends have anything to do with all this. Please forget what I said."

Amy wanted to demand that Pinkie tell her the names, but respected her friend's wishes and did not insist. Maybe when Pinkie had fewer worries on her mind, Amy would ask again. But she couldn't resist saying, "Do you think their doing what they did back then is tied in some way to the deaths of Thurmond and Mercer?"

Pinkie sighed and shook her head. "I don't see how, Amy. For many years now Walter and Don have lived their lives as productive citizens, running very successful businesses, and making scads of money. I've not heard a hint of scandal involving either one since they settled down. I think that if someone wanted revenge, he probably wouldn't have waited all these years. Maybe the killer just happened upon the two of them?"

"I can't believe it's mere coincidence that they both were killed," Amy said. "No. I believe that whoever did this had a special grievance against them."

"You may be right. I'm afraid I'm much too distracted over Tim to think that clearly about anything."

"I can certainly understand that." Amy's heart went out to the older woman.

For the sake of distraction, Amy said, "Pinkie, what do you think of me asking Mary to manage the shop? I need to be on the road right now, looking for antiques, but there's no way I can leave for that long. Barney has his hands full with the refinishing and repair work."

"That may be a good idea, Amy." Pinkie nodded her approval. "Mary seems dependable and quite bright, and she probably could use the extra money. But what about her painting? Do you think she'd be willing to lose more time from that? I know she said her real reason for coming back to Ashley Springs was to pursue her art work."

"I've thought of that. Of course, I haven't fully made up my mind to ask her," Amy said. "If I do, what would be wrong with letting her fix up one of the front rooms of the new building as a studio away from home?"

"Nothing, I'm sure," Pinky answered. "But you have doubts?"

"I have to remind myself that I don't really know her. We were mere children when we were in school together. Were you acquainted with her family?"

"Only in an impersonal way. You probably remember that Mary lived with her mother and grandfather in the house she's in now, and she always had to work hard. I told you about that, I think, back when she first applied for a job with you. I can remember her as a very young child, bringing eggs into town to sell house-to-house. I bought them because I felt sorry for her. She was such a shy little thing. Several years later, when someone told me that Mary had left home, I thought it was a good thing.

"It's her grandfather that I remember best," Pinkie continued. "He was a stern, self-taught minister, with none of the Christian love you see in a true believer. He preached 'the end of the world' on street corners on Saturday afternoons. Mary and her mother would stand next to him with their heads bowed in shame at the spectacle he made, waving his arms around and shouting hell and damnation. Did you know Mary's mother?"

"No," Amy said. "I don't think I ever saw her."

"Irene Griffith was a thin, timid woman who died in her early forties, not long after Mary left home. I remember Irene sometimes had ugly bruises on her face and arms, as did the child. Nowadays, the man would be reported for child abuse, but back then, short of killing someone, a man could do just about anything he wanted to his family without fear of reprisal.

"One day she came with Mary to deliver the eggs. She had some pretty bad bruising across her forehead and down one arm. I suggested that she tell the sheriff about the beatings. I thought the poor woman would faint. She turned white as a ghost, grabbed Mary's arm, and backed away from me as if I were the devil himself. She and Mary never came back after that. I truly regretted having said anything."

"Then what happened?" Amy was fascinated with Mary's history.

"Sad to say, when Mary got old enough and left home, Irene hanged herself from a tree in the front yard. I may be wrong, but I don't think Mary came home until after her mother's funeral. The family seemed bound to bad luck. A few months before Irene killed herself, the grandfather was found in an alley behind an old honky-tonk, stabbed to death. The police never did find out who did it.

"I know Mary didn't come home for that funeral, because Tim was among the group of men who volunteered to be pall bearers. Then when Irene died, Mary got the farm which she arranged to lease. After all the horrid things she went through in that place, I was very surprised to learn that she had moved back there."

"As I said, I remember her in elementary school," Amy said. "We were in the same grade for a while, then Aunt Leigh sent me to St. Albins Catholic School. I realized even back then that Mary was a very private person, and now I better understand why," Amy said. "Has she ever said anything about knowing you back then?"

"Not a word. But then I'm sure she wouldn't want to talk about those times, and I certainly wouldn't say anything about them." Pinkie shook her head. "I didn't recognize Mary, you know. She's changed quite a lot in her growing up."

"I guess most of us don't realize how fortunate we were as children," Amy said.

Pinkie noticed the clock on the cafeteria wall. "My land! I've been gone for almost an hour. Ellen will think I've forgotten her and Tim."

When the two of them got back to the hospital, Ellen was holding a glass of water while Tim sipped from a straw. He looked pale and weak, but he greeted them with a smile. "Did you girls have a good lunch?" Tim asked, as he settled back on the pillows Ellen rearranged for him.

"We ate enough, but mostly we gossiped," Pinkie said. "I see you didn't eat."

"All this dope they have me on takes my appetite." Tim held out his hand to Amy, who took it in both of hers. "And how are you, Beautiful Lady?"

"Great, and flattery will get you everywhere," she said. "Is there anything I can do for you?"

"As a matter of fact, there is." Tim caught his breath. He obviously was in pain. After a moment he said, "You might call Simmons House and tell Amos Hardiman that my newest copy of *Engineering Today* is on our hall tree."

"Be glad to," Amy said, patting his hand, then releasing it.

Ellen picked up her purse from the chair where she'd been sitting. "I'll be on my way," she said. "I'll be back this evening, Pinkie, so you can go eat supper."

In spite of Pinkie's protests, Ellen repeated firmly that she would be back. She told Amy again that she was happy to meet her, and quickly left the room.

"Ellen is a jewel," Pinkie said. "We are first cousins, but I only met her after our children were grown. She read in the newspaper about Tim's appointment as chief engineer of the dam project and called me. We've become close friends since then."

A nurse came into the room to check Tim's vital signs. "Dr. Lee has started his rounds," she told Pinkie. "He should be here in a few minutes."

"Then I'll leave now," Amy said. "See you tomorrow."

She left with a heavy heart.

CHAPTER 14

▼

The town had settled back into its normal routine, as one day blended into another and though the two murders were still on everyone's mind, their effect became less oppressive with the passage of time. Amy thought it was an added relief to everyone that the news crews no longer walked into stores, cafes, and any other place they thought a good interview could be had. The absence of their abrasive ways and their noisy equipment brought a modicum of peace to the town.

In spite of her wishes to the contrary, the word had spread that Amy found Thurmond's body. For several days, microphones were stuck in her face every time she came to town. Barney had gotten pretty good at protecting her from the press at the shop. He would put himself bodily between the reporters and Amy, then move them toward the door.

Between Barney's discouragement, and her single response that she had nothing to say, Amy's popularity did not last long. One reporter covered her role in the news event by printing garbage saying, "Amy Bordeaux breaks down, unable to speak of the horror of her discovery," An asinine lie. Naturally, some of the townspeople were curious too. A few of them asked her questions. She would just shrug and say, "It's over now. Let's forget it." They also gave up.

Although the sheriff and the police had nothing to say, other than that they were working on it, there was a noticeable increase in the number of out-of-town official vehicles that were driven in and out of town, or parked around the courthouse. Even with all that help, Amy got the gut feeling that the sheriff was no closer to the killer than he was at the beginning.

Today, Amy was helping Barney put the finishing touches on Nadine Benson's desk. He was ready to begin the cleaning process on Gayle's bed frames and wanted the desk out of his way. After they had put on the last coat of shellac, Amy called Pinkie. Tim had been out of the hospital for a few days and under the watchful care of the home hospice group. Pinkie could not praise the nurses enough. Volunteers, which included some of the residents at Simmons House, took over while Pinkie got out of the house, or just rested for a few minutes.

"Just checking to see if there's anything I can do today," Amy told Pinkie when she came to the phone.

"Not a thing I can think of, thank you, Amy. Just a minute." Pinkie came back on line chuckling. "Tim said that a minute or two of seeing you would be good therapy."

"Tell him I'll stop by after work, as usual."

Barney went back to the workshop and sounds of moving objects told Amy that he was clearing a space to work. Hannibal, who had been staying in back with Barney, must have decided it was safer on his cushion behind the counter. He flopped down with a sigh and started another nap.

While Amy occupied herself with waiting on customers and ringing up sales, her thoughts focused on what Pinkie had told her of the gang rape. She realized the heinous act showed a particularly callous attitude on the part of the young men. But also, callousness on the part of their parents. They were the ones who probably paid to keep their sons from being prosecuted by the law. With their families' support, the young mens' inhuman act was, in their minds, an acceptable expression of their own superiority. A dangerous attitude that could allow for even meaner behavior to be justifiable.

She found herself wondering what else they might have done. As she wrapped packages for her customers, Amy didn't see how a man could wait this long if he thought his daughter, or sister, or wife had been so horribly mistreated.

Amy felt a tightness gathering in her stomach as a sense of urgency came over her. She felt that she had to do something immediately. On the tail of that thought, followed her memory of promising Leigh to have nothing to do with the Thurmond case.

But what about the dream she had the night after finding Walter Thurmond's body? It was more of an impression than a memory, but it left her with a weird feeling of being connected in some way to the murders. Amy removed her smock and put it under the counter.

"Mary, could you and Nancy handle things for a little while?"

"Sure, Amy. Taking a coffee break?"

Reluctant to tell her where she really was going, Amy said, "Yes, I think I will. I'll be back shortly, then you can take one too."

She walked the four blocks to the courthouse building, then climbed two flights of stairs to the sheriff's office. "Hi, Marlene," she said, as she opened the door into the reception area.

"Hey, Girl Friend!" Marlene took off her head phones and swung around from the radio. "Everything going good for you?"

"Sure, things are great. I just had a couple of ideas I thought I'd talk over with the sheriff if he has a minute."

"Honey, I can hear that brain humming from here!" Marlene flashed her good-natured grin. "If you can wait until he gets off the phone, I'm sure he'll see you. Have a seat, and I'll get us a cup of coffee."

Marlene's short figure filled her uniform shirt and skirt until there wasn't a square inch of cloth that wasn't stretched to its limit. Her fondness for food was legendary, and when any of the other deputies wanted a special favor, they knew to bring her a box of candy, or promise her a free lunch at Sadie's. Marlene's good nature and generosity made her the most popular person in the court house. Sheriff Morgan had been quoted as saying that if Marlene ever quit, he would be gone the same day.

"Here you go." She handed Amy a plastic cup of steaming black coffee. "Guaranteed to perk up your spirits and cure whatever ails you." The smile faded and sympathy filled her dark eyes. "I hear Mz. Pinkie's husband has a bad problem. How are they doing?"

Amy shook her head, sadness gripping her again. "As you probably know, chances aren't great that he will survive for too much longer. Pinkie's being her usual calm self."

The two women sat quietly for a moment, the silence broken only by the static that issued from the radio. "Doesn't that thing drive you crazy?" Amy said.

"Sometimes, but thank goodness I don't have to work it on my night shift." Marlene said. "Everything switches over to the police station when we close at six o' clock. Just knowing I'm leaving it behind every evening keeps me sane!"

Amy put her cup down on the battered coffee table which held worn copies of *Field and Stream* and several brochures on the prevention of AIDS. "Do you think they're getting any closer to knowing who the murderer is, Marlene?"

"The Good Lord only knows because Sheriff sure don't confide in me." Marlene rolled her big eyes. "If somebody don't come up with the answer to this thing real soon, I think a bunch of folks will march on us. And the good Lord also knows that Frank Morgan is doing all one man can do! And that's enough said by me." Marlene stood up and looked at the telephone on her desk. "He's off the phone now. Wait just a sec."

She disappeared through the office door. A moment later she was back. "He's got to be in court in fifteen minutes, so you'll have to say your piece fast."

Sheriff Morgan rose from behind his desk and reached across to shake Amy's hand. His face looked drawn and more wrinkled than she remembered. She knew he probably hadn't had a decent night's sleep since the whole nightmare of killings began.

"Have a seat," he said, motioning toward two wooden chairs across from his desk. Amy took a seat, as the sheriff settled his large bulk back into his own.

"I'll be quick," Amy said. "I was talking to a friend of mine several days ago, and she was telling me how Walter Thurmond, Don Mercer, and some others had gotten into some sort of trouble back when they were young men. Something about a girl they had raped and the whole business being squelched by their families. Sheriff, you knew them pretty well back then, didn't you?"

"Are you implying that I was one of the rapists?" Sheriff Morgan leaned forward, his eyes dark, his face flushing with quick temper.

"No, of course not." Amy said, hastily. "I know you're busy and I was trying to hurry, so I didn't say that very well. It's just that I know that you were a deputy back then and thought you, better than anyone, would know details…." Her voice trailed into silence.

As Frank waited for Amy to finish her sentence, he saw her face slowly drain of color, and her eyes turn blank and staring. The last time Frank had seen a similar expression on someone's face had been on his long-dead brother's just before an epileptic seizure.

"What's wrong, Amy?" Frank got up from his chair and started around the desk to her. She looked ready to pass out.

She didn't answer, but her expression became one of fear and revulsion, then tears rose in her eyes and began to roll down her face. Really alarmed now, he considered pressing the intercom button for Marlene. "Please, Amy, tell me what's wrong."

When she still didn't answer, he moved around his desk and reached for the button on his phone.

"Sheriff Morgan." Amy's voice stopped him with his hand on the receiver. She had risen from her chair and stood there, shivering like a puppy in an icy wind. "You've got to find the killer right away because he's going to kill again." Her teeth chattered so hard, she could barely get the words out. She was facing him, apparently fully aware of her surroundings.

Galloping jackasses, he thought with alarm, *her seeing that mess that was Walter Thurmond has finally taken its toll!* "Now, Amy, we don't know that he'll kill again," he said softly, trying to reassure the obviously hysterical woman. "We have law men crawling all over the place, and I don't think he'll be trying anything again. We'll catch him."

Amy's expression became one of anger. "Don't patronize me, Sheriff. I said he will kill again. In fact, he's already chosen his next victim. You don't have much time." Then, as quickly as her anger had come, it was gone. Confusion filled her face, as she slowly shook her head. "Why did I say that?"

She rubbed her face with both hands, then stepped past him to the door. "To answer my own question, I don't know. But I do know that you don't have much time to stop him."

Frank felt the acid begin to burn its way into the back of his throat. He dug into his shirt pocket for the ever-present roll of anti-acid lozenges. Popping two into his mouth, he made another attempt to get the woman to see sense.

"I don't know why you said what you said either, but I do know why you're confused right now. You held onto your nerves for a lot longer than most women could, even longer than some men I know. But you've got to realize that we have things in a lot better control than it might appear to you. You've also got to forget all this and go on with your own business."

Amy didn't answer, she just opened the door and walked out.

Frank reached for his Stetson and jammed it onto his head. He left his office in time to see Amy close the outer door.

"What in the world did you do to Amy?" Marlene asked, raising her eyebrows. "Don't tell me you bawled her out. Now why would you do that?"

"No, I didn't *bawl* her out." Frank was in no mood to answer to his deputy. "She's beginning to come loose around the edges, so I told her to just get on with her life and let us handle the crimes. Anything wrong with that?"

"No, sir." Marlene didn't often see Frank Morgan in a defensive mood. Whatever had happened between him and Amy had to be something out of the ordinary. She wisely decided not to pursue the subject for the moment. Instead, she said, "You're going to have to hurry if you make it into court before the second 'Hear Ye'."

But Frank was already closing the door behind himself.

CHAPTER 15

▼

Amy stood on the sidewalk in front of the courthouse, still trembling from the strange episode she had just experienced. She had no idea what happened in there. One minute she was having normal thoughts about how she would get the sheriff to open up to her, then she was on another plane, seeing and hearing things she did not understand.

She walked the few feet to a bench which was usually filled with whittlers, men who gathered to talk while they carved chips of wood from small sticks with their pocket knives. Evidence of their industry, shavings of multi-colored wood, lay thick on the ground around the bench. Amy felt strangely drained of energy. The strobe-like flash of mental pictures she had seen in the sheriff's office were gone, but the frost of fear still lay on her spirit. The feeling was familiar, like something she'd had before, but Amy couldn't think where or when it was.

As she rested, the comfort of the day's warmth seeped into the cold places among her bones and her immediate world resumed its familiar coalescence of sight and sound. With the return of normalcy, came the memory of her behavior in the sheriff's office. He undoubtedly thought her one of those hysterical females for whom so many men felt disdain. And she had left without a word to Marlene. It wouldn't be easy to answer the questions her friend would have for her the next time they saw each other.

Amy stood up and began walking back toward her shop. She had blown it with the sheriff, and now he would avoid her at all costs. But she needed more information, and Amy thought she knew the one person who would be willing to talk to her.

Mary and Nancy assured her once more that they could handle the business. Now Mary wasn't the only one looking at her curiously. Nancy seemed interested in her unusual behavior too. Amy said nothing to satisfy their curiosity, but walked to the back to tell Barney.

"I'm going on an errand and should be back in about an hour." She waited for him to ask her what errand.

Instead, he said, "Gayle called just after you left. She asked that you call her when you got back."

"I'll do that now." She picked up the workshop phone instead of going back up front.

Gayle answered on the third ring. "I was wondering if you'd want to go to the Sheep Pen for dinner this evening," she said. "I know this is late notice, but we both seem to be on the run most of the time, and I thought I'd take a chance."

"As a matter of fact, I think dinner out tonight is exactly what I need." Amy didn't want to spend a lonely evening worrying over the strange experience she'd had at the courthouse.

Gayle said she would pick her up at eight o' clock.

Barney, who was rubbing wax on an old cedar chest, said, "Looks as if you have a friend. Just be sure the two of you keep a sharp eye out, and don't flirt with strangers." He smiled, but Amy knew he was concerned about her being out after dark.

"I only flirt with men I know, Barn. But since most of those are married, that could prove more dangerous than winking at a stranger."

"You know what I mean. You're leaving now?"

"I'm going to run a couple of errands. Mary and Nancy are doing fine up front."

Amy felt guilty for not telling Barney the whole truth, but she didn't dare let him know what her real mission of the moment was about. She drove out of the alley and onto First Street which led toward the lake area.

A few minutes later she stopped in front of a house in one of the more exclusive suburbs that fringed the shore side of town. Nadine Benson's red Cadillac Seville was in the three-space garage, and her husband's black BMW was parked next to it. But the '86 Chevy truck he drove around town was gone. William was probably hard at work at his real estate office. Amy pulled in behind the Seville and cut her motor.

"Amy, how nice to see you." Nadine, dressed in a skirt with a red and pink floral print and a bright red blouse, stood in the side door that Amy knew from previous visits led into a cavernous den. Nadine's purse was under her arm, and car keys in her hand.

"I see you're on your way out," Amy said. "Don't let me stop you. I can come back at a more convenient time. I should have called first." She backed up a few steps.

"No, no," Nadine said. "I'm going to Grace's, but I really need to wait a while. I ordered some barbecue ribs for her from Mitchell's and they won't be ready for another half-hour. I was going to wait in the store, but I'd rather spend the time with you. Come on in and we'll have a glass of iced tea."

"If you're sure, Nadine. As I said, I can come back another time."

"Of course I'm sure." She led Amy into the den and over to one of the two overstuffed sofas that flanked a massive stone fireplace. "I stopped by yesterday to see the desk, but you weren't there at the time. William will be beside himself with joy when he sees what I'm giving him."

Amy seriously doubted that William Benson got beside himself with joy about anything, but she knew that Nadine loved her own fantasies.

"Please, sit down and make yourself comfortable," Nadine said, already on her way back across the large room. "I'll fix our tea. It won't take a minute."

Before Amy could protest any further, Nadine had disappeared down the short hallway that led to the kitchen. Amy found herself alone in the big room with its atrocious furnishings.

Nadine's taste in clothes extended to her surroundings. Large chairs and big square tables were placed about the room in no particular order. Prints, stripes, and flowered backgrounds clashed on a jumble of chairs, sofas, pillows, and drapes. A variety of knick-knacks covered every flat surface. The total effect was one of confusion. In one corner of the room a massive television set and the single recliner facing it seemed to make a lonely statement. Amy thought that a lot of soap operas were watched from that chair.

"Here we are!" Nadine caroled. She was carrying a tray that held two tall glasses of tea and a sugar bowl. Amy hurried to clear a space on the huge oak coffee table in front of the couch where she sat. Nadine busied herself, seeing that Amy had a coaster for her glass, then dipping a generous amount of sugar into her own. As she vigorously stirred her tea with a spoon, Nadine turned to Amy with anticipation.

"Have you heard anything new about our murders?" she asked. "I can't bear to think what may happen next if Sheriff Morgan and the police fail to catch that crazy person very soon."

Amy was questioning her own wisdom in asking this woman for information, even though she knew time was critical. And while she couldn't say why, Amy felt there was more to the men's culpability than the rape of a girl. She had to use any means possible to discover if she was right. Nadine's capacity for absorbing information, then spilling it to everyone she met, made her a good news source, but a worthless confidant. Amy opted for curiosity over caution.

Ignoring Nadine's question, she said, "I was talking to a friend of mine the other day and she told me that when Walter Thurmond and Don Mercer were just young men, they had gotten into some sort of trouble. She didn't know exactly what the trouble was, but the group of young men the two had run around with had broken up shortly afterwards. Do you know what it was they did?"

Nadine's face lit up with a big smile. There was nothing she liked better than for a person to come to her for information. She leaned toward Amy and lowered her voice as if someone might overhear her. Amy found herself glancing back over her shoulder to make sure they were alone.

"Well, it's not for me to say anything negative about the dead, you know," Nadine began in a righteous tone, "but it was a long time ago, and boys will be boys. William knew I didn't approve of his running around with that bunch. After all, you're a married man, I told him. Some of the other young men were married at the time, too, but that didn't slow them down."

Nadine sat back and clasped both hands in her lap, pleased that she had taken a stand against whatever it was that she had not explained yet. Amy was dying to ask if William had also been part of the group when they allegedly raped that girl, but didn't dare. Nadine seemed unaware that she may have implicated her own husband in the wrongdoing.

"Do you think any of them were involved in something illegal?" Amy asked, to nudge Nadine into opening up more.

"I think they were." Nadine nodded her head vigorously. "Now mind you most of the talk was only rumors, but I believe where there's smoke, there's fire. If those men had been innocent, there wouldn't have been such awful things said about them. Grace and I are friends, so I don't want to be uncharitable, but I have to say that Walter was the ringleader. They pretty much did whatever he said do."

Amy, feeling frustrated with Nadine's meandering around the subject, was ready to ask her point blank what it was that the men had done.

"Good afternoon, Amy." William Benson's soft voice spoke from behind her. She jumped, but not as high as did Nadine. Amy turned to face him. His eyes looked huge and gargoyle-like behind the thick lens of his glasses. She managed to say, "Good afternoon, Mr. Benson."

"Oh, William." Nadine was on her feet, obviously upset at seeing her husband. "You can be quiet as a cat sometimes, can't you? Amy and I were just having a little tete-a'-tete, so to speak." She giggled nervously.

"I thought you were going to Grace's." William had a pleasant expression on his face, but Amy got the strong feeling that all was not well with this husband and wife team.

"Yes, I am, and I need to go pick up that barbecue right now. My goodness, the time has gotten away from us, hasn't it? Ready, Amy?"

Amy watched Nadine's performance, fascinated by the woman's complete loss of control. Many of the townspeople laughed about William Benson's being henpecked and submissive to his wife's every whim, but Amy was seeing a side of him she thought few other people had.

She gladly followed Nadine's swift passage to the garage. "I'll see you later, Nadine," she said, then turned back to see William standing in the doorway watching the two of them.

"Goodbye, Mr. Benson," Amy called, as she started toward her car.

He briefly lifted his hand.

Amy knew it had been a mistake trying to get information from Nadine. She hoped Mr. Benson didn't treat Nadine badly over the incident. She also hoped he hadn't heard enough to know what she was after.

"No indeed, not a smart move at all," Amy muttered, as she drove off.

But what really shook her was the expression she had seen on his face before he pretended to be friendly. It wasn't an expression she'd seen before in her many encounters with him over the years. Benson had always appeared smiley, friendly. She might be reading more into this than was there, but darn if the little man didn't seem downright sinister for a second or two.

"Well, let's not get overly dramatic with this," she said, aloud. "He was probably just aggravated that Nadine was gossiping again."

Amy sure hoped so.

CHAPTER 16

▼

Anita Waggoner stood in the bedroom door, watching Nancy tie her tennis shoes. "Where do you think you're going?"

"I promised Alicia I'd go over and help her with a home permanent. I'll be back before eleven." Nancy picked up her change purse and stuffed it into her jeans pocket.

"Does it ever dawn on you that you should ask me before you make plans?" Anita frowned, as she watched her daughter's unconcerned preparations to leave.

"I'm sorry, Mom." Nancy kissed her on the cheek. "I knew you wouldn't mind me just going over to Alicia's, so I forgot to ask. I'll ask next time, okay?" She was already walking down the hall.

"Just be sure you're home before eleven, do you hear me?"

The front door was already closing. Anita sighed. Nancy was much too independent for her own good, but Anita didn't seem to impress her daughter much with the few rules she tried to impose. If only her father were here instead of on the road almost every night of the month.

Nancy ran down the steps and across the yard. Actually, Bud Purefoy was parked at the end of the block some three houses away, waiting for her. Tonight was just another of the many times Nancy had lied about her whereabouts so that she could meet him. She just hoped Anita wouldn't decide to check up on her. She never had, but who knows when she might start. Mothers! Sometimes they could be a pain.

Bud, as usual, remained behind the wheel of his truck, revving his motor and leaving Nancy to struggle with the passenger door which always stuck. Her tight

Levis made the climb up to the seat difficult. Bud had installed risers that held the truck above its frame to make it look like Big Foot, the crashing, smashing derby winner of truck-wrecking fame.

Truthfully, and Nancy wouldn't dare say it out loud, she thought the truck looked ridiculous and awkward. But even one word of criticism would win her Bud's scathing diatribe on the stupidity of women. She told him once that he was a macho misogynist. Having no idea what she meant, he had laughed at her for calling him a dirty name.

"Why don't you buy a ladder for getting into this friggin' truck?" Nancy said, pulling at the seat of her skin tight jeans to loosen the pinch between her legs.

Bud's answer was a tire-screeching take-off that flung her back against the seat and popped open her door. For a second she thought she would slide out onto the pavement, but Bud grabbed her arm, then slowed down enough to reach across and help her get the door shut.

"That's it, make enough noise to get the neighbors out" she said. "They can tell Anita who I'm with. You are such a jerk," Nancy grabbed her seat belt and buckled it as she griped. "Between you and my mom, I'm not going to live long. She says she's going to kill me if I don't quit hanging with you, and you're trying to run me over."

"Hey, baby, it's cool." Bud tossed back the greasy wings of hair that hung on each side of his face and grinned at her. "Your momma been on you again, huh? You make her any promises?"

"No, of course not," Nancy lied. "She knows I'm not scared of her, but the bitching gets tiresome. I wish Daddy was here, he'd get her off my butt."

"You think your daddy is some kind of special, don't you?" Bud looked at her and grinned. "Well, he may not be nearly as great as you think, woman. Not that I'm saying anything."

"I told you before, Bud Purefoy, don't you make up anything about Abner. He works hard to make my mom and me a living and I don't want you bad-mouthing him."

"Okay, okay! I got other things to think about anyhow. I don't need no hassle."

"Yeah? Well, what is tonight all about?" Nancy asked. "What's with the, 'don't tell nobody we're going out tonight,' thing? You're on a secret mission, or something?" Nancy laughed at the thought.

"Go ahead and laugh," Bud sneered. "You wouldn't think it was so funny if you knew what I know."

"You are driving me crazy, Bud Purefoy." Nancy crossed her arms at her waist in disgust. "You sound like a little kid, for cripes sake. What do you need me along for?"

"You're making me wonder, myself." Bud was beginning to lose his temper. "It's business, Babe. You understand business? You don't have to know every-thing, and I'll tell you what you do need to know when it's a done deal. I just wanted someone along to help keep an eye out and their mouth shut. Can you handle that?"

Not completely satisfied with his answer, Nancy settled back into her seat. She couldn't resist tweaking him, though. "A secret mission, huh? The FBI hired you, or maybe the CIA?"

"I ain't as dumb as you think I am," he grouched. "You'll change your mind about 'ole Bud when I get this thing nailed tonight."

"But why can't you say who it is that you're meeting? You said I can keep my mouth shut, so why can't you tell me what's so important?"

"Are you gonna' make me sorry I brought you along?" Bud's top lip went into its favorite snarl mode, as he glared at her through the curtain of his stringy hair. "This is big bucks for me, and better not nobody mess me over on this."

"Well, not no one's gonna' mess you over," she said, mocking him. "Get real, Bud. There's no way to make big bucks in this hick town unless you're selling dope, or you're born into a rich family. The first had better not be what tonight is about, and your family isn't noticeably wealthy, right?"

"You do have your smart mouth on tonight, don't you?" Bud stomped the brakes as he spoke, throwing Nancy against her seat belt which tightened across her stomach. "You can walk home from here, you know."

"To heck with you, Purefoy! My mother's right, you're nothing but a jerk. I'll be glad to walk home. Then I won't have to listen to any more bull about all the money you're going to get from a pie-in-the-sky scheme you dreamed up. I don't want any part of it."

Nancy unbuckled her seat belt and wrenched open her door. Before she could slide off the seat, Bud grabbed her wrist and said, "Get back in the truck, or you're gonna' make me late. Come on now."

She hadn't realized they'd gotten so far out of town. Bud had turned off onto the narrow highway leading up to the top of Bitterweed Mountain. Thick woods lined both sides of the road and it was very dark. She let Bud pull her back into the truck. Once more, he reached across her and slammed the truck door shut.

"Look," Bud said, "I'll tell you what it's all about as soon as I know it's safe and we're out of here."

Nancy studied his face in the reflected lights and wondered about the word 'safe'. She thought he looked worried. If he was worried that meant Bud wasn't as sure of himself as he should be, and that in turn worried her.

"Right now I just need you to be with me and not ask questions. Okay?" Bud actually sounded as if he were pleading with her.

Nancy didn't like the feeling she was getting. "This someone you're meeting with, do I know them, too?"

"I told you to never mind who it is." He was back to using his normal rude tone. "Just do as I say when we get there and be cool."

The road they were traveling obviously hadn't seen any repair work in a very long time. Trees and bushes grew to the very edges of the road, and clumps of grass sprouted in the multitude of holes in the neglected roadway. To Nancy, it looked like a scene in one of those cheap horror movies, all deserted and spooky.

"Where are you taking me? And why did you choose such a godforsaken place, anyway? Does someone you know live up here?" When he didn't answer, Nancy said, "Why don't you just run me back home?" A note of mounting panic crept into her voice.

"Women!" Bud hit the potholes without slowing down, bouncing Nancy around and causing her seat belt to squeeze down again. "Nothing but questions all the time. No, no one lives up here, to answer one of them. Ain't been a house up here for as long as I know about. Back before I was born, the country club was here. The buildings are still standing, but they ain't in too good shape."

They had been climbing steadily since they left the highway. Through the openings in the trees, Nancy could see the sparkling lights of Ashley Springs scattered up and down the valley far below. She wished she were back home in her bedroom, talking on the phone to Alicia or Brenda about all their usual topics, like boys, what to wear to work the next day, and how much fun they would have when they went off to college.

Although she'd never admit it to her mother, Nancy didn't like being around Bud much anymore. The pull of infatuation, and the fun of doing things her mother didn't want her to do, had begun to wear thin. Lately, she'd found herself looking at him with critical eyes. Bud's crude manners and style of speech had become more irritating than entertaining. They left her with faint feelings of disgust. He wasn't the least bit attractive to her anymore, she decided.

Nancy's new point of view had developed in the past couple of weeks. Since she started working at Bordeaux's, as a matter of fact. Her new feelings had something to do with her admiration of Amy. Nancy wished she could be more like her.

Amy was beautiful, but that wasn't what impressed Nancy. She knew she was pretty enough her own self. It had more to do with the way Amy conducted her life. She stood on her own two feet, made a very good living, went where she wanted, when she wanted, and answered to no one.

Of course, there was Barney Scott, but he was more like a big brother and very good friend to Amy. Nancy had heard him make suggestions, but only after Amy had asked for his advice. This was so different from the way Abner treated Anita, and the way Bud treated her.

Her mother was always quoting Abner, as if she didn't have a thought of her own. And the way Abner talked to Anita proved he had no respect for anything she said or did. They had terrible arguments, or rather, he would rage on for the longest time about something Anita had done, or forgotten to do, while her mother retreated into a meek silence. Sometimes her mother would try to defend herself, but she was never allowed to say more than a few words before Abner was back at her again. He was out of the house a week at a time, sometimes longer, but he expected Anita to do things exactly as he wanted.

Nancy had always adored her father and sided with him in his demands on Anita. But lately, she had moments of wishing her mother should stand up for herself. She found herself wondering why Anita couldn't take pride in herself as Amy did. Why couldn't she make a decision without worrying about whether or not Abner would approve?

Nancy also wondered if what Bud had said about her dad going with other women could be true. Remembering how much Abner stayed away from home, and how little her parents interacted when he was at home, made it seem possible that Abner really might have another woman. This was a new way of thinking for Nancy. One she had yet to fully explore.

"We're here." Bud's voice jogged her back to her present unhappy predicament. She was sorry she had let Bud talk her into coming up here. He was really nervous now, drumming his thumbs against the steering wheel and jiggling in the seat as if he had to pee. Bud braked to turn between two brick pillars that had once held a gate between them. When the headlights swept past, Nancy could see the large hinges that were still fastened into the bricks.

They drove along a large circular driveway which was overgrown with tall weeds.

The truck lights revealed a huge, two-story building that was literally falling apart. The roof sagged at one corner, and the peeling, dirty paint on the walls gave a scabrous look to the broken boards. That and the dark lonely location, made Nancy think of chain saws and werewolves.

Bud drove around the curve of the driveway to where another set of brick posts marked the exit from the front lawn. He pulled the truck into an opening between the trees near the pillars and plowed through bushes and tall grass until the entire length of the truck was enveloped in the brushy woods. When he killed the lights, they were immediately covered with a thick, seamless black that seemed to smother the very air. Nancy had a panicky moment of claustrophobia.

"I don't like this," she said nervously. "Why do we have to be way out here?"

"Shut up," Bud snapped. His own doubts about the place increased by the minute. The place was more desolate than it appeared when he had checked it out that afternoon.

"Now listen," he said, his voice cracked with tension, "you stay in the truck. There's no way anyone can spot you in here, but if you hear anything, you duck down. Got it?"

"But why, Bud? Why mustn't anyone see me?" Nancy was practically babbling. Something bad was going to happen, just as her mother had warned her it would if she kept going out with him.

"This is not a good idea," Nancy insisted. "Please take me home."

"I told you to shut your mouth." Bud sounded ready to hit her. "I wish to hell I had left your butt at home, but it's too late now. You'll do exactly what I tell you to, *comprende*? Keep your eyes peeled, and when you see headlights down the mountain, give the horn a tap to let me know he's on his way up here. You got that?"

He didn't wait for an answer, but issued more orders, "When he pulls into the driveway over there, you make sure you stay quiet, and don't do nothing to call his attention to you. That way he won't see where I'm parked."

Again, he didn't wait for her to say anything, apparently taking for granted that Nancy would obey. Again, she thought of how much he sounded like Abner. Her eyes had adjusted to the dark enough that she could now see shapes of trees outside the truck windows. Bud opened his door and slipped out of the cab, then closed the door behind him. She heard the scrape of limbs against the truck as Bud moved toward the tailgate. Nancy could actually see him as he ran toward the old building, his light green sweat shirt giving off a faint glow. Dumb Bud, she thought, didn't know enough to wear something dark.

"Typical Purefoy thinking," she muttered under her breath.

Nancy hadn't worn anything dark either, but then she hadn't known there was a reason to when she left home. She promised herself she would not leave the truck, as she slid farther down in her seat, getting her head below the back glass.

CHAPTER 17

▼

Meanwhile, Bud was wishing he'd stayed in town, too. In broad open daylight his plan had seemed foolproof. He'd get to the country club first, hide, and wait quietly until the person left the money and then drove away. It occurred to Bud now that the killer might not just simply drive away. He was also remembering that he'd let the other person decide where they would meet. Not exactly smart, he admitted to himself.

"Damn!" He cursed out loud. He'd gone off and left his flashlight in the truck. He didn't have time to go back, retrieve the flashlight, spook Nancy into yet more griping and carrying on, and then get hidden again before his mark arrived. He'd just have to feel his way through to the room he planned to hide in. Anyway, he decided, the person would use a light of some kind to reach the assigned place in the building, and that way, Bud would see him first.

He had made contact by phone, not giving his own name, of course. He had demanded that the huge sum of ten thousand dollars in exchange for Bud's not telling the sheriff he'd seen that person's car in the lane behind Walter Thurmond's house on the night of the murder.

"I recognized your vehicle," Bud had said. "I saw you when you sneaked back to your car and drove off without turning on your headlights. If you'd turned them on, you might have seen me parked not far up the road from you." Then he'd added, "I saw what you did." Bud had heard that line in a movie and thought it was cool. The person, after calling Bud a few choice names, had agreed to his terms.

To Bud, the quick willingness to pay meant admission of guilt. Actually, he'd seen nothing except a vehicle which he recognized, driving out of Thurmond's back road that night. It was a stroke of luck, being at the right place at the right time. If this really was the killer, Bud wasn't worried because he'd disguised his voice by putting a folded handkerchief over the phone. He had also been careful not say anything that could identify him. Sweat rolled down Bud's cheek as he briefly considered what could happen if the killer learned who he was.

That afternoon, the flimsy lock on the front door had been easy to break, and he had scouted around until he found the best place to hide. Now, as Bud re-entered the old building, he stopped just inside the door to orient himself. He then made his way, as silently as the squeaky old flooring allowed, up a flight of stairs to the large room that had once served as a private club room. Bud managed to get across it without running into anything. He'd chosen a huge old leather sofa to hide behind. It was an ugly affair, large enough to seat twelve people comfortably. He didn't wonder that it had been abandoned.

Positioning himself behind one end of the sofa, Bud faced the door which was the only opening to the front stairs. He was certain that the person would come from that direction. Behind him was a door that opened to an outside set of stairs. They led down to what was once a large open veranda, but was now a tangled briar patch. Bud figured that after he got the money, he'd slip down the back way and keep to the trees until he got back to his truck. Then he'd wait for the other person to leave.

He knew Nancy wasn't about to tell anyone about tonight, and the killer sure couldn't say anything without giving away his terrible secret. Bud was sitting in the cat seat, and it felt good. With that last thought, Bud's confidence returned full strength. Any doubts he had about his scheme to get rich quick faded with knowing that he'd covered all the bases. His plan was perfect.

Bud's eyes had adjusted enough so that he could make out the darker shapes of the furniture and junk that littered the large room. Bud was pleased to see the lighter grey of the door, which meant that even without a flashlight, he'd be able to see the person enter and leave. Nancy's signal would give him time to be on the look out. Satisfied he'd chosen the best possible position, Bud settled down to wait.

Only a few minutes had passed when there was a light squeak behind him. He felt a small draft of air near his cheek before he felt the cool touch of metal above his right ear. A voice behind him said, "You shitty little bastard. Don't you know ain't nothing free?"

In the second before he died, Bud realized that the voice speaking in his ear was not the voice he'd heard on the phone.

In the truck, Nancy was whimpering, she was so scared. She had stared into the darkness for what seemed to her a very long time after Bud left. Gradually, her eyes adjusted even better to the dark and she began making out the lighter openings of the truck windows and the dim form of the truck hood stretching before her to the bushes. She could even see the darker patterns of the trees surrounding her. A light breeze caused small bumping, scraping sounds when the limbs and leaves brushed against the truck.

Each sound brought the hope that Bud was returning, and the fear that it was the mysterious person he was meeting here. Nancy swore to herself that if God would only let her get back home safely, she would tell Bud Purefoy to shove off. She never wanted to see him again.

Close to where she sat, a loud screech suddenly shattered the quiet. Nancy jumped so hard, she banged her head against the door facing. She was in a blind panic until the following, "who-who-whooo," told her it was only an owl. "Damn that Bud," she muttered, rubbing the side of her head. "He'd better get back soon, or I'm leaving without him." In his haste, he had left the keys in the ignition.

The next sound she heard turned her blood to ice. A single gunshot came from the old building behind her. "Oh, my god, Bud! What have you gotten us into?" Tears rolled down her face. She was almost positive that he didn't have a gun, so it had to be the other person who did the shooting. And that other person must have been here all along. What if he knew she was here too?"

The moment she'd heard the shot, Nancy had dropped to the floor board. She stayed huddled there, straining to hear any further sounds, like Bud running to the truck, or calling her name. But after a few moments, the need to see forced her back into the seat. Nancy looked through the back window of the cab toward the road and saw nothing moving.

Screwing up her courage, she slowly opened the truck door and climbed down to the ground, leaving the door ajar knowing that Bud always kept the inside light turned off. No doubt a habit formed from his life of crime, she had decided long ago. The limbs and leaves scratched her bare arms as she made her way to the tailgate of the truck, where she hunkered down behind the bushes that grew to the edge of the old driveway.

"Please don't let Bud be shot," she prayed desperately. From her position, she could see the building's front door. She stood up, but was afraid to step out into the clearing, knowing that her light blue sweater would show up just as had Bud's shirt.

She froze as her eyes caught a movement. Someone was running swiftly along the side of the building. The figure stepped out onto the driveway and ran toward the opposite end of the country club, but was no more than a dark shadow against darker shadows. It was quickly lost to Nancy's view.

A moment later she heard a motor start, and for a second or two saw nothing, then she realized a vehicle with no lights was moving around the circular drive toward her. Nancy scrambled farther back into the bushes and knelt by the truck again. She hid just in time. The headlights came on and as the truck followed the curve of the drive, its lights swept past where she had been standing. As it passed her, the reflected glow from the headlights and dashboard shone on the driver. Then the truck accelerated and disappeared down the old road.

Before she could fully absorb what she'd just seen, her eyes were drawn back to the old building. Flames were leaping out of the second-story windows. Whoever that was in the truck must have set the building on fire. Her stomach gave a wrench as she realized that Bud must still be inside. She ran toward the burning building, calling his name. Struggling with the warped front door, Nancy finally got it to open. A dreadful crackling sound came from overhead, and heavy clouds of smoke were settling down into the lower floor. She forced herself to move farther inside.

"Bud! Bud! Where are you?" she screamed, as she stumbled toward a doorway that was backlit by the fire. She found a set of stairs, but had only gone up for a few steps when she realized that flames filled the room at the top and she could go no further. Coughing and choking, blinded by the acrid smoke and fumes, she turned back. She heard timbers falling overhead.

Afraid of being trapped in the burning building, she rushed toward the front door and ran into something immovable. Her left knee took the blow, knocking her down. As she got up, excruciating pain stabbed through her leg, and she sank back to the floor. The roaring of the fire, as it devoured the rotten wood of the old building, filled her with terror. Nancy forced herself to get up and limp out into the blessed fresh air of the night.

Sobbing and coughing, she stumbled back to the truck. Nancy knew she had to get help for Bud. After a couple of false starts the motor kicked over, and she rammed the truck into reverse, shooting backward onto the grassy area. The flames had already eaten through the roof in places and sparks were shooting up into the black sky. The glow from the fire filled the nearby woods with a wild, flickering light that made her think of demons dancing in celebration. She gripped the steering wheel with both hands, and burned rubber on the old driveway.

Nancy drove down the mountain with reckless abandon, once banging her head hard against the roof of the truck, as the tires hit an especially large pot hole. By the time she reached town and parked across the street from the police station, people were already outside and pointing at the flames on the side of the mountain. A policeman ran out of the station for a look, then hurried back inside. In just a few seconds, both of Ashley Springs' fire trucks were wailing and flashing their way up toward Bitterweed Mountain.

There was nothing she could do. If Bud could be saved, the firemen would do it. She drove the truck to a Seven-Eleven store only two blocks from her house, parked it on the far side of the lot, and put the keys under the floor mat. Then she limped toward home.

It took her twice as long as it normally would to get to her house. Her knee was already swollen and hurt worse than anything she'd ever had before. Finally reaching her home, she slipped into the front hallway. Jay Leno's show was in progress behind her mother's closed door. Relieved at not having to face her, Nancy hurried into her bedroom and locked her door, just in case Anita decided to check on her.

Her knee was a real mess. Not only was it bleeding, it was also red and swollen, with a bluish looking area around the cut. As bad as her injury was, the pain seemed minor compared to her fear for Bud. She knew that if he had been able, he would have gotten out of that building. Then, like a cold stone, fear settled into her stomach when Nancy remembered that other truck. She was glad she hadn't gone to the police. At least no one knew she had been up there, and Nancy was certain that the driver of that truck had not seen her. She fell back on her bed, covered her face with a pillow, and gave over to her tears.

Later, she slipped into the bathroom to shower away the smoke odor that clung to her. The water stung her knee almost unbearably, but she stayed with it until she felt clean again. She rinsed out her sweater and put it on a hangar to dry. She'd tell Anita that she spilt a malt on it. Nancy ran a little water in the tub and used hand soap to wash the blood off her jeans. She would wring them out with a towel to get them as dry as she could, then hang them in her closet until she had a chance to sneak them into the clothes-hamper in the washroom.

Finally, tired and in pain, Nancy limped back to her room, put on her pajamas, and climbed into bed, knowing that her world had been forever changed. In spite of the two aspirins she had taken, the pain in her knee kept her tossing and turning until almost dawn. She couldn't stop thinking of Bud, and she cried until her head felt feverish and her throat sore and dry. The hellish scene of fire, smoke, and shadows, with the dreadful sounds of crackling flames and falling timber, replayed over and over in her mind. When she finally did fall asleep, she dreamed of being surrounded by the flames and screaming for Bud to save her.

CHAPTER 18

▼

The Sheep Pen was almost twenty miles east of Ashley Springs, not far from Place City. The name of the restaurant hardly did justice to its cuisine. Amy told Gayle its menu included a variety of ethnic entrees that would please the palate of most gourmets, but that the house specialty and the decor were Mexican. The public was served on a first come, first seated policy, so the waiting lines could be quite long, especially during the tourist season.

Amy and Gayle sat on one of the padded benches that lined the maroon and grey foyer and people-watched, as they waited for their table call. Since the dress code required shoes, shirts, and no shorts, the customers here were less casually dressed than were some of the vacationers who normally gathered at franchise eateries across America. There were no shorts revealing white legs and varicose veins. The men wore casual slacks, some with sports jackets, and the women wore pant suits or dresses.

Even so, they were both conscious of heads turning to watch their progress through the room when the hostess escorted the two of them to their table. Gayle's white linen sheath, unadorned except for a heavy gold locket and gold hoops at her ears, accented her long blonde hair and tanned skin. Amy's turquoise silk suit was matched with turquoise earrings which highlighted her blue eyes and black hair. Together, they were more than enough to turn men's heads and make wives snappish.

The Sheep Pen was literally arranged in pens, copies of those once used on this location where sheep were dipped to rid them of ticks and other insects before they were shipped off to different parts of the country. Horizontal slats enclosed each table on three sides giving the illusion of privacy, while also providing a view of the room. To further suggest seclusion, the lights were so dim that the features of other diners were difficult to make out.

Candles flickered in red glass holders on each table, and the wagon wheel chandeliers were outfitted with low wattage bulbs. These provided a soft light that erased wrinkles and created a veneer of youth for the older women. In her first quick scan of the room, as they were being led to their table, Amy didn't see any familiar faces.

"Your waiter will be with you in a moment, ladies," their hostess told them, as she seated them in one of the pens midway of the room.

"This has a more interesting atmosphere than the usual Mexican places I've seen," Gayle said. "The decor looks authentic."

"Perhaps that's because Mr. and Mrs. Wyndos, who own the place, lived in Mexico for many years before they came here to retire," Amy said. "Some of the furnishings and art are things they had in their own home there."

"Good evening, ladies. I'm Andrew and I'll be your server for the evening." A waiter, dressed in tight black pants, white shirt, and a bolero jacket began unloading his large round tray. He placed tall goblets of ice water before them, a stainless steel stand holding three bowls of different dips, a basket of tortilla chips, and two menus.

"May I get you something from the bar?" he asked, solicitously.

"I'll have the house white wine, please," said Amy. She was already reaching for a chip and spooning cheese dip onto it. Gayle ordered a vodka martini sans olive. Andrew was back almost immediately with their drinks. Saying he would return to take their orders, he left them to relax.

"Ah, now this is what a wine good should be," Amy said. "Body enough to lift the spirits, and silky smooth going down." She held her glass toward Gayle, "Here's to our friendship."

Gayle touched her glass to Amy's. "Hear, hear! I feel very fortunate to have met you, Amy. I know we'll continue to get along famously."

For a moment they both sat quietly, glancing around the dim room at the other diners. Amy looked again at a couple she hadn't noticed at first glance. They were seated almost directly across from them, on the far side of the room.

"See someone you know?" Gayle asked.

"I think I know the man sitting across from us," Amy said. "That being the case, I certainly wouldn't expect to see him in here with that woman."

Gayle reached for her drink. A beautiful gold bracelet on her arm sparkled with each move of her arm. A distant memory stirred just below the surface of Amy's mind.

Gayle was looking in the direction Amy had indicated. She said, "He's married, right?"

"He is if it's who I think it is." Amy laughed. "Would you listen to me? I sound just like those old biddies who tend to everybody's business but their own. So to change the subject, I think your iron beds will be beautiful. Barney will get the rust and old paint off, then put an anti-rust coat on them. Did you decide what color you want them painted?"

"This sounds a bit dreary, but I think I want them done with black, high gloss enamel."

"That's not dreary." Amy said. "They will be beautiful."

"Thinking about the beds reminds me of Mary Griffith," Gayle said. "I'm curious about her living on that farm by herself. Does she have anyone in particular she's interested in? Like a boyfriend? Or what about family?"

"She has neither that I know of." Amy shook her head. "You know, Mary could be quite attractive if she'd take the trouble. She's apparently not interested in things like make-up, hair styles, and clothes. I've hinted a couple of times that I'd help her with a make-over, but she always changes the subject. I think she would be very pretty if she'd just make a little effort."

Andrew, their waiter, was back at their table. "Are you ladies ready to order?"

"I'm ready if you are, Amy," Gayle said. "I'm famished."

Both ordered a green salad, then Amy asked for a medium-well done sirloin steak with baked potato, and Gayle ordered Italian meatballs, with homemade spaghetti, and a bottle of Arsenio's Cabernet Sauvignon to be served with the food.

After Andrew had brought their salads, Gayle said, "If you don't mind my asking, is there a man in your life at the present time?"

Amy laughed. "No, I seem to be in between male friends right now, and to be honest, I'm quite comfortable with the situation. What about you?"

"I don't have a boyfriend at the moment either. Are you okay with going out with another woman?"

"Why, of course I am." Amy looked at Gayle curiously. "Why do you ask?"

Gayle smiled. "Oh, nothing. Some women prefer the company of men in public. If they're with another woman, they're afraid people will think they can't get a real date."

"I'm afraid we're a bit backward here in our small part of the world. It's very common for women to have dinner together." Amy laughed. "I certainly prefer it myself given the choice of men around here."

"Sorry," Gayle said. "I didn't mean to make this sound like a second rate outing."

Amy smiled. "So, how is your book coming along?"

"Very slowly, I'm afraid. I've developed writers' block. You know, when ideas won't come, and words won't flow. It's like your brain turns to mush, and you can't write two decent sentences consecutively. I'm not in the same league with a writer like Leigh, who doesn't have that problem, as evidenced by the number of books she's written."

"Oh, yes, she does," Amy said, emphatically. "Not often, but sometimes."

By the time they had finished their salads, Andrew was there with their food. He poured each of them a glass of wine, then left the bottle in a cooler next to the table.

"It looks and smells wonderful!" Gayle said, as she used her spoon to wind spaghetti around her fork.

They ate in silence for a few minutes, then Gayle said, "We were speaking of Mary a moment ago. Didn't she live here as a child? I think Nadine Benson said she did."

"That's right, she did." Amy said, as she wondered at Gayle's continued interest in Mary. "We were in the same grade in elementary school, but Leigh sent me on to St. Albin's Catholic School, and I never saw her again after that."

"You didn't say anything about that the day I met her," Gayle said.

"I know. Maybe that's because I feel sort of protective of her," Amy said. "As a child, Mary didn't seem to know how to involve herself with other kids her age. Not any of us, her classmates, were of help to her. We pretty well had our own groups and did all our after school things together. You know how that goes."

"Yes. I certainly do," Gayle said.

Amy continued, "I do remember one time when I tried to be friendly with her. I think we were about ten years old at the time, and I decided I would ask her to my house to play. But she shied away from me like a whipped puppy, like she was afraid to talk to me. Her grandfather, who we all thought was a weird old man, was waiting for her as he did every school day. He drove a team of mules, hitched to an old wooden wagon.

"Of course, all of the families I knew had a car or two, and most of the high school students owned cars, so a wagon and mules seemed archaic to us. I could tell by the way Mary walked with her head down, never looking at anyone, that she was ashamed. Anyway, on that particular day he yelled at her to get there at once, and she ran all the way to the wagon. I'm sorry to say that, other than speaking to her, I never again tried to make friends with her."

Gayle had been listening with an intense interest. When Amy finished speaking, she sat back in her chair with a thoughtful look on her face. "You had an unusual capacity for mercy for someone so young," she said. "I'm sure she remembers you with kindness."

"Oh, I don't know," Amy said. "I was no more merciful than the other kids, except that I never made fun of her. She avoided me after that day, like the offer of friendship had embarrassed her. Occasionally through the years, I have thought about Mary and wondered what became of her. Then about two months ago she walked into my shop and asked for a job. I was very glad to give it to her and she's proven herself to be a very dependable worker." Amy shook her head. "You never know, do you?"

"That must have been strange for you, seeing her after all these years."

"It was like having the past walk into your door, bringing back all sorts of memories."

"Did she look much like the young Mary you remember?"

"No, as a matter of fact, she didn't. Of course, she's a grown woman who has lived on her own for many years, and that would naturally change a person. Maybe I expected to see the same fearful, shy person I saw when she was young. However, though not fearful, she is somewhat reclusive which can be interpreted as shyness, I suppose. All I know is, I'm glad she came back and is working at the shop," Amy finished, determined not to say any more on the subject of Mary. She couldn't get over Gayle's unusual interest in a woman she'd only met once.

CHAPTER 19

▼

As Gayle refilled her wine glass, her conversation took a different course. Amy was relieved that she wouldn't have to say anything more about Mary.

"About that man-thing we were talking about," Gayle said, smiling in amusement. "Mrs. Benson, and every other older woman I've met, with the exception of your wonderful aunt, wants to introduce me to all the unattached, 'suitable' males in the area. The ladies mean well, but from what I've seen so far, I have to agree with you that interesting male company is a scarce commodity here."

Amy laughed. "I know what you mean. When I first came back here to live, I was introduced to every single male over twenty years of age. I even went out with a few of them, just to satisfy my older friends. Most of the dates were pretty dull affairs. Finally, I just said, 'no more', and that ended that."

"Didn't any of them intrigue you?" Gayle leaned forward, lacing her long fingers together in front of her.

"There was one man," Amy admitted. "A lawyer; who was nice looking, good company, and 'upwardly mobile,' as they say," Amy laughed again. "Very mobile, as it turned out. After we dated a few times, he accepted an offer to join a firm in Seattle and left with a fond farewell. Now I'm very grateful I didn't have the chance to make yet another mistake."

"Another mistake?" Gayle raised her eyebrows questioningly.

"Yes, but that was a long time ago." Amy grimaced. "I'll tell you about it one of these days. It's not something I'm proud of, by any means."

"Why not now?" Gayle said. "The evening is still young."

"If you wish." Amy took a sip of her water and settled back into her chair. "When I was teaching at the university, that was four years ago, I met Prince Charming. He was a professor of archaeology. A handsome, charming, attentive man. He was just about perfect, or so I thought. I fell for him hard. After a brief courtship of eight months, he asked me to marry him, and I accepted. Leigh gave us a beautiful wedding in the cathedral there.

"Then shortly after we were married, Stephen began working late at his office. I thought nothing of it since I had a lot of paper work with my classes, too. The difference was, I brought mine home. Anyway, I didn't notice anything wrong until after he told me he was taking a trip to South America to an archeological dig there.

"He had said that the conditions would be too primitive and uncomfortable for me to go with him. This was during a summer term when I didn't have classes, but I concurred. Besides, he'd only be gone for a couple of weeks. Instead, he was gone four weeks.

"It was after his trip that I noticed a certain Jane Levy was at his office a lot. Once I saw them in the staff coffee shop together. She was just around, you know?" Amy smiled, and shook her head. "Stephen always had a plausible excuse for her presence, like, she was doing a paper and needed his input. She was helping tutor some of his students and needed to check with him on schedules, etcetera, etcetera. I learned that her parents were Abraham J. Levy and Muriel Strauss Levy, who had financed the building of the Levy-Strauss Research Center on campus in honor of their parents. Jane stood to inherit one of the largest fortunes in the South. Some competition, don't you think?"

"Sounds overwhelming," Gayle agreed.

"After a while, Jane made no secret of her interest in my husband. I ignored the rumors and the advice of my friends and did nothing. Looking back, there was probably very little I could have done, anyway. I returned from a week-end visit here with Leigh to find the two of them in our house, in our bed! So, I filed for divorce.

"Stephan and Jane went on an extended tour of Europe, and when they came back, they had a huge wedding. End of tale. With my added failure in holding the interest of the afore mentioned lawyer, you can see why I'm a bit leery of men. I would find it very difficult to trust any of them."

"Men can be total rats, can't they?" Gayle said.

Amy didn't mention the call she'd recently gotten from her former husband. Except as a item to share with Leigh, his involvement in her present life was a non-issue.

"Good evening, Ms. Bordeaux. Did you ladies enjoy your meal?"

Amy turned to see Abner Waggoner, Nancy Waggoner's father, standing there with a woman, who definitely was not his wife. Amy felt a wrench of dislike at the sight of Abner's greasy smile, but she kept what she hoped was a bland expression.

"I'd like you to meet my cousin, Margaret Finch," he continued, smoothly. "Margaret, this is Amy Bordeaux who owns a nice gift shop in Ashley Springs."

"It's nice to meet you, Ms Finch," Amy smiled at the older woman standing quietly at Abner's side. "This is my friend, Gayle Armbruster."

While a polite exchange of remarks was being made, Amy could see that, in spite of her calm demeanor, Ms Finch was uncomfortable. After saying again how nice it had been to see them, Abner steered his 'cousin' toward the exit.

"His daughter works for me at the shop," Amy said, as she frowned at the couple's retreating backs. "He's a salesman for a pharmaceutical company and travels a lot. Nancy said he only gets home about once a week. He could get home more often if he wanted to."

"I'll repeat myself," Gail said, not smiling. "Men can be total rats. I'm not rushing you, but are you ready to leave?"

As Gayle drove back toward Ashley Springs, they both were silent. The return trip lacked the spark of high spirits that had colored their trip to the restaurant.

Overeating, Amy thought, has a way of settling a person down. She glanced over at Gayle, who was concentrating on the road in front of the rapidly moving car. "You know," she said, "the murders have added more stress than I'd like to admit. It's as if a black cloud is hanging over the town."

"What did you say?" Gayle looked over at Amy, then back at the road. "Sorry. I'm afraid my mind was elsewhere."

Amy laughed. "Nothing really, I was just saying how tense life has gotten lately." She recognized again the thread of fear that had continually run through her thoughts since she'd found Thurmond's body. It was always there, like a power line humming with its own energy. Amy wished for at least the hundredth time that she could go back and erase that day from existence.

"Look over there!" Gayle said. They had completed one of the long curves in the three-mile descent into the valley. She was pointing toward the flank of Bitterweed Mountain, which sheltered the town on the southwest side. Huge flames were leaping above the trees. The women momentarily lost sight of the fire, as they made the last curve which took them to the stretch of road passing below the fire. From this new perspective, the fire looked much larger.

"I think that's about where the old country club building is located," Amy said. "It was replaced by a new one on Candlestick Island at least twenty years ago."

Curiosity-seekers lined the highway with their trucks and cars parked on each side. Groups of teenagers were sitting on the tops of their vehicles, while others had gotten out for a better look. From the laughter and shouting, they appeared to think the fire was a spontaneous bit of entertainment. They, together with the gawkers in passing vehicles, were causing a serious congestion around the road leading up the mountain. Gayle slowed to a crawl to get past them.

The woods were extremely dry from the long drought the area was suffering, so the trees were like tinder, ready to explode into flames. It filled Amy with dread to think of the devastation the fire could cause if it should go farther out of control. Literally hundreds of homes were built on the wooded slopes of the ridges surrounding the valley and Ashley Springs. Those who had chosen Bitter-weed Mountain for their location were now in danger of losing it all. The Thurmond house was one of them.

A fire truck roared past Gayle's car, braking hard to turn into the road that was now behind them. The Ashley Springs Fire Department had evidently called nearby towns for help, because yet another fire truck came barreling past them, horn blowing and lights flashing. Amy saw the logo of the Place City Fire Department as it sped past.

"This is awful," she said. "We've always had a peaceful community, and now everything seems to be going wrong."

Having left the crowded scene behind them, Gayle picked up speed until they were once again skimming swiftly through the night toward Amy's home. She looked over at Amy briefly before returning her eyes to the road. For one split second, Amy thought she saw hate in her new friend's eyes. It left her wondering if the feeling had been directed toward her.

Then Gayle said, "Sometimes there are things that go on in a community that no one will admit is happening. That way, it's not their responsibility to do anything about it."

Amy didn't know how to reply, so for several minutes they were silent. She wondered if Gayle had been thinking of something specific, or if her words were just a chance remark a person makes when their thoughts become philosophical.

"Do you believe in karma?" Gayle asked, jumping to an entirely different line of thought.

"I've heard of it, of course, but I'm not sure I know what it means or how it works," Amy said. "Why do you ask?"

"Nothing really. I just find that its theory of, 'what goes around, comes around' interesting. In other words, every person is ultimately held accountable for their actions."

"I do believe that," Amy said.

A few minutes later, Gayle turned into Amy's driveway. She looked over at Amy and smiled. "I enjoyed the evening so much," she said, as she shifted into Park. "I hope we can do this again in the near future."

"Me, too," Amy agreed, as she opened her car door. "Come by the shop soon and let Mary show you her paintings. We can have a cup of coffee." Amy got out and closed the car door, then leaned down to the opened window. "Aren't you a little nervous about being alone at the Anderson place? I mean, it's so isolated. The killer seems to be picking people who are alone, and he's striking at night"

"Again, I don't think he's interested in our type, but I have a gun and I know how to use it," Gayle said. "What about you? Do you have one?"

"Yes, but I don't think I could shoot it even if I needed to." Amy stepped back from the car so Gayle could leave. "Thanks again for the delicious dinner and nice evening."

Gayle gave a last wave as she drove off.

Hannibal bounced out to meet Amy, preceding Barney, who was coming down the garage apartment stairs.

"I think the old country club is on fire, Barn," she said, as she scratched Hannibal's ears. "We came past the place on our way home." She turned, looking back toward the southwest. "You can see the glow from here."

"It will be hell putting that out," he said, "with everything as dry as it is."

The black night sky above the fire was colored a deep pink. A breeze stirred the air around them, making Amy shiver. "It scares me to see that. I wonder how it started?"

"Campers, maybe," Barney said. "Or it could have been some kids. I've heard that's one of their favorite parking places. You're shaking like a leaf, are you cold?"

"Just tired, I guess. I know you want to go help with the fire, Barn, so don't worry about me. They need all the help they can get up there."

"I'll get up early in the morning and do what I can, but I'm not leaving you out here alone this late at night." Amy argued with him, trying to convince Barney that she had Hannibal and would be okay, but he stood firm. "They've got a lot of men up on that mountain by now," he said. "They'll need fresh help early in the morning."

Amy's mind was whirling with too many thoughts to allow her to relax. Hannibal, sensing her unrest, alternated between lying next to her on the couch in the den, and padding out to the kitchen where she could hear him slurping at his water bowl. She watched the eleven o' clock news, then made herself a cup of warm milk, hoping that would help make her sleepy.

But her thoughts kept going back to her strange experience in the courthouse that morning. Amy recalled the feeling of extreme cold that had come over her, and the brief moment in which she'd heard a gunshot, followed by the choking odor of smoke. But thinking about it answered nothing. She still had no idea why it had happened.

Finally, too tired to stay up any longer, she and Hannibal trudged up to her bedroom. Amy checked the view from her window, but she couldn't see the glow from there. *Maybe they've gotten the fire under control*, Amy thought, as she got into bed and curled up beneath the covers. She dropped off to sleep almost immediately, worn out by the emotional and physical demands of the day.

On the sheepskin rug next to Amy's bed, Hannibal put his large head down on his front paws and promptly began the pleasant task of chasing squirrels in his dreams.

CHAPTER 20

▼

Amy had the coffee made well before daylight. Barney whistled from the garage for Hannibal, and she let the dog out for his potty run. In less than ten minutes, the two of them were in the kitchen.

"I'm going to Sadie's first to see what's happening," Barney told her over his cup of steaming coffee. "Even if they have the fire under control now, they'll still need an extra hand watching for hot spots."

"I won't be far behind," Amy said, as she buttered her toast. "I want to work on the shop books before I open. Sure you don't want a bite to eat here?"

"No, in town I can get the news and one of Vera's doughnuts at the same time. Lock your doors when you get in the car," Barney ordered, as he stood up to leave. "Since the world has gone crazy, there's no need in you taking even the slightest chance of someone being where they shouldn't."

Thirty minutes later, Amy snapped Hannibal's leash onto his collar and led him to the car. Once they were both inside the car, she locked its doors, then opened the garage door with the electronic button. No one was lurking about outside that she could see, and Hannibal wasn't edgy in the least. He was sitting calmly in the front seat, waiting for her to get the car moving.

By the time she reached the highway, a golden glow was spreading quickly across the sky, as the light from the rising sun began to touch the clouds to the east. Amy had a good view of Bitterweed Mountain as she drove toward town. She saw no visible flames, but there was still plenty of smoke drifting above the mountainside. She thanked the Lord that there had been no wind last night. A gray pall of smoke hung over the section of valley nearest that mountain, which included the downtown area of Ashley Springs.

The smell of burning wood seeped through her car's filtering system. As she entered the town's city limits, a fine ash had settled in delicate layers on sidewalks, trees, and stores alike. People stood in small groups, huddled together in conversation, apparently in no hurry to start their work day. Amy parked as near the front of her shop as she could, intending to go into Sadie's for her second cup of coffee and to find out for herself what the situation was on Bitterweed Mountain. She knew Barney was probably long gone by now.

"You stay here," she told Hannibal. "I'll only be a few minutes." Amy rolled down one window enough to allow the dog to stick his nose through. She had just slammed the car door when she heard a shrill voice shouting, "Amy! Amy Bordeaux!"

She turned to see Nadine Benson mincing painfully across the street, her short fat feet jammed into high heeled, too small shoes, and her round belly wagging to and fro in the front center of her pink pants suit. As Amy watched Nadine's limping approach, she thought how typical it was of Nadine to take the time to dress up before six in the morning when most of the people she knew would just slip on an old pair of jeans.

"Oh, my goodness," Nadine gasped, as she stepped onto the curb where Amy waited for her. "Isn't it just awful? Why, our small town vies with Chicago for its sheer brutality."

Amy wondered why Nadine was concerned with the crime statistics of Chicago. The woman seemed to be in a state of near panic over two killings that were now old news. Admittedly, the horror of them could still make a person shudder, but Nadine should have been past the panic stage by now.

Noticing Amy's puzzled look, Nadine said, "You mean you haven't heard? That poor Purefoy child was found burned to a crisp in the fire last night. William told me this morning that the boy had been shot in the head. What is this world coming to!"

Her last words, shrill enough to attract the attention of several people on the street, were lost to Amy. She felt as if someone had punched her in the stomach. She recalled the odd spell she had in the sheriff's office yesterday, and her recollection last night of the gun shot and the choking odor of smoke. Amy wondered if she was going totally nuts. She couldn't have known what was going to happen!

Amy heard her name called and realized Nadine was practically in her face. "My dear, are you all right? I didn't think the news would be so upsetting to you, or I wouldn't have just blurted it out like that."

"No, no, I'm just fine." Amy forced herself to smile. "I guess the thought of that young man being killed upset me for a moment." She put her hand on Nadine's arm and began to lead her down the sidewalk. "Why don't we have a cup of coffee and you can fill me in on the details. Of course, I know the fire was in the old country club area, but that's all I know."

When they reached Sadie's Café, Amy led Nadine to her usual booth at the back of the room. Several men, with soot on their faces, were sitting at one of the larger tables. They looked exhausted, as they talked quietly among themselves. From the very fact that the men were relaxing here in the café, Amy surmised the fire was either out, or under control. Barney was probably helping patrol the area to make sure no new fires started up.

"I don't really know anything else," Nadine said, continuing her too-loud monologue, as if there had been no interruption. "William called me from the Masonic Lodge where he was attending a meeting and said that when they heard the alarm, he and other members of the lodge went outside. The volunteer firemen were already leaving with the fire trucks by that time. William and the other Masons went up to help. When he came home around four o' clock this morning, he said the firemen had found what was left of Bud's body."

Amy felt her stomach roil at the picture the words formed in her mind.

"These young people are ruining themselves with all the drugs they take," Nadine prattled on. "Poor Bud Purefoy included. That daddy of his always did let him get away with anything."

Amy noted how Bud, the scourge of the town, according to Nadine several days ago, was now that 'poor little boy.' She interrupted, "Nadine, did Mr. Benson know how the country club caught on fire?"

Nadine shook her head. "All he knew was what I told you," she said, and then actually lapsed into silence. Amy took advantage of the break to think about Bud's death, and to try again to make sense of her 'foretelling' another murder, right down to hearing the gun shot and smelling the fire. But the scene she had experienced in her mind gave her no clue as to why Bud died, or who wanted him dead.

The normally noisy crowd, that gathered here daily, was subdued and thoughtful this morning. There was none of the kidding and laughing that usually went on among the daily coffee-drinking bunch. Even Vera was uncharacteristically quiet, walking around the room refilling cups without her usual loud joking with the men. She worked her way to their booth.

"Are you girls as upset as everyone else?" Vera asked, as she refilled their cups, then propped one elbow on the back of the booth. "They tell me that Bud was shot. It was a mercy that he was dead before the fire got him. Don't seem right for a young person's life to end that way, though. I mean, lots of us wanted to see him get his comeuppance, but not like this. You know what I'm saying?"

"Well, I'm going to tell William he's to load every gun he's got before night-fall!" Nadine said, her double chin quivering. "The evil loose in our little town must be stopped, even if it requires every one of us to arm ourselves."

"Now, Miz. Benson," Vera soothed. "I don't think we're in all that much danger. Bud lived life on the edge, and it caught up with him, that's all. Probably some dope deal that went bad. As for the other killings, I feel sure the sheriff will find that maniac pretty quick. If everybody starts wearing a gun, then we'll sure 'nuff be in danger."

Raised voices at the front door drew their attention.

"Speaking of guns," Amy said, her voice full of quiet alarm.

Elmer Purefoy had entered the café holding a rifle. It was obvious he had been drinking heavily. His round face was flushed deep red, and he swayed as he walked.

Nadine let out a shrill shriek when she saw the gun and pushed toward the end of the booth to get up. Amy grabbed her by the arm to prevent the woman's standing up, and said in a low voice, "Nadine! Stay still. You don't want him pointing that gun at us, do you?" Nadine quickly saw the sense in that and settled back as far as she could on the booth seat.

Elmer headed toward the large table where the firefighters were seated. He waved the gun and yelled. "We gotta' go find the pervert that done this to my son. There's a mad dog loose and we gotta' run 'em down before he gets any one else. Now get off yore butts and get yore guns. We'll have us a hanging and put an end to all this namby-pamby pussy-footin' around the sheriff's doin'." Elmer had apparently regressed to his earlier years as a Ku Klux Klansman.

The men's eyes were fastened on the gun Elmer waved at them. He had bragged many times about how he kept only loaded guns in his house, so they figured this one was loaded as well. They could see his finger was on the trigger and knew this was a serious accident waiting to happen. The men began to move slowly away from the table, not sure how to handle the distraught man.

"Now, now, Darlin'." Vera had come up behind Elmer while he was concentrating on the men. "I hate to see you so upset, but you sure do have every reason to be."

She put one arm around his waist and her other arm through his rifle-bearing arm, effectively stopping his waving it about. She held him still until everyone moved from in front of the wavering gun barrel, still speaking to Elmer in a soothing voice.

"We're going to help you, ain't we, fellas'?" Vera began to ease him toward the counter where the cash register sat, putting more distance between her customers and Elmer's gun and getting him closer to one of the empty tables. "You just come have a seat so we all can talk this over. We need to sit down here and plan how to go about this thing. Come up with a good answer, you know."

Elmer's expression relaxed, as he fastened his eyes on Vera's calm, sympathetic face. He allowed her to steer him to one of the chairs.

"My heart's broke for you, Elmer." Vera had managed to insinuate her fingers behind the trigger, thus preventing his accidentally depressing it. She kept up a stream of talk to keep him focused on her. "Poor Maggie Lou must be tore completely up, but honey, you gotta' be tough for her now. It's gonna' take your strong arm and good heart to help both of you make it through this terrible thing. Losing a child's gotta' be the most painful thing in this world. Here," she said, sliding the rifle from Elmer's loosened grip. "Let me just put this out of the way while we talk."

Vera had the rifle in her hand now, she jerked her chin at Cliff Herman, who had slipped up behind them, prepared to wrestle the gun away if necessary. He quickly placed the rifle behind the counter.

Everyone there heaved a collective sigh of relief, and most of the men went back to their coffee and talk, which now included whispered opinions on Elmer's behavior. Then, while Cliff and a couple of the other men continued talking to Elmer, Vera called his brother, Manny, to come get him.

Since Manny lived only a few blocks from the café, he was there within minutes. As the two men went out the front door, the roar of everyone trying to talk at the same time, filled the café with the sound of relieved people, who had forgotten how depressed they were only moments before. Several of the men complimented Vera on the way she had handled Elmer.

"Anyone grieving like he is can do crazy things," she said. "Lord knows he's likely to go sure enough crazy if he ever finds out who shot Bud."

No one there disputed her words. Silence fell across the room, as each person gave over to his or her own thoughts about all of the dreadful events happening in their own little part of the world.

Nadine had let out only an occasional whimper, until the gun was safely put away. She fanned herself with a paper napkin, trying to recover from the shock Elmer had delivered. She reminded Amy of Scarlett's Aunt Pitty Pat, who was prone to the vapors any time she became emotionally upset.

Amy set down her cup, and scooted out of the booth. "I have work to do at the shop before I open," she said. "Why don't you come over and take another look at your desk, Nadine? It's completely finished."

At the shop, Amy pulled the protective covering off the desk and Nadine practically danced a jig in her pleasure. All thoughts of guns, death, and danger forgotten for the moment. After promising she would deliver the desk in a day or two, Amy said goodbye to Nadine at the shop door. She then went to the cooler to check the number of fresh flowers and green plants she had on hand for yet another funeral.

Amy knew that people who would ordinarily let Bud's death pass unremarked, would be ordering arrangements. In her mind, and probably in most people's minds, Bud was a victim of the same killer who had caused the horror of the past few weeks, and therefore, could not be ignored as he would have been if he'd died in a car wreck. They could have said it was his fault because everyone knew how recklessly he drove. But to be murdered by the same monster who had killed Thurmond and Mercer was very different.

CHAPTER 21

▼

Much later, Amy looked up at the huge antique Regulator clock hanging on the wall above the walnut chiffonnier which held the lingerie displays, wondering why Nancy Waggoner had not come to work yet. Amy was alone except for Barney, who arrived shortly after Nadine left. He told her that the fire on the mountain was completely out. An arson team was working with the sheriff's department, looking for clues as to the origin of the fire and wanted the area cleared of everyone except their people. Amy had told him of the scene in Sadie's.

"Good Lord," Barney had said. "If it's not one thing, it's something else."

As if her thoughts had drawn him to her, Barney appeared at the workshop door. "You're all by yourself up here?" he asked.

"Nancy was supposed to come in at eight-thirty. It's almost nine now and she hasn't shown up, or called. That's not like her. She seemed to be happy to work in Pinkie's place, so I wouldn't think she'd miss work without saying something."

"Maybe she overslept," Barney suggested.

Amy was already dialing the Waggoner's telephone number. "Hello, Mrs. Waggoner? This is Amy Bordeaux at the shop. Is Nancy still planning to come to work this morning?" She listened for a moment, then said, "I'm so sorry. No, that's quite all right, so don't worry about it. If there is anything I can do, please let me know."

"What's wrong?" Barney asked, as she hung up the phone.

"I knew Bud Purefoy was interested in Nancy," Amy said, "but I didn't think she was seriously interested in him. Her mother said that one of Nancy's friends called to tell her about Bud's death. Nancy became hysterical and wouldn't stop screaming, so her mother called Dr. Thompson, who ordered something to help calm her down." Amy rubbed her forehead. "I feel as disoriented as poor Nadine was this morning. Everything has gone very strange."

She was about to tell Barney of her premonition in the sheriff's office the day before, when Mary walked in. Amy did not want to share those strange moments with her co-worker. She didn't understand what had happened herself, so she certainly couldn't expect anyone else to. They would only think her weird.

"What's wrong?" Mary asked, as she put her purse underneath the counter. "You look as if you're upset about something."

Amy managed a smile. "Not really. I just called Nancy's house and her mother said she was too emotional to come to work. I'm sure you've heard about Bud Purefoy's death."

Mary nodded. "Poor Nancy," she said. "I hope she'll be all right. He hardly seems worth such grief from a nice girl like her."

Amy raised her eyebrows in surprise. She had never heard Mary express her feelings about anyone before, and certainly not in such negative terms.

"I didn't realize you knew Bud that well," she said.

Mary's face reddened. "I don't, really," she admitted. "Only what I've seen of him around town, and what I've heard about him. I shouldn't speak ill of the dead like that. I'm sorry." She hurried to the closet to get her work smock. Neither of them mentioned Bud again.

Amy called a friend of Nancy's, Alicia Morgan, to ask if she could fill in for Nancy.

Alicia agreed to come as soon as she could get ready. As the day progressed, the floral requests for the upcoming Purefoy funeral kept all of them, Barney included, too busy to discuss Nancy's dilemma any further. At Amy's request, Alicia called a friend of hers, Brenda Woolcott, to ask if she could help them out for a few hours. Fortunately, she agreed to come, too.

At five-thirty, after everyone had left for the day, Amy drew the blinds, put the CLOSED sign in the window, then cleared the register. She put the money and receipts into her safe, ready to go to the bank the next morning. Barney had left a few minutes earlier to drive down to Little Rock for a load of flowers. They had used almost every stem they had in the shop, both real and artificial.

Before he'd left, Barney said, "I'm sure I'll be back before dark, but you keep the doors locked and Hannibal with you, okay? You might keep your gun in a convenient place too."

Amy promised she would, even though she thought he was going a little overboard on the safety issue. After he left, she chose a small music box that Nancy had admired and gift-wrapped it. A few minutes later she knocked on the Waggoner's door.

"Come in, Ms. Bordeaux. How nice of you to stop by." Anita Waggoner brushed a strand of brown hair from her cheek. She opened the door wide for Amy to enter.

"I can't stay but a minute, so don't let me keep you from what you were doing." The delicious aroma of baking bread filled the house. She thought Nancy's mother looked relieved to see her. Amy figured it must have been a strenuous day for the woman. Handling an upset teenager who is trying to deal with the death of a peer, probably required a lot of patience on the mother's part. The, 'I will live forever,' syndrome, common to Nancy's age group, had been seriously compromised for the young girl.

"She's in her room," Anita said. "I'll show you the way." But instead of walking down the hallway, she stopped and faced Amy again. Lowering her voice to a near whisper, she said, "Nancy has absolutely lost it. The way she's been acting is almost scary. Dr. Thompson gave her medicine to help calm her down, but she's still cried most of the day. I'm at my wit's end. If her dad were home, he could do something with her. She listens to him much better than she does me."

Amy wondered what Anita would think if she knew her husband had been less than ten miles from home the evening before, and that he'd been with another woman. Amy hoped that neither Nancy, nor her mother would hear of it.

Anita was a pretty woman but, not having seen her for a while, Amy was surprised at the changes she saw in her. There were new wrinkles around Anita's eyes and at each side of her mouth which emphasized the sadness Amy saw in her face. But Amy figured it might not be as much sadness as it was disillusionment. Anita could know more than Amy thought she did.

Anita was twisting her hands in a wringing motion. She plainly needed someone to confide in about her daughter's predicament, but Amy didn't feel their relationship was close enough to serve that purpose. They were in the same Sunday school class, but other than seeing each other about town occasionally, that was the extent of their interaction.

"Isn't there someone who could come over and distract Nancy for a while? Perhaps one of her friends?" Amy said.

Anita shook her head. "She's gotten several calls from girls in her class and from two of her closest friends, but refuses to talk to any of them. That really worries me because Nancy has always shared everything with Brenda and Alicia."

"Then she probably won't talk to me either," Amy said.

"Yes, she will." Anita lifted her chin in determination. "She needs someone besides me to distract her. Come this way." She led the way down the hallway to the last door on the right. Anita knocked, then opened the door, saying, "There's someone special here to see you."

Amy entered the room of a ten-year-old. The pink curtains at the windows were deeply ruffled, their tie-backs fastened with small, stuffed teddy bears. The four-poster bed had a matching canopy with corner curtains that also sported little teddy bears. The over-all impression was one of overweening care for the young woman who lay curled in the fetal position with her back toward them.

"Sweetheart," Anita's voice took on a begging quality. "Look who's here to see you. Ms. Bordeaux was nice enough to come by."

Nancy, whose back was to them, reached down to yank the top sheet over her legs, but not before Amy caught a glimpse of a white bandage that didn't quite conceal the angry red skin surrounding it. Anita motioned for Amy to move closer, then retreated back into the hallway, leaving Amy to stand alone near the bed.

Feeling uncomfortable at Nancy's unfriendly reception, Amy said, "I stopped by to see if there's anything I can do."

There was no response, so Amy decided she's say her piece, then leave. "Look, Nancy, I don't want to impose on you, but I think you probably need help in dealing with Bud's death. Sometimes just talking about a situation can ease the pain. If I can be of help in that way, I want you to know I'm ready to listen at any time. And please don't worry about your job until you're completely well."

Amy placed her gift on the side of the bed and turned to leave the room. "I'll come back when you feel better."

"Don't go." Amy looked back to find Nancy sitting up in the bed, looking as if she had been crying for hours. Her nose was red, her eyes swollen, and her hair hung in strings.

"Oh, Nancy, I'm so sorry you're having to go through this." Amy walked back to sit on the side of the bed. When she did, the sheet pulled away from Nancy's leg. It looked bad. Before Amy could mention it, Nancy began to cry again. Amy put her arms around the girl's shoulders.

"There, there," she said, soothingly. "It's so very hard to lose someone you care about, but it will ease with time, as trite as that may sound now."

"You have no idea how hard it is," Nancy said, still crying. "I don't know what to do. No one can help me."

"Help you with what? You know your mother will help you, your friends are more than willing, and I am too. Just let us know how we can make it easier for you."

"Yeah, right." Nancy blew her, then said, "I'm sorry, I didn't mean to be rude."

Amy had the feeling that however horrible Bud's death was, the young woman was reacting to more than that. She sensed an element of fear in her young employee's words. "Your knee is awfully red and swollen," Amy said, thinking that Nancy could be worried about that. "It looks as if it's infected, so I know it's painful."

Nancy wouldn't look at her. "No, it's fine. I fell yesterday and twisted it."

The knee may have been twisted, but Amy knew that the damage she saw wasn't caused by a simple fall. "Has the doctor seen that?" she persisted.

Nancy pulled the sheet back in place, looking very upset that Amy had mentioned it. "Please, Ms. Amy, I said it was okay," Nancy insisted. "I just need more rest, that's all."

Amy wanted to ask what Anita thought of it, but knew that saying anything more on the subject might ruin any chances she might have of getting Nancy to open up to her later.

She stood up to leave. "Your mother probably has your dinner ready by now, and Hannibal is waiting for me in the car. Please don't hesitate to call me if there is anything I can do."

The young woman looked so forlorn and sad that Amy hated to leave her.

"Thanks for coming, Ms. Amy," Nancy said, "and thanks for the gift. I mean that."

Amy went by the kitchen to say good-bye to Anita. With a promise to come back soon, she then headed for her car.

Enormous black thunder heads were building to the southwest. From the looks of them, Amy thought they might be about to get some relief from the dry spell that had plagued the area for so long.

CHAPTER 22

▼

The courthouse, free of its daytime bustle, surrounded Frank with its enormous emptiness. He listened to the breathing of the ancient building, sounds that mimicked retreating footsteps, doors closing, and murmuring voices in inaudible conversations. He thought they might be the haunting echoes of the past, released from the walls like a thin vapor during the silent hours.

He removed his hand from the phone he'd just put down, then rubbed his eyes and aching temples, trying to release some of the tension that was building toward one of his ferocious headaches. Nausea stirred in his belly. Whether it came from the headache or from the information he'd gotten in the past two hours of phone calls, he didn't know.

For a brief moment, Frank wished that he had let Ben Edwards stay when the detective offered to work late with him. Ben's ability to see a situation clearly without bringing his personal feelings into the problem, made him one of the best detectives Frank had ever known, but he realized now that he really didn't want Ben into this yet. Eventually, the detective, and all the other men working on the case, would have to know everything, but only when Frank was ready to share. There were a few things he needed to do on his own.

Frank had known on the morning of Thurmond's death that he should not delay in making the phone calls he'd just completed, but his deep-seated reluctance to open that particular can of worms had held him back. Young Bud's death last night had been the kick in the teeth he needed to verify his suspicions. The violence was spilling over onto people who had nothing to do with the killer's motivation, and that had to be stopped.

He looked down at the notes he had hastily scribbled on the writing pad before him. There were three people listed, two dead by someone using the same modus operandi. This absolutely nailed down his worst fears. The person who had murdered Mercer and Thurmond, and probably Bud Purefoy, had also killed Roy Haversham in California and Marvin Schnieder in Florida—both former residents of Ashley Springs.

The mens' throats had been deeply cut, their penises and scrotums excised, placed in their mouths, and their mouths sewn shut with black silk thread. Mercer and Thurmond had been mutilated in the exact same manner. Coincidence was no longer a possibility.

Frank believed that each of the murdered men had been involved in acts of cruel and criminal behavior in the old country club, back in the days when these same men had thought themselves to be above the law. A different kind of justice was in force now. The men who had either committed, or had witnessed, unspeakably inhumane acts in those earlier days, were now being systematically executed.

The sheriff had one more out-of-state person to call. There was a chance he was still alive. Frank also had to contact the three members of the group who still lived in Ashley Springs. Although they may have figured it out for themselves by now, Frank felt obligated to warn them of the very present danger they were in. Two other members of Thurmond's group had died many years ago. Alton Greenway was killed in Korea, and Dr. Henry Anderson, along with his wife, had been murdered in 1979. Frank, since Walter's death, knew now that the couple's deaths were connected to the present day killings.

He vividly remembered the day the doctor and his wife's bodies were discovered. When the call went out for Sheriff Maurice Riley and his deputies to go to the Anderson home, Frank had been on a county road not far from the house. He was the first lawman to reach the scene of the crime.

When he got out of his unit, he heard a strange noise coming from the large attached garage. Frank found the Andersons' daughter, eleven year-old Rosalind, crouched in one corner of the garage behind the doctor's Silver Cloud Rolls Royce, clutching an old rag doll. Her clothes were filthy. She even had dirt on her arms and legs. Frank imagined that at some point, she had been running away from the house and fallen in the dirt. She must have decided to come back and hide in the garage.

Her shrill keening was more that of an animal than of a human being. When Frank tried to pick her up, she hissed like a snake, spraying a froth of spit into his face. She fought his touch so strongly that he was forced to leave her on the con-

crete floor. He stayed by her until other law officers arrived. Later, Frank understood the condition of the girl when he saw the carnage she must have witnessed
in the second floor master bedroom.

The housekeeper, Carmen Sanchez, had found her employers' bodies when
she'd come to work that morning. The Andersons had given her a key to the back
door, so that she wouldn't have to disturb them if they wanted to sleep late.
When Carmen entered the house, she thought they were doing just that, sleeping
late. But then she saw what looked like smears of blood on the kitchen floor, and
she followed the trail of spots up the stairs to their bedroom. The door had been
open, so she entered the room, calling out their names. Mr. and Mrs. Anderson
were obviously dead, as blood covered their heads and bodies, as well as the head-
board and bed linens.

When Carmen pulled herself together enough to stop screaming, she called
the sheriff's office. Then she looked for the two children. The Andersons also had
a son two years younger than Rosalind. Carmen said she never thought about
going into the garage. At that point Mrs. Sanchez began to cry.

"I guess I didn't want to look too much," she told the sheriff. "I was afraid I
would find the children dead, too."

The housekeeper seemed truly heartbroken over the fate of her employers, and
claimed to have no idea why anyone would commit such violence against the
Andersons. After more questioning, Sheriff Riley allowed Mrs. Sanchez to
accompany Rosalind Anderson to the hospital. The child had not spoken to anyone. The doctor would allow only Sheriff Riley to question her, and then for just
a few minutes. Rosalind did no more than stare into space, either unwilling or
unable to answer his queries.

She remained in the hospital until her father's sister, a Mrs. Pennington, came
up from Mobile, Alabama, to take Rosalind home with her. The sheriff was
present when the aunt came to the room and he told Frank the doctor strongly
recommended that Mrs. Pennington seek psychiatric help for Rosalind.

Sheriff Riley formed a search party, and they scoured the surrounding area for
the boy. Frank, like most of the men who joined in the hunt, believed the killer
had probably taken Henry Anderson III, called Hank, to some secluded place
and gotten rid of him as a witness, though they were puzzled as to why Rosalind
was left alive. One of the men suggested the killer saw the girl as too crazy to
identify him. That sounded weak to Frank, but no one came up with a better
idea.

Bulletins went out to surrounding states, but nothing turned up. There were
the usual sightings reported by well-meaning people, but none of them were pro-

ductive. The son was never found. The killer, or killers, had also disappeared without a trace. The case was on file as an unsolved double murder.

Frank considered those killings to be past history, that is, until Thurmond's death. Now he believed that Hank had not been killed, but had fled to escape being charged with his parents' murders. It wasn't too much of a stretch, Frank thought, to credit one small boy with the killings. Not when his parents had been very drunk, which they knew from a blood alcohol test done during the autopsy, and very sound asleep. The autopsy also had shown that he had wielded a hammer to their heads first, and had then stabbed them which could also explain how the young boy was able to render such brutality on their bodies.

Hank had probably ingratiated himself into some family with a sad tale of being abandoned by his parents. A lot of people did not have television back then, so Hank's picture wouldn't have been shown in almost every home in America. He could remain anonymous in a way that was impossible today. There were any number of scenarios that could explain why Hank was never found. At any rate, Frank believed him to be alive and well and back now to exact revenge against men, who, with the permission of his father, played sex games with him and his sister.

Frank felt a flush of familiar guilt. What he'd known back then, and the part he'd played in allowing the heinous crimes to continue, had haunted him all these years. Rumors started among the deputies that something very unsavory was going on at the country club. Frank didn't remember how the speculation started, whether someone had seen something they thought was wrong, or if it was just idle talk that had spread.

At first, when he overheard the men talking, Frank ignored it as just being trashy talk. Adultery was nothing new in his county. The number of divorces witnessed to the hanky-panky among the randy and the witless. Frank had spoken harshly to the men, warning them that they could get into serious trouble talking such garbage.

"You can get sued for defamation of character if it gets back to some of our leading citizens that they are being accused of committing adultery," he'd said.

One of the deputies made a parting remark, as if he had to have the last word. "Adultery ain't what I heard was going on," he'd said. "I'd kill a man if he messed with my child." When Frank pressed him to say more, the deputy refused by shaking his head and walking away.

Frank heard nothing more on the subject, but couldn't get the man's remark out of his mind. Later that same night he went to the country club by a road that was seldom used and parked in the shadows of the thick woods which surrounded the building. A set of stairs led from the bricked patio at the back to the second story and allowed entrance by other than the more public indoor stair-case. Frank got out of his truck and hid in the bushes nearest the steps.

A few minutes later, Dr. Anderson drove his Cadillac into a parking space close to those steps. The doctor had reached into the back seat and pulled his two children out. He held them each by an arm, as he forced them up the steps to the private rooms. Frank could hear the boy's voice raised in protest, begging his father not to make them go in there. The little girl said nothing, but Frank stepped back into deeper shadows when she turned her head and seemed to look directly at him.

He drove back to town to continue his regular patrol, choosing to say nothing, and thus keep his job. He had been haunted every day since then by the memory of the little boy's pleas, and his sister's wordless acquiescence.

Heaving a deep sigh at the awful memories of that long-ago time, Frank turned his swivel chair to face the long windows behind his desk. Hank would be something over thirty years old, and Frank knew he could run into him on the street and not know him. The question now was, why had he waited so long for revenge?

Lightning stabbed the night sky over Oak Tree Ridge to the northeast of town. There were still a few vehicles on the streets below. The driver of one car switched on his headlights as Frank watched. The halogen lights along Main Street were beginning to make pools of yellow in front of the darkened store win-dows. Most of the people of Ashley Springs were home with their families, prob-ably enjoying a nice, home cooked meal.

Since his wife had died five years ago, Frank had no one to go home to. He spent long hours on his job just to avoid spending even lonelier hours in Mari-anna's house. In his mind, it would always be her house. Frank hadn't changed a thing since her death. Her sewing basket still sat next to her rocker, and her bifo-cals still lay on the lamp table.

A new thought popped into his mind that had nothing to do with Marianna. What if Anderson thought that he, Frank, was guilty by association? After all, he was the only law officer left in Hickorytree County that had been involved in the Anderson case. Would he come after him too? "Not if I can help it," Frank mut-tered to himself.

Turning back to his desk, Frank looked once more at the notepad with its list of names. The last name was Bud Purefoy's with a large question mark beside it. He knew in his ulcer ridden gut that Purefoy's death was connected to the other killings. Bud, in his nocturnal wanderings, had probably heard or seen something that, in his mind, connected someone to the murders. That would explain his death, particularly if he confronted that person.

Frank sighed heavily again. Not only did he have to worry about searching out evidence that would substantiate his theory on Purefoy's death, but he had to worry about who would be the next possible victim, and how Amy Bordeaux could know another person was about to die. He didn't even want to make a stab at that last one. There were too many other very real situations to worry about, such as, the political and economical ramifications of the murders. Mayor Lester Harvey Lumley, had been waiting in Frank's office when he'd gotten back from a meeting in Little Rock. Lumley was in a sweat, his face as red as a turkey's wattle.

"You've got to get to the bottom of this immediately!" he had yelled. "Guests in our city must feel safe in order to enjoy themselves. With some nut killing our citizens and burning down buildings with poor little ole' boys in them, they can't feel too safe, now can they, Sheriff?"

The windy old jackass had forgotten that he'd been standing in the same spot not two weeks ago, demanding that Frank do something about that "terrible Purefoy boy," who was nothing but trouble. Bud's apparent determination to become a member of the Cummins State Prison population had caused grief for many a business man whose merchandise went missing after Bud had been in their store. They'd also lost more than one night's sleep listening to Bud roar around town with his exhaust pipes popping and his tires screeching. The city policemen were fed up with running him down and giving him tickets.

Apparently all was forgiven now that Bud turned up murdered. Forgotten was the fact that every time the police arrested him, Elmo Purefoy would show up to harangue the police for "picking on my boy" before he paid the bail. Bud would stand there with a sly grin on his face, enjoying the show his daddy put on.

And Bud wasn't merely a petty thief. Frank and Chief of Police, David Spratlin, had been working to get some solid leads on Bud's dope dealing connections. They knew he was selling, but wanted to find out from whom he was buying his supplies.

But Bud's future in serious crime was over and they could close those files on him. It was Frank's opinion that if Elmer Purefoy had made his son admit his guilt when Bud was several years younger, he might still be alive today. Too bad, he thought, that parents can't see their own duplicity in their children's wrong doing.

The mayor had tried to sanctify the young man in order to push for a quick end to what he had reduced to a 'threat' to the local economy. Frank had fought to hold his tongue and assured Lumley that the law officers of the town and county were doing all they could to get a lead on the killer, but that he couldn't promise him when there would be an arrest.

A much disgruntled mayor had walked out, muttering about the incompetency of improperly trained law officers. Frank would have liked to take Lester by the collar and push his face into the diplomas and certificates on his office wall that witnessed to the extensive training Frank had received, most of it at his own expense.

Shrugging his shoulders, he dismissed the old fool from his mind. The enormity of what he had learned tonight, put the mayor's rudeness into a bottom drawer category. Frank focused instead on what he had to do in the next few days. Tomorrow, he planned to question some of Bud's friends.

He especially wanted to talk to Abner Waggoner's daughter, Nancy. His deputies, over the past two months, had reported seeing the girl with Bud many times. Frank would bet that Abner didn't know his daughter was dating Bud. But with Abner on the road all the time, and his wife being the kind, timid woman she was, he'd also bet that Nancy could slip out of the house any time she wanted.

Someone had parked Bud's truck on the Seven-Eleven parking lot. Frank didn't figure it was the killer, so there was the distinct possibility that someone else had been up on that mountain with Bud, and that possibility could be Abner's daughter. He would talk with Bud's male friends first and if nothing likely turned up, he'd talk to Nancy.

Frank heaved yet another deep sigh. He still had one more phone call to make. He dialed the Louisiana number for Chester Plummer, another former buddy of Thurmond's. On the third ring, a woman answered.

"Hello. Is this Mrs. Chester Plummer?" Frank asked.

"Yes, this is she." Chester's wife's voice was faint, as if she wasn't feeling well.

"I'm Frank Morgan, sheriff of Hickorytree County in Arkansas. May I speak to Chester please?"

The voice on the other end became instantly shrill. "Chester is dead. He's dead! Why are you asking for him now?"

The woman began to cry, then Frank heard a scuffling sound and a man's voice came on. "Who is this?" he demanded.

Frank repeated who he was, then asked, "And who are you?"

"I'm George Matthews, Mrs. Plummer's son." The voice was deep and authoritative. "Why are you asking questions about my step-father's death?"

"Was Chester murdered?" Frank asked, abruptly. He could be authoritative too.

"Yes, and rather horribly, as it happens. My mother found him and I can tell you, she doesn't need a reminder of that particular nightmare, Sheriff."

"It is a nightmare, Mr. Matthews," Frank said. "It's the same frigging nightmare we're having up here. I'm sorry to upset your mother, but I thought maybe the killer hadn't gotten to Louisiana yet. Do you know if the police have any clues as to who killed Chester?"

"Not a one," Matthew's voice was filled with contempt. "The police decided it was one of the crazy street people who wander about near my mother's apartment, and they're not doing very much to find the nut. She was just beginning to adjust some, and now you've brought it all back to her." The man sounded deeply angry. "I don't appreciate this, Sheriff. You should be asking the police your questions."

Matthews apparently had forgotten that Frank had called there because he hoped Chester was still alive. He could understand the man's hostility and tried for a more friendly voice. "Would you ask your mother if Chester ever mentioned seeing someone he knew in earlier years? We think the killer may have known Chester pretty well."

"I certainly will not." Matthew's voice was hard. "If you have any more questions, you can direct them to the Shreveport police." The receiver slammed down, hurting Frank's ear.

"Rude bastard," Frank said, his hair trigger temper getting the best of him. Giving himself a moment to cool down, he punched in the area code and number for Louisiana information, then dialed the number for the Shreveport Police Department. After being passed from one extension to another, he finally reached the department he wanted. However, the detective in charge of the Plummer case wasn't there. Frank left his name and number.

The large Westclox on the wall struck ten o' clock. It was time for him to go home. A couple of stiff shots of Seagram's VO would help dispel the scenes of violence that filled his mind and numb the ever present sense of guilt. He might even get a few hours sleep.

Frank reached over and snapped off the green-shaded lamp on his desk. In the dim reflection of the lights from the lobby below, Frank made his way out of his office to the broad staircase. He felt extremely tired. The low back pain that plagued him every waking moment, sent a sharp message down his left leg. Frank had long since decided that growing old consisted of few pleasures and multiple problems.

He paused at the top of the stairs on the third floor. The marble walls and floors of the ancient courthouse literally made an echo chamber of the huge open center of the building. He had heard the click of a door somewhere below him. Leaning over the bannister, he scanned what he could see of the first floor. The lights were bright enough for him to see all the doors on the right side of the lobby. The one nearest the bottom of the staircase was ajar. Frank eased down the steps as quietly as his hard heeled cowboy boots and the marble steps allowed.

He knew the maintenance man, Bob Hatcher, always locked the doors so that they could be opened from the inside, but not from the outside. The ground floor windows had been covered with insulated glass when air-conditioning had been installed several years ago, so no one could enter through them without major destruction. A quiet entry was impossible.

Frank had reached the second story level when he heard the solid thump of the rear courthouse door. He ran recklessly down the remaining steps, but by the time he got outside, no one was in sight. He heard the squeal of tires at the north end of the building, then the diminishing sound of a truck motor. Frank's back gave a savage stab that made him wince. He knew he'd be lucky if he could climb out of bed in the morning.

Pulling his key chain from his pants pocket, he let himself back into the building. Frank went to the door he'd seen open and flipped on the overhead lights. Nothing seemed out of place. In the morning he'd ask Sandy O'Leary, the county clerk, to see if anything was missing.

Frank checked all the exit doors to be certain they were locked, then let himself out of the rear door where his Suburban was parked only a few feet away. He rattled the door behind him to make sure it was locked and, favoring his back, he got into his vehicle. The thought occurred to him that anyone who saw his Suburban would know that he was still in his office.

A brilliant flash of lightning lit the interior of Frank's truck cab as he pulled out into the street and turned toward home. He'd bet storm warnings had been issued.

Then, like the flash of lightning, he had a sudden insight. The person probably hadn't been in the courthouse to steal anything. "I'll bet that son-of-a-bitch was right down there listening to my calls!" Frank felt outraged that the killer could pull a trick like that on him. He slammed his fist into the steering wheel and continued cussing the sneaky bastard. Then another thought occurred to him. Had his life been in danger? Had that person been there for more than just listening?

"Naw." Frank reassured himself. "If he'd wanted me, he could have gotten me."

Not a happy thought.

CHAPTER 23

▼

By the time Amy had stopped off at Merlin's Grocery for milk and bread, and listened to fifteen minutes of nonstop gossip from Mrs. Merlin, the storm had moved much closer. Sudden spates of rain foretold the coming deluge as she drove home. To the accompaniment of blue-white bolts of lightning, and ear splitting bursts of thunder, Amy parked her car inside the garage and quickly unlocked the door that opened into the mud room. A nervous Hannibal pushed past her legs into the safe haven of the house.

"I don't blame you, boy," Amy said, as she struggled to get past him to unload the groceries onto the kitchen table. "It looks as though we may have a rough night of it." To get Hannibal away from her feet, she poured Choice Bits into his bowl. "I need to get a weather report in case there are tornado warnings. If there are, we'll make our beds on the ground floor tonight."

She flipped on the small television set which she kept in the kitchen, and punched in the local weather station. The weatherman was just giving a report. She had missed the first part, but heard him say that a line of thunderstorms was headed their way with hail, dangerous lightning, and possible high winds. He advised listeners to stay tuned for further reports.

Hannibal lapped a mouthful of water and took a bite of the food while watching Amy to be sure that she didn't leave him alone in the kitchen. When she went back into the mud room to hang up her raincoat, he abandoned his food to follow her every step.

"Before the weather gets any worse," Amy said, hoping her calm voice would reassure him somewhat, "I'll take a quick shower and change, then we'll have a bite to eat, okay?"

The big dog followed her upstairs and lay next to the bathroom door while Amy showered. She was nervous about being around water pipes during a thunderstorm, so she made her shower brief. Dressed in her pajamas and robe, she trekked back down the stairs, with Hannibal close at her heels. He was practically hugging her knees as the thunder and lightning became nearer and louder. When satisfied that Amy was in the kitchen for a while, he settled down to do some serious eating.

She toasted a pimento cheese sandwich in an iron skillet on top of the stove, and put together a small salad. Amy took her food and a glass of iced ginger ale to the work center where she kept a couple of stools. She sat on one and propped her bare feet on the other. Only then did she allow herself to think about the thing she had tried to not think about all day.

Each time the crazy scene at the sheriff's office popped into her mind, which must have been at least two hundred times, Amy would immediately find something else to distract herself. But there was no avoiding it now. It was time to examine what had happened. What she had experienced in that brief moment, as it flashed like a waking nightmare before her eyes. The icy knot tightening in her stomach reminded her of the freezing cold that had seeped into her bones during that brief episode.

She had seen a very dark room, then someone moving toward a barrier of some kind. If felt as if she'd been crouching behind some object. There had been a movement behind her. The sound of the gun shot had been deafening, very close to her right ear, and the strong odor of smoke had choked her, so that she could not get her breath. This morning, when Nadine told her Bud had been shot in the head and the building burned down with him in it, she knew it was exactly that experience she'd had in her vision.

Pushing back the untouched sandwich, Amy wrapped her arms around her waist and rocked to and fro. Questions formed, then floated away to be replaced by others. She had no idea why such a thing happened to her, so what did it mean? Was she becoming some kind of freak? She'd always had the ability to pick up on other people's thoughts, but it never seemed that unusual to her. Especially since Leigh was almost as sensitive to Amy's thoughts as Amy was to hers. Her aunt had said, "I think we were supposed to have been born identical twins, but there was a mix-up in heaven." They had treated it as a private joke.

This was no joke. She needed to talk to someone, but Barney wasn't here and Leigh was in New York. Actually, Amy preferred that no one know about her weird experience until she could better understand what was going on, herself

"This is getting me nowhere," she said. Hannibal looked up at her with his eyebrows in their questioning mode. "You can't help me, fellow, as much as I know you'd like to."

After dumping her sandwich into the disposal, Amy carried her ginger ale up one flight of stairs to the den. As she settled on the couch, she thought about other things that had happened. For one, she was regretting her visit with Nadine, especially after William Benson had come home and caught them gossiping. Amy had felt as if she'd committed a moral wrong on seeing his obvious disapproval. It had been a very uncomfortable moment.

Nadine probably knew something about Thurmond's and the other men's pasts, but after her husband got through with her, Amy doubted she would talk freely again. However, Nadine had acted her old self this morning. The shock of Bud's death had probably canceled, for the time being, any reticence her husband had tried to instill.

It was the change in Mr. Benson that was the most puzzling to Amy. There was nothing weak or indecisive about the man who had interrupted Amy's fact-finding mission. Instead, his stealth and his frozen expression still made her uneasy when she thought about them. The gossips in town claimed he was a henpecked husband because during different community projects the couple had helped with, Nadine always seemed in charge, telling him to do this and to do that. But what Amy saw yesterday afternoon belied the henpecked theory. For a split second, when Amy faced William, she had felt a faint stirring of revulsion.

Then there was Nancy's situation. When Amy had seen the injured leg and the fear in the girl's eyes something clicked, and she became certain Nancy had been with Bud at the old country club. Which meant Nancy knew more than she let on, and possibly knew something that could get her into serious trouble.

Simultaneously, there was a flash of lightning and the heavy boom of thunder that rattled the windows. Amy jumped, and Hannibal tried to climb into her lap. "Hey, we're okay, Hannibal," she told him. She put her arms around his neck, and he licked her cheek. "We're safe and dry. Nothing to worry about." Nonetheless, he leaned against her legs for moral support.

Amy wished Barney were home. He should have been back from his flower buying mission at least an hour ago. She hoped nothing had gone wrong, what with the weather being so bad that driving would be very difficult on the crowded, rain-slick interstate.

"He probably just stopped somewhere to eat," she said aloud. But her own reassurances still didn't ease the undercurrent of worry.

When the two of them were settled again, Amy said, "Life can become too complicated to fathom, Hannibal. Be glad that you're a dog." He lifted his head from his paws to whine and sweep his feathery tail across the carpet to show Amy that he felt the same way.

"Sitting here is driving me crazy," she said. "I might as well be doing something useful." Amy stood, and walked to her desk, Hannibal right behind her. From the desk drawers, she took out her business journals, a stack of bills for her shop, and her checkbook. For the next several minutes the only sounds were the rustling of papers, the rumble of thunder, and the rush of pouring rain as it beat on the roof. The telephone rang, making Amy jump and Hannibal whine. It was Leigh.

"Amy, darling! Are you all right?"

"Yes, Aunt Leigh, I am. My protector is with me."

"Who? Barney?"

"No, Hannibal. I could get used to his being around. What's up?"

"I should ask you that. For some reason I felt the need to check on you." Leigh said, demonstrating again the mental link between the two of them. This wasn't the first time she had called when Amy was particularly burdened about something.

"They haven't caught the killer yet?" Leigh said.

"No, they're not even close. In fact, there's been another murder." Amy went on to explain how Bud Purefoy's body was found in the ashes of the dilapidated old country club building. "They're saying that he was shot in the head and was probably dead before the fire was set. That was a mercy."

"I am absolutely horrified!" Leigh said, when Amy had finished giving all the details. "You should pack your bags and come up here until they catch that monster!"

"I would almost agree with you, except that I have a business to run. Unfortunately, there's been one funeral after the other, and we've been inundated with orders for flowers. So we're much too busy for me to leave." Amy changed the subject, hoping to distract her aunt from worrying about her safety. "Gayle took me to the Sheep Pen for dinner yesterday evening. I really enjoyed it. She is very pleasant company."

"I'm so glad, darling. You haven't been out much for quite a while, and it's good for you. It would be especially good if you could find an interesting man to go out with, too."

"As a matter of fact, I have met a man that I think could be interesting."

"Who is he? Has he asked you out yet?"

Amy laughed. "Not yet since I only met him a few days ago. He's Ben Edwards, the detective. You know, the one who questioned me at the Thurmond house. He's good looking, the right age, and seems to be confident without being arrogant."

"A lawman?" The excitement left Leigh's voice. "Not the type I'd choose for you, I'm sure, but he's all right for you to have a date or two with, I guess."

"Thank you for your permission, Auntie. The problem is, I don't see him as a normal person." Amy laughed. "I can hardly say his name without adding detective to it. But then, everyone seems different in the light of what's been happening around here." Amy laughed again. "I even saw William Benton as a latent macho man, if you can believe that."

"You really are misinterpreting things, aren't you?" Leigh said. "You'll have to explain that one some time. So, where is Barney? I thought he was staying in your garage apartment."

"He is, but he had to run down to Little Rock late this afternoon to pick up a load of flowers and plants. What with so many funerals, and them so close together, we are out of every kind of flower we carry. Barney should have been back at least an hour ago, so something's delayed him. He'll be here any minute now."

"You mean you're there by yourself?"

"Hannibal would be insulted to hear you say that. He is very vigilant and brave when he isn't cowering from the storm we're having right now. I think he can hear your voice because he's wagging his tail and grinning. You want to speak to him?" She held the receiver close to Hannibal's ear while Leigh said something. In his happiness at hearing his beloved mistress' voice, he woofed and danced about, wagging his whole rear end.

When Amy reclaimed the phone, she said, "Leigh, there's something I need to discuss with you, but not on the phone. When do you think you'll be home?"

"That's part of the reason I'm calling. Plans have been changed here, so I should be back there either tomorrow afternoon or early the next morning. You can't give me a hint now?"

"I'd rather not. I need your opinion on something, so give me a call when you get in, okay?"

"I have to say, you're worrying me a bit here," said Leigh. "Are you sure you don't want to at least give me a hint of what this is about?"

"If I gave you a hint, you wouldn't want to stop there. It's nothing for you to worry about. Just a matter of interpretation."

Leigh didn't want to settle for that, but Amy refused to say any more on the subject. With repeated promises to be careful, to lock up, and to keep her gun with her at all times, Amy hung up and got back to her bill paying.

The roar of the heavy rain had eased up during her phone conversation, but rumbles of thunder indicated that another wave of storms was approaching. She didn't mind, as long as the storms did no damage. People had been praying for rain for weeks now. Also, any hot ashes up on the mountain still simmering would be forever drowned in the downpour.

Amy thought how she should be counting her blessings, feeling as she often did a deep gratitude for her lovely, secure home, and for Leigh and Barney who loved her. Whoever the killer was, he probably has never had a decent home, or someone to love him. She looked up from her paper work.

"What an odd thing for me to think!" she said, aloud, causing Hannibal to come to his feet. To the dog's anxious whine, she said, "It's okay, boy. Just the muddled thoughts of a somewhat insecure female. No insult intended to you, my man, but I do wish Barney would come home!"

After Amy finished signing the last check, she rose and stretched, thinking that a cup of hot tea would be good. Hannibal, who still lay on the floor, gave a low growl. His floppy ears perked to their maximum ability, and he looked down the steps toward the kitchen. Amy had opened her mouth to ask him what was wrong, when he jumped to his feet, the hackles on his neck bristling, and his nose wrinkling back to reveal a ferocious set of fangs. The rumbling in his chest gave way to sharp barks.

"Hannibal, what is it, boy?" But he was already down the stairs and in the kitchen. Barking steadily now, the dog was really frantic, scratching and leaping onto the double glass doors that led out onto the lower deck. Amy, who had run down the steps behind him, managed to pull back one of the curtain panels that covered the doors. The deck was illuminated by repeated flashes of lightning, but she saw nothing that should alarm the dog.

Just as quickly as he had run down the steps, Hannibal ran back up, barking at every breath. He continued on up the second flight of stairs, but then midway, he slowed his pace and barked at the wall as he ascended. It appeared to Amy that he was following the passage of something, or someone, up the outside set of stairs that led from the lower deck, up to the front lawn.

"It's just an old armadillo," she told Hannibal, trying to reassure both herself and him, but not feeling any better.

Ignoring her completely, he now turned and ran back down the stairs. Again he was at the lowest level, still barking steadily while scratching at the deck doors. Amy felt certain that Hannibal's frantic actions were caused by more than a mere four legged animal.

She turned back to go upstairs to get her gun, but saw lights sweep past the front windows. Hannibal left the door downstairs to join her as she ran into mud room. He growled and whined, pushing against her legs, wanting her to let him outside.

CHAPTER 24

▼

"No, you're not going out there, Hannibal." Amy pushed at the big dog. "Now get back." The dog obeyed, but kept up a low growl until they both heard the familiar sound of the Suburban's door slamming. Amy opened the door for Barney.

"Thank goodness, you're here," she said. "Come in before you drown."

He came across the garage to where she stood in the doorway. "I'll drip all over everything," he protested. "I've been in and out of that truck so many times, that I'm soaking wet."

"That's what the mud room is for," Amy said. She reached out and pulled on Barney's arm to urge him in, then shut the door behind him. He stood in the middle of the floor while she got a large towel from the adjoining half-bath. She put his dripping raincoat on a hanger as he dried his face and hair.

While she put the kettle on for tea, Hannibal diverted his attention from the direction of the river and came to greet Barney. The dog seemed to have forgotten his earlier frenzy, and in the safety of Barney's presence, Amy decided it had been an armadillo after all.

"Man, what a mess!" Barney said, as he settled down at the kitchen table. "It rained its butt off all the way from Little Rock to here. I'll bet flash flood watches are out everywhere." He stopped to take a closer look at Amy. "You're sure everything's okay? I have worried myself into another ulcer over your being here alone. If I hadn't known Hannibal was with you, I'd have two more ulcers."

"And I was worried about you," Amy said, as she poured hot water over their tea bags. "I didn't expect it to take you this long."

"There was a bad wreck on the I-30 bridge." Barney shook his head. "All four of the north bound lanes were blocked by an eighteen-wheeler lying on its side. Apparently, it had been going too fast to stop for a car that pulled in front of it from an on-ramp. It was a mess. I'll bet traffic was backed up all the way to Pine Bluff by the time they got one of the lanes cleared."

"I'm glad you're home, Barn." Amy leaned down to hug his neck. "So many bad things are happening, I couldn't bear it if anything happened to you."

He smiled. "I appreciate that." She knew he meant it.

Amy went over to the sideboard to slice a piece of pound cake she had baked the day before. She slid it onto a dessert plate and put it in front of Barney.

"I got enough flowers to take care of the Purefoy funeral," he said, after he'd taken his first bite of cake. "I put the fresh flowers in the cooler, and set the pot plants and silk flowers in the workshop. I'll help you get them set up in the morning," he said, looking down at Hannibal, who had placed his head on Barney's knee. "How is this fellow getting along?"

"He was pretty upset just before you drove up." Then Amy told him about the way Hannibal had run up and down the stairs, and how he had barked and growled.

Barney put down his fork. "You say that happened just before I drove up?"

"Yes. As a matter of fact, he spooked me so badly I was on my way to get my gun when I saw your headlights. He seems fine now."

Barney got up from his chair. "Do you have a flashlight handy?"

Amy objected to his going back out into the rain. "It probably was an armadillo," she said. "You know how he hates them. You'll get soaking wet again, Barn."

But Barney already had his raincoat on and was opening the door into the garage. Hannibal was outside before either of them could stop him. He disappeared around the west end of the house where the stairs were located.

"Lock the door behind me," Barney ordered, before he rapidly followed Hannibal's lead.

The rain had abated to a lighter, but still steady downpour. The storm was quickly moving to the northeast. Amy had finished rinsing their cups and putting away her paper work when Barney tapped at the door.

"I didn't see anything," he said, as he worked his way out of his muddy boots. "Nothing is missing that I can tell. You don't have much out there except the wrought-iron furniture, and I doubt anyone would be stealing that."

"As I said, it was probably just another armadillo," Amy said, laughing.

Hannibal's continuing frustration with the strange animals that trundled across the lawn at night, rooting and digging holes in the ground in their search for worms and bugs, had been comical to watch. He would catch one, then spend several minutes growling and trying to get a grip on the animal with his mouth. Eventually, all he could do was watch his tough shelled nemesis waddle off, unharmed.

Now the dog was standing patiently next to Barney, having the good manners to not make muddy tracks into the house. His paws and legs were dirty and his fur dripped water.

"Best I work on you before you go any farther, Old Boy," Barney said. "Amy, if you have some rags, I'll get the worst of it off."

When she returned with a large towel, Amy heard Barney say, "Hello! What's this?"

Hannibal had something in his mouth. Barney held out his hand and the dog obediently dropped a wristwatch into it. It was gold-colored with a brown leather band and it looked expensive.

"Hannibal's spook may have been a thief, sure enough. Either that, or a peeping tom," Barney said, as he held up the watch for Amy to see. "I'll turn it over to the sheriff in the morning." He pulled a handkerchief from his jeans hip pocket and dropped the watch into it. "I doubt there'll be any fingerprints after its being out in the rain, but then you never can tell."

They discussed possible explanations for someone being outside her house on a stormy night, but neither could think of any that made sense. Their unmentioned fear was that the person snooping around Amy's house might somehow be connected to the killings.

Seeing that he was already worried about her, Amy had decided she would say nothing to Barney about her strange experience at the sheriff's office. He wouldn't be able to deal with such a weird circumstance tonight, so she'd tell him at a more suitable time. Like after Leigh got home.

"Oh, Barn, I forgot to tell you that Leigh called tonight. She said her plans had been changed and that she would be home either tomorrow or the next day. I didn't ask how long she'd be staying this time, but maybe we'll get in a few days of her company."

Barney smiled his pleasure. "It will be good to have her home again, for however long."

Amy yawned. "Sorry, Barn. There's been too much excitement for me today."

"You need to be in bed, anyway. It's very late," he said, unconsciously falling into his "father" mode. Amy didn't mind. "Turn on the deck lights and keep

Hannibal in your room," he ordered. "If he gets upset again, call me on the intercom."

After she locked the door behind Barney, Amy went to the den to get a book. She chose a Koonz novel to read, hoping the imaginary horror in the story would distract her from her real fears. Happily, before she'd even finished the first chapter, Amy found herself nodding. She turned off her lamp, and heard Hannibal readjusting himself on the mat by her bed, preparing to catch up on his own sleep.

Amy woke up shivering. The room felt as cold as the inside of a refrigerator. She groped until she found the bedspread and pulled it up over her, bundling down into the covers. She waited to warm up, but after a few minutes passed she felt even colder than at first.

Trying to make sense of the very chilly air, Amy thought she must have set the thermostat too low. She raised up on one elbow to see if the cold was affecting Hannibal, but he appeared to be sleeping soundly. Evidently, he was worn out from his earlier excitement because ordinarily, when she stirred even a little, he would open his eyes to check on her.

She lay back down and pulled the covers up around her ears. That was when she heard the sound of glass breaking. She raised up again, still shaking with cold, and looked toward her bathroom. But the bathroom door was not there. In fact, Amy was looking at a room she'd never seen before. A window across from her bed let in enough light from an outside source to show her a dresser with a large mirror above it on the wall across from the bed. She did not recognize it, or the bedspread she gripped to her chest, or the television set, or the overstuffed chair which sat in one corner of the room.

Amy threw back the covers to step out of bed. Hannibal was no longer on the floor. Before she could call his name, a dark figure stepped through a door on the opposite side of the room and walked swiftly toward the bed. Amy flung herself onto the floor and opened her mouth to scream, but no sound came from her throat. For the first time she noticed that a foggy haze blurred the scene around her. In the split second it took for her to analyze her surroundings, the figure had reached the other side of the bed and bent over the pillow. Then the room was gone and everything went black.

Amy realized she had her eyes closed. At Hannibal's whine and the touch of his rough tongue on her arm, she opened her eyes to discover that she was back in her own room and in her own bed.

CHAPTER 25

▼

Nancy swung around on the toilet seat, put her right foot on the edge of the tub, and peeled off the large band-aid to get a better look at her knee. The injury looked worse, and was more painful than before. The skin was dark and puffy, and there was a red streak that ran from the knee cap to about midway of her thigh. Nancy knew from the first aid course she'd taken in high school that her knee was infected. The teacher had shown them films of blood poisoning cases, and the place on her knee looked the same as the injuries in the pictures. She had to do something.

She rummaged through the medicine chest and the plentitude of bottles her mother had collected, looking for something that might stop the upward movement of the red streak. She found a lot of over-the-counter medicines for everything from coughs to hemorrhoids, but nothing for infections. Then she remembered the cases of sample medicines her dad kept in his closet. As a salesman for a pharmaceutical firm, Abner had always kept cases of different medicines at home. Nancy also knew, from his repeated warnings in the past, that she'd be in serious trouble she opened one of them.

But Abner wasn't at home and she was desperate to stop the infection. She couldn't go to Dr. Thompson. She'd have to answer his questions about how she'd hurt herself. So far, she had kept Anita from knowing how serious the cut had gotten. Her mom had believed her when she'd said it was a small cut gotten from bumping into a glass showcase at work, but Dr. Thompson would know better.

Nancy stuck her head out of the bathroom to make certain that her mother wasn't in the hallway. She could see the line of light under Anita's door and hear the television. Thunder rumbled, a deep, threatening sound. Nancy shivered with nerves. She quietly eased open her dad's bedroom door. Her parents had used separate bedrooms for so long that Nancy could barely remember a time when her parents had slept together. Her clearest memory was the times when she would get into the bed with them on a stormy night such as tonight. That was a very long time ago.

Lightning flashed brilliantly, illuminating the room before she flipped on the lights. Feeling guilty for just *being* in her father's room, Nancy quickly went to his closet and folded back the two louvered doors. Three black cases sat side by side on the top closet shelf, much too high for her to reach. She rolled her dad's desk chair over to the doors and clumsily climbed onto the seat, trying to spare her knee, but the pain stung sharply as she was forced to bend it. Carefully, Nancy pulled one of the cases from the shelf.

It was heavier than she expected, but she managed to get down from the chair and put the case on the floor without dropping it. Nancy sat on the floor, wincing again when she forgot and bent her knee. Straightening the injured leg, she unlatched the two metal fasteners on the case and folded back the top to reveal what looked like hundreds of packages containing a variety of medicines.

She wasn't sure just what she was looking for, but figured she would recognize something with an antibiotic in it. Most of the names were familiar to her. Nancy began taking out packages of pills in plastic bubbles, and boxes and bottles of pills, glancing at each list of ingredients. One or two looked as if they might be what she wanted, even though the labels didn't list any antibiotic that she recognized. The print on some of the smaller packages was so small that Nancy had a hard time figuring out what some of the words were. She kept digging.

Near the bottom of the bag were some folded pieces of paper. Glancing at them before she set them aside, she saw that one was a piece of newspaper, and the other a folded sheet of lined tablet paper. Digging deeper into the case, she hit the jackpot in the last layer of packages and boxes. Twelve small boxes contained tiny plastic tubes.

The print on the side of the boxes read, "Use as a topical application for mildly infected injuries. NOT for internal use." She removed all of them and began the tedious job of fitting the hundreds of items back into the case.

It took a long time, but finally Nancy had them all in approximately the same order in which she'd found them. That was when she discovered she'd left out the newspaper article and the sheet of paper. Nancy groaned in despair. The

storm had gotten much worse while she had been occupied with finding the medicine. The brilliant flashes of lightning, deafening claps of thunder, and stronger
winds were sure to bring her mother out of her room. Anita knew Nancy had
always been scared of storms and their violent pyrotechnic-audio displays.

Trembling with nervousness, Nancy decided the best thing to do was stuff the
papers into her pocket, along with the ointment, then get back to her room. She
would sneak back here later to restore the papers to her dad's case. As quickly as
she could, Nancy lifted the heavy case back onto the shelf and shut the closet
doors. After she put the chair back under the desk, she peeked out into the hallway and once again found it empty.

As Nancy quietly closed her own door, she heard Anita open hers. Ignoring
the pain in her knee, she jumped onto her bed, jerked the covers over her legs,
and grabbed her diary and pen from the bedside table. At almost the same
moment, a soft tap announced her mother's arrival.

"Was that you in the hallway just now?" Anita asked, as she opened the door.

"Yeah, I had to go to the bathroom," Nancy said, as she slowly moved her leg,
seeking a position to ease the pain. "I can't sleep with all that racket outside, so I
thought I'd write in my diary." She held up the book.

Anita lifted her nose and sniffed. "Is that smoke I smell?" Anita looked at
Nancy with accusing eyes. "Have you been smoking? It does smell more like
wood fire, though."

Nancy thought quickly. "Me and Alicia burned trash for her mother. We sat
outside watching it for a while."

Anita looked relieved. "I see. Well, the storm is getting worse by the second.
The weather station says we are under a severe thunderstorm warning. Want to
come watch TV with me?"

"Thanks, but I'm okay here. Maybe you should turn off the television until
the lightning stops."

Nancy almost laughed out loud, as she realized *she* was sounding like a mother
now. She assured Anita again that she was okay with the storm then said good
night as Anita left the room. She wondered briefly if her mother was the one who
needed company during the storm.

She waited until she was sure Anita was in her room before she threw back the
covers. She had bumped her knee when she'd jumped into the bed, and it had
been all she could do to keep a grimace of pain off her face. Nancy pulled up the
bandage to view the damage. The wound had a small tear in it and some
nasty-looking gunk was oozing out, along with a bit of fresh blood.

She pulled out several tissues from the box near her bed and cleaned her knee as well as she could, then unscrewed the cap from one of the tiny sample tubes. Nancy squeezed the entire contents onto the wound, wrapped it in a clean bandage which she'd gotten from the bathroom medicine cabinet, and put tape over that. The red streak seemed redder and higher than when she'd checked it earlier. The pain was pretty awful.

Exhausted, and feeling a little nauseated, Nancy sank back against her pillow. That's when she felt the crumple of papers in her pajama pocket. She unfolded the piece of newspaper first. Nancy didn't see a date, but she could tell the paper was really old. There was a small picture of a boy below the heading which read, "Anderson Boy Still Missing."

According to the article the boy, Henry Anderson, III, was eleven years old and had disappeared after his parents were brutally murdered. The state police and the sheriff's department gave a list of phone numbers to call for anyone who knew of the boy's whereabouts, or knew anything about the boy's disappearance.

Nancy put the newspaper clipping aside and unfolded the other piece of paper. It had something written in pencil on it, the words faded and hard to read. Nancy held it closer to the lamp to make out the words, "*You wouldn't help me, so you'll be sorry some day.*"

Questions whirled through her mind. Why had Abner saved the two items? Was the boy in the picture someone her dad had known when he was young? What had been important enough about the newspaper article that he had saved it, hidden away, all these years? And the note. It sounded like a threat, but why would a child threaten her dad?

As she thought about the mystery of the two pieces of paper, Nancy realized she was feeling much worse. She had that miserable hot and cold feeling she got whenever she ran a fever. The aching in her knee had spread to the rest of her leg so that Nancy couldn't tell which hurt the most, her knee or her hip. And the nausea was getting pretty bad.

"Well, shoot!" Nancy said, in disgust. Everything was going wrong. Tears welled up and she began to cry again. The pain, the rotten feverish feeling, the guilt she felt over Bud's death suddenly seemed more than she could bear. She needed to talk to someone, and she knew it couldn't be her mother. Anita would tell her dad, and he'd bawl her mom out like it was all her mom's fault. Then he would turn on her, accusing her of being totally stupid for going out with Bud. He'd be right, of course, but she didn't want to hear it.

An idea that Nancy had earlier, grew in her mind. She could tell Ms. Amy, and she would know of a way Nancy could let the sheriff know what she'd seen at the old country club without revealing her identity. That's what she'd do. She would tell Ms. Amy. Feeling a tiny bit better for having made that decision, Nancy thought again about the strange papers she'd found in her dad's case. Before she could rest, she needed to hide them from her mom.

Feeling both a little dizzy and slightly sick, Nancy decided that her bottom bureau drawer would be the safest place. That was where her winter socks were kept, and Anita wouldn't be looking in there for a few months yet. Nancy tucked the papers as far to the back of the drawer as she could reach and made sure they were covered completely by pairs of socks before limping back to her bed. The pain in her leg was growing by the minute.

Nancy wished she'd thought to get some aspirin while she was in the bathroom. She didn't feel like getting up again. She turned her pillow over, looking for a cool spot to put her head. Outside, the rain was making a steady roar on the roof, and lightning flashed repeatedly and contrary to her former thoughts, Nancy now wished her dad were home. She would feel safer with him here. If only he weren't so condemning of her, she could talk to him about her problems.

Then, looming in her mind was the picture of Bud's light-colored shirt as he ran away from her toward the old country club building. Nancy heard again the sound of that single shot that had changed forever her small, safe world. She cried tears of fear and grief as she prayed, "Please help me!" She had never felt so alone in her life as she did now.

CHAPTER 26

▼

Abner Waggoner pounded on the door of number eleven at the Economy Stop Motel. The roof had no extension to provide shelter from the pouring rain, so by the time Margaret fumbled with the lock and got the door open, Abner was soaked. This did not improve his already foul mood, which he immediately made apparent to her. "It took you long enough, didn't it? You should have been at the door ready to open it. I'm damn near drowned!"

Margaret grabbed a towel from the bathroom and handed it to him, but he would not be soothed. "This is a helluva' night to meet," he groused, as he scrubbed at his wet hair and made a frizzled mop of it. "What's so urgent it couldn't wait until Wednesday night?"

She had backed up to sit in one of the chairs that matched the bed and the particle board table. Abner's bad moods with her were increasing, making a drastic change from the romantic, sweet-talking sales man she thought she had fallen in love with. For almost a year now, she had been sneaking about, meeting Abner at whatever place he chose. For the last two weeks, that had been this roadside motel only thirty-five miles north of Ashley Springs.

The cheapness of the motel was a slap in the face for Margaret. At first she had tried to justify his downgrading of their relationship, by telling herself that he was pushed financially because he was saving for his daughter's college expenses. Nancy was supposed to enter LSU this coming fall semester. But Abner had cut back on the money he spent on meals they had together too, and he'd changed the number of times they 'dated', from twice a week, to once a week, and lately he'd missed a couple of those.

He claimed he had to spend more time on the road to boost his sales, and that his wife and daughter were making more demands on his time as well. Margaret was supposed to understand what a strain he was under and to not expect the same treatment she'd gotten during the first few months of their affair. She accepted his excuses out of a deep sense of guilt and shame for her own behavior.

The first time Margaret consented to have dinner with him, Abner assured her that he was filing for divorce. Over time, they talked less and less about his leaving home until finally, neither of them mentioned it anymore. Added to that, he began to find fault with almost everything she did or said. Margaret, already sick of her own duplicity, recently admitted to herself that she was seeing the real Abner these past few weeks.

He put his wet jacket on one of the hangers fastened to a metal rod next to the bathroom. With practiced ease he shed his pants and shirt, putting them on hangers as well. He had on blue boxer shorts, embroidered with black geese. Margaret watched his disrobing in silence. Abner finally looked at her, a frown on his face. "Aren't you going to undress?"

Margaret felt a mixture of pain and disgust. Pain at being treated like a whore, and disgust with herself for having been so stupid. "No, I'm not undressing," she said quietly.

"Then why the hell are we here?" Abner plopped down on the side of the bed. His sullen mood pulled down his mouth and formed deep lines that reached his chin. The expression served to emphasize his drooping cheeks where developing wattles altered the shape of his face.

"To talk, Abner, remember? That's what I told you when I called."

Margaret had to raise her voice to be heard above the drum of heavy rain on the motel roof. The room filled with a brilliant blue light and almost immediately thunder jarred the thin walls. The rain began to pour even harder, the sound shutting the two of them off from the rest of the world.

"You got me out in this god-awful weather just to talk?" Abner put his hands on his hips. "I thought you'd at least want to go to bed first."

Margaret couldn't imagine wanting to go to bed with him ever again. But in spite of her new feelings, or her lack of feelings, tears spilled down her cheeks. She had allowed herself to be enticed into going with a married man simply because she'd been lonely for a very long time. Margaret had let her selfish feelings lead her instead of her good sense.

She had been a church-going, God-fearing person until she let her baser needs take control. Like so many other women who found themselves alone, Margaret had no social life to speak of after John's sudden death of a heart attack. That was four years ago, and the occasional outing with other widows hardly had substituted for a male-female relationship.

She had first met Abner in the town of Connerlyville, in a café which was next to the boutique where she worked. He had asked one of the waitresses to introduce them. His bright, friendly personality had ultimately dazzled her into his bed. Margaret was able to pacify her conscience for a long time. She repeated to herself his claims that, his wife wasn't really a wife anymore. She told herself that she deserved male companionship again. Not until she began to see him for the shallow person he was, did she realize the depth of her own wrongdoing. Margaret hoped that God would forgive her.

"I want to end our relationship," she told Abner now. "I thought it only fair to tell you to your face. I didn't know that it was going to storm."

"*You're* telling *me* our relationship, as you put it, is over?"

Abner came around the bed and leaned over her, causing the flab around his waist to roll over the elastic waistband of his shorts. He thrust his face so close to hers, she could see the fine web of broken capillaries covering his nose and cheeks. The liquor on his breath was stale and mixed with the odor of unbrushed teeth. Margaret turned her face away. She saw him clearly now, as a middle-aged Lothario only a few years away from becoming a lecherous old man.

"No one quits on Abner Waggoner, missy," he declared. He jabbed his chest with his forefinger. "I do the quitting, and if I weren't so damned nice, you would have been out of here six months ago!"

The outraged Abner, clothed only in his blue goose shorts, struck Margaret as being comical. Her giggle shocked her as much as it did Abner. She quickly put her hand over her mouth to hide her unexpected smile.

"You find this funny?" His voice squeaked in his indignation.

Abner stomped, as best he could with bare feet, back around the bed to the hangers that held his wet clothes. He put one of his arms into the sleeve of his shirt and the wet material clung to his skin, coldly uncomfortable.

"You can't leave now, Abner." Margaret felt something like pity for him. "You would drown before you could get into your car. We can just sit here until it lets up some."

He stopped to listen to the roar of the storm overhead. "It's a fact I'm not going back out in that." He glanced at his wrist watch. "It's after eleven already, and I can go home in the morning. I might as well sleep here." He peeled the one sleeve off his arm.

Abner's rage at Margaret's saying she was through with him seemed to have completely vanished. His self-serving statement brushed aside the fact of Margaret's leaving in the downpour and dealt only with his personal comfort. He turned down the covers on the nearest side of the bed and climbed in. Giving his pillow a punch, he reached over to turn out the lamp.

He was beginning his night's sleep as if she were not in the room, making it very plain that Margaret had dropped to the bottom of his list of priorities. She felt deeply embarrassed at even being in the same room with him. Margaret knew with certainty that he was thinking of getting some other woman into his bed. She couldn't wait to get home and wash the smell of him out of her hair.

She gathered up her purse and car keys from the bedside table. Without saying a word, she opened the motel door wide, and walked out into the deluge of cold rain. If Abner called out to her, she did not hear him. Drenched to the skin, she got into her car and drove out onto the highway, barely able to see through the heavy curtain of water that poured solidly down her windshield. Even with her wipers working at full speed, she could barely see the middle line of the highway.

The road was dark and deserted at this late hour and ordinarily, Margaret would have been fearful and nervous at being out in a storm. Instead, she realized that she felt really good! In fact, she felt free.

"Why didn't I do this months ago?" Smiling, she punched in her Eagles CD and began to hum along with the band as they sang, "Take It Easy." Margaret knew she would, "take it easy," before she let herself become entangled in another relationship. She had been entirely too anxious to be with a man to think clearly about what the repercussions might be. *If* she ever dated again, the man would be single.

In her rush to get to her car, Margaret had not noticed the vehicle parked only a couple of spaces from her own. Nor did she know that someone in it had been waiting for her to leave. It would have really upset Margaret if she'd known that for the last two times she had met Abner at this motel, the same person had followed them. The person had noted that Margaret usually left first. But whether she had left tonight or not, a matter of business would be brought to a conclusion. Margaret would never know how lucky she was.

Abner did not call out after Margaret. Cursing her thoughtlessness, he got up and slammed shut the door, but not before the rain had blown all the way to the foot of the bed. His bare feet were wet from squishing over the soaked carpet. Again, muttering imprecations against Margaret's gross inconsideration, he dried his feet on the towel she had handed him earlier, then went over to where his clothes hung and took several swigs from the ever-present flask of whiskey he kept in his jacket pocket.

It stung a bit that she had beat him to the punch by saying their affair was over, but the more he thought about it, the more relieved he was that Margaret had taken the initiative. He'd been trying to find a good time to tell her they were through. But this way, and Abner felt a swell of anticipation, when she begged him to take her back, he could point out to her that she walked out, not him.

Little Molly Gerstag at the Piedmont Café in Sundown was more than willing to take Margaret's place, and Abner was more than ready for a younger lover. Feeling satisfied that he had handled things very well, Abner turned off the lamp on the other side of the bed and plumped up his pillow again. Floating comfortably on the sensations of near inebriation and self-satisfaction, he was asleep with the next breath he drew.

The cacophony of the elements covered the light tinkle of breaking glass at the back window. Neither was Abner aroused when the beam of a small halogen flashlight located his head on the pillow. But a sharp prick on his neck was enough to startle him awake. He reached for the lamp and the prick became a cut.

"Don't move, Abner, unless you want to die now," a voice whispered near the ear where the burning pain worsened.

"What do you want?" Abner held very still, hoping to pacify whoever it was. "You want my money, is that it? Get my billfold out of my pants. Just please don't hurt me."

"It's different when the pain is yours, isn't it Abner?" The anonymous whisper came again. "Have you forgotten that time when I said you'd be sorry some day? You laughed at my note and stuck it into your pocket. I was no more to you than a piece of dirt."

A terrible fear rose to clog Abner's breathing. He knew he was about to die, but begged anyway. "Please don't kill me! I'll do anything you want, just please don't do this." His heart beat so hard he felt it might burst.

"I begged for mercy too, remember? I was totally helpless while you did those terrible things to me. You didn't ask what I wanted then, and I'm not granting you what you're asking now. Good bye, you slime bag. May you burn in hell forever!"

Abner realized his throat was being cut milliseconds before he died.

CHAPTER 27

▼

"You're moving too fast."

"I move when the opportunity presents itself."

"You've never executed three of them in three-month's time, let alone in three weeks!"

"Because there's never been so many criminals in one place before. Abner needed to go. He probably should have been the first one, anyway."

"I think you need to lie low for a while and let things cool down. You're making mistakes, and mistakes can get us caught."

"Mistakes? I don't recall making any mistakes."

"What about Bud Purefoy?"

"What about him? He was the one who made the mistake. What was I to do? Let him tell the sheriff that he saw my vehicle at the back of Thurmond's house that night? That would have been a mistake for sure."

"No, of course I didn't mean that. But you could have gotten rid of him in a less spectacular way, like having him overdose. Everyone, including the police, knew he was both selling and using drugs. Shooting wasn't all that bad. Could have been the result of a drug deal gone bad, but setting the place on fire? That attracted everyone in two counties."

"I thought that was a nice touch, myself. So, that's one mistake according to you. What are the others?"

"Being so close to Amy Bordeaux could be a mistake. You could inadvertently say something that could connect us to the murders."

There was a silence that got deeper as the seconds went by. Then the anger flared. "Did I ever tell you you're too damn pushy for your own good? Talk about me making mistakes—what was that about you going out to Amy's house? And you weren't planning to let me know that, were you? If I hadn't seen the wet clothes, I wouldn't know it yet. Maybe you're the one who will 'inadvertently' give something away. You knew my agenda when you followed me here and I'm not changing it now. Must I worry about whether or not you can hold yourself together? And if I have to worry, what should I do about that?"

Silence settled like dust between them. Ghosts of the past rose to revive memories that caused deep emotions to roil and twist, stirring the poison of hate in one, and the chill of fear in the other. The absolute quiet strained at the nerves until there was a relenting—and a warning.

"Okay, I'll let things cool down, as you say. But you keep in mind what's to be done here. And you keep yourself far away from that Bordeaux piece, or you may get the two of you killed."

"I'm not interested in Amy. She's just a nice person and I have no reason not to be friendly with her. If I suddenly stopped being friendly, she would have a reason to be suspicious of me, you know."

"Don't give me that asinine garbage!" Temper flared like crimson flames. "You can't wait to be around her. Think you're fooling me? Well, I've got news for you. I have ways of making her think you're total trash. She won't be able to look at you, let alone be friendly. Push me and I'll show you."

Silence filled the room again. Only one would win. It had been that way for a very long time. It would be fatal to try to change that now.

CHAPTER   28

▼

Barney tapped on Amy's kitchen door. Earlier, she had buzzed him on the intercom to tell him she was cooking his breakfast. As he waited for her to let him in, Barney looked out at the yard which was covered with leaves and limbs that had been torn out of the trees by last night's heavy winds and rain. The flowers were battered to the ground, looking as if they'd been trampled by a herd of cattle. They gave mute testimony to the power of Arkansas thunderstorms. Barney had talked several times to Amy about having a storm cellar built, but she firmly refused to give up a portion of her front lawn to a "hidey-hole".

"Not only are storm shelters ugly," Amy argued each time, "but they make a perfect home for spiders and snakes. I'll take my chances above ground, thank you just the same."

She opened the door and motioned Barney in. He could smell bacon cooking and felt his belly rumble in anticipation. As he took his place at the kitchen table, he thought what a homey place it was. Sunlight lay in strips across the turquoise *Congoleum* floor. The white kitchen cabinets had turquoise tile counter tops, and the bright yellow curtains at the bay window matched the tablecloth on which he propped his elbows. He liked the combination.

"You sleep okay?" he said. Amy looked a bit pale, and Barney figured she had a hard time going to sleep after all the excitement.

"When I finally got to sleep, I slept okay," she said, confirming his thought.

Amy served his bacon, toast, and eggs on a creamy *Lenox* plate with a gold rim. Amy told him once that she believed in using the best dishes daily, instead of saving them for future generations to break. It had sounded like a sensible idea to Barney.

"I slept with one eye open," he admitted. "Not that I thought anyone would be so foolish as to come back. I did patrol around the house a couple of times before dawn, though. Didn't Hannibal tell you?"

"If he said anything, I didn't hear him," Amy said, smiling.

"Smart dog." Barney scratched Hannibal's ears. "He knew it was me. I saw him push the curtains back to get a look. You wanted out, didn't you, boy?" Hannibal waved his tail in assent.

Amy gave the dog a generous portion of Choice Bits, then sat down to her bowl of raisin bran and sliced banana. "Did you find any other evidence of a prowler?" she asked.

"No, but that watch Hannibal found is expensive," Barney said, as he chopped his eggs to bits, allowing the yellow yolks to puddle into his bacon strips. He then shook enough pepper onto them to turn them black. Amy had to look away. "Somebody's going to miss it," Barney continued, in reference to the watch. "It may already be reported as stolen."

She remained quiet, as she slowly ate her cereal. He thought she seemed a little pre-occupied, but figured she was worrying over her prowler.

"I've thought about last night's episode," he said, after swallowing a large bite of his eggs, "and it doesn't make sense that a person would choose a stormy night to come prowling around here, if you know what I mean. But say he was almost here when the rain began and he just kept coming, then what were his intentions? He may have meant to break into the house before Hannibal sounded the alarm. If so, then it was someone who didn't know he was here."

"Yes, I agree, Barney," Amy said. "It was some jerk looking for something to sell for dope, probably."

"Yeah, some jerk with a boat."

Amy looked up, surprised. "How do you know that?"

"You said Hannibal tracked him down the steps just before I drove up, and whoever it was certainly didn't run back up and through the front lawn. I would have seen him in my headlights as I came up the driveway. The dock was the only way he could escape without being seen. When Hannibal got outside, he went straight to the boat dock where I believe he found the watch. He took a terrible chance what with the river running as high as it was."

Amy shook her head slowly. "You know, I've never thought about someone coming in from the river," she said. "But then I've never had this kind of situation before. It makes me feel even more vulnerable." Her appetite gone, Amy got up and dumped the remainder of her cereal into the garbage disposal.

"It won't happen again," Barney said confidently. "He knows now that you have a dog to warn you. You have the Purefoy flowers to do today, right?"

"Right. Brenda Woolcott is coming in again to take Nancy's place, so I'll have plenty of help. I thought that after we get most of the flower orders taken care of, I would go to the public library to do some research. I also have to call Pinkie some time today, and go by to check on Nancy."

"Sounds like a full day to me." Barney took his dishes to the sink of sudsy hot water. He washed his plate, fork, and cup and put them into the yellow dish drainer. "I'll take that watch to the sheriff today."

"I hope Leigh comes in today," Amy said.

"Yeah, I miss her too. Do you know if she'll take Hannibal home with her?"

Amy shrugged her shoulders. "Leigh didn't say, but I guess that's what she'll do. I was hoping he'd be here for a while, myself."

"But if you tell her what happened last night, she'll insist that he stay here," Barney said, as he fastened Hannibal's leash to his collar, preparing him for his morning run.

Amy watched them go out the door, again wondering if she should tell Barney about the weird hallucinations she'd been having, first at the sheriff's office, and again last night. She knew it would upset him terribly, maybe even make him think she was losing her mind, but he would be upset anyway when he learned she'd held it back from him. However, Barney wouldn't have a clue as to what to do about it. Amy didn't have a clue, herself. The last two episodes hung over her like a dark cloud because, she had to admit, they scared her.

"No," Amy said out loud. "I won't tell Barney, at least not until Leigh and I decide how to handle it." She felt a little easier, knowing she might have her aunt to talk to soon.

Later that day at her work station in the back room of her shop, Amy tied the bow on what she hoped was the last order of flowers for the Purefoy funeral and said, "Okay, Barn, get these over to the funeral home, and we should be finished with one more unpleasant job."

Alicia and Brenda helped Barney load everything into the Suburban and, along with Amy, they heaved a collective sigh of relief when he drove off.

"Working on these funeral orders is so depressing, especially this one for Bud," Brenda said. "I wish none of this dying stuff had ever happened."

"I know what you mean," Amy agreed. "Which reminds me, are you or Alicia going to the funeral?"

Brenda looked at Alicia and they both shook their heads. Alicia said, "If Nancy wanted us to go with her, we would, but Mrs. Waggoner told us last night that Nancy wasn't feeling well enough. The doctor had said it would be better for Nancy if she stayed at home in bed. Since we don't know Bud's family, we're not going either."

"Then why don't we adjourn to Sadie's for a few minutes?" Amy said. "We deserve a break, don't you think? As soon as Barney gets back from the funeral home, we'll leave."

When Barney returned, he said he'd be glad to sit up front for a while. "That's the easy part of running this establishment," he teased Amy. "At least I'll get a few minutes rest."

At the café, Amy led the way to her favorite spot, a booth near the back. This morning, a larger group of men than usual sat next to the front window at the big table reserved for the regular coffee drinking crowd. Most of them smoked, so Amy always got as far away from them as she could.

"Good morning, ladies." Vera placed glasses of ice water in front of them. "That is, as good a morning as it can be, what with another funeral about to take place. Ya'll goin'?"

"No, Vera," Amy said. "I think the four of us have done as much as we want to by getting all those flowers ready."

"I don't blame you, honey." Vera turned her attention to Brenda and Alicia. "Ya'll been staying some with Nancy? I hear she's all tore up, poor thing!"

The two girls looked uncomfortable, not sure how they should answer Vera's obvious bid for a little inside information. Surprisingly, Mary was the one who came to their rescue.

"They're doing everything Nancy's asked them to do. So, are you closing for the funeral?" Mary asked, tossing the conversational ball back into Vera's court.

"No. I know poor old Elmer, but I don't ever remember seeing his wife more than five times in the many years I've lived here, so I won't be going. Elmer hardly ever comes in here except to ask a favor of someone. He sure don't buy anything. A bunch of the men plan to go, though." Vera nodded toward the coffee drinkers.

They all wore glum expressions, and none of them were cracking jokes or ribbing each other as they usually did. Amy thought their mood was reflective of how most of the townspeople felt.

Vera turned her attention to Amy. "You were here when Elmer come in with that rifle, weren't you? He like to scared us all to death. Still, I feel sorry for him and his wife. It's gotta' be a terrible thing, losing your child."

After Vera left them to wait on other customers, Amy brought up Nancy's name again. "Had either of you girls gotten to talk to her about the night of Bud's death?"

"I've called her every day," Brenda said. "But she won't talk about that night."

"The same for me," Alicia said. "She cuts me off when I ask questions. She just cries and says she can't talk. It's like she's scared, or something. Once when I called, Nancy said she was thinking about leaving town."

"Why would she want to leave?" Mary asked. "Surely Bud's death wouldn't be reason enough for her to leave home."

"I can't see her father allowing her to leave," Alicia said. "He wants her to stay at home all the time as it is. He wouldn't let her go some place just because she's upset."

"Well, Nancy's emotions are a mess right now," Amy said, "and there's no accounting for what she'll say. Give her a few more days."

Just then Amy was distracted by the sight of the sheriff's tan Suburban speeding by the café, followed by a police car. A sense of *de 'javu* made chills creep up her arms. She had been sitting in the same place the day Don Mercer's body was found. Amy had watched as the police cars rushed by on the street, just as they were doing now. And Barney had said *he* was in Sadie's when he saw them speed by on their way to Thurmond's.

Please, she prayed silently, *don't let it be another one.*

As if to mock her plea, Jim Arnold burst through the front door with a wild look on his face. He was chalky white, and seemed hardly able to walk to the table where the group of men sat. A hush fell across the room, every eye on Jim. Amy felt dread tighten her stomach muscles.

"He got Abner Waggoner too!" Jim's voice quavered. "That son-of-a-bitch done killed Abner." Tears were rolling down his cheeks. Jim was Abner's uncle on his mother's side, and had always treated Abner like the son he'd never had. Jim slumped down into a chair that one of the men pulled out for him.

By then Vera had found her voice. "You sit right there, honey. I'll bring you a nice cup of hot coffee." Having said that, for a moment she just stood there, looking as if she might cry, too. "Lord, Lord, what are we to do?" Vera said, as she started toward the coffee machine.

"Poor Nancy," Brenda sobbed. She reached for a napkin to wipe her eyes. "She loves her daddy so much. This will kill her."

Alicia was rocking back and forth, saying softly, "Oh, no. Oh, no."

Mary was doing her best to comfort the two of them, but Amy knew nothing could be said that would lessen the horror they all were feeling.

The men began to recover from hearing the terrible news, and their outraged voices filled the café with the sounds of their anger and fear. Almost as one, they rose and started toward the front door. Mixed phrases drifted through the room as they erupted out of the door and onto the sidewalk.

"Something's got to be done," one of them shouted.

"We need to shake Sheriff Morgan up!" yelled another. "He'd better do something fast, or we will."

"I'm going home and get my gun," said yet another. "We gotta' find that bastard before he kills the whole damn town!"

Amy felt drained. The events of the past few weeks were taking an enormous emotional toll on everyone. The memory of last night's dream, or whatever it was, returned and like cold water pouring down her back, the icy feeling that had accompanied that nightmare, trickled down her spine. *Surely,* she thought, *what I saw last night doesn't have anything to do with Abner.* But, in her heart, she knew it did.

Shaking off the now familiar feeling of dread, she offered Brenda a napkin to dry her tears with, and said, "All we can do now is let Nancy and Mrs. Waggoner know we're ready to help in any way we can. You might want to go to your friend now. Even if she won't talk to you, your being there would help, I'm sure."

"I think that's a good idea," Mary agreed.

Amy paid their bill, and they all went back to the shop—Mary to work, and Amy to get her car to take Brenda and Anita to Nancy's house. She told Barney what Jim Arnold said, explaining that they had no details, just that Abner had been murdered. Barney was as shocked as they were, but said very little. What could a person say in face of such mind-numbing news?

She drove the girls to the Waggoner house and waited in the car while Brenda and Alicia went to the front door. After knocking several times and getting no response, they had started back toward the car when a voice called out, "Hello there! Are you girls looking for the Waggoner's?" An elderly lady stood on her porch at the house next door. "Mrs. Waggoner took her daughter to the hospital early this morning."

"Oh, no!" Brenda wailed. "What else can go wrong?"

"Thank you!" Amy called to the neighbor, who waved before going back into her house. When Brenda and Alicia got back into the car, she said, "I'll take you to the hospital."

CHAPTER 29

▼

The receptionist at the hospital told Amy that no visitors were allowed in Nancy's room at the moment. "The sheriff and one of his men are in there with her right now," she said. "That poor woman. Her child sick, and now her husband's been murdered!"

Barney was fond of saying that bad news traveled faster than a freight train in a small town, while, on the other hand, he said, you might not hear about someone's good luck for several months. Amy thought he was probably right. "Could you tell me anything about Nancy Waggoner's condition?" she said.

The clerk seemed to realize she may have said too much. She adopted a stern expression, as if unfriendliness on her part would make Amy forget how unprofessional she had been. "We're not allowed to give that information, ma'am. You can have a seat in the waiting room, if you wish. It's straight down this hallway."

Not so easily dismissed, Amy said, "Then would you tell someone in the Waggoner's room that we are here?" Amy wrote Brenda and Alicia's names on one of her business cards, handed it to the woman, and then led the way to the waiting room. For several minutes the three of them thumbed through old copies of *House & Garden* and *Redbook* in silence, then Brenda got up to pace about the room.

"Ms. Amy, what will Nancy do now? She was crazy about her dad, you know. Everything seems to be going so wrong!" Tears trickled down Brenda's cheeks. She looked much younger than her seventeen years, and sounded much like Amy felt; scared, confused, and sick at heart.

Not having an answer to the girl's question, she changed the subject "Maybe you both had better call your mothers to let them know you're here," Amy suggested. "When they hear of Mr. Waggoner's death, they'll probably call you at the shop."

Amy gave them each a quarter and then walked up the hall toward the nurses' station. She needed physical activity, something that would work off the nervous feeling in her stomach.

"Ms. Bordeaux?"

Amy jerked around to face Sheriff Morgan. Detective Ben Edwards stood nearby.

"I didn't mean to startle you," the sheriff said. "Seems I do that a lot."

He had taken off his hat, and Amy noted again how very tired he looked. She was too filled with her own feelings of fear and dismay, however, to have much sympathy for him.

"Sheriff, I was hoping I could have a word with you alone." She looked past him to Ben who was smiling in a friendly manner. Amy thought he looked a little frayed around the edges, too. She thought not many people she knew were getting much sleep nowadays.

The sheriff turned to Edwards and said, "I'll be back at the office in a few minutes. Tell the State boys I want to talk with them before they leave."

"Sure, Frank." Ben smiled again, as he looked back at Amy. She thought he was trying without words to reassure her. "Real nice seeing you again, Ms. Bordeaux," he said, then strode rapidly away from them toward the elevators.

Amy walked back toward the waiting room so that the nurse, who was back at her post, couldn't hear them. Near the waiting room entrance, Amy turned to face him. "I had a prowler last night at my house." The sheriff's expression did not change. "If it had not been for Hannibal," Amy continued, "that's my aunt's dog, someone might have broken into my home. But his barking, and the fact that Barney drove up at that time, made whomever it was run away."

"Barney was out last night?"

Amy thought he was focusing on the wrong piece of information, but explained anyway. "He went to Little Rock yesterday evening to get flowers that I needed for the Purefoy funeral. A wreck on the interstate held him up for hours." Determined that he understand the position she was in last night, she explained once more, "If Barney had not come back when he did, and if Hannibal hadn't raised Cain, whoever it was could have gotten inside."

"Why did Barney go to your house so late? Doesn't he live in that apartment over your store?"

Amy was losing patience with the sheriff. He was asking useless questions about Barney, instead of paying attention to the fact that someone had prowled around her house. "For your information, Sheriff Morgan, Barney has stayed in the apartment over my garage ever since I was unfortunate enough to find Mr. Thurmond's body."

"Are you thinking it was the killer at your house last night?" His face mirrored his skepticism. "It couldn't have been, because he killed Abner almost fifty miles away from where you live. It's not likely he stopped by to break into your house."

"No, of course I'm not saying that. All I *am* saying is, someone wanted to be at my house awfully bad to come out in such terrible weather." She stopped abruptly to get a grip on her emotions, then asked, "Would you tell me where it was that Mr. Waggoner was killed?"

He looked at her with interest for the first time. "At a motel. Why?"

"Then tell me one more thing. Did the killer break a window?"

"How did you know that?" Morgan's face flushed with anger. "Who's been talking to you? Was it someone from my office?"

"No, no," Amy said quickly. "No one told me anything. It was just a lucky, or rather, unlucky guess. Please forget I asked."

But his famous temper had already taken over. "Look, Ms. Bordeaux, I asked you nicely to keep your nose out of police business. We have to keep such information strictly to ourselves, and I mean to find out how you came to know about that window. You're meddling into something that could be bad for you, and disastrous to the case. I'm done with your interference, understand?"

Adding fuel to Frank's anger was the fact that William Benson had told him about Amy's asking Nadine questions. Frank felt that her getting involved in the case could backfire on her. The last thing he had wanted was for the killer to take an interest in Amy, and that may have already happened. As suddenly as he had lashed out at her, he calmed down.

"Ms. Amy," he said in a quieter voice, "please let the professionals handle this. I'll look into the prowler being at your house, but I have to tell you, if someone was there in all that rain, there's probably nothing left in the way of clues, such as footprints. Just go about your own business, and I promise we will do everything we can to get this thing stopped."

Amy became aware that Brenda and Alicia had gotten back from the pay phone and were standing near enough to hear the conversation. She wanted to tell the sheriff about the strange scene in her bedroom the night before, how she'd awakened at the sound of breaking glass, and how a shadowy figure had approached her bed, only to disappear before she could see what it was going to do. Amy certainly didn't want the two girls to hear her crazy story.

The sheriff had seen them too. Almost as if he had read her mind, Frank said, "And we will talk about that window later." He tipped his hat, then turned to walk to the elevators.

"What's his problem?" Brenda gawked at the big man's retreat. "He looked pretty upset. Was he mad at you, Ms. Amy? What window was he talking about?"

"Oh, I don't think he was mad at me." Amy ignored Brenda's last question. "He's understandably upset about all the murders he's having to work on. Some of the victims were his friends, you know."

"Well, I just hope he never gets mad at me." Brenda made a comical face, "He scares me just to be near him." Alicia nodded her head in agreement.

"We're lucky to have him as sheriff, even if he is a bit unfriendly at times," Amy said. "Being a little scarey isn't bad for a man in his position. What did your mothers say?"

"Mom said she was glad we came to see Nancy, and to try be home in an hour," Alicia said. "She's pretty upset about Mr. Waggoner's death."

"Momma told me the pretty much the same thing," Brenda said.

"Ma'am." The receptionist at the desk was waving for them to come her way. "Mrs. Waggoner said you can come up now. She's in room two-sixty-nine."

When they walked into Nancy's room, the blinds were closed, making the room dim. Nancy lay still and quiet, a small shape under the white sheets. First Brenda, then Alicia went to Anita and hugged her. The three of them cried softly, then Anita wiped her eyes and held out her hand.

"I'm so sorry about everything," Amy said in a whisper, patting the distraught woman's hand. "It must be terribly difficult."

Anita reached for a clean tissue from the box on the table next to the bed. She wiped her eyes and blew her nose before speaking. "Thank you, but there's nothing anyone can do. Right now I have to be strong for Nancy. She's so sick."

Nancy's face appeared flushed, and there was an IV drip was in her right arm.

"She's been delirious with a high fever," Anita said. "Early this morning I heard her calling out. She was talking wild and crazy, and when I touched her, she was so hot it shocked me, and then I saw her knee. It was badly swollen and very red all around her leg. I called Dr. Thompson. He told me to take her to the emergency room. They put an I.V. into in her arm and brought her to the room." Anita's voice broke with a sob.

"The sheriff and the detective came to tell me about Abner. I had been expecting my husband any minute because he said he would be home this morning. Anyway, they took me out into the hall." Anita caught her breath with a small gasp, the reality of her husband's death still not fully absorbed. "When I came back in with the two men, Nancy was awake. She sat up in bed and began screaming. She seemed to be afraid of them for some reason. I guess the fever affected her mind so that Nancy didn't know what she was doing."

"I'm sure that's what it was," Amy said, trying to reassure Anita. "Fever can do that to a person."

"I didn't know she had hurt her knee until I walked into her room yesterday morning without knocking. I thought then it looked bad, but she was determined to make nothing of it. She said she hit it on the walk-in cooler at your shop, but surely if Nancy hurt it that badly, she would say something, or be limping. Did you notice anything?"

"Nothing at all. Maybe she fell, or something, and didn't want to admit it." Amy knew that sounded weak, but she didn't know what else to say. She felt certain that Nancy had good reason to not tell her mother what really happened.

Anita leaned close to Amy and whispered, "They gave her something to make her rest, so I haven't told her about her father's death. She's much too sick to deal with that right now."

"I think you're right," Amy reassured her. She looked over at the bed where Alicia and Brenda stood silently, one on either side. They each held one of Nancy's hands. "Wouldn't you like to get out of here for a few minutes?" Amy suggested, "We can stay with Nancy. A cup of coffee, or maybe something to eat to help keep your strength up."

Anita straightened her shoulders and wiped tears off her face with the lump of soggy tissue in her hand. "Thank you, but I'm all right. I don't want to leave Nancy because she may wake up and need me."

"I don't blame you," Amy said. "I'll go down and get something for you."

Anita said she'd like a cup of coffee. From the pay phone in the waiting room, Amy called Barney to tell him where she was.. "Mrs. Waggoner is alone, so I'll stay with her for a while. Is everything all right there?"

"Not to worry," he said. "Mary and I are just sitting here. I don't think there'll be much going on in town today. By the way, Leigh called about thirty minutes ago."

"She's back home?"

"Yes. She said to tell you she would be here at about four o' clock, and if that's not okay, to call her."

"That's perfect. But back to what's going on here. Sheriff Morgan and Ben Edwards were here when we got to the hospital. I told him about my prowler. I also told him you came in just in time to chase off whoever it was, and he wanted to know where you had been and what time you got back." Amy laughed. "I think he's getting so desperate to find the killer, he's imagining everyone looks guilty. Even you."

Barney didn't reply immediately, then he laughed too. "You'd better watch out or he'll be accusing you next," he said. "By the way, I took the watch over to his office, but he wasn't there. I left it with Marlene. She said she would give it to Frank as soon as he got in. And don't worry about the shop," he reassured her, "because Mary and I've not been busy at all."

Nancy awoke from her induced sleep feeling, she said, a little better. A nurse brought in her lunch tray and she ate a few bites of the orange gelatin at her mother's insistence. She did, however, drink almost a whole glass of milk without any urging. "My head's not hurting like it was," Nancy said. "Would you raise my bed so I can sit up?"

Anita obligingly pushed the right button, then put her hand on Nancy's forehead. "Your fever's gone down, so you're getting better." Amy could see the frown lines disappear, as Anita realized her daughter might be over the worst of her illness.

"Brenda and Alicia were here earlier," Anita said, as she fluffed up Nancy's pillow and straightened the bed covers a bit. "Ms. Amy was kind enough to bring them, and I have to say, you really have them worried."

"I wish I'd been awake to talk to them," Nancy said. "I'm afraid I've given them a hard time for a couple of days."

Anita laughed. "They aren't the only ones you've given a hard time."

"Yeah, I know." Amy saw the haunted expression return to Nancy's face, as she slumped down in bed and pulled the covers to her chin.

"I feel awfully tired," she said, as she rolled over on her side, facing away from the two of them. Amy knew Nancy didn't want her mother to see the tears that had sprung to her eyes.

CHAPTER 30

▼

Amy went back to reading a book she'd brought with her, and Anita to paging through a new issue of *O Magazine*. Anita had left Nancy's side only once since Amy's arrival, and that was to call her aunt, Martha Evans, who lived on a farm above Cartersville. The aunt said she would pack a bag and be on her way within the hour. At two-thirty she walked into the room.

Martha Evans was a tall woman, taller than Amy's five-eight, and almost painfully thin. Her hair was snow white, but her posture was as straight as that of a teenager. She gave the impression of a quiet strength, as she held her niece's hand and spoke softly to her. Amy slipped out into the hallway to give the women some privacy. Later when Amy reentered the room, Anita introduced Amy to her aunt.

"I've heard a lot of nice things about you, Ms. Bordeaux." Martha Evans shook Amy's hand firmly. "My grandniece admires you greatly."

Nancy lay very still and relaxed, apparently asleep once more from the residual effect of the sedative they'd given her earlier. As Martha smoothed back a strand of hair from the girl's face, Amy could see that the older woman's fingers were knotted with arthritis.

"We, at the shop, think a lot of Nancy," Amy said. "She's such good help, and we enjoy having her around. I just wish she weren't so ill."

"My grandniece is young and strong," Martha said. "She will bounce back from this in an amazingly short time." She looked up to smile at Anita. "You'll see."

"I'll leave now," Amy said. "If there is anything the two of you need, just give me a ring. I'll be more than happy to get it for you. I'll stop by later this evening." After reassuring Anita that her staying with her had not been an imposition, Amy left the hospital.

She drove back to the shop where she found Mary puttering around in the front of the store, dusting knickknacks on the glass shelves. Barney was in the back where he had just finished removing paint from an old cedar chest which the owner wanted refinished.

"I need to call Pinkie," Amy said. "She'll think I've forgotten her."

It took a minute for her friend to get to the phone. Pinkie said she had been trying to coax Tim into eating a snack. Amy told her about Nancy's illness and her own involvement at the hospital. Someone at Simmon's House had already called the hospital and told Pinkie of Abner's death.

"I'm sure that right now Anita's feeling as if the seven plagues of Egypt have fallen on her," Pinkie said. "Trouble does seem to come in bunches sometimes. How is she?"

"Anita is handling everything amazingly well, considering what she's been through. The few times I've been around her, she seemed so timid and meek, but today Anita seemed to be in control. She isn't saying anything to Nancy about her father's death until the infection is under control. Anita's aunt, Martha Evans, is with her. That should help a great deal."

"I've known Anita ever since Abner married her and brought her to Ashley Springs," Pinkie said. "She is a very nice person." Amy heard her friend draw in a deep breath before she said, "Amy, whoever the killer is seems to have gone completely wild. Please keep someone with you all of the time. You never can tell what direction he might take next."

Amy assured her friend that she was being very careful. She was glad she hadn't said anything about last night's prowler, it would only add another worry to her friend's already heavy load.

After she put down the phone, Barney said he had gotten as far as he could on Gayle's beds. "I have to wait for the primer to dry before I can put on the first coat of enamel," he said. "Are you going to be here for closing time? I thought I'd go work in your yard for a while. There's a lot of leaves and limbs down from last night's storm. Hannibal needs exercise too, so I'll take him with me. Tell Leigh I'll see her later."

It was still a couple of hours before Leigh was due, so Amy figured this would be a good time for her to go to the library. "You don't mind, do you?" Amy asked

Mary. "I want to do some research which shouldn't take much more than an hour."

"Research?" Mary suddenly looked interested.

"Oh," Amy had to think quickly. "I thought I'd look up the history of early Ashley Springs. I've been asked to do an article for the historical society about early businesses located on Main Street." She wasn't exactly lying. Amy had been asked to do an article for the historical society, but she had already done the research on it.

Mary seemed satisfied with her explanation. All she said was, "I'll be fine, you go ahead."

Amy mentally kicked herself as she drove to the library. She shouldn't have mentioned the research part. She hated to lie, but Amy certainly couldn't tell Mary the whole truth because then Barney would find out and all heck would break loose. After Sheriff Morgan's repeated insistence that Amy practice caution, and that she not involve herself in police business any further, she felt guilty about what she was doing now. But the flashes of visual intuition she had experienced again last night, convinced Amy that she was somehow tied to the killings. She was determined to dig up a plausible reason for the men to be dying the way they were, and for her own ability to mentally tune into that violence.

Amy hoped that when she talked with Leigh, her aunt could help her understand what was happening to her. Meanwhile, she didn't want Mary, or anyone else wondering why she was so interested in the murdered men.

Thinking about Mary, Amy realized that her best helper was not the most comfortable person to be around. Mary was reserved to the point that it was hard to know what she was thinking. It left the impression that she didn't approve of most people.

Not even me!" Amy thought, as she turned into the library parking lot.

Ruth Stover, the head librarian, took Amy back to the room where the microfiche machine was kept and asked if Amy knew how to work it. When Amy assured her she did, Ruth showed her where the newspaper films were for the years she wanted. When Ruth was satisfied that Amy had everything she needed, she went back to her station behind the counter.

Amy decided to start with the year, 1970. When the newspapers had been committed to film, the oldest of them were yellowed with age, so the print was blurred. Amy had to squint at some of the poorer films, but she had managed to cover almost a year's span of time before one of them caught her eye. It was an article with a picture on the society page. A very young Walter Thurmond was standing beside an also very young Don Mercer. The headline read, "Thurmond and Mercer Families Build New $150,000 Men-Only Area For The Country Club.'" Twin smirks on their faces expressed their delight with themselves.

According to the brief article under the picture, the two families and a third contributor, who wished to remain anonymous, had financed the addition of a second floor to the original building. Amy was curious as to whom the unnamed donor was, and wondered who among the wealthy in her town owned such modesty. The characteristic fit no one she knew.

She read the rest of the article. It said that the new addition included a smoker's room complete with a bar, restroom facilities, and two bedroom suites for "special guests." The addition even included an outside staircase which only gold card members could use.

"That stinks," Amy muttered. "The good old boys could sneak whatever or whomever they wished up those back stairs and their wives would be none the wiser. I'll bet there were a lot of 'important' meetings up there."

She moved to the more recent papers, swiftly checking front pages, society pages, and police reports, finding nothing else of interest until she came to the issue for June 7, 1972.

Banner headlines announced the murders of Dr. and Mrs. Henry A. Anderson. Amy read slowly to absorb that distant chapter of violence. The housekeeper, a Mrs. Carmen Sanchez, had discovered the Anderson bodies.

Mrs. Sanchez had come to work that morning to find the back door closed, but unlocked. She was quoted as saying, "Dr. And Mrs. Anderson always kept the doors locked at night. They have all kinds of valuable things in the house, you know. They had given me a key because sometimes they liked to sleep late and didn't want to bother with letting me in. I thought they were up at first because of the unlocked door, so I went to the kitchen to start their breakfast. Then I saw something red on the kitchen floor, and I followed what looked like bloody smears upstairs, calling out for Dr. and Mrs. Anderson as I went. Their bedroom door was open, so I looked in and, oh, *Madre Dios!*" The article ended with the statement that Mrs. Sanchez had been unable to talk any further.

She wondered where Mrs. Sanchez was now. She would like to talk with her, Amy was thinking, as she continued reading about the murders. The thirteen-year-old daughter, Rosalind Anderson, had been found by a deputy. She was scrunched down in a corner of the attached three-car garage, hidden behind the couple's Silver Cloud Rolls. The child was covered with blood, according to the deputy who first discovered her. The law officers had guessed that the child was the first to find her parents. The reporter of that piece, a Herman Saddler, said the child was so traumatized, she had not spoken a word. She was taken to a hospital to be treated for shock.

Other news reports were about the son, Henry Anderson, III, who was missing. Both the police and sheriff departments conducted an immediate search of the premises for the young boy, thinking that he would be found dead somewhere in or near the house.

That not being the case, they had extended their search to the considerable number of acres that made up the Anderson estate, and on to surrounding properties. They had also searched for several miles along the river, but did not find him. They concluded that the killer may have kidnaped him, or killed him, then moved his body to another location. Perhaps even to another state.

In the following week's paper, Amy found an article with a picture of the young Henry. It showed a young boy with nondescript features, a butch hair cut, and wearing dark rimmed glasses. She was struck by the fact that butch haircuts were not in vogue among kids his age back then, and how nerdy he looked. All the other teenagers pictured in sports photographs, or other occasions, had fairly long hair. If she knew anything about young people, because his hair cut made him different in appearance from the other boys, Henry was probably the brunt of many jokes. The article went on to say that no clues had been uncovered as to the boy's whereabouts. Sheriff Riley was quoted as saying that he and all his men were working to find new leads.

Amy paged ahead for another three weeks without seeing anything new. The story disappeared from the headlines and the front pages. It was moved to the inside pages where the articles became smaller and less detailed. On the society pages, the Thurmonds, Mercers, Bensons, and other prominent families, smiled their way through teas, dances, and charity events. Their world was untouched by the tragedies.

The Anderson deaths slowly faded into the anonymity of old news. The headlines on July 19, 1976, one year after the murders, told of Sheriff Maurice Riley being killed in a one-vehicle accident. He was returning from Cartersville late one night, lost control of his truck, and had slammed into a tree. He died instantly. Deputy Frank Morgan would take over as acting sheriff until the regular election was held.

Her back was aching and her eyes burning, as she put the rolls of film back into the canisters and returned them to the shelves. She still was no wiser as far as anything involving Walter Thurmond and his friends that would anger a person to murder. Amy felt that their families' powerful influence had squelched everything unpleasant, including whatever it was that had set the killer off.

When she left the library, Amy glanced at her watch. She had just enough time to run by the hospital to see if Nancy's condition had improved any further. She drove out of the parking lot and headed for the hospital. She didn't notice the truck which was parked on the opposite side of the street in the shadows of a large magnolia tree. Its driver waited until Amy reached the corner, then pulled away from the curb to follow her.

CHAPTER 31

▼

Nancy was again sleeping peacefully when Amy entered the hospital room for the second time that day. Martha Evans sat in a chair pulled close to one side of Nancy's bed, while Anita reclined in the lounge chair on the other side. Anita got up and motioned for Amy to follow her out of the room. They walked a short distance down the hallway before stopping to talk.

"I hope you don't mind my bringing you out here," Anita said, as she shrugged her shoulders. "I don't know how much Nancy is sleeping, and how much she's pretending to be asleep."

"Of course I don't mind," Amy said. "How has she done this afternoon?"

"The fever broke completely not long after you'd left." Anita's face was drawn with worry, which seemed odd since Nancy was doing better. Then she said, "Nancy woke up and seemed really happy to see Aunt Martha, but then she became upset again. She's suddenly crying again and telling us she doesn't know what she'll do. When we asked her what she was talking about, she became even more upset, repeating that there's nothing anybody can do. We decided that the nightmares she's having are so realistic, that she doesn't realize they're just dreams."

"You're probably right," Amy said, though she didn't believe that for a minute. "I'm sure Nancy will realize that as soon as she's over this terrible infection."

"It hurts to see her so frightened." Tears came to Anita's eyes.

Behind them, they heard someone say, "Amy! There you are." Amy turned to see Gayle walking toward them.

"I've been looking for you for most of the afternoon," Gayle said, when she reached them. "I finally got Barney at your house, and he said I might find you here."

"But Mary was at the shop. She could have told you where I was."

"I drove by there and saw that both your car and Barney's truck were gone, so I didn't stop." Gayle was looking a little embarrassed. "I'm sorry, I didn't mean to be so rude. Please forgive me for interrupting you like this." She smiled at Anita.

"Don't worry about that, I'm glad you found me." Amy turned to Anita. "This is Gayle Armbruster, a friend of mine. Gayle, this is Anita Waggoner, the mother of Nancy Waggoner."

Gayle reached out to shake Anita's hand. "You must think I'm terribly crude, coming in here like this. I want to say how very sorry I am about you husband, and about Nancy being so ill. How is your daughter doing?"

"Thank you for your concern," Anita said. "Nancy is some better, but still pretty sick."

"I'm sure she's in good hands here. Again, excuse me for barging in as I did. Amy, I'll call you later this evening, okay?"

"I'm leaving in just a moment if you'd like to wait."

"I'll wait down in the lobby. Nice meeting you, Mrs. Waggoner. I'll be checking on Nancy." Gayle lifted her hand, as she turned and walked swiftly back toward the elevators.

"She's a beautiful woman, isn't she?" Anita said, as she watched Gayle's slim figure disappear into one of the elevators.

"Yes," Amy agreed. "For some reason I always feel dowdy in her presence." She laughed. "Or at least a little wide in the hips."

"You have absolutely nothing to complain about, Amy." Then Anita said a bit wistfully, "We need friends, don't we? I just never seemed to have the time for making friends. That doesn't speak well for me, I know."

"Well, it's never too late," Amy assured her. "I'd feel honored if you'd consider me your friend."

Anita began to cry again, shoving tissues against her mouth to choke back the sound. "Sorry. I just can't seem to stop crying."

"You have a lot to cry about, Anita," Amy said. "I think crying helps us deal with sudden changes, don't you?"

"But, I keep asking myself, who would want to kill Abner?" Anita shook her head. "I don't know what to do now. This whole thing is so unbelievable. The sheriff even said there might have been a woman with Abner earlier that evening.

I wonder if *she* killed him?" Amy didn't know what to say, so she remained silent. Anita continued, "And I have to tell Nancy that her father is dead. How do I tell her that he was murdered?"

"If you don't mind my saying so, I don't think I'd tell her just yet that he was killed by some person. Of course, she'll want to know how he died. Maybe you could say he was found dead in bed and that they haven't completed the autopsy yet. That would be the truth without the brutal details that will have to come later. I wouldn't wait *too* long though, because someone is bound to say something about her father's death."

Anita straightened up, then blew her nose vigorously on the already damp wad of tissues. "I think you're absolutely right, Amy. Thanks for the idea. I may as well face the storm, because turning my back on it won't make it go away." She gave Amy a shaky smile. "I think I hear Nancy's voice. She must be awake."

She put her hand against the hospital room door and paused. "I appreciate everything you've done, Amy. You really are a friend. I'll talk to you later."

As Anita pushed the door open, Martha Evans was saying something in a quiet voice. Again, Amy thought it was good that Anita had her aunt. If anyone could help her through the rough times ahead, Martha could.

Gayle was waiting for Amy in the lobby across from the elevators. "I'm sorry that I interrupted you the way I did," she said, as she walked with Amy to the front door. "It's just that I wanted you to have dinner at my house tomorrow evening, and didn't want to wait until the last moment to invite you."

"Don't worry about it. I was ready to leave, anyway. I only ran by to see if Nancy's condition had improved since I was here earlier. It has, thank goodness."

Amy pushed open the heavy glass door, and they walked out into the cooler air of the late afternoon. The sun had gotten below the ridge of mountains to the west, and the wind was blowing in vigorous gusts that caused newly fallen leaves from the oak trees to scurry around their feet. A tinge of fall was in the air, forecasting the coming change of seasons. The two women walked down the broad sidewalk which divided the parking lot into two large areas.

Amy stopped to fish in her bag for her keys. "And I do appreciate your invitation Gayle, and I'd be happy to accept. Where are you parked?"

Gayle pointed to the farthest section to their left. "This must be the peak visiting hours. I could only find that spot over near the street."

"My car is right here. Let me drive you over to yours."

After they'd gotten into the car, Gayle said, "So what happened to Nancy? She must be really sick to have been put in the hospital."

"I think she's going to be okay now." Amy started the motor. "It's one of those dreadful infections that go from a benign situation to a very serious one in a brief span of time. You know how young people are. They seldom pay attention to their bodies' warning signals."

"What caused the infection, do you know?"

Amy shook her head, as she backed the car out of the parking space. "All I know is, when I went to see her night before last, she had some kind of injury to her knee. There was a bandage on it, but I could see it was red and swollen. When I asked Nancy how she got hurt, she yanked up the covers and gave me some story about falling and cutting it. Then she changed the subject as if she didn't want me to say any more about it. Her mother told me that Nancy said she hurt her knee at my shop. I know that she didn't."

"So Nancy was trying to hide the injury?"

"Or just resenting my asking about it. I was more concerned at the time about her emotional state. I realize now how attached she must have been to Bud Pure-foy, as hard as that is for me to understand. She's been terribly upset since his death."

"Young girls' emotions can certainly blow up all out of proportion to the occa-sion," Gayle said. "But I wouldn't have figured a girl like her getting that ripped up over someone like him. He didn't seem to be her type, if you know what I mean."

Amy glanced over at Gayle, realizing for the first time that the woman seemed to know about Nancy and Bud. Gayle was much more acquainted with their lit-tle community and its cast of characters than Amy would have expected. Amy chided herself, thinking that Gayle had only lived in the town for a few months and could be a whole lot friendlier with the local people than she would have at the same point in a new place.

Aloud, she said. "My thoughts exactly. Anyway, Anita was concerned enough about Nancy's state of mind to call Dr. Thompson. He went to the house and gave Nancy a tranquillizer before I got there. She remained nearly hysterical and poor Anita was worn out with trying to calm the girl down."

Gayle shook her head and laughed. "I'm glad I'll never have children. They are wonderful as babies, but teenagers are too tough for me to handle. You never know what they'll do or how they'll act. Their good sense seems to fluctuate with their hormones."

Amy pulled up behind Gayle's car. "I was in the library earlier looking for some material for an article I'm planning to write. I looked at newspapers almost twenty years old and guess what they were full of then?"

Gayle smiled. "I can't imagine."

"The Anderson murders. You know, I asked if you minded living in a house that had such a violent and sad history? It really was awful. The daughter apparently was affected mentally by the trauma of finding her parents dead and, of course, the son was never found."

Gayle clicked her tongue. "Finding your parents all bloody and chopped to pieces is enough to send anyone over the edge, let alone a young girl. When you asked me how I felt about living there, I did a little research of my own. It would make an excellent plot for a novel. I just might see what I can do with that."

"That would work," Amy agreed.

As Gayle opened her door preparing to get out, Amy asked, "What time do you want me to arrive tomorrow evening, and what may I bring?"

"Bring only yourself at eight o' clock. I hope you like Chinese food. I found a new recipe for stir-fried pork I want to try."

"I love Chinese." Amy assured her.

She waited until Gayle was in her car before she drove away. When Amy checked her rear view mirror, she saw another vehicle's back-up lights come on just two car spaces from where Gayle's car was backing out. The fleeting thought of not having seen another person approaching their car vanished as her mind was filled with thoughts of the gruesome material she'd read at the library.

Amy wondered what had happened to the young Anderson boy. And she thought it would be interesting to talk to the housekeeper, providing Mrs. Sanchez was still alive. Amy pressed on the accelerator and drove swiftly down the street. She was anxious to get to the shop where Leigh was due any minute.

The truck which had been parked outside the library earlier that afternoon, again followed Amy at a discreet distance.

CHAPTER 32

▼

Leigh's burgundy Lexus was parked near the shop's front door, so Amy pulled into the space behind it, and hurried inside. Her aunt was taking pieces of old jewelry out of an antique glass case to show an interested customer. Amy waved to Leigh, as she walked over to the cash register where another customer waited to pay for a floral wreath.

"I'm sorry to keep you waiting," she told the woman, as she made change. Amy slipped the large wreath into a plastic bag and apologized again for the delay. The woman left, apparently happy with her purchase.

Amy walked back to look first into the flower arrangement room and then into the workshop area. Mary was nowhere to be seen.

Her aunt had finished wrapping a large brooch in tissue paper for her customer and was making change when Amy got back to the cash register.

After saying goodbye to her customer, Leigh turned to give her niece a brief hug and a hard look. "You look a little pale," she said.

"I'm fine. Just didn't sleep well last night, is all. Where is Mary?"

"I got here much earlier than I had expected. Not long after you left, in fact. Poor Mary was bored out of her mind, not having had a handful of customers all afternoon. She said that she'd like to get home to a painting she was working on, so I told her to go ahead, I could take care of things until you got back. I hope you don't mind."

"Not at all," Amy said. "I'm sorry I wasn't here, but I thought it was a good time to do a couple of things. Let me lock up and then we can talk in my office."

She turned over the sign in the window so that it read "Closed," and then locked the front door. Amy went to the refrigerator in the work room and took out two Diet Dr. Peppers. Leigh had settled into a comfortable overstuffed chair across from Amy's desk. After handing Leigh her drink, Amy went around the desk to her swivel chair.

"How was your trip?" she asked. "Was Mr. Phillips pleased with the new manuscript?" Martin Phillips was the editor of the Martin-Anchor Publishing Company which had published Leigh's last four books and, according to Leigh, one of the best editors in the business.

"Yes, he was. Martin said he already had a movie contract in the works for it, but right now he's more interested in my making a tour for my book, *Murder Made Easy,*" Leigh said, naming her latest book to hit the best seller's list.

"That sounds exciting. When will you leave?"

"Martin said he'd already arranged for book signing appointments in England and France for the end of this month, so he wants me in New York by Friday of this week. That's why I'm home now. I'm not happy with the idea of going that far away when things are so deadly here at home." Leigh took a last sip from her drink, and placed the can on the floor next to her chair.

"Okay," she said, "let's talk about why you look a mere shadow of yourself. I can tell something's going on with you that isn't positive."

"Have you talked to anyone since you got home from the airport?" Amy asked.

"No one but Mary, and she had even less to say than usual. Matter of fact, I thought she seemed somewhat preoccupied."

"Okay, so that means she didn't catch you up on the latest mayhem in our small community."

"That sounds ominous."

"First, let me tell you about something that happened to me after you called last night." Amy told Leigh about the prowler and the way Hannibal had turned into a snarling beast, racing up and down the stairs, and how the dog had gone outside and found the watch. "So you can see that Hannibal was the hero in the scene," Amy finished.

Leigh shook her head. "This whole business is a nightmare."

"More than you know," Amy agreed. "Thanks to the men in my life, I am safe enough, but on to something much worse. Abner Waggoner was murdered."

Leigh's eyes stretched wide with shock. She slumped in her chair as if the weight of all the bad news was too much for her to support. "When did that happen?" she asked.

"Last night, also," Amy said. She went on to relate the meager details she knew. "And then, Abner's daughter, Nancy, was put into the hospital. She had an injury that involved a nasty infection, so poor Anita Waggoner is coping with a very sick daughter, while trying to deal with the murder of her husband. And the sad thing is, she may have even more unpleasant things to deal with."

"I'm afraid to ask why you said that."

"I believe that Nancy was with Bud Purefoy in the old country club building the night he was killed. When I went to see her, Anita told me Nancy was in hysterics over Bud's death. I know Nancy liked him, but not enough to become unbalanced by his death."

"What are you thinking?" Leigh raised her eyebrows.

"I went to see Nancy before she was put in the hospital, and that girl was scared out of her wits about something. She kept saying things like, 'I don't know what to do', and, 'No one can help me.' Those are not words of grief." Amy sighed, as if wearied of her thoughts. "I strongly suspect that Nancy knows more than she should about Bud's death."

"Have you told Frank Morgan about this?"

"I went to his office yesterday with that intention, but he was so angry with me for asking questions about Thurmond and Mercer, that he wouldn't listen to anything I had to say. Then by the time I saw him at the hospital today, I had decided it was best to not say anything yet. After all, it is only a suspicion, and Nancy and Anita have enough problems without Sheriff Morgan harassing the two of them."

"Perhaps when Nancy's better, and if she is involved in some way, she will tell him herself," Leigh said. "So what have Frank and his group learned about the killings so far? Are they giving the public any kind of reassurance that they know what they're doing?"

Amy shook her head. "As far as I know they haven't a clue as to whom the killer is. But this morning the town was virtually flooded with law men. I don't know where they're from, or what agencies they represent, and I don't care." Amy gave a brief laugh. "I wouldn't mind seeing the National Guard move in. I know that they're doing all they can, but things have happened so fast that Sheriff Morgan and Detective Edwards hardly have time to deal with one thing before something else goes wrong. Besides, I think perhaps they're not looking in the right direction."

"And what direction would that be?" Leigh said.

"From something I overheard him tell Detective Edwards, Sheriff Morgan is looking into things like business deals and who may be mad at whom. Situations that could have caused very bitter feelings in recent times. I can't tell you why, but I feel strongly that the sheriff should be looking for something that may have happened many years ago.

"For instance, you said in our last talk on the subject that the way in which the bodies were mutilated could indicate that the killer suffered serious abuse when he was very young. What if some of these men were guilty of that kind of behavior and the killer is just now getting his revenge? And maybe he's been in prison, or even—"

"Whoa, just a minute." Leigh sat forward, her brows drawn together in alarm. "I know you're upset by all that's happened and I can't blame you, but this is just a lot of wild speculation on your part. I refuse to think of the trouble you'd make for them, and for yourself, if you even suggested such a thing. You've got to promise me, Amy, that you'll stay out of the way and let the experts do what needs to be done."

Amy understood her aunt's feelings, but Leigh had yet to know the whole story. "I can see how you'd feel that way," she said, "but, for my own mental well being, Leigh, I've got to do something. I've come to believe I'm much more connected to the killings than just having found one of the bodies. That's the real reason I need to talk to you."

She got up from her chair and paced back and forth between the desk and file cabinets. "What I'm going to tell you next, I haven't told anyone else, and you will think I'm crazy before I finish, but believe me when I say this really happens." Amy swung around to face her aunt, who was still sitting on the edge of her chair. "I've been having some kinds of dreams, or maybe they're visions. Whatever you call them, they are very real."

"Good Lord, what are you telling me now?"

"I'm telling you that I've been having some kind of visual foreknowledge of things that I don't want to know about." Amy's eyes grew large and filled with tears. "It happened again last night. I have no idea why I am doing this, and I'm afraid that it will happen again."

Leigh was horrified by the very real fear she saw in Amy's face. She stood up and walked around the desk. Putting her arms around her niece, she said, "I don't know what you're talking about, but we'll work it out together. You'll have to tell me about these things you've seen, of course."

Before Amy could reply, they both were startled by a metallic clank that came from the rear of the building.

"What was that?" There was an edge to Leigh's voice.

"It sounded like the workshop door. Maybe Hannibal and Barney have come back."

When neither Hannibal nor Barney made their presence known, and only silence issued from the rest of the building, Amy rose and walked to the office door. "Barn, is that you?" she called.

The silence continued.

Until that moment, Amy hadn't noticed how dim the light from the windows had gotten. The sun had dropped below a bank of clouds in the west, cutting off the direct rays of light and making the day seem older than it was. Her office and the areas beyond it, were filling with deep shadows. As she flipped on the lights, Amy thought she heard a vehicle motor starting up in the direction of the alley. She hurried to the back of the building, fishing her key ring out of her jeans pocket. Unlocking the door that opened onto the alley, Amy looked in both directions. If there had been anyone there, they were long gone now.

"The door was locked," she said, as much to reassure herself as Leigh, who was right behind her. "No one other than a regular member of our staff could get in. It may have been someone searching through the trash bins just outside the door. That happens more often than you'd think."

"I guess I was spooked from listening to the terrible things you were telling me." Leigh managed a laugh. "But I have a suggestion."

"I do too," Amy said.

Simultaneously, they said, "Let's get out of here."

Leigh said they should adjourn to a public place that still would afford them some privacy. "We can get a quiet table at McCarney's Marina, have something to drink, and talk. What do you think?"

Amy knew it was still a couple of hours before the dinner crowd arrived at the marina restaurant and agreed that it was a good place. "We'll take both our cars to keep from driving back here later," she said.

The truck, which had followed Amy from the library, now sped out of the alley just seconds before Amy had opened the workshop door. It waited at the corner of the block. When Leigh and Amy drove away from the shop, it followed a few car lengths behind.

McCarney's was located at the edge of the lake, just past the Perry Dam Park. The lake was visible through the wide glass windows that made up almost the entire wall facing the water.

While they waited for the hostess to attend them, Amy watched boats of different types moving about the lake's shiny surface, some skimming across it at high speeds, their powerful motors throwing up tall 'rooster tails' of foaming white water, while others proceeded at a more leisurely pace across the broad expanse of Perry Lake. It was pleasant to watch, and Amy found herself wishing she had no more to think about than steering a boat.

"Good afternoon, ladies." A woman with a pleasant smile greeted them. At Leigh's request, the hostess led the two women to a corner table which afforded them the privacy they wanted. When their waitress arrived, Amy ordered a glass of white wine and Leigh a pilsner.

"And bring us a plate of your delicious fried ravioli," Leigh added.

Until their food and drinks were served, they sat in silence. Amy could see that Leigh was thinking of the things she had told her, and probably nursing a dread of what she was yet to hear. But Amy was feeling relief that she could finally share this terrible burden with someone she trusted.

"Please eat at least one of the ravioli before you begin," instructed Leigh, common sense ruling. "You're still looking pale, and I know you haven't been eating properly."

Amy was surprised at how good the food tasted. She actually finished a third meat pastry before wiping her fingers on her napkin and asking, "Leigh, do you believe that someone can see in their mind an event before it happens?"

"I believe the mind has powers of which most of us remain unaware," Leigh said. "For example, you and I pick up on each other's thoughts too often for it to be dismissed as mere coincidence. On a few occasions, I've known what another person is going to say before it's said. This is not an uncommon occurrence for a lot of people. But you're talking about something quite different than that, right?"

"I'm talking about seeing, hearing, and smelling events in the future."

Leigh frowned as she pushed back her plate. "When did this happen?"

"Once in broad daylight at the sheriff's office, and again last night in my bedroom." Amy hesitated, then said, "Actually, I had a very brief episode, that I didn't recognize at the time, when I found Mr. Thurmond's body. It was extremely brief and nothing like the last two."

"Start with that," Leigh said.

"Remember I told you that when I got down to the gazebo, there was this dried, black blood everywhere? Well, just for a split second, the blood wasn't black, it was a bright red, as though it were fresh. For those few seconds, the air felt icy cold." Amy shuddered at the memory. "Then, in a snap, the blood was dark again, and the sun was as hot as ever. I thought afterwards it was only my reaction to seeing that horrid body, but now I don't think so."

"Now tell me about the other two times," Leigh said.

"I went to see Sheriff Morgan, thinking he might tell me something about Mercer and Thurmond's younger years," Amy said. "As a law officer, he'd know if anything out of the ordinary had taken place back then. But he became very angry and told me to mind my own business. That's when it started." Amy looked down at her hands in her lap, her shoulders drooping in despair. "Of course, I had no idea what was happening to me. I didn't really pass out. It was more as if a dark cloud made of ice cold air had covered me. I knew I was with the sheriff, but at the same time, I was someplace else.

"Anyway, I heard a gunshot very close to my right ear, and at the same time, I was choking on heavy smoke. Then I heard myself tell the sheriff that the killer was going to strike again and that he needed to do something quickly. Then the cloud went away, but I still felt as cold as if I'd walked into a freezer. I literally ran from his office and out into the sunshine. All I could think of was getting warm again."

"That ended the episode?"

"Yes, except that it took me several minutes to feel normal again. That same night Bud Purefoy was shot in the head and left to burn to a crisp in the old country club building." Tears of stress filled Amy's eyes. "I don't understand what's happening to me."

Leigh's face was drawn with worry, but her voice was calm as she said, "Tell me about the other episode, Amy, then we'll talk."

Several couples had been seated in the dining room and their subdued conversations added to the semblance of privacy. No one seemed to notice Amy's distress. Outside the large windows, the day had darkened. The sun was setting below the rim of trees that covered the hills in the near distance. The underbellies of the clouds were now tinged with orange, making them seem even darker and more ominous.

When Amy didn't say anything for several seconds, Leigh asked, "Do you want to continue this here, or had you rather finish at your home?"

"No, let me tell the rest of this while I'm into it," Amy said.

She took a deep breath and told Leigh about her vision, or whatever it was, the night before. "The feeling of extreme cold woke me up. I sat up in bed and was shocked to find myself in a strange room with different furniture, different curtains, and a different bed. Hannibal wasn't on the rug next to my bed, in fact the rug wasn't there either. The floor was covered with carpet, and you know, I have no carpet in my house. That room was so cold my teeth were chattering, and I had goose bumps all over.

"Then I heard glass breaking, and a moment later, a man came through what I think was a bathroom door, and walked towards me. I scrambled off the bed onto the floor on the other side, but he acted as if he didn't see me—as if I wasn't there. He came straight to the side of the bed which I had just vacated. He used a very small flashlight to find his way, then he leaned over my pillow and began doing something with his hands.

"In a flash, I was back in my own bedroom and Hannibal was licking my arm and whining as if he knew something had happened to me. My room was warm and everything was normal, except that the chill stayed with me for several minutes. Isn't that strange? Each time it happens, I nearly freeze to death..." Amy's voice trailed off as she stared out the windows where only a trace of daylight was left.

"I think we should go to either your house or mine," Leigh said briskly, as she put her napkin next to her plate. She motioned to their waitress for the check. "Do you want to go up to Eagle's Nest?"

"I'm certain that Hannibal would be hurt if you didn't go see him. Besides which, you'll probably want to take him home with you." Amy's smile was weak. "Furthermore, I need you to help me explain all this to Barney."

Leigh's eyebrows rose. "I know you said that I'm the first you've talked to, but somehow I thought he'd know something about it."

"You know Barney. He doesn't like to talk about things he can't see, or put his hands on. He's about as pragmatic as you can get. He would be a hopeless case, trying to cope with my visionary imaginings."

"You've got him pegged, haven't you? Then your house it is."

Over Amy's protests, Leigh paid for their food. When they'd gotten into their separate vehicles, Amy led the way onto the highway.

The truck remained where it was for a minute, then its driver pulled out behind the two women once again. This time the driver followed only long enough to be certain as to where the two women were headed, then made an U-turn and drove back toward town.

CHAPTER 33

▼

"I told you! Bordeaux is going to be the death of us."

"Please, I can't listen to you while you're pacing back and forth like that. Sit down and tell me why you're so upset."

"I took the opportunity to listen in on Bordeaux's conversation with her aunt not an hour ago. Bordeaux suspects that Nancy Waggoner was with Bud the night at the country club, so Nancy apparently knows more than she's told so far. She may have seen the two of us leaving after I set the building on fire. Even if Nancy says nothing, you can bet that Bordeaux will feel it her duty to tell the sheriff what she suspects. Then he'll force the girl to talk."

"Maybe there's some way we could scare them so they won't say anything."

"I can do more than just scare them. Nancy is no problem, but Bordeaux is going to be harder to get to. She's either got Barney with her or that damn dog."

"Wait a minute. Are you saying that you plan to kill them?"

"What else do you think I mean? It's a matter of their necks or ours, and I don't choose to be put to sleep forever."

"But isn't there another way? Neither of them has done anything wrong."

"That Waggoner girl did wrong for having anything to do with that stupid Pure-foy kid. And Amy's more wrong that you know. Not only is she nosy as hell, but she's figured out more than any ordinary person should. There's something about her I haven't figured out yet, so Amy's got to go and you're going to help get rid of her."

"Oh god, don't get me into something like that. You know I couldn't actually kill anyone. I'd be sure to mess up some way."

"Stop your whining. You make me sick. Must I keep reminding you that it was your own romantic notions that made you follow me. You're going to do your part for a change, so cut out you damn complaining and listen."

For the next several minutes, a plan was made that would allow them to get to Nancy, and use her to lure Amy into their web. No more objections were made by the weaker partner. Death lurked too closely.

CHAPTER 34

▼

Barney and Hannibal were in the yard when Leigh and Amy drove in. Barney looked around, but kept weeding the bed of flowers he was working in. But the dog recognized Leigh's car immediately and went daft with joy. He showed his good training by not jumping up on her when she got out of the car. The greeting between mistress and dog took precedence over greetings between humans until Hannibal was certain that Leigh knew just how much he had missed her.

"I admit that makes me feel a little jealous," Amy said, when the frenzy was over. "He's put on a pretty good show of enjoying my company since you left."

"His heart is big enough for the two of us," Leigh said. She clicked her tongue and pointed to her heels. Hannibal obediently fell behind and followed them toward the house. Only his wildly waving tail told of his continuing excitement.

"May I greet you now?" Barney said. He put one arm around Leigh's shoulder and gave her a squeeze. "Pretty tame next to old Hannibal, but just as sincere."

Once inside, Barney and Leigh settled down on the couch in the den with Hannibal at their feet. While Amy put a large frozen pizza in the oven, and rinsed the lettuce for a salad, the two of them caught up on each other's activities. As she entered the den and seated herself across from them, Amy thought how natural they looked together. Barney had just finished telling Leigh the few details he knew about Abner's death.

"I think Amy has some things she needs to tell you, Barney," Leigh said, after a few minutes of small talk. "Please do her the favor of listening before you react. We both know you worry about her, but right now she needs our best advice."

Barney eyes widened with. "Are you in trouble?" He sat up from his relaxed position.

"No, I'm not in trouble, Barn." Amy wished Leigh had let her lead him into the subject a little less abruptly. But her aunt's no-nonsense attitude was probably the best. No telling when she would have gotten the courage to begin. Amy plunged in and repeated what she had told Leigh about her visions.

As with Leigh, Barney couldn't immediately think what to say. If Amy was having dreams, or visions, or whatever they were about the murders, he didn't want to think where that might lead. He proceeded to say so in such sharp tones that Hannibal raised up to look at him.

"Barn," Leigh said in a soothing voice, "Amy's not having these premonitions on purpose. It is a gift, though not one you'd ask for. I have a theory as to why she's having them, and you're not going to like that either."

Amy left for the kitchen to check on the pizza. She reappeared a few minutes later to announce that the food was ready. "I think we should eat now before we get into the details. I can't believe it, but I'm actually hungry."

At the kitchen table, Leigh deliberately turned the subject of conversation to herself. She told Barney about her upcoming European tour. Barney looked a bit glum at the news that Leigh would be out of the country for so long. He wouldn't say it, but with all the bad things going on here at home, he felt Amy would be safer if Leigh was around to help him keep an eye on her.

As if reading his thoughts, Leigh said, "You know, I think I should put this tour on hold for a while. I really don't want to be gone right now, and it's not as if this is the first book I've had to hit the best-seller list. I don't need the publicity as badly as I did in earlier days."

"Oh no, you don't." Amy dropped her fork with a clatter. "We won't go there, Leigh. I will not be treated like a child who has to be watched every minute."

"See, Barney, she thinks all I have to do with my life is to look after her." Leigh shook her head, then turned to Amy. "What if I just want to stay home because I just want to stay at home?" Leigh raised her eyebrows. "You're going to tell me I can't?"

"You're not fooling me one bit." Amy pushed her chair back and stood up. She began retrieving their empty plates and putting them into the sink. "Besides, you know how publishers are. If you don't give them one hundred per cent, they won't care how many books have hit the best seller lists. They'll stop giving you special attention and work with some neophyte who is just dying to take your place in the lime light."

"She sounds as if she's been talking to my agent," Leigh said, as she began helping Amy to clear the table. "Why did we raise her to be so self-sufficient and strong-willed, Barn?"

After Leigh had made a pot of coffee and left it to perk, they resettled themselves in the den. Amy sat next to Leigh this time, and Barney sat in the recliner. Hannibal happily placed himself between the two women and neither of them scolded him for getting onto the leather couch.

"And now let me tell you why I think you're having these visual premonitions, or precognitive events," Leigh began. "I have to tell you, or at least remind you, of some very unpleasant things in the past, Amy. I believe your distant past is affecting you now. Some of them will be familiar to you, others will not. Barney, most of what I'm going to say will be new to you. Amy, I'll begin by asking you a question. How far back in your childhood do you have a clear memory of things that happened to you?"

"I remember playing in the yard of the house on Myrtle Street here in Ashley Springs. I was about four years old then, wasn't I?" Leigh nodded. "I remember your telling me we had moved from Chicago when I was a baby. You told me stories about how deep the snow got there in the winter and how cold it was." Amy felt goose bumps run up her arms. "I don't think I actually remember anything about Chicago, but then I couldn't if I was only a baby."

"Then what really stands out for you among your earliest memories?" Leigh said.

"Mostly just what you've told me through the years. But I do remember that when I was still very young, sometimes at night, just as I drifted off to sleep, I would have an odd feeling come over me. It was like this sweet presence was drifting just beyond my touch and sight, and I could feel the love radiating towards me. I wanted very much to see this person, whom I later decided was my guardian angel. As I grew older, it happened less and less. I don't remember exactly when it stopped, but I always wished she would come back to me. I'm sorry. That sounds maudlin."

"I'd hardly call it maudlin to remember your mother with love, Amy. And I believe that's who it was."

"The memory of that is still so strong," Amy admitted.

Leigh hesitated. She was having some reservations about pushing her niece recall the past.

Again, Amy sensed what she was thinking. "Don't try to put me off, Leigh. I need to know what is happening to me before I have another premonition. It may help me to know what I should do when it happens."

"But you also understand that I could be wrong."

"You're not," Amy said, confidently.

Barney had gone to the kitchen and returned now with a tray holding cups of fragrant Columbian coffee, creamer, and a bowl of sugar. When they had fixed their coffees to their individual tastes, Amy looked expectantly at Leigh.

Leigh nodded and put her cup on the side table. "First let me say this. Your mother had psychic abilities far beyond the regular ESP that most people have. She tried hard to conceal it from our parents, but she told me many times about that things were going to happen. They nearly always did. You have inherited her psychic sensitivity, Amy. I believe your finding Walter's body triggered the depth of the fore-visions that you began experiencing. That's because, as a small child, you witnessed Laura's murder. She had been stabbed repeatedly with a large knife, and you saw the pools of blood those fatal injuries made. The police found you in your crib, screaming for you mommy. They said Laura had been terribly mutilated and that you had watched it all.

"Later the police learned that the killer had moved from city to city and applied for jobs as a delivery person for home fuel companies. The job gave him the opportunity to choose his victims and arrange entry into their houses. Actually, his wife turned him in. She had kept the murder weapon when he had given it to her to clean up. She hid it and when he beat her within an inch of her life. After she had recuperated, she took it to the police. They discovered that the common denominator in all of the cases was that the victims had their fuel oil tanks refilled not more than two days before they were killed."

Amy had not heard the story told this way before. Leigh had always avoided the details of Laura's death, and Amy had never pushed for anything more. But her aunt obviously believed they were connected to Amy's present dilemma, and could be a possible explanation for the visions she'd been having.

"You had nightmares from the first night you went home with me," Leigh continued. "You would wake up screaming for your mommy, shaking all over as if you were freezing. It would take a very long time to get you calm and sleepy again. For the first few nights, I put you in your crib to sleep, but when you continued to have the bad dreams; I let you sleep in my bed. It didn't stop you from waking up scared, but you calmed down much more quickly, knowing that I was where you could touch me. The nightmares occurred less and less often as you got older, but you still had them until you were eight years old. Then they stopped all together."

"You know," Amy said, looking surprised. "I *do* remember when they stopped, and I remember why. When that man was executed, you went as the family witnesses to his death. I remember you saying that you had requested to be there. When you came home, you handed me the newspaper that announced that his death had occurred at eleven p.m. two nights before. You said, and I quote, 'Amy, that son-of-a-bitch is in hell now. He'll never hurt another living soul,' end of quote. I knew you were telling the truth, and so, no more nightmares."

"One other thing," Leigh said, "and then I'm finished. You say you experience a freezing cold each time you have an episode. The night of your mother's death, she fought furiously. She managed to throw a dresser bench out of the window, breaking the glass. There was a blizzard that night. The police woman who took you to the station said your whole body was blue and that you felt like a block of ice. I think you're psychically re-experiencing the cold you felt that night."

Amy felt a shifting of the air around her, and as Leigh's voice faded, and her surroundings dimmed, she saw two people fighting. The woman's arms and hands were bloody as she picked up a piece of furniture and threw it at the window, at the same time screaming for help. Instantly, cold air poured in and the window curtains flapped wildly in the wind that blew with force into the room. The man and woman continued to fight for a brief moment before the woman fell to the floor a second time. She turned her head toward Amy, her face full of pain and sorrow. Amy watched the man's arm rising and falling long. She looked back at her mother and saw that she was smiling.

Like a saving echo from her real life that reached out to her in that far away place and time, she heard Barney's voice saying, "You're all right now, Amy. The past can't hurt you."

Much later, after Leigh left, Barney sat at Amy's kitchen table. She knew that he was reluctant to end the evening. Leigh had carried Hannibal home with her at Barney and Amy's insistence. Neither of them felt comfortable with her going alone to an empty house, even though the evening was still young. Now Barney hated to leave her without Hannibal on watch.

The three of them had decided that should Amy have another of what Leigh had labeled, visual premonitions, she was to call Barney and Leigh and the three of them would go to the sheriff.

"I don't think I told you," Barney said now. "The watch belonged to Bud Purefoy."

"No!" Amy was shocked. "How did the person who was sneaking around my house get Bud's watch?"

Barney shook his head, a frown made deep creases between his eyebrows. "It could have been taken when Bud was murdered."

"Great! You're saying that Bud's killer was prowling around here?" Amy did not like the direction his guess work was taking.

"If that's true, and I'm not saying it is, he has become very interested in you for some reason. Have you been discussing the murders with anyone other than Leigh?"

"I talked to Pinkie," Amy said defensively. "She's the one who told me about the men getting into trouble back when they were young. The same ones who are being killed."

"So now you've dug into the men's past, and coming up with information the murderer doesn't want exposed," Barney accused. "That would get him interested, all right."

"Barney, Pinkie would never tell anyone that she told me what she did. The only other person I questioned was Nadine."

"I don't want to believe this," Barney said, a little louder than necessary. "You know Nadine is a motor mouth. She couldn't keep a secret if she would be hung for the telling of it, and you know it."

Amy tried to calm him down. "I did not tell her a thing! And Mr. Benson came in before she could tell me anything. He seemed to be in a bad mood and reminded Nadine that she was supposed to be at Grace's house. I must say, I didn't know he could be so assertive."

"He probably gets sick of his wife's gossiping ways." Barney shook his head. "The point is not the time frame you're asking about, but that you're showing an interest in the dead men."

"Nadine probably won't tell anyone about my visit because Mr. Benson was so upset with her. Anyway, I did learn about the past from the old newspaper files at the library. Back then, the Anderson murders were a very large item. However, there was nothing about the men having gotten into trouble, so it may be I'm on the wrong track. Maybe there's no connection to the murders and the mens' pasts."

"There may be some connection to your own murder, if you're not careful," Barney said. Amy could see that he was deeply worried, and felt a twinge of guilt. "Oh, hell, Amy," he said. "You're having premonitions of the murders, and you feel that it's your responsibility to do what the sheriff and all the other law enforcement officers haven't been able to do. You know that's a ridiculous way for you to look at this."

Fortunately for Amy, the phone rang. She answered on the kitchen extension. "Hi, Pinkie. Is everything all right?"

Realizing he'd said all, if not more than he needed to say for the evening, Barney got up and waved his hand to indicate he was leaving.

"See you in the morning, Barn," Amy called after him, blowing a kiss in his direction to show she wasn't angry with him.

She learned from Pinkie that Tim was doing worse. After talking several minutes, she bid her old friend good night. She made her lonely trek up the stairs to bed. She really missed Hannibal.

CHAPTER 35

▼

Amy struggled awake, fighting for breath. Something covered her face and crushed her nose, the weight of it so heavy that she couldn't even turn her head to seek air. She clawed at the thing on her face, but it didn't move. Flailing about, her hand came in contact with a bare arm, and pushing hard, she felt it give slightly. She dug her fingernails into the flesh, then scratched downward as hard as she could. She felt the tear of flesh just as the arm jerked away.

As suddenly as she had felt the pressure against her face, it was gone. Amy sat up gasping for air, pushing aside the pillow that now lay loose on her chest. She gathered her knees underneath her, prepared to fight her attacker, but could see no one. The faint glow of the night light near her bed showed the room to be empty and the bedroom door shut. Again, as it had been the night Abner Waggoner was killed, the air in the bedroom was so icy the air seemed gelid in consistency, making it difficult for her to breathe.

Amy shivered as she scrambled out of bed and grabbed her gun from her bedside table, then hurriedly checked the bolt on the door. It was in place, just as it had been when she went to bed. She cautiously opened the double doors to the closet, prepared to shoot if necessary. No one lurked behind the hanging clothes. She then searched the bathroom and its closets, and again found no one. Puzzled, but very relieved, Amy stood still for a moment, her heart pounding from tension. She vividly remembered the desperation of not being able to breathe, and of being unable to move her head to get air.

Shaking so hard her teeth were clenching together, Amy felt cold to the bone, just as she had during the other nightmarish episodes. She took her heaviest robe from the closet and slipped into its welcome warmth, then went back into the bathroom. She ran the shower until the steam coated the glass door, peeled off the robe and pajamas, and stepped under the water's warmth.

Gradually the shivering stopped and she began to feel warm again. After scrubbing herself dry with a large towel, she put on her pajamas and wrapped herself in the robe, then brushed her teeth. Warmer, but still upset, Amy again tested her bedroom door to be certain it was locked.

The digital clock readout showed that it was only one thirty in the morning. If her past experiences were really connected with Bud and Abner's deaths, then someone else had been hurt, or worse, tonight. Amy recalled her promise to call Barney and Leigh, but quickly decided she would wait until daylight. Neither of them would know where to go with this thing, and the sheriff, even if he believed them, would be angry that she could give no more information than that someone had been smothered with a bed pillow.

The room was back to its normal temperature once more and Amy felt warm enough to take off her robe. Climbing back into bed, she piled her pillows high behind her head, punching them with a ferocity that showed her frustration and her anger. What *really* made her furious was the fact that the visions, the experiences, were not helpful to anyone because they contained nothing that would identify who was in danger or where the person was located.

Knowing she dared not go back to sleep, Amy turned on the lamp nearest to her and got out the new novel she'd started a couple of nights before. Amy had turned a half dozen pages before she realized she hadn't absorbed a word on any of them. She had decided to go downstairs and make a cup of tea when the phone rang.

Feeling certain that the call would bring more bad news, she grabbed at the phone, dropped it, then got it to her ear to say, "This is Amy."

"Ms. Bordeaux, this is Sheriff Morgan. Don't be alarmed. No one is hurt. I'm calling at the request of Nancy Waggoner. She would like you to come to the hospital so she can talk to you. Would that be possible?"

"Yes, I can do that." Amy swung her legs off the side of the bed. It was now two o' clock. "Why does Nancy want to talk to me at this hour, Sheriff? What's wrong?"

"About thirty minutes ago there was an attempt on Miss Waggoner's life. She won't talk to us. She insists on talking to you."

"Someone tried to suffocate her, didn't they, Sheriff?" she blurted out.

"How did you know that?" The sheriff's raised his voice, causing Amy to take the receiver from her ear. "Just a lucky guess, right? Like the motel window?

What have we got here, our own gypsy who can tell the future?" His sarcasm could have etched metal.

Wishing she hadn't mentioned the suffocation, Amy said, "Yes, that's what it was, just a guess. Do you know who did it?" Amy hoped to divert his attention from her blunder.

Sheriff Morgan apparently decided not to pursue her supposed gift of fore-knowledge at the moment, but Amy was pretty sure he'd get back to it later. "We hope she will tell you something that will be helpful toward finding that out," he said. "After you talk with her, you will talk to me." The sheriff's voice was very firm. Then he added, "I don't want you driving in alone, so I'll send a car out for you. Can you be ready in about twenty minutes?"

"That won't be necessary, Sheriff. Barney will drive me in."

For a full minute after she put down the phone, Amy sat rocking herself back and forth. She had experienced what Nancy had gone through when someone tried to suffocate her. "My God, am I going crazy?" She felt confused and deeply afraid. It was as if the killer had been in *her* room with the intent of murdering her. He was so close to her, yet she hadn't the slightest clue who he was.

Amy pushed the buzzer next to her bed which connected her to the garage apartment. She lifted the phone just as Barney came on the line.

"What's wrong?" His voice was sharp with alarm.

"Nothing's wrong over here," she said quickly to reassure a nervous Barney. "The sheriff just called and said someone tried to kill Nancy Waggoner. For some reason she wants to talk to me, so Sheriff Morgan asked that I come to the hospital."

Barney hung up in her ear.

Amy quickly pulled on jeans and a tee shirt, then slipped her feet into a pair of sandals. Before she got downstairs, Barney was at the kitchen door. They hurried out to his truck. When they were on their way, he asked, "Did Sheriff Morgan say anything other than someone tried to kill Nancy?"

"He had very little to say, actually. He just said he'd talk to me when I got there. He offered to send a car for me, but I told him you would bring me in."

"The sheriff needn't worry about that," Barney said. "I want to hear for myself what they have to say about this mess."

Amy silently promised herself she would tell Barney about what she had experienced tonight, but only after they were with Leigh. Her aunt could help keep Barney under control when he found out she'd actually felt the pillow on her face. A shudder ran over Amy when she remembered how she struggled to get air, and felt the arms of the person who held her down.

In only a few minutes they pulled into the empty parking area at the hospital and quickly made their way to the building. No one was in the lobby when the two of them hurried inside. It had a deserted air that is common to public buildings at night, when the flux and flow of pedestrian traffic ceases, and people are asleep.

When they stepped off the elevator on the third floor, Archie Ledbetter and a uniformed policeman were facing them. Amy glanced down the hall and saw yet another policeman standing in front of the door that led into Nancy's room. She wondered how the attacker had gotten past the nurses station without being seen. But the hospital was a veritable warren of hall ways and empty rooms, so she supposed he could have hidden in almost any nook and cranny, then when he thought the time was right, he went to Nancy's room.

"Ms Bordeaux," Archie said, although he had called Amy by her first name since they were in high school together. "Sheriff Morgan and Chief Spratlin are in the waiting room. They said to bring you there as soon as you got here. Barney, you can wait here."

"No, I will not wait, Archie," Barney wore his fighting look, jaws clenched and eyes dark. "Where Amy goes, I go."

Archie stared at Barney for a second, debating the wisdom of pushing the issue, then shrugged his shoulders. "I guess Sheriff Morgan can handle you." While the policeman remained in front of the elevators, Archie led them down the hall.

Sheriff Morgan, Police Chief David Spratlin, and Detective Ben Edwards were talking to a nurse when they entered the waiting room. The nurse was managing to look both indignant and frightened at the same time.

"I'm telling you," she was saying, "we had no idea that anyone was on this floor except our people. But with as many doors, hallways, empty closets, and laundry rooms as there are in this place, a dozen people could hide and we might never see them."

"Yes, that's possible, Mrs. Arnold," the sheriff reassured her. "Please go on."

Looking a little less tense, she said, "One of the nurses answered the pay phone. It's unusual for it to ring so late at night, but the person said he was a close friend of Nancy's, and he had just heard about her father's death. He said he had something to tell Mrs. Waggoner about her husband's murder that she needed to hear. So my nurse went to tell Mrs. Waggoner. The aunt had left earlier in the evening, and Mrs. Waggoner was the only one in the room with her daughter. Nancy had improved to the point that I didn't think it was necessary to have a nurse stay in the room with her, so I told Mrs. Waggoner we'd watch out for Nancy while she was on the phone." The woman looked down at her spotless white shoes. "I guess we didn't."

"You couldn't have known what would happen." Amy was surprised at the softness of the sheriff's voice. "That's all for now, except I need to know where that pay phone is located."

"Go down this hall," Mrs. Arnold pointed back toward the elevators. "Make a left, and then look closely, because it's in a niche near the stairwell exit."

"We'll let you get back to your patients now," Chief Spratlin said. "As we've already said, we'll call your people in, one at a time, after we've talked with Ms Bordeaux here."

Ben Edwards walked Mrs. Arnold to the door where Amy and Barney stood. He stopped next to them and thanked the nurse again for her help. Mrs. Arnold hurried back to her station.

"It was good of you to come so quickly," Ben said, smiling at Amy.

"Sorry to get you out like this," Sheriff Morgan said, his dark eyes saying much more.

Amy dreaded the talk she knew she would be having with him. "Miss Waggoner refuses to talk to any one else."

"I don't mind, Sheriff. I'm only concerned for Nancy."

Frank Morgan looked at Barney. "You may step down the hall until we're through here."

"I'm not stepping anywhere, Frank," Barney was tensed, ready for the sheriff's objections. "What you have to say to Amy, I intend to hear."

Frank looked at Barney, a trace of a smile matched the amusement in his eyes. "Since we don't want a fight on our hands, I suppose we won't argue with that. Right, David?"

Chief Spratlin wasn't hiding his broad grin. "Sure, Barney, we have no secrets," he said. "Let's all sit over here." He waved them over to a group of chairs. Barney and Ben sat in chairs on either side of Amy, while the sheriff and police chief sat in chairs across the cocktail table from them.

David Spratlin looked at Ben. "Would you please explain to them what's happened up to this point?"

Ben turned to face Amy. "I think you heard what Mrs. Arnold said, right?" When Amy nodded, he went on, "While Mrs. Waggoner was out of the room, someone came in, placed a pillow over Nancy's head, and attempted to suffocate her. Fortunately, her mother had insisted Nancy have the call button in her hand before she left. Nancy managed to punch it when the man put the pillow over her head. We're guessing that when the nurse's voice came on, asking Nancy what she needed, the would-be killer knew the nurse would come to the room if the girl didn't answer, so he ran out of the room. The nurse said she got just a glimpse of someone turning the corner down the hallway as she was running to Nancy's room in response to the girl's screams. One of the pillows from Nancy's bed is missing."

"The nurses said you were the last person to visit with the Waggoners after the aunt arrived," Frank spoke. "Did you see anyone hanging around that struck you as being out of place, maybe? We think someone had been here earlier, checking out Nancy's room and looking for a place to hide. We're grasping at straws right now," he admitted.

Amy shook her head. "Just Gayle Armbruster. She came here looking for me. I was in the hallway, talking to Mrs. Waggoner when she found me."

"How did she know to look for you here?" David asked.

"She called me at home and Barney told her I was probably here at the hospital. She wanted to invite me for dinner at her house." Barney was nodding in agreement.

"She couldn't leave word with Barney for you to call back?" Ben asked.

"I'm sure she could have, but what was wrong with her dropping by here since she was already in town?" Amy asked defensively.

"Not a thing," Ben spoke quickly.

Amy's voice was tight with impatience, as she turned to the sheriff and said, "You told me on the telephone that Nancy wanted to talk to me. When may I see her?"

Instead of answering her, Frank said, "Do you know what she wants to talk to you about?"

"No, I do not." Amy was getting very tired of the officiousness of the three men. "And I won't know until I get to talk to her."

Unruffled by her belligerence, the sheriff continued. "If she tells you anything connected with how she got the injury to her knee, or who she thinks is trying to harm her and why, you have to tell us. Otherwise, you could be charged for withholding evidential information, understand?"

Amy stood up. "Whatever that means. May I go in now?"

"I'll walk you to the door," Ben stood up and held out a hand to help her up. Once they were out of ear shot of the others, he said, "You're not asking for advice, but I'd like to suggest you not go any place by yourself from now until the killer is caught. He will probably find out that Nancy called you in tonight, and he may think she's told you something she's not telling us. You seem to be in a unique position with this case."

"What do you mean?"

"I mean you found Thurmond's body, you've been asking questions, and you seem to know something about the situations before we do." Ben took a deep breath, then said, "I know how you're going to hate me saying this, but in view of all that's going on you probably shouldn't even be going to Gayle Armbruster's house for dinner. Most especially without someone to go out there with you. It's a pretty isolated spot."

Amy stopped walking and turned to look at Ben with astonishment. "You're absolutely right, I do hate you saying that. Are you saying that my social life should be put on hold until one of these days you catch the murderer, the identity of whom you haven't the faintest clue?"

"If I can figure out what you just said, the answer will probably be yes," Ben said, smiling. He thought Amy was beautiful, even when she was upset.

"I have no intention of having you, or anyone else, tell me where I may, or may not go, with or without an escort," she said, her eyes flashing with temper. "And neither of us knows at this point what Nancy wants to see me about. At least, you claim you don't." Having said that, Amy whirled around and walked rapidly to where Pete Hammond was now standing in front of Nancy's door.

Ben stood silently, while Pete looked on with interest, as Amy walked around the deputy and put her hand against the door. Just before pushing open the door, she said, "Call me later."

She spoke so softly that Ben wasn't sure he heard her correctly, but the wise-ass grin on Pete's face told him that he probably had.

CHAPTER 36

———————▼———————

Nancy was curled into the fetal position, her back to the door. When Amy entered, she jerked around to see who it was, fear making her eyes wide and dark. For a second the girl didn't seem to recognize Amy.

"See, Sweetheart, Ms. Amy is here." Anita stepped to the side of the bed and smoothed her daughter's hair back from her forehead. "It's so kind of her to come at this hour of the morning." Nancy lay back down, not turning away from them, but she drawing up into a knot, with her face close to her knees.

"Nancy wants to speak to you alone," Anita said, leaving Amy to wonder how the woman felt about being excluded. "I'm going to get a cup of coffee, then I'll go to the waiting room. The sheriff asked that I come talk to him, so this will be as good a time as any to get that chore over with."

She nodded for Amy to follow her to the door. In a low voice, Anita said, "Nancy's refused to take anything to help calm her. She said that if she hadn't been awake when that person came in, she would be dead." Anita's lips were trembling, "I know I shouldn't have left her alone."

Even as Amy reassured Nancy's mother that there was no way she could have known what would occur, she understood how Anita could feel responsible for what happened to her daughter. "I'll be back as soon as the sheriff's finished with me," Anita said in a louder voice.

Amy walked back to the bedside and waited for Nancy to speak. After a few seconds had passed and Nancy still did not move, Amy said, "I came to help. Please tell me what I can do."

At her words, Nancy straightened her legs under the bedspread and sat up, favoring her injured knee. She gathered the bed sheet under her chin, using one corner of it to wipe tears from her cheeks. Amy saw that Nancy's hands were trembling, and her expression could only be described as one of total fear.

"I know you've been terribly frightened by what happened," Amy said, hoping to make the young woman feel secure. "Anyone would be. There is a guard just outside your door, and the building is full of police. No one can get in here unless its your family or staff. Please don't be so upset. You really are safe now."

"I'll never be safe again!" Nancy blurted, the tears again pouring down her face. "They got in here this time, so they can get to me again. They'll kill me just like they did Bud."

"You said 'they.' Was there more than one person in your room? Did you see them?"

"I didn't see anything," Nancy answered the second question. "I had my eyes closed and my back to the door. I heard the door open and started to turn around to see who it was, then the pillow was over my head and I couldn't breathe. I pushed the call button I happened to be holding in my hand, and scratched at the arms I felt holding me down. It was horrible." The tears came faster. "What will I do?" The last words came out in a wail.

Amy put her arms around Nancy and hugged her close. "I promise you, Nancy, no one is going to hurt you again. You won't be left alone for a minute, even after you go home, until the person that did this is caught. Please believe that." She held Nancy until the sobbing subsided, then reached for a handful of tissues from the box on the bedside table and handed them to her.

"But they think I know something, and they mean to kill me," Nancy said, rubbing her eyes hard with the tissues. "Maybe not right away, but later they will."

"So you think there could have been more than one person in here tonight?"

Again, Nancy ignored the question, as she followed her own thoughts. "They must have figured out I was with Bud that night," she said, confirming Amy's suspicions. "I hadn't told anyone, so I didn't think they could find out. But they must have because of what happened tonight. Maybe Bud told some of his friends before we went up there and some of those guys blabbed it around. But that doesn't make sense because Bud made it plain that I was the only one in on his deal, as he called it."

Amy felt as if she had swallowed a cold stone. She was guilty of having said that Nancy might have been with Bud. She couldn't at the moment remember just who she had said it to, but had her own 'blabbing' caused Nancy's present danger? Amy felt nauseated at the thought.

"It's extremely urgent that you tell the sheriff what you just told me, and anything else you might know about that evening. Then maybe he can put a stop to this whole nightmare."

Nancy shredded the tissues in her hands. "You just don't understand."

"No, I don't understand, but I'm willing to try. If you can't tell me who the person was, can you at least tell me more about that night? Like, why did Bud go to the old country club? Did he tell you that?"

Nancy shook her head. Now that the tissue was in tiny pieces, scattered on the sheet, she was wringing her hands together. "Like an idiot, I agreed to meet Bud that evening. I had absolutely no idea that he meant to go up there. I wouldn't have gotten in his truck if I'd known. Mom had tried to tell me Bud was headed for bad trouble and I was risking being with him when that happened. Well, I was. Now I'm in the worst trouble I've ever been in."

Tears choked up her voice again, and Nancy stopped speaking for a moment to regain control. Amy was reminded of her visit with Nadine, and how she had skirted around the issue, never answering Amy's questions.

Nancy sighed heavily. "I love my mom very much, Ms. Amy, but I guess I don't act it. If I'd listened to her, I wouldn't be here now. I had actually meant to tell Bud that night that I wouldn't be going out with him ever again. Great timing, huh?" Her face was white with worry and fear. "So I went with Bud, and then I couldn't even help him. I couldn't get through the fire. Oh, Ms. Amy, I couldn't help him get out of there."

The torture in the girl's voice shook Amy to the core. "Nancy, please listen to me. There was nothing you could have done. The autopsy showed that Bud had died of the gun shot wound. He was already dead when the fire was started." Amy mentally flinched at what she had just said. She hadn't meant to lie, but the words just came out with certainty, as if she really did know what the autopsy report had said.

Nancy didn't seem to find much comfort in Amy's words, although the hard crying had lessened. "Bud always thought he was smarter than the cops," she said. "Even though he was always getting caught for doing something dumb. Now he's dead, and he'll never have the chance to do better."

Amy thought Nancy had touched on one of the hard truths of the situation. She wished that everyone, but especially young people, could fully realize that we only have one chance to get it right. She was jerked from her thoughts by sounds of people running and yelling.

"Get him!" someone yelled, not too far from the room.

Nancy grabbed Amy's arm in grip like a vise. "He's back, he's back!" she screamed, as she flung the covers back meaning to get out of her bed.

Amy blocked Nancy with her body. "No, no. There are too many people out there to allow him back in. It's something else, Nancy. It's not him, I'm certain it's not."

The sounds diminished, though they could still hear loud voices farther down the hallway. A moment later, there was a brief tap on the door, and Chief Spratlin entered.

"Excuse me for interrupting you two ladies, but I have some news that could be very good. We caught someone, Nancy. He may not be the one who was in here, but if he isn't, we believe he knows who was."

"Can you tell us who the person is?" Amy said.

"We'd rather not say until we've had a chance to get a lot more details than we have now. Sheriff Morgan is taking him down to the jail for questioning. We'll know something later today." He spoke to Nancy again. "A man will be outside your door for as long as you're in the hospital, and we have men on every floor. No one will enter or leave the hospital until we know who they are and what their business is. You're safe here, Nancy."

After Chief Spratlin left the room, Anita came back in. She walked over and put her arms around her daughter. "We can relax now, sweetheart. The police are doing a wonderful job of keeping you safe." She kissed her daughter's cheek, then turned to Amy. "Perhaps now they can put an end to all this craziness and get the person who murdered Ab-uh, Walter Thurmond."

Amy spoke quickly to help cover Anita's slip. "Surely they can."

"I was in the waiting room talking to Barney when we heard a commotion in the hall," Anita said. "When we stepped out to see what was going on, Sheriff Morgan was pushing someone ahead of him to the elevators. I saw it was a man, but that's all." Then Anita seemed to realize that Nancy and Amy may not have finished their disrupted conversation. "I'll go back to the waiting room and let the two of you continue. You probably weren't through talking yet."

"No, Mom," Nancy said quickly. "We were finished so don't leave." She scooted down into the bed and pulled the covers up to her chin. "Ms. Amy is tired after me getting her out at crazy hours. Thank you for coming, Ms. Amy, and I'm sorry I bothered you."

"It was no trouble, Nancy," Amy said, realizing that for now, she had learned all she would from this very frightened girl. "Whenever you feel like talking, just call me."

Anita walked out into the hallway with Amy. They moved a few feet away from the door and the police officer who sat near the door. Anita faced Amy and said, "Did she tell you what she's been so upset about? I mean, besides being attacked tonight."

Amy couldn't tell Anita the things that Nancy had confided to her. This time, she wanted to be very certain she was not responsible for anything happening to anyone, especially not to Nancy again. Also, Anita was walking the thin line of exhaustion, grief, and worry. She did not need the added burden of knowing that her child may have seen the killer.

"Nancy is very upset over what happened tonight, of course," Amy said. "She also wanted to talk about Bud, and thought you might not be receptive to hearing about him." Amy knew that sounded weak, but it was the best she could come up with for the moment. She could see the mother's need to be reassured of her rightful place in her daughter's life, and said, "Nancy loves you very much, Anita. That was part of what she said to me. I think she was afraid her actions the past couple of days might have made me think otherwise. Of course, I didn't."

Anita's face twisted with emotion. Her voice was a little quavery. "I know she loves me. It's just that she's trying to grow up, and I'm constantly worried for her. I need to back off and let her have room to do that." She straightened her shoulders, and took a deep breath. "I've decided to tell Nancy about Abner when I go back into the room. I'll be taking her home sometime today and I can't wait for someone to blurt it out just as I almost did. I think she's physically strong enough to handle it now. I just don't know what it will do to her mental state."

"She will be emotionally devastated, I'm sure," Amy said. "But Nancy is a strong person, and all these experiences are pushing her toward maturity. These are terrible things for her to have to cope with, but with your support she'll be just fine."

Privately, Amy hoped she was right about Nancy's being able to stand the strain without falling completely apart. As she said goodbye, Amy reminded Anita that she was available whenever she was needed.

Amy felt tired to the bone. The excitement and tension were gone that had kept the adrenaline flowing. The long day, marked with the news of Abner's death, the dreadful visions she'd experienced, and Nancy being attacked, had worn down her reserves. Amy's legs felt heavy with fatigue and her head ached.

She had almost reached the waiting room door when she heard Nancy cry, "Oh, no!" and knew that Anita had told her of her father's death.

Amy walked into the lounge where Barney met her at the door and put a sheltering arm around her shoulders. "Come on, Boss," he said. "You're going to bed.

And I don't think you need to worry about going to work today, either. After all you've been through, I would like to see you take it easy for a few days."

"I'll second that," Ben said.

Amy had heard Sheriff Morgan give orders for tightened security measures at the hospital. He had told Pete to pass the word that all of the waiting rooms, linen closets, and supply rooms were to be checked on every round the men made. She knew he wanted no more slip-ups where Nancy was concerned. She also knew that Anita would be wide awake for the rest of the night. Amy felt she could sleep with an easy mind for what was left of the night.

CHAPTER 37

▼

Frank leaned against the wall of the interrogation room watching Maxie Suth-erland. At best, Maxie was a pitiful sight, with tears and mucus meeting to drip from his grey stubbled chin.

"Okay, Maxie." Frank had enough of the old man's sniveling. "Let's go over this one more time. You tell me what I need to hear, and I'll let you go back to your rag picking. And you'll promise that you won't try sleeping where you don't belong, right?"

"But I done told you, man," he quavered. "I ain't seen nothing. I ain't lying! You know I was drunk, man, you know that."

"I know you found that pillow in the hospital hall, and I know you didn't try to kill Miss Waggoner, *and* I know you're lying. Either you'll tell me what you saw, or I'm reserving a room in back for you to spend a few nights in. By this time tomorrow night, you'll be seeing spiders all over the walls, and it'll go down from there. You want that, Maxie?"

"No, man! Please! You know my old heart ain't gonna' hold up to that. Why you pickin' on old Maxie, anyway?"

Frank thought he might actually feel sorry for the old bum if he weren't so smelly and dirty. His clothes were greasy with filth. There were some very old food stains on them. Frank never excused anyone, no matter how poor they were, for being habitually dirty. He would leave orders for the deputies to personally conduct Maxie to the showers out back before they closed him away for the night.

"Okay." Frank pushed himself away from the wall. "I'm tired of fooling with you. I'll have Archie put you in a cell."

Archie got up from the end of the table where he had been sitting silently during the questioning. He took a set of handcuffs from the side of his belt as he moved toward the old man. Maxie broke into deep sobs. His whole body trembled with the force of his crying. Frank could tell he was genuinely afraid.

"You're trying to get me killed, that's what you're doing. If I tell you what I seen, I'm dead."

Frank sat down at the table across from him. "You'll be dead if you don't. The only way I can protect you, is if I know what you know. Are you ready to tell me the truth?"

"I ain't telling you nothing with him in here."

"Who? Archie?"

"Yeah."

"No problem," Archie said, as he moved toward the door. "See ya'."

When the door closed behind the deputy, Maxie leaned toward Frank. "You can't *never* tell it was me that told. He'll come after me, and he's a mean person."

The odor of stale wine washed into Frank's face, causing him to lean back in his chair. "So, I won't tell. It will be strictly between you and me," Frank promised, knowing he lied. "I'm going to put this on tape, okay? That's so I won't forget anything later." He pointed to the cassette recorder sitting in plain view on the table.

Maxie's poor mind muddled that over for a second or two and apparently decided it was harmless to him. "Okay," he said, "as long as you don't tell nobody else."

Frank pushed the recording button and spoke the date and time, then said, "O.K., you can talk now."

What he heard in the next few minutes stunned him. After asking a few questions, Frank rewound the tape and took it out of the machine. He didn't want anyone else hearing this until he had checked out a couple of things. Retrieving his hat from a chair next to him, Frank jammed it onto his head, then went to the door and yelled down the hallway. A policeman, on duty in the office, came to the door to see what the sheriff wanted.

"Is James still here?" he asked.

"Yes, sir. He has contact duty tonight." That meant James was the one who handled the incoming and outgoing calls on the radio from the law men on night duty.

Mitchell walked down the hall to where the sheriff stood.

"I want Maxie locked up in one of the cells back there," Frank said. "No one is to talk to him. And I mean *no* one. Check on him once in a while, will you? And make sure he takes a shower before you lock him up. There should be a clean orange coveralls around here that will fit him."

Frank walked swiftly toward the back door with Maxie's whining protests drifting after him, "But, Sheriff, you promised me you weren't gonna' put me in no cell."

The sheriff drove to the courthouse, let himself in, and stomped up the stairs to his office. He wouldn't have suspected Billy Joe Smith in a million years. However, Billy Joe, better known as B.J., had made no secret of the fact that he hated Walter Thurmond and his friends. Thurmond had headed the group that fired B. J. some six months back for stealing from the country club. Frank arrested him, but before a time could be set for his hearing, Walter, who was a close friend of the judge that B.J. was to appear before, called Frank and said the country club board members didn't want to press charges against Smith. They thought firing him was enough punishment. With no one to testify to his guilt, the matter was dropped.

After that, B. J. told all over town what he thought of those "big shots," a term that seemed to cover all people with money. He also stated publicly that he hated Thurmond in particular. At the time, Frank figured it was just his way of saving face. Later, Dr. Rash, the veterinarian, had hired B. J., and the talk had died down. The gossips moved to more current town news and had, as in Frank's case, generally forgotten the incident.

If what Maxie said was true, B. J. had a motive, albeit a rather weak one, for getting back at the men. Still Frank couldn't see him being as attentive to detail as the killer was. Also, the persona of Billy Joe Smith didn't seem to fit into the slash, carve, and sew modus operandi of the perpetrator. But what if he were actually Hank Anderson? Then his motive would go far beyond just being fired, and his hatred would be fueled by a much stronger sense of injustice. The B.J. that Frank knew would be a mere disguise for a more deadly purpose.

Frank sighed and scratched his head. The only fault he could find with that line of reasoning was in B.J.'s doing something so inane as stealing from a billfold carelessly left in the men's locker room at the country club. Why would he risk his cover for a few bucks? Frank couldn't answer that. But they had ole' B.J. for attempted murder and maybe a whole lot more.

Maxie saw B. J. in the hall outside Nancy's room just as she had started screaming. He said B. J. ran toward an exit door, and disappeared just as the nurse came around the corner to see about Nancy. He had dropped the pillow in the hall near the laundry room door behind which he was hiding. Maxie had grabbed it as the nurse entered Nancy's room and had put the pillow into the laundry bin where he planned to spend the rest of the night. Being more than a little drunk, he was sound asleep when one of the policemen found him. Maxie had put up a small struggle, even managed to run a few feet before Pete got the handcuffs on him. He was too feeble to give them any real trouble.

Frank switched on the overhead lights in his office's reception room. It seemed extra quiet without the radio sputtering its almost constant stream of communication between deputies and police. He was looking for a particular report he had forgotten about until Maxie had mentioned Billy Joe's name. Everything on the recent murders was kept in one cabinet. Frank rustled through the top drawer until he came to Archie's folder of reports on the first three cases. Frank had told all his men to include in their reports everything they found on Bud Purefoy. They were to consider the young man's death connected to the older men's murders until he told them differently.

He took Archie's file over to Marlene's desk and turned on her lamp. He looked for a report on the date of Walter Thurmond's death. He found it on the second page of that particular day's record. Archie had written that when he was on his way to carry out Frank's orders to locate Grace Thurmond, he saw Billy Joe Smith and Bud Purefoy coming out of the woods not three-quarters of a mile from the Thurmond house.

Archie had stopped and asked the two men what they were doing so far out of town on foot. Billy Joe said they had been fishing in Corbin Creek, and held up two small brim to prove it. Then Archie had given the two men a lift to where the veterinarian's truck was parked a quarter of a mile further down the road. Archie had asked Billy Joe if Dr. Rash knew he used the truck for pleasure. Billy Joe smarted off that what the doctor didn't know wouldn't hurt him.

Frank got up and went to a large map of the county where it hung on the wall behind Marlene's desk. He traced his finger along the track of Corbin Creek from the Thurmond house to the approximate place Archie had seen Billy Joe. They could easily have been hiding in the woods next to the lawn and watched the police, the deputies, and all the other personnel who had gathered to search the grounds.

But why would they want to watch? Frank figured if they were sick enough to slaughter men like that, they could be sick enough to gloat over the aftermath. Frank knew that Bud sometimes hung out with Billy Joe, even though he was a lot older than Bud. But then Bud wasn't known for his appropriate choices in anything, much less the company he kept.

Frank also knew both men were into drugs. He hadn't figured Bud for a killer, but he was easily influenced, so Anderson, aka Billy Joe Smith, could have persuaded him to help out with the promise of big money. That would explain Bud's death. If he got cold feet, Anderson would shoot him.

Another factor that could make a stronger case against B. J. was that he had bragged to a number of people how Dr. Rash let him do some of the surgical procedures on the animals. Frank felt that with B. J.'s set of values, a human being would hardly rank any higher with him than one of the horses he'd claimed to have gelded.

Yes, Frank thought, Smith had motive, possible expertise, and opportunity. A little third degree should determine whether or not Smith was who he claimed to be, or if he was Hank Anderson. For the first time since Don Mercer's death, Frank felt that things were coming together. He sensed that the end of this horrible puzzle was near.

CHAPTER 38

$$\blacktriangledown$$

"Everything has been so weird for the past few weeks!" Amy told Barney, as she slumped down in the passenger seat. "People getting slaughtered like cattle, Stephen's calling out of the blue, and then tonight, someone trying to kill Nancy."

"Hold it," Barney interrupted her. "Repeat that please."

"I said someone tried to kill Nancy. But you knew that, Barn.'

"No. What you said before that about Stephen calling. You wouldn't be talking about Stephen Abramson, would you?'

"Oh, Barn, I'm sorry. Everything's been in such confusion that I forgot to tell you. Let's see, I was about to leave the shop to go to Leigh's for dinner when the phone rang, and it was Stephen. I couldn't believe my ears when I heard his voice."

"What did he want?" Barney's tone of voice was hostile. He remembered well how much Abramson had hurt Amy. So much so that she had been distrustful of all men since then.

Amy shrugged. "He said he wanted to see me, though I can't imagine why. I told him that I didn't want to see him and ended the conversation."

"I'm glad you forgot to tell me," Barney said, his smile back again.

"Why?" Amy said. She had expected a lecture because she *hadn't* told him.

"Because that proves more than anything you might say on the subject, that Stephen no longer has a place in your mind or heart. I have wondered about that."

Amy looked more cheerful than she had since she found Thurmond's body. "You are absolutely right. Stephen is history; God bless him."

Barney went inside with her to do the same safety check he'd done nightly since the event of the intruder. After he satisfied himself that her house was secure and had left, Amy took a long soaking bath to unwind. But she couldn't stop her mental wheels from turning. She was most concerned about Nancy, who seemed to know who had killed Bud.

The scary thing was that the attack tonight meant that the murderer knew that Nancy had seen something he didn't want her to see. Or knew something she shouldn't. Amy's only comfort was that there would be a guard on Nancy's door for the rest of the night. She felt strongly that Nancy needed to tell the sheriff everything she knew as soon as possible.

Amy tossed and turned until she realized that sleep had eluded her, despite being tired to the bone. She got up, put on her robe, and tracked wearily back down the stairs. She missed Hannibal because he would be keeping her company right now. Amy put milk on to heat and pulled one of the stools near the stove to keep an eye on it. On top of worrying about Nancy, her psychic visions kept replaying themselves in her mind. All of it together was driving her to distraction.

Amy poured her milk into a mug and added a drop of vanilla and a teaspoon of sugar. It was a brew Leigh had fixed for her many times when Amy was growing up. It provided her a comfort all its own. Sipping the hot milk, she deliberately made herself think of something more pleasant. Ben Edwards was a pleasing subject with which to distract her unpleasant thoughts, and she did like him, Amy admitted to herself.

He was, however, a dedicated lawman and that gave her pause. She could imagine their conversations being full of blood, gore, and crime statistics; that is, if he hadn't developed depths that went beyond law keeping. She was intrigued enough to want to know such things.

The warm milk was working its magic and Amy found herself yawning. After rinsing out her cup, she made her way back up the stairs and to bed. She was asleep before her head settled on the pillow.

Amy woke with a start. The sun, streaming through her bedroom window, signaled that it was late morning. While shoving her feet into slippers, Amy looked at the clock on the bedside table and panicked. It was nine twenty-five. Then the events of the night before came flooding back. It had been after three this morning before she went to bed that last time Amy also remembered that she'd told Barney she wouldn't go in to work today. She laughed in relief, as she turned on the shower, stripped off her shortie pajamas, and stepped under the steaming water.

After dressing in an old pair of jeans and a tee shirt, Amy went down to the kitchen and put the coffee on to perk, then walked out onto the lower deck. The dam was generating, so the river was high and swift. Amy always enjoyed the rush of the bluish-green water which made shishing, tinkling, glubbing sounds as it circumnavigated rocks, trees, and its banks along the way. Amy felt a sense of untamed freedom in the way it recklessly sought its lowest level and its ultimate goal, the open sea. She found a certain satisfaction in the fact that no matter what man did to control it, the river still met its natural fate.

When she walked back into the kitchen to pour a cup of coffee, Amy wondered if Barney was also sleeping late. She hadn't heard him mowing, or working on his truck, or any of the other piddling things he did on Saturday mornings. Then she saw the note propped against the micro-wave oven. It said he would be cleaning the lot she owned across the road from the house. He had called Mary, who had called Alicia Brown, who had said she could work today. The last part of the note said that Gayle had called and asked to be excused from her invitation to Amy for dinner tonight. Something had come up and she had to leave town. Gayle said she would call again when she returned.

After reading the part about Gayle, Amy felt a release of tension, as if she had unconsciously dreaded going to Gayle's. It seemed strange that she'd feel that way, but in being honest with herself, Amy admitted to feeling a little bit pressured by her new friend. It was as if Gayle wanted more out of the relationship than she was willing to invest.

Amy didn't know when her reluctance to get closer to Gayle began, since she only now recognized it. Shaking her head in puzzlement at her newly discovered feelings, she was nonetheless pleased that she didn't have to make the effort that being pleasant company would have taken. Gayle probably would have noticed.

The long day stretched pleasantly in front of her. Amy thought she would work on the large metal tray she was Tole painting, and maybe do some weeding in the flower beds. She called the shop to reassure herself that she wasn't needed. Mary said that, although they were busy, everything was going smoothly, so Amy wasn't to worry.

"I sold my painting of Sugarloaf Mountain," Mary added.

"That's wonderful, Mary. I wanted that one myself, just as I've wanted most of your paintings." Amy laughed. "But you know that I am one of your most enthusiastic patrons."

"Yes, and I thank you for that." Mary sounded pleased.

Satisfied that things were going well at the shop, Amy then called the hospital to check on Nancy. Anita told her Nancy was being released that afternoon.

"I was really worried about going home," Anita said. "But Chief Spratlin came by and said they are posting a full-time watch at the house until they're certain they have the right man." Anita paused a moment, then said. "Nancy has behaved so strangely since I told her about Abner. She was so hysterical about Bud's death, that I naturally expected a much worse reaction over her Dad, but after the initial shock and tears, she's been very quiet. I have to admit this worries me."

Amy was afraid Anita had reason to worry. "Would you ask Nancy if she would see me again after she gets settled at home?" she said, "I need to talk to her."

"Of course, Amy. Is there something I can tell her?"

"Thanks, but it's just a small matter we didn't finish discussing last night— actually, this morning! Nothing to worry about," she reassured Anita.

She intended to insist that Nancy tell her mother everything, as well as talk with Sheriff Morgan. Amy knew it was not right for Nancy to make her a confidant and keep secrets from her mother. Especially not after the murderous attack made at the hospital. Nancy was scared all right, but Amy felt that the girl was placing herself in serious jeopardy by not letting the people around her know why she was in danger. The time for such secrets was over.

Next, Amy called Pinkie. After asking about Tim and explaining that she was not working, Amy gave an edited version of Nancy's harrowing escape. After answering as many of Pinkie's questions as she could, Amy then asked her if she knew what had become of Mrs. Sanchez, the housekeeper.

"Actually I don't," Pinkie said. "She left here with a daughter, but I don't know where the daughter lives, or if Mrs. Sanchez stayed with her. Tell you what. I'll ask Tim. He may have heard something." Pinkie promised to call back.

The doorbell rang just after Amy put down the phone. When she opened the door she wasn't surprised to see Leigh and Hannibal standing there.

"I suppose," Leigh began, as she walked past her niece, "that if I hadn't called for you at the shop, I wouldn't yet know what happened last night."

Amy felt a twinge of guilt at not having called Leigh first. "I slept very late this morning," she said. "I fully intended to call you as soon as I'd gotten other calls out of my way." She bent down to hug Hannibal. "At least someone still loves me. Coffee?"

But by then Leigh was already at the kitchen counter and pouring her own. She turned to look at Amy, a look of contrition in her eyes. "Sorry I'm so rude this morning," she said. "I was already steamed at those New York people when I called the shop. The news that there had been an attempt on Nancy's life, and that you were involved really upset me." Leigh said, as she and Hannibal followed Amy back onto the deck. "So what happened?"

Amy told Leigh what she knew. At the end of her monologue, she said, "They caught some man in the hallway, but Chief Spratlin wouldn't tell us who it was, and I could understand that. But I haven't heard anything more this morning."

"Dear heaven above," Leigh murmured. "Where will it end?"

"I had another dream experience," Amy said.

Leigh turned to face Amy. "You saw something?"

"No, but I felt something." Amy then told her of the smothering sensation and how she'd fought to free herself, then had scratched the arm of the person holding the pillow over her head. "But when the sheriff told me about Nancy, I knew I'd experienced the same feeling she had." Frustration, mixed with despair, filled her voice. "Why, if I've got to have these things, can't they be detailed and happen soon enough for me to be able to prevent their happening?"

"Wait now," Leigh said, her brow wrinkling in concern. "You can in no way blame yourself because the premonitions aren't working that way. And I'm not willing to think of what you might get into if they did! This is a no fault situation here, you understand?"

"As I've said before, if the visions and sensations aren't meant to help, then what's the point of having them?"

"Let's hope you'll have no reason to experience any more."

"Amen!" Amy agreed fervently.

"We agreed that we would go to Frank Morgan about them if you had another episode. You didn't tell him, did you? What changed your mind?"

"I started thinking about what I would tell him. That I'm seeing and feeling things that are of no benefit to his solving the murders? The sheriff is such a realist that I'd have to actually see the killer and tell him who it is. Then he'd not believe me unless the killer confessed to him."

"You're probably right," Leigh said, "but I still think you should tell him. What if you do see something ahead of time? If you haven't said anything to Frank about all the others, he might not feel compelled to act on it even then."

"That's true, and I will tell him very soon. Nancy is not the only one who needs to get things out in the open. Let's change the subject, okay?" Amy sighed, and Leigh's heart went out to her niece at the unhappiness in her face.

"Well, I do have something else to talk to you about," Leigh said. "Remember I said I was disgusted with my agent and publisher?"

"I think you called them, 'Those people in New York', didn't you?" Amy smiled at her aunt. "What's going on?"

"I told you I wasn't leaving until Friday, but it seems they want me to be there in the morning. That means I must fly back this afternoon. From there I go to London. I've already told Barney that I'm making you a gift of my adorable Hannibal." She held up her hand as Amy started to object. "We both know it's unfair to him for me to be gone more often than I'm here. He doesn't like to travel by plane. Not only does his size make him a problem at times, but it insults him that he has to stay in cargo when he knows he's supposed to sit with me."

Leigh stroked the dog's broad head which he had placed in her lap as soon as she mentioned his name. "I think you need him with you, and he deserves more company than I can give him." Leigh leaned down to kiss Hannibal on top of the head. "You be sharp and keep my Amy safe." Her voice was shaky. "Understand?" Hannibal gave a gruff woof to say that he did.

Leigh stood up to leave. "As always, I've still got more packing to do, and I have to pick up my cleaning yet, so I'm off."

With their arms around each other's waist, aunt and niece walked to the kitchen door. "Promise me that you will go to Frank." Leigh insisted. "Even if he is an old grouch, he's plenty smart. Just because he doesn't appear to go along with what you tell him, doesn't mean he won't give it serious consideration."

After giving Amy the address of the hotel where she would be staying in London, her first tour stop, along with more advice on how to stay safe, Leigh left.

Hannibal whined softly after his mistress, while Amy wiped tears from her cheeks. They both watched as Leigh stopped her car across the road where Barney stood, rake in hand. He leaned down to talk with her and, after a minute or two, backed away to watch her drive off. Amy knew Barney hated Leigh's leaving as much as she and Hannibal did.

CHAPTER 39

▼

Amy turned back to a house that seemed much more empty than it had twenty minutes before. Hannibal gave her leg a nudge to remind her that he hadn't abandoned her.

"It's you and me, kid," Amy said in her best Humphrey Bogart voice. "Let's get something to eat. Barney should be coming in for his breakfast in a few minutes."

She filled a bowl with Choice Bits for Hannibal, and then put bacon in the microwave oven to cook. After scrambling two eggs and frying a couple of pieces of sausage, Amy put the food on a plate and covered it with plastic wrap, then placed it on the warming tray until Barney got there. She poured raisin bran for herself and added a half cup of skim milk. Amy walked up the stairs and out onto the upper deck to eat her breakfast.

The loftier view was like one you'd expect to see from a tree house. The upper limbs of the surrounding trees afforded shade and privacy, while allowing her to watch closely the comings and goings of birds and squirrels. Although she had seen many beautiful sights in her travels, Amy still thought her own place was the best of the best. Several real estate companies, and individuals, had called to ask if she'd sell. Amy's answer was always no, and would remain no.

After finishing her cereal, she leaned back in her reclining deck chair while Hannibal chose a spot in the shade not far from her. They both dozed off. The ringing of her cordless phone jerked her up in her seat. It was Pinkie.

"Tim remembered Mrs. Sanchez," she said, "so I've got a little information for you. He heard that she went to live with her daughter, a Mrs. Wendale Richards, and as of last year, they lived in Pemlington, which is only a few miles west of Mount Veda. Perhaps you could call the daughter to find out if her mother is still with her."

"That's what I'll do, Pinkie. I'm not sure just what I'll say my reason is for calling, but I'll think of something."

"I guess I'd better not ask why you're calling her," Pinkie chuckled, then her voice became serious. "Amy, I'm not sure I approve of your looking into those long-ago affairs. Please don't do anything that could cause you to get into trouble."

"I won't," Amy promised. "And I'd appreciate it if you and Mr. Tim wouldn't say anything to anyone else about this. Sheriff Morgan isn't happy with me now, and I don't want to get him upset with me again. It may turn out to be just another wild goose chase, so there's no point in saying anything until I talk with her."

With Pinkie's promise to keep quiet, and her own promise to not do anything that might compromise her own safety, Amy hung up. She got the Richards' number from information and in a matter of minutes Mrs. Richards had answered. She couldn't understand why Amy would want to talk to her mother.

"You say you don't really know my mother, so what is it you want to talk to her about?" the woman persisted.

"I am interested in the history of the old Anderson house," Amy said, stretching the truth. She made a mental note of how often she'd been doing that lately. "A friend of mine has renovated it, and I thought I might do an article on it for the local newspaper. I knew Mrs. Sanchez could tell me a few things about the house since she had worked there several years ago." Her words didn't ring true even to her own ears.

"My mother don't need to talk about no Anderson house, or what went on there," Mrs. Richards said harshly. "You shouldn't be bothering her, anyway. I don't know what you think you're up to, lady, but my mother's an old woman now and living at the nursing home. Her mind ain't working too well most of the time, and you'd just confuse her. I don't want you visiting my mother, and I don't want you asking her no questions." The clunk of the phone spoke as bluntly as had the daughter.

Amy was disappointed. She thought the old housekeeper had probably kept up with the Anderson girl for a few years after the tragic deaths of her parents. Maybe Rosalind was dead, or maybe she was living out her existence in some mental institution, or maybe she was married and had a family. Whatever had happened to her, Amy would bet Mrs. Sanchez knew something about it. The phone rang again.

"Amy?" It was Ben Edwards. "I hope I didn't disturb you, but I went by the shop and Mary Griffith told me you were home today. I was glad to hear you decided to take Barney's advice to take the day off."

"I'm glad I did too. I could get accustomed to this." Then with a small feeling of dread, Amy asked, "What's wrong?"

"Nothing at all, although I can see why you'd ask that. I'm calling to say that I've got to drive to Mount Veda this afternoon to pick up some things from the police station up there. I wondered if you might like to ride up with me?" He hurriedly added, "I know you have a dinner date this evening, but I can have you back in plenty of time."

"As a matter of fact, the dinner date is off," Amy told him. "Gayle was called out of town unexpectedly."

"I'm sorry I didn't know that sooner, or I would have renewed my invitation to dinner. Unfortunately for me, I've already set up an interview with someone for this evening. But if you'll go with me this afternoon, I certainly would feel better."

"I think I would enjoy that," she told him, thinking it would be more fun than the Tole painting or the weeding. "But you're going on business, you say?"

"That won't take long. I'll need to talk to someone for a few minutes, and pick up a package. I thought if you wanted to, we'd stop at Justin's for pie and coffee." Amy smiled at the hope she heard in his voice, as he said, "You'll go, then?"

"Only if Hannibal may go too," Amy qualified.

"He will make an impressive chaperon," Ben willingly agreed.

Amy hung up, feeling more lighthearted than she had in days. "I'm afraid," she told the big dog who was sitting at her feet, listening to her end of the conversation, "that I'm feeling entirely too pleased that Ben is wanting my company. Who knows what it could lead to?"

Hannibal stood up, the better to wag his feathery tail. He certainly didn't seem worried about the outcome.

CHAPTER 40

▼

Barney came in for his breakfast a few minutes later. Amy told him about Ben's invitation. "Good for him." He was smiling. "You need to get away from this place for a while. And you'll be in safe hands, too."

"And you can do something besides hang around to watch over me." Amy put his food in front of him, then poured herself a glass of orange juice. "I'm hoping that we can make a different arrangement very soon that will allow me to lead my own life."

"Don't get smart with me, Missy. I will admit, now that you have Hannibal to follow you around, I'm not as uptight as I was. So he's going with the two of you, huh?" Barney was smiling again. "How did Ben feel about that?"

"He knew I wouldn't go without Hannibal, so it's all right with him."

"Uh, oh, I think he's really interested."

"Of course he is," Amy said, arching her brows. "He'll be here any minute, so I'd better get ready." With a quick hug for Barney, she ran up the stairs to her bedroom. Barney was still smiling a full minute later.

When Ben drove in, Barney walked out with Amy to speak to him. "You boys have anything new on last night's fiasco?" Barney asked, after greeting Ben. "Is the sheriff telling who he picked up last night?"

"No to the first question, and no to the second one as well, Barney. With all that's been happening, Frank wants as little information made public as possible. I'm sure you can understand that."

"Yes I can," Barney said, as he backed away from the Bronco to let Ben get out of the vehicle. Hannibal, who had come out with Barney, sniffed at Ben's pants leg.

"Let me make room for the big guy here." Hannibal waved his tail as if he knew Ben was referring to him. Ben reached into the back where evidence of his occupation, mostly papers, covered the seat. After he had gathered everything up and put it on the floor, he bowed to Amy, who had been standing nearby watching it all.

"Mademoiselle," Ben opened the front door for her with a sweeping gesture.

"Thank you, Kind Sir." Amy climbed into the high seat with as much dignity as she could manage. At a motion of Ben's hand, Hannibal jumped onto the back seat.

"You take care of my girl, there." Barney called, as Ben started the engine.

"She's safe with us," Ben assured him.

As they drove out onto the highway, Hannibal, who was sitting in the center of the back seat, thrust his big head forward between Ben and Amy, handily blocking their view of each other.

"He's not the least bit jealous, is he?" Ben peered at her around the big animal, laughing. "I could learn to really love this guy."

With Amy's permission, Ben left the windows down to let the air flow through the vehicle. After a few minutes, Hannibal forgot about his chaperon duties and withdrew to the back so he could watch the landscape zip by on all sides.

Typical of a person who spends a big portion of his work hours asking questions, Ben had plenty for Amy. He was keenly interested in her childhood, as well as her recent years. She found herself telling him things she had shared with few people. Such as, how Leigh had adopted her after her mother's death, although Amy did not tell him the manner in which Laura had died.

Finally Amy said, "You're really good at this, aren't you?" He glanced at her, his eyebrows raised in a quizzical expression. "Asking questions," she added.

"I'm sorry." When Ben smiled, an unexpected dimple revealed itself in his right cheek. "I do it without thinking, I guess. Especially if I'm really interested in learning what I can about a person. And I must admit I've had an interest in knowing you better since the first time we met."

Amy was pleased at his professed interest, but preferred not to think about the manner of their first meeting. She quickly changed the subject. "Turn-about is fair play, you know, so you can answer questions now."

"Whatever you want to know," he agreed amiably.

In the next several minutes, Amy learned that Ben was born in Iowa, moved as a young child to St. Louis where he graduated from high school, then had gone on to earn a degree in criminology at the University of Colorado. "How in the world did you come to Ashley Springs?" she said. "I mean, I love the place, but it's not exactly the size town that you'd expect to find someone with your credentials working."

"It's been a step-by-step process in my search for a more peaceful existence, and still be able to stay with my profession. I know that sounds odd for a person who's in the business I'm in, but I just wanted a place that had fewer heinous crimes, if that makes sense to you." His laugh was unexpectedly bitter. "I thought Ashley Springs would be that place, but instead, we have a major crime wave going on. A serial killer in a supposedly peaceful small town."

"That must be a real disappointment to you," Amy said. "But we who live here are even more disappointed, if such a mild term might be used for this living nightmare."

Ben looked over at Amy, his face showing his chagrin. "Look, I'm not trying to characterize what has happened to your town as merely something that let me down." He reached over to touch Amy on the shoulder. "God knows, I'm absolutely determined to find the madman who is terrorizing this very nice town full of people. In fact, I feel a very personal sense of outrage that he's chosen to destroy the peace and security of everyone who lives here."

"And I didn't mean to be so defensive," Amy said. "I know you weren't minimizing the killings, Ben. I've seen you at work, remember?"

He looked over at Amy and smiled, the very nice dimple showing itself again. "I also remember being struck mute by the lovely young woman who inadvertently became involved in such an ugly situation. I'm not happy about the circumstances, of course, but I'm very glad that it led to us being together this afternoon." Ben's eyes told her he meant every word.

"Flattery is lovely, but please continue with your story."

"Okay." Ben focused back on the road again. "I worked with the Los Angeles Police Department for five years, then moved back to St. Louis to work in the detective bureau there. I was investigating a case that involved whole families being killed by some nut with a double-barreled shot gun. I heard through the grapevine of an opening in Little Rock, applied for it, and got it. Although there was a lessening of volume in homicides committed in that city, there were still more than I wanted to deal with. The case loads were so heavy at times, I wasn't sure which case contained what facts. So I decided to try for a really small town, and here I am."

Amy could hear the frustration in Ben's voice and felt touched that he would reveal so much about himself to her. Not knowing how to respond, she remained quiet. After the brief silence, they went on talking about inconsequential matters, neither of them wishing to ruin their first time together.

By now, they were driving into the outskirts of Mount Veda. It was even smaller than Ashley Springs, but it had a special air about it, as if time had stood still here. There was an aura of friendliness such as was practiced two generations ago, when neighbors were more than neighbors, and hard work an accepted way of life.

Tourists flooded the small town during the vacation season, and the local people seemed perfectly comfortable in their company. Amy suspected them of feeling superior to the gawking crowds of invading strangers.

As they neared the center of town, which was the courthouse square, Amy and Ben saw and heard the local music makers. They were gathered in groups of four or five, and sat under large old oak trees that shaded the courthouse lawns. There were even more small bands sitting in front of old houses that faced the courthouse. These structures had been converted into small shops. Kentucky bluegrass tunes, some of which were as old as remembered time, were being played in a collage of sounds that featured banjo, fiddle, and guitar.

Stopping every few yards to allow clots of tourists to cross the street, Ben drove away from the busy courthouse square to a quieter area only three blocks away. He stopped in the parking lot of the Mount Veda Police Station, managing to find a rare spot in the shade.

"I won't be long," Ben said. "Do you want to come inside, or wait out here? It's fairly comfortable in the shade."

Amy sensed that he preferred her to stay in the car. She, on the other hand, had no desire to accompany him. "I think I'll walk Hannibal back to the square, so if you'll tell me about how long you'll be, we can be back by then."

"It may be as long as thirty minutes," Ben opened the driver's door. "I'll drive you back to save you the walk." Amy assured him that she much preferred walking. Ben acquiesced and said, "When I'm finished, I'll cruise the square for you."

After Amy fastened the leash to Hannibal's collar, they walked the three blocks back to the square, then wandered from one group to another, watching people as much as listening to the music. Hannibal was something of a distraction because of his size and his apparent willingness to be petted by strangers. Across the street from the courthouse was a two-story yellow house, and on its porch was yet another group of musicians.

Amy walked over to the house, and through the crowd of people who stood listening to the music, and others who made their way in and out of the building. At her command, Hannibal obediently sat down near the porch railing and allowed her to tie the end of his leash to one of the posts. Amy went inside to look through the cluttered collections of vases, musical instruments, old books, bottles, dishes and other objects, similar to those that could be found in hundreds of shops throughout the Ozark area. She then climbed the steep stairs that led to the upper floor which was also crowded with a variety of objects.

She walked over to a shelf of glassware. On the top shelf, a green bottle in the shape of a dog sat partially hidden behind other bottles. Amy was immediately intrigued by the shape of the head which looked exactly like a little black dog named Alex that belonged to friends of hers. Carefully lifting the bottle down, she carried it downstairs to the lady at the cash register. To her surprise, the bottle cost only four dollars. Amy was very pleased with her find. It would make the perfect gift for Kathy and Ron, the owners of Alex, a wonderful little black dog that grabbed the heart strings of everyone he met.

When she got back outside, Amy rescued Hannibal from an enthusiastic toddler whose mother apparently didn't know her little darling shouldn't beat a dog over the head with his toy truck. Hannibal, grateful to escape the abuse, quickly followed her to one of the unoccupied benches on the courthouse lawn.

They sat down to enjoy the coolness of the shade and the pageantry of the summer crowd. The ebb and flow of people, dressed in bright colors and comfortable outfits, the trademark of American tourists, made interesting watching. One elderly couple held hands and talked animatedly to each other. The woman's face reflected the contentment of knowing she was attractive to her male companion. It was a feeling that Amy knew to be a very pleasant experience.

A sudden movement across the street caught her attention. A woman, dressed in jeans and a sleeveless denim shirt, moved quickly to a shop door and entered the building. She wore a cap pulled low over her face, and had on dark sunglasses, but in the brief look Amy got before the woman disappeared, she had the impression that she had seen that woman before.

Just as Amy decided to walk over to the shop to check the person out, she heard the staccato tap of a horn and saw Ben pull up to the curb across from where she sat. She picked up the sack which held the green bottle and walked over to the vehicle, Hannibal close to her heels.

Ben leaned down to speak to her through the open window. "You two looked very content where you were. Do you want to stay a little longer?"

"No, thank you," she said, as she unsnapped Hannibal's leash and opened the back door for him. Ben reached over and opened her door. "It was nice for a short while, but I'm ready to go." Before fastening her seat belt, she settled the green bottle in its bag on the floor between her feet.

"Souvenir, huh?" Ben said.

"A gift. It's a green bottle that reminded me of someone I know," she said.

"Someone looks like a green bottle?" Ben had a big grin on his face.

"Yes, my friend is a little green dog from Mars."

Amy was surprised at how good she felt in his company, and how much she enjoyed his sense of humor. She realized at that moment that humor was the one important ingredient that had been missing from all her other involvements with men.

Ben drove to Justin's Restaurant, where they both ordered chocolate pie and coffee. Amy ate every bite, then scraped the plate clean of crumbs.

"Would you like another piece?" Ben asked.

"Waste not, want not, as the old saying goes," Amy smiled, taking a last sip of coffee. "I'm ready to leave when you are."

After they had driven a couple of miles toward home and Ben still had made no mention of his visit, Amy could contain her curiosity no longer. "So, you got what you came for?" She looked back at a package that lay on the seat beside Hannibal.

Ben glanced at her, his face revealing nothing. That seemed to tell her that he thought his business was none of hers. But after a moment's pause, he said, "As a matter of fact, I did. In that box is a very interesting artifact from an investigation held many years ago. One of the deputies who worked on that case had taken it home with him after the authorities decided it was not an evidentiary piece. The sheriff thought it may tell us something about our current cases."

"The deputy was the person you wanted to talk to?"

"That's right. He lives in a remote area up on one of the mountains near here and was nice enough to meet me at the station."

"What is the object? Can you tell me?"

"You're pretty good at asking questions yourself, you know that?" He smiled at her. "Maybe you should be an investigator. But I can't tell you what it is. Sorry." Then he added, "I shouldn't have said what I did, but I'm sure you won't mention it to anyone."

"Of course I won't." Amy felt good about his revealing a bit of information that no one else had. It made her even more certain that the detective really liked her.

Ben was silent for a minute. When he spoke again, it was on a different subject. "Are you and Gayle Armbruster pretty good friends?" he glanced at her, his eyes serious.

"We are new friends, yes. I don't know her that well, but what little I've been around her she seems to be a very nice person. You brought this up once before. Why? Is there some reason why you think that we shouldn't be friends?"

"No, just my terrible habit of asking questions taking over again. I would like to hear how much you know about the woman, however."

"What should I know?" Amy again felt the surge of resentment at Ben's apparent disapproval of her choice of friends, calling Gayle 'the woman.' "She's friendly, nice to be around, and she's about my age."

Amy crossed her arms over her chest. An outward sign of her resistance to Ben's line of questioning. "In case you haven't noticed," she added, "there aren't that many single women who are my age in Ashley Springs. So I was hoping the two of us could be good friends, okay?"

She wasn't about to reveal her recent doubts about having Gayle as a friend, because Amy didn't really know why she was having those doubts. Gayle had done nothing to deserve them, but Amy still felt that sense of reservation deep inside.

Ben looked into the rear view mirror, then slowed down the speed of his vehicle. He reached over to touch Amy's shoulder. "I've done it again, haven't I? Please don't be upset with me. I wouldn't deliberately insult your intelligence, believe me. It's just that in a case like this one, a law officer finds himself looking at every person within the circle of acquaintances and friends of anyone even remotely involved in the situation. Your finding the body has made you a part of the circumstances surrounding Thurmond's murder."

Ben lightly pressed his fingers to make firmer contact with the woman he found so intriguing. "I promise I won't mention the subject again, but I also urge you to tell me if you think of anything I should know."

Amy wasn't certain how she did feel toward Ben at the moment. She heard the sincere concern in his voice, but she had never allowed anyone to dictate her choices or her friends. No detective was going to start now. She took a deep breath, then turned to smile at him. "I'll hold you to that promise, but I'm not making any of my own. Let's not talk about this any further."

"You've got it," Ben said, as he pressed down on the accelerator and got them back up to speed again. "Do you suppose I'll ever learn to carry on a conversation like an ordinary person without asking questions?"

"Not a chance." Amy couldn't keep from laughing. "You just asked another one."

For the remainder of their trip, Ben managed to talk about things that didn't require questions. Amy was surprised at his knowledge of music. He told her he had been an amateur singer/actor in the community theater in Los Angeles. "I also took part in our police benefit shows. A regular ham, I am," he declared. "Though not a green one."

As he turned into Amy's driveway, Ben said. "May I ask you one last question?"

"Only one."

"If I can get tickets to the opening night of *Cats* would you go with me to see it? You know the play is coming back to Little Rock."

"What about Hannibal?" She smiled at him teasingly.

"I'm not sure I could find a tux that would fit him," he said, with a straight face.

When Ben came around to open her door, Amy said, "I will give it my serious consideration."

After he saw her to the door, Ben backed his vehicle into the turn around space and drove out to the highway. Amy caught herself smiling as she and Hannibal entered the house. Except for that short moment of resentment, it had been an exceptionally nice afternoon. She wondered why she hadn't liked Ben when she first met him. Right now, she couldn't imagine.

CHAPTER 41

▼

"You're inviting her to dinner again."

"I have to, don't you see? Otherwise, she's going to suspect something, and I know you don't want that."

"Don't patronize me, you slut. I told you to stay away from her and what do you do? You still want to ask her to dinner, for god's sake. I need to teach you a lesson, one that will convince you that I mean what I say."

"Please don't be upset. After tonight, I promise I'll have no more to do with Amy. I plan to tell her that I'm moving back to New York very soon, and then I'll get too busy to see her again. You want me out of here, right? After the dinner tonight, it will be over."

There was a long moment of silence and she couldn't tell how her suggestion had gone over. After a few seconds, the decision was given.

"You're right. It will be over. Since they've arrested Billy Joe, it's only a matter of time until it dawns on him he's been used." An obscene giggle escaped. "What a fool he is. I should have killed the bastard before he bungled the Waggoner job, but it's too late to remedy that. Now he'll blab to save his own hide, and they'll know who we are. If I get the chance, I'll fix him so he can't talk. Maybe they'll let him out on bail."

She listened quietly, relieved that the slaughter in Ashley Springs was coming to an end. She prayed no one else would die before the two of them left. Her hope was short lived as the monologue continued.

"I have business in California, so you be ready to leave for New York day after tomorrow. Meanwhile, I'm planning a little surprise for the sheriff and that Nancy person. When that's done, I'm out of here. I'll come back in a year or two and finish *the executions. By that time everyone will have settled back into their routines and will have forgotten about us.*

"And you're right, we don't want our little Amy to get suspicious, plus, it gives you the opportunity to say goodbye in a friendly manner. I want that woman completely at ease."

Dread balled up in her stomach as she listened to the last words. Capitulation didn't come this easily. She looked up and saw the smile and cold fingers tickled her spine. She had seen that smile several times before, always when a deadly plan took form. It told her that someone was going to die quite soon. She wondered when her own time would come.

CHAPTER 42

▼

Amy leaned back in her recliner, feeling tired even though the day was still young. Depression had that effect on her. It sapped the juices of her vitality like the hot sun on a plant. She watched as leaf patterns danced across the red Spanish tile floor where the morning sun found spaces to penetrate the shade.

The day was too bright for yet another funeral. The sky should be weeping rain tears for the mourning that filled the town. Today, Abner Waggoner would be buried. She vividly recalled how smug he was that night at the Sheep Pen Restaurant when he brazenly introduced his girl friend as his cousin. He'd known that Amy was aware of the lie, but seemed confident that she would say nothing.

Gayle's presence apparently hadn't mattered to him, either. What really angered Amy every time she thought about his disgusting attitude, was the fact that he knew his daughter occasionally worked in her shop. She felt as if he'd made her an accomplice to his adulterous behavior.

Amy shook her head. She was not sorry that Abner was dead, only sorry for his family.

Some people lead trashy lives, believing that they'll never get caught. Which was mostly wishful thinking on their part, especially when they lived in a small town like Ashley Springs. No matter how much the sheriff and his people tiptoed around the fact that Abner's body was found in a seedy motel, it didn't take a genius to figure out why he was there.

Sheriff Morgan would locate the woman Abner had been with, if he hadn't already, and it would be open season for the gossips. Anita and Nancy probably already knew about Abner's duplicity. That had to make it even harder for the two of them.

Amy had gone to the Waggoner home earlier that morning. She delivered the coconut cake she had baked the evening before. Anita had said that her sister, Janice, was due at the Little Rock International Airport at eleven o' clock. Barney volunteered to drive Anita to meet the plane. Two of Abner's cousins, Mitzi and Mazie, had driven over from Memphis the evening before.

They seemed disinclined to help Aunt Martha with the household chores. They sat comfortably at the kitchen table with their cups of coffee, still in their housecoats, and gossiped about some young woman in their church who had 'set her cap' for their very married preacher. So while Martha prepared breakfast for them and Nancy, Amy had loaded the dishwasher, swept the kitchen floor, and dust mopped the living room and front hallway. She left when Martha took a tray to the bedroom for Anita and Nancy.

Dr. Thompson had told Anita in no uncertain terms that Nancy was not to go to the funeral service. Although he was sympathetic with Nancy's wish to attend, he said that Anita had enough on her hands without Nancy's being put back into the hospital. He had left a bottle of antibiotic capsules. Nancy was to take every one of them, even when her knee looked and felt better.

Amy asked to stay with Nancy while the family was gone. She rose now from her recliner and walked over to the open patio doors, taking in a deep breath of the fresh morning air. *Lord, give me the strength to be of help today,* she prayed as she turned to go upstairs to change her clothes. Amy wanted to leave early so she could go by the shop to check on things there before going on to the Waggoner's.

According to Mary, only a few customers had been in, and unless a tour bus pulled into town, there was not likely to be enough business for even one person to handle.

"The whole town is quiet," she said. "I think everyone's giving a lot of thought to what's going on here, don't you?"

"As well we all should," agreed Amy.

She went to her office to get some bookkeeping done, but found herself staring into space instead. Rousing herself from the morbid thoughts that were growing in number, Amy reached for the phone on her desk and punched in the numbers for information. She learned there was only one nursing home in Forest Grove, and dialed that number.

A crisp female voice answered, "Peaceful Valley Nursing Home."

A chill ran over Amy as she thought how the name of the nursing home would be very appropriate for a funeral home. "Good morning," she said. "I was wondering if Mrs. Sanchez is feeling well enough to have company tomorrow?"

There was a brief silence at the other end, then the voice became even more formal.

"May I ask who is speaking, please?"

"This is Amy Bordeaux in Ashley Springs. I thought I'd visit with Mrs. Sanchez for just a few minutes if she's up to having company."

"Are you family?"

"No, I'm not, but I..."

"Then I'm sorry, Ms. Bordeaux," the smoothly official voice interrupted. "Mrs. Sanchez expired late yesterday afternoon."

"Expired!" Amy quickly toned down her voice, and said, "You mean she's dead?"

"That's exactly what I mean. Good day." The dial tone sounded in Amy's ear, effectively ending the conversation before Amy could think of her next question.

She put the receiver down, feeling even more depressed. The poor woman probably died without anyone to hold her hand, or to say a last comforting word. Amy shook herself, trying to break the dreadful hold that all the deaths in Hickorytree County was having on her mental well being. No matter which way she turned, Amy's efforts to learn something that might help to identify the killer were thwarted.

The sad death of Mrs. Sanchez probably had cut her off from some very essential information that only the housekeeper could provide. It seemed strange to Amy that her death should occur at exactly this point in time. It was one more break for the killer.

Although Ben had not said anything when they went to Mount Veda, Amy wondered if he or the sheriff had thought to question Mrs. Sanchez. If they had, she would like to know what the housekeeper said. She might ask Ben the next opportunity she had.

She became conscious that the shop door bell had been ringing intermittently while she was wool gathering, so Amy walked over to see if Mary needed any help. She didn't, so Amy waited until the last of the customers straggled out, then went back to the refrigerator in the flower workroom. It was a mess from all the flower parts and pieces that had been trimmed to put together the many arrangements that people had ordered for Abner's funeral. Amy was in no mood to deal with the clutter now.

She went to the refrigerator and got out two Cokes. Amy put ice into two large plastic cups and took them up front.

"Come over to my office and get off your feet for a few minutes, Mary. There's something I've been thinking about for a while and I'd like to talk to you about it."

After they'd both poured their drinks over ice, Amy broached the subject she'd intended to talk about for several days now. "I like the way you handle the business here, Mary," she began, smiling at the pensive look on her friend's face. "The way you handle customers and get along with the other staff members.

"I'd like to have more time to attend estate auctions, garage and flea market sales, and so forth, but what with having to keep up with the book work, plus help Barney with refinishing furniture, and all the other things that seem to take up my time, I'm always behind on something. The antique sales are increasing every month, so we need another sales person, too. I was wondering if you'd consider taking over as store manager, for lack of a better term. Of course, a raise would go with the position."

Pleasure flushed Mary's face, but then it faded as she took a deep breath and cleared her throat. "I'm flattered that you've asked me, Amy," she said, not meeting Amy's eyes in her shy way. "But I would feel obligated to put in more than the eight hours I work now, and I promised myself when I came back to Ashley Springs that I would focus more on my paintings. You can understand that, I'm sure."

"I certainly do, Mary," Amy said. "I believe you should concentrate on your painting also, so I gave that a great deal of thought and wondered how you'd feel about setting up a studio of sorts in that large room on the other side of my office. Those huge windows should make it a wonderful place to paint, and whenever the business slacks off enough for the other staff members to handle it, you could spend that time painting. Not ideal, I'd admit, but you could keep one project going here and a different one at home. Do you think that would work?"

Mary looked not at all as happy about the proposal as Amy had hoped.

"You are very generous, but I'll have to think it over." Hearing the front bell jangle, Mary rose to go back to the shop. "Thank you for asking me."

Amy stood, too. As an afterthought she said, "I had thought about asking Gayle Armbruster to work a few days each week. She knows something about design and color, which would be a plus in this business. But she's busy writing…" Amy's voice trailed off at the expression on Mary's face. "What? Did I say something wrong?"

Mary's face had flushed a deep pink again, but this time not with pleasure. Her eyes were dark with anger, and her mouth pulled down in a soured expression. A startling change from the passive responses that Amy usually got from her.

"What's wrong?" Amy asked again, when Mary did not answer immediately. Both had forgotten the waiting customers.

Mary dropped her eyes, visibly struggling to get her feelings under control. "It's just that I don't think that Gayle would be a very good choice, that's all. She doesn't strike me as the type who would settle for being a mere clerk."

Amy's concerned look faded. "I never thought of anyone working here as a 'mere' anything, Mary. I think of all of you as my friends. Except for the younger girls, most of the women who have worked here in the past haven't done it because they needed the money, but because they wanted something to keep them busy for a part of each day. But for whatever reason a person works here, they receive nothing but friendship and respect from me."

Mary looked up at Amy, her face drained of color now, as if she knew she'd overstepped the boundaries of diplomacy. "I don't know what I was thinking, Amy," she said, apologetically. "It's entirely your business whom you ask to work here, so I shouldn't have said anything. Please forgive me, and I'm honored that you asked me to be manager."

She walked quickly into the shop, while Amy stood where she was for a moment. Then she turned back to her desk, feeling a little angry and more than a little confused. Mary had never shown her anything but a willingness to go along with whatever she suggested. The woman's strong reaction to the possibility of Gayle's working here was unusual, to say the least. She wondered why Mary had developed such a strong dislike for someone she barely knew.

Amy would not bring up the subject of the manager's position to Mary again. Someone with such strong prejudices might take a dislike to someone else who came to work at the shop. If Mary were in a position of authority, things could get pretty sticky.

She sighed, as she sat back down at her desk. She was determined to find someone to help run the shop for her. Truth told, there were times lately when Amy wished she could just walk away from the shop and its sometimes onerous responsibilities. She realized, though, that her feelings probably sprang from all the dreadful things that happened in recent times. Amy hadn't had a solid night's sleep since she discovered Thurmond's body. If this horror didn't end very soon she would go nuts, of that Amy was very sure.

The phone on her desk rang, saving her from any further desperate thoughts. It was Amy's private line that she'd had put in, both to have a modicum of privacy and to not disrupt the shop business.

"Hello, Buttercup." Her aunt's cheerful voice sounded like a healing balm to Amy's unhappy state of mind. "How is my favorite niece doing?"

Amy knew that meant Leigh wanted a full report on everything she had done, or had been involved in since her aunt left town. She told Leigh that the Waggoner funeral was being held that afternoon, and then learning of Mrs. Sanchez's death. "I've been so depressed this morning, I don't have the energy to work on the books. Every time I turn around, someone else is dead. But at least I have the comfort of knowing Mrs. Sanchez died of old age and not from the venom of someone's hate."

"Are you certain that it was old age that killed her?"

"You sound as paranoid as I feel," Amy said. "Ben said it was natural to feel suspicious of almost everybody, what with the psychic trauma of murder in the air."

"Ben said?"

"Maybe I did leave out a detail or two," Amy admitted, then she told her aunt about her afternoon with Ben, and his call last night. "He really is a very nice person, Leigh, and he's interesting to talk with. Believe it or not, he talked about many things just like a regular person and without once mentioning the murders."

"But murder is his business, Amy, and so he's not just a regular person. I will say though, that you are probably safe in his company. From murders, that is." Leigh laughed.

"Well, Auntie, that's what Barn said too. I'm glad you're not downright hostile toward him, because I fully intend seeing more of him. He's already asked if I'll go to see *Cats* with him, if he can get the tickets. And, he asked me to have dinner with him Saturday night."

"Sounds as if your man has a serious crush on you, Pumpkin, and I'm awfully glad you have something so positive going on in your life. Now, change of subject. Hannibal is due for his check up at the vet's. Could you take him? Dr. Rash has his records, so he'll know which shots are necessary."

Amy promised to make an appointment as soon as their call was over. Leigh caught Amy up on how her book was doing in the British Isles, which was great. After warning Amy to be careful and not to do anything foolish or dangerous, Leigh said goodbye.

Amy immediately called the animal clinic and made the appointment for Hannibal. The receptionist said she could bring the dog in at ten o' clock the next morning. Amy looked at her watch and saw that she barely had time to eat lunch before going to the Waggoner's.

Determined not to allow her moment of anger with Mary make a difference in their relationship, Amy walked over to the shop area and approached her. "Would you like to close the shop for lunch?" Amy asked. "We can eat at the new LeBlanc's Cajun Cookin' if you like."

"I don't care for their food, Amy," Mary said, making Amy wonder if she was still upset about Gayle. "I'm not very adventuresome with my taste buds, I'm afraid. I'll get a quick sandwich at Riley's Drug Store in a little while. Thanks for asking me, though."

"We'll get together another time, then," Amy said. "Barney will be in the back if you need any help with the Waggoner floral arrangements. I'll be at Nancy's house by twelve-thirty. If I don't get back by closing time, just put the cash in the safe, along with the receipts and I'll finish everything in the morning."

Barney had delivered Anita's sister to the Waggoner's house and was now busy sanding on a large cedar chest. She said, "Leigh called me a few minutes ago." She told him the content of their conversation.

"I'll handle the appointment for Hannibal in the morning," he said. "You may still have your hands full helping the Waggoner's."

At the mention of his name, Hannibal raised his head from his paws and grinned, beating up dust motes with his tail. But to his disappointment, Amy told him to stay with Barney. She took time to scratch his ears and hug his neck before rushing out to her car. If she was lucky, LeBlanc's wouldn't be too crowded. It was two hours until the Waggoner funeral. Amy's stomach clenched involuntarily as she thought of how many funerals this small town had suffered in the past few weeks. She couldn't help but wonder who would be next.

CHAPTER 43

▼

Amy arrived at the Waggoner's and was immediately caught up in a whirlwind of confusion. The cousins were running about in their robes, hair still in curlers, literally wringing their hands. They seemed to think they were going to be late, but were doing nothing to prevent that. Martha was at the ironing board pressing the poorly packed dresses for the two women. She looked at Amy and rolled her eyes heavenward before suggesting that they go do their hair.

A steady wail issued from the direction of Nancy's room, so Amy opted to go back there.

At Anita's invitation, she opened the bedroom door. Anita looked at her with something akin to desperation in her eyes. Nancy, dressed in denim shorts and black tee shirt, sat in the middle of her bed crying her heart out, her words barely distinguishable.

"But if I don't go to Daddy's funeral," she was saying, "how am I going to know he's really dead? And I won't ever see him again if I don't go!"

Anita shook her head in despair, tears running silently down her own cheeks, "But, Sweetheart, you know you're not able to sit through the funeral service. Dr. Thompson said your knee would start swelling again and you'd wind up back in the hospital."

Amy sat on the edge of the bed next to Anita, and said, "May I make a suggestion?"

"Please do." Anita's voice was thin with exhaustion and tattered nerves. "I can't think straight with all that's been going on. Mazie and Mitzi have been up since the crack of dawn making trouble, and Janice is still sick with a migraine.

Aunt Martha is about past her limit of endurance, and Nancy is inconsolable. What do you suggest?"

"I don't know what you can do about your sister or the cousins, but why couldn't someone take Nancy down to the funeral home before the guests arrive and let her have a few minutes with her father? She needs to be able to say good-bye."

Nancy, who had stopped sobbing to hear what Amy said, broke into tears again. "Please, Mom. Ms. Amy will take me there, won't you?" Nancy looked at Amy, her eyes begging her to agree.

Amy hadn't thought about who would actually take Nancy to the funeral home, but knowing the other women had to get ready for the services, she could see where her doing it made sense. She nodded.

Anita sighed heavily. "I should have thought of that. All I could think about was what Dr. Thompson said. I couldn't take it right now if Nancy had to go back to the hospital. Do you think I should call him to see if it's okay?"

"We don't have much time," Amy said. "I personally think Nancy will be better off going to the funeral home for a few minutes than she will be staying here in this emotional turmoil."

"I agree." Anita rose from the bed, her voice decisive. "But we need to get her out of here without Mazie and Mitzi seeing her. They'd probably insist on going too. If you'll help Nancy get her shoes on, I'll go out there and arrange a distraction to keep them out of the way. When you hear a door slam, the two of you leave fast." Briefly, a mischievous grin played across Anita's face. "Sorry you'll miss the show," she said.

Nancy sat on the side of the bed while Amy helped get the Nikes on her feet, then tied the shoestrings for her. She braced Nancy with one arm around her waist as they waited for her mother's signal. Suddenly a door slammed, and at the same time they heard Anita yelling, "I need a little peace and quiet here! Do you think that could be arranged?"

Not losing a second, Amy snatched open the bedroom door and helped Nancy hobble through the hallway and out of the house. It sounded as if Anita was finally expressing some long overdue truths, and Amy smiled at a mental picture of the two busybody cousins cowering before a no longer meek Anita. *Give 'em heck, girl!* Amy thought.

She helped Nancy into the car and ran back around to get under the wheel. As she drove away, Amy glanced at her rearview mirror in time to see a police car pull out behind her. True to the sheriff's orders, they were keeping a close watch on Nancy.

The next thirty minutes were some of the most painful Amy had ever spent. No matter how poor a relationship a child has with her parents, at their deaths, there is a ripping of emotional ties that changes forever the child's space and place in life. The remnant of childhood that remains as long as even one parent is living, disappears with their death. Losing the protective shelter of the older generation leaves the son or daughter with the cold wind of mortality blowing in their own faces. A mere breeze at first, it grows stronger with each passing year.

Nancy had told Amy that she and her dad were very close until the past two years. The young woman had a lot of memories intertwined with her father, and each one would cause her pain until enough time intervened to soften the sharp ache of loss. A quieter Nancy returned home, and a quieter house greeted them.

Amy didn't see the two cousins, but she could hear them talking in their bedroom. They no doubt, were agreeing that poor Anita had finally lost it.

Martha, wearing a black silk dress that emphasized her white hair and beautiful eyes, had a smile on her face as she came into the living room. "Your mother is getting dressed now, Nancy," she said. "Let me help you back to bed and make you comfortable before we leave." Martha turned to Amy. "There is fresh coffee in the kitchen. Help yourself to any of the food that appeals to you. The neighbors have been most generous."

Amy wasn't the least bit hungry, but thought coffee would be good. When she reached into the refrigerator for milk, she saw that the shelves were crammed with bowls, plates, and pans of food. Neighbors and other friends in town were showing their sympathy and concern for the Waggoner family. They had brought enough food so that Anita wouldn't have to cook any meals for at least a week.

In a few minutes, Amy was joined by the cousins, dressed in their similar Matisse-colored dresses, the same dresses that Martha had been ironing earlier. They flitted about the table and counters, practically salivating over the tempting dishes, but spoke in near whispers. Anita had definitely gotten her point across, Amy noted. Then Aunt Martha came to the door and quietly told them that the limousine was there for the family. It was time to leave. Amy went to Nancy's room where Anita was giving her daughter a last hug. After the front door had closed on the last of the women, Nancy drew a deep breath and then scooted to the edge of the bed, showing her intention of getting up.

"Maybe you should stay in bed," Amy suggested, as she placed Nancy's slippers where she could reach them.

"I'm sick of this bed," Nancy replied, already shuffling toward the door. "Besides, I'm hungry now." She limped out of her bedroom and into the kitchen where she sat in one of the chairs, then propped her injured leg on another.

Amy dished up the different foods Nancy said she'd like; a small piece of pecan pie, a slice of ham, fruit salad, and a glass of milk. The girl ate every bite, then while Amy removed the dirty dishes, Nancy stared into space, a frown on her face. Amy could feel the tension building in her, as the quiet continued.

Amy spread the dish cloth on its bar, then broke the silence. "If you're going to sit up for a while, I think you'd be more comfortable in your mom's recliner," she said. "You could put that knee up to keep it from swelling."

Nancy got up and limped into the living room, and after she settled into the recliner looked at Amy. There was still a residual fear in Nancy's eyes, but Amy could also see the look of determination in her drawn brows and clenched jaw.

Clasping her hands together, Nancy got immediately to the subject. "I know my Dad was murdered. Mom had to tell me because she knew either Mitzi or Mazie would let it slip." Nancy seemed comfortable calling the two older women by their first names. "I wasn't that surprised when she told me, though. It was like I already knew. I know that his death is somehow connected to the others who have been murdered, and that Bud's death is part of it, too. If I could just figure out *why* these awful things keep happening, I might could handle it better."

Suddenly her face crumpled and the tears poured down her cheeks again. "Ms. Amy, maybe I could have kept my dad from dying if I had told the sheriff about that night at the country club."

"Oh no, honey," Amy said, moving quickly to kneel beside the chair and put her arms around Nancy. "I'm sure it wouldn't have made any difference at all. Whoever is doing the killing wouldn't be put off by your telling the sheriff that you were with Bud." Amy handed Nancy some tissues. "This is a very cruel and twisted person whose agenda has nothing to do with you. I know you'll agree that we should do everything we can to help catch this person and prevent someone else from being hurt. I'll listen to whatever you have to say, and then we'll figure out together what would be the best thing to do. Okay?"

Nancy blew her nose and sat up straight. "As I've said before, if I had listened to Mom I wouldn't be in the fix I am, and I wouldn't know what I know. I never dreamed that what Bud was up to that night could have anything to do with the murders."

"Do you believe he was attempting to blackmail the killer?"

Nancy took a shuddering breath. "I've thought and thought, and I know now that had to be what he was doing. He kept talking about the big money he would have, and how everyone would respect him and think he was as good as they were. The silly jerk. Like dishonest money would bring him respect." Nancy dropped her head. "I know I shouldn't speak ill of the dead, Ms. Amy, but Bud was a long way from smart. If I had known what he was doing that night, I would have killed him myself."

"Considering the fact that he could have gotten you killed too, I understand how you can feel that way. Do you want to tell me about the rest of that evening?"

Nancy wiped her eyes again and took a deep breath, as if fortifying herself for what was to come. "When I heard the shot, I was in a panic. I knew Bud didn't have a gun, so it had to be the other person doing the shooting. I got out of the truck and squatted down in the tall weeds that grew close to the driveway.

"That's when I saw someone running from the building and in the opposite direction from where I was. I saw headlights come on, and a few seconds later, a truck drove past my hiding place. It had an emblem on the door, but it wasn't until later that I realized it was the veterinarian's truck. You know, Dr. Rash."

Amy felt a shock as the thought occurred to her that Nancy might be saying that Dr. Rash was the killer. She had to restrain herself from interrupting Nancy's story.

"Right after that I saw flames in an upstairs window. By the time I got inside, the fire was spreading through the whole place and smoke was so thick I couldn't see. Part of the ceiling started falling in, so I turned to run out.

"That's when I hit my knee on something sharp. I managed to get back outside and to the truck, and then I drove back to town. I still had the idea I could get help for Bud. By then people were out in the street looking at the fire, and the fire trucks were already driving out, so I parked the truck and walked home." Nancy began to sob like her heart would break. "There was nothing I could do to help Bud. I wanted to, but I couldn't."

Amy knew this fact tortured Nancy, even though the situation had been all Bud's idea. "There really was nothing you could do, and at least he didn't suffer."

Nancy didn't seem to take much comfort from Amy's words, but she did get a better grip on her emotions. "He thought he was smarter than the cops, even though they were always catching him. I guess he thought he was smarter than the killers, but they caught him too." Worry and fear creased her forehead. "And now they've come after me. They know I was with Bud that night, and think I know more than I should. What can I do?"

Amy was adamant. "We have to call the sheriff *now*. There is no way you can sit on this any longer. I don't mean to scare you any more than you already are, but if the killer thinks you know who he is, the chances of another attempt on your life could be growing by the minute."

Nancy nodded and said, "You're right, I can't handle this alone any longer."

"I just have one question for you, and I promise I won't say anything to anyone about it. Did you see Dr. Rash in that truck?"

Nancy shook her head vigorously. "No, ma'am. It was not Dr. Rash."

Amy's stomach gave a lurch when she realized that Nancy had just admitted she had seen the face of the killer.

The girl was in more danger than even she had thought. She went to the kitchen phone and dialed the sheriff's office. "Marlene, this is Amy. Is the sheriff in?"

Her friend explained that Sheriff Morgan was helping with the traffic at the funeral. "He should be here in another thirty minutes." Amy then asked if Ben Edwards were there. "No, he's out on some kind of search order. Can I help you?"

"You can tell the sheriff that I need to talk to him as soon as possible." She couldn't keep the urgency, and growing anxiety, from her voice.

"Sounds serious. Are you okay?"

"Yes, it is, and yes, I'm okay." Amy said. "But more than that I can't say right now."

"Hey, that's the business I'm in," Marlene said. "Give me the number where you can be reached."

Amy gave her Nancy's number, as well as the shop's number. "I'm at the Waggoner's right now, but I will be at the shop within the next hour. If he doesn't reach me here, I'll wait at the shop until I hear from him."

She talked Nancy into going back to bed and kept herself busy for the next hour rearranging dishes of food to make room for the ones that were still being delivered by more kind-hearted souls in the town. When she checked on Nancy, she was relieved to see that the girl had fallen asleep.

Amy had no sooner gotten back to the living room, than she heard car doors slamming, which meant the family had returned. The two cousins went straight to the kitchen and hovered over the new dishes of food like two bees over honeysuckle blossoms. Amy put on a pot of fresh coffee for Anita and Martha, then said her goodbyes. She asked Anita to follow her to the door so she could speak with her privately.

"Nancy has decided she wants to talk with the sheriff about some things she'd rather not discuss with anyone else right now." Amy took one of Anita's hands in hers. "Please trust her for a short while, and when the time is right, Nancy will tell you everything. I think she is doing the right thing by confiding in the sheriff, and I hope you'll have the strength to remain in the dark for a little bit longer."

Anita's face twisted with fear for her daughter. "Does she know who tried to kill her?"

Amy felt sorry for her, knowing that Anita would need to call on all her reserves before the ordeal was over. "Not exactly," she qualified, "but the things she will tell the sheriff will help him find that person. The sooner he does that, the sooner you can stop fearing for her safety."

Anita managed a smile, and promised she would let Nancy handle it her own way.

Hannibal gave Amy an enthusiastic welcome when she walked through the shop's back door. The phone began ringing, so Amy hurried up front. It was Gayle.

"I wanted to apologize again for canceling on you," she said. "And I wondered if you could come out tomorrow night?"

Amy was surprised to find herself looking for an excuse to not go to the Anderson house. "I've been trying to help Anita and Nancy Waggoner a little," she hedged. "Neither of them is feeling well, and they have house guests. If the visitors leave tomorrow, then I probably can. Do you mind if I call you back on this?"

"Not at all," Gayle answered graciously. "I have all my preparations made. It won't take but a few minutes to put the dinner together. You call whenever it's convenient."

They chatted a moment about the sad situation the Waggoner women found themselves in, then Gayle said, "I wanted to tell you now, Amy, that I'll be moving back to New York in a couple of days."

Amy was shocked to hear that, since Gayle had given no hint before now that she didn't plan to stay in Ashley Springs for a very long time.

"I'm surprised, Gayle. What's happened that made you decide to move? I thought after you renovated the Anderson house it would become a permanent residence for you."

"I thought so too," Gayle's voice sounded sad. "You know I left a message that I would be out of town and broke our date? I flew back to check on an aunt of mine and learned she is much more feeble than she admitted to me on the phone. I'm going back to take care of her."

Amy felt certain that Gayle was lying about her reason for moving. It was just a feeling Amy had, but she recently had come to believe in those feelings. Whatever the reason for Gayle's leaving, she knew it wasn't for a sick aunt.

"I will try very hard to be there tomorrow night and as promised, I'll call to let you know for certain."

Hannibal had stood beside her patiently during the phone call, but now wanted his friend's attention. Amy obliged by scratching his ears. Barney had come in while she was talking to Gayle.

"I think Hannibal has a sixth sense where you're concerned," he said. "Minutes before you drove up, he was at the window watching for you. "So how did things go at the Waggoner's?" Barney asked. "I know Anita's sister was half blind with a migraine headache when I picked her up at the airport. Did she go to the funeral?"

"No, Dr. Thompson came over and gave her a shot. She slept the whole time I was there. Not much help to Anita, I'm afraid."

"An altogether bad day, huh?"

"One of many lately, Barn. Do you think this nightmare will ever end?"

"Not until they catch the killer, I'm afraid."

But when will that be? Amy thought, despair filling her heart, as she waited for a call from the sheriff.

CHAPTER 44

▼

Someone was knocking at the workshop's door. A voice called, "Hello!"

Amy called back, "Come on up front, Ben."

As the detective entered the gift shop, Barney waved toward a couple of stools as an invitation for Ben to sit. But Amy got up from hers and headed toward the back. "If you don't mind, Barn, I'll talk to you later, okay?" she said apologetically. "Right now there's something I have to do." Her eyes begged him to understand.

"Sure, Boss." Barney shrugged his shoulders and stood watching the two of them disappear into the back. Amy wondered what he was thinking. No where near what was really going on, she knew.

As they left out the back door, Ben said, "Let's ride around a few minutes and talk, then I have something I want you to see." After they were seated and both belted in, he started the motor and drove out of the alley into Court Street. "Marlene said you were looking for Frank, but that you'd settle for me." His eyes twinkled with humor. "Just so happened I was on my way to find you when I checked in and Marlene gave me your message. Anything you can tell me?"

"As much as I know. I stayed with Nancy this morning while her family attended the funeral. She talked about Bud's death and her guilt at not being able to help him. She admitted that she was with him the night Bud was killed."

Ben whistled. "Do you think she saw the killer?"

"I'm sure she did, although she didn't come out and say so."

"That certainly explains the attack on her. Frank said he intends to question her, but there's been so many other problems to keep him busy, that he hasn't gotten to it yet. He will now.

"Did Nancy give any specifics?"

"She said she saw the truck of the person who killed Bud and set fire to the building. She said the truck was white and had a symbol painted on the door like the one Dr. Rash has on his."

"She's not saying that Dr. Rash is the killer?" Ben didn't seem excited over that idea.

"That was my question and she said definitely not."

"That means she got a good enough look at the person to be able to identify him. Hot damn! She might have saved her own father's life."

"Please don't even hint at that to her. She is eaten up with guilt as it is."

"Sorry, that just jumped out. Do you think she would talk with me?"

"No, she was very adamant. She said no one but Sheriff Morgan."

Ben took his radio phone off its hook on the dash and hit a button. Amy heard Marlene's voice say, "Sheriff's Department."

"Ben here. Is Sheriff Morgan still out on the river?"

"Yes, he just called in. Said he needed to talk to you. He's still waiting for the forensic team to arrive, so he may be out there for some time. You'll get in touch with him?"

"Yeah, I'm headed out to the river myself. Thanks, Marlene."

Ben put the phone back on its hook. "We had some very interesting things happen this morning," he said, accelerating as they headed out of town. "Frank arrested Billy Joe Smith, booking him for assault with intent to kill. From what you just told me, it's a possibility that he also killed Bud. You said Nancy described Dr. Rash's truck. B.J. works for the man and was probably driving the doctor's truck that night. If Nancy can place him at the old country club, we've got him dead center on that one. Bad news is, he's got an alibi for two of other killings."

Amy felt her spirits fall down somewhere near her shoes. She had quickly gotten her hopes up that the dreadful events of the past were over for good.

"Okay," she said. "You said 'things.' What else happened today?"

"A skeleton was found out near the river."

Amy thought she would never be surprised by anything else in her life. "Do they know who it was? But then probably not at this point," she answered her own question.

"As soon as we have an approximate time line, we'll know how far back to look at old missing persons files. Forensics will try to match dental records, things like that. We don't even know if its male or female at this point. Sheriff thinks its either a small woman or a child."

"Who found it?"

"Jim Arnold. He was going fishing instead of to Abner's funeral. He said he'd had all the bad stuff he could put up with for a while. Seems he came around a bend in the river to see a very big oak tree lying half-way across the water. It must have been downed by that storm the other night.

"Anyway, he said the dam wasn't generating so the water was too shallow to take his boat around the tree. He pulled his boat up onto the bank and was dragging it around the enormous root wad, when he almost fell into a hole. What he thought at first to be a stone and white sticks, turned out to be a skull and a pile of bones."

Amy shuddered. She felt a painfully familiar cold creep over her body.

"Are you all right?" She could hear the concern in Ben's voice. "Maybe I shouldn't have told you all of this, but I knew you would hear about it before the day was over anyway."

"No, I'm glad you told me," Amy hurried to reassure him. "I just thought of how that person must have felt being in that dark hole all by himself."

"Oh, so you've decided the gender, have you?" Ben smiled.

"Of course not. I just said that for no reason." Amy realized that she was warming up. That made her wonder if she could somehow prevent having the spells of her own volition.

"Another reason I told you, I thought you may have some feeling for what happened there. You've had pretty good instincts on some other events."

She smiled back at him. "So now my visions are mere instincts, are they?" She was very pleased with herself that she could joke about her problem.

"Do you remember, or hear about, many years ago a Dr. and Mrs. Anderson being brutally murdered in their home? The killer or killers were never caught."

Amy felt a stab of guilt. If Ben found out she had researched that very subject, he would probably get all preachy over her trying to do his job. So she said, "Vaguely."

Unaware of her lie, he said, "According to Frank a girl of about twelve and a boy of nine were at the house at the time of their parents murders. The girl was mentally out of it from the shock of seeing her mother and father dead. Frank said it was a blood bath.

"The boy, known as Hank, was missing. Frank has thought since Waggoner's death that the boy ran away and has now returned as an adult. Seems he and the girl were both sexually abused and Hank came back for revenge. If the skeleton is Hank, that theory is blown to bits. But here is an intriguing item. The burial cave is at the very back part of the Anderson property. That makes it even more likely that he's in there. If you get any ideas, will you tell me?"

Amy didn't answer immediately. She was wondering why she knew for a certainty that the small skeleton was the Anderson boy. His killer was the same person doing the killing today.

"Amy?"

"You know I will, Ben. I want the killer to be caught just as badly as you do."

Ben turned off the asphalt highway onto a narrow gravel road. It was full of pot holes, making for a very bumpy ride. After about five minutes, he turned again. This time they were driving down what once had been a road, but bore little resemblance to one now. It was only a grassy opening between trees and bushes vying with each other to close the small space between them. Broken limbs and crushed weeds showed that other vehicles had recently traveled this same lane.

They finally made it out of the woods. They entered a small clearing that ended at the bank of the river. There were two other vehicles parked nearby and Ben parked behind one of them. The sheriff's Suburban was parked further up near a huge tree lying with its bushy limbs in the river. The dam was generating and the water was almost level with the bank. The large tree limbs swayed in the current as if they were alive. The sheriff was standing near the enormous chunk of roots and dirt that had given up to the strong winds of the storm.

Ben turned to Amy and said, "I'm sure you don't want to get chiggers and ticks all over you. Wait right here and I'll tell Frank you need to speak to him."

Amy was sure too. Not only did she not want the blood-sucking creatures on her, but she didn't want to get anywhere near to the little cave where the boy had been. She was claustrophobic and couldn't bear to think of the young child being down in that dark hole with no hope of getting out. Was he killed first? Or did he die slowly of dehydration and starvation? She realized with a jolt that she was actually seeing him in there. He was curled up into a small ball, as if trying to keep himself warm. Amy began to cry.

To distract herself from her thought pictures, she watched as Ben pointed to his Explorer, and the sheriff turned his head to look at her. They walked off a distance from the other three men at the tree. The conversation went well for a few seconds then must have heated up. They both began waving their arms and talk-

ing vigorously. Ben was first to quiet down. He was very still as the sheriff continued talking, and after a space of a few minutes, turned and walked back toward
her.

Ben climbed back into the vehicle. "I'm sorry," he said, as he turned to face
her. "I had to tell Frank what you wanted to talk to him about. You know how he
can be sometimes." Amy nodded with complete understanding. "He wants you
to go to the Waggoner's and wait for him there. As soon as the guys from Little
Rock get here, he'll come talk to you and Nancy. He wants me somewhere else."

"Why on earth does he want me at the Waggoner's?" Amy was dismayed. "I
have to get my car, then I need to go home to see about Hannibal."

"I only know that you need to do as he says, Amy. He wants you both for
questioning. You can call your partner to get your car to you. Tell ole' Barn he's
to keep a close eye on you when you do get home." His laugh was reassuring. She
thought he must not be too concerned.

"That's not funny, Ben," she fought not to smile back. "I'm not a mere child
who has to be watched every minute."

"You're not trustworthy, and you know it." This time he wasn't amused. "I'm
worried for you, Amy. Please stay with Nancy until Frank gets there. He'll tell the
two of you what needs to be done. Promise?"

"Okay, okay. I'll stay there."

They were back on the asphalt road by now. Both of them fell silent, occupied
with their own worries about what could happen next. It was only minutes until
they arrived at the Waggoner house and just in time to see the sisters, Mitzi and
Mazie, drive off in their Lincoln Continental. Amy was relieved to see them go.
She could just imagine how Anita felt.

After a brief goodbye, and a reminder for her to never be alone, Ben drove off.
As she walked slowly up the sidewalk to the porch, Amy felt pretty depressed.
Complication after complication seemed to create new worries every day. It
would be a while before Ben and Frank Morgan could unknot the latest problem
of an unidentified skeleton. Even if she told them what she knew, they would still
have to have proof. And now the sheriff was worried not only about Nancy's part
in this, but hers as well.

Sighing from the burden of it all, Amy knocked on Anita's front door. She
heard her call, "Just a minute," then Anita came to the door. "You don't have to
knock," she said. "You're like family around here now. Come to the kitchen. I
want you to meet someone."

Amy followed her to the kitchen where a very tall state trooper stood.

"Trooper Angstrom, this is Amy Bordeaux. Amy, the officer says he's on duty here until Pete gets back from his break. I don't know whether to feel safe or scared." Anita's smile was shaky.

"No need to be afraid, Ma'am," the trooper assured her. "Just remember what I said about the phone. Don't hesitate to call if you see or hear anything suspicious. Also, I would lock the front door. You don't want someone walking in, like Ms. Bordeaux could have." With a tip of his hat, the trooper left by the back door.

"What is going on?" Amy said.

"Seems we're being guarded twenty-four hours a day," Anita said, as she dropped int a nearby chair. She placed a small cell phone on the table. "Not by the trooper. He just came by to leave me this." She pointed to the phone. "He has this set so that all I have to do is punch zero, and someone will come running."

Tears welled up into Anita's eyes. "They're not giving me the whole story, but of course I know that Nancy is in danger. Can you tell me just how this all came about? Nancy refuses to talk to me until she talks to the sheriff."

Amy felt sorry for the woman. It was bad enough to be on the outside of the family and involved, but to have your own daughter threatened was an unimaginable worry. "I don't really know myself, Anita. It seems that the man they put behind bars and thought was their murderer may not be. Since Nancy dated Bud, and Bud was murdered, and since she was attacked, they think the safest thing to do is keep a very close eye on her. I agree. The sheriff even asked that I stay here until he could come. Until they catch the mad man causing all this mayhem, we had better do as the officer said."

"You're right." Anita wiped her eyes. "I've got coffee on if you want some."

"That sounds good to me. What do you say we get a card game going? Think Nancy is up to playing gin rummy?"

The three women were soon settled at the kitchen table, all of them playing the worst game ever. Their concentration wasn't on the cards, but on each sound and movement in the house.

CHAPTER 45

▼

After Ben dropped Amy off, he drove to his apartment and packed an over-night bag. Frank had already made arrangements with Slade Angstrom to fly Ben to Memphis. Slade owned a Cessna 172 four-seater which he kept at the Ashley Springs Municipal Airport. From Memphis, Ben would take a connecting flight to Mobile, Alabama. Sheriff Morgan expected Ben to get the information he needed and to be back the next day.

As he placed his overnight bag into his Bronco, Ben thought of Frank's last words to him. "Others could be at risk here beside the men who were involved with Walter and Don and their filthy acts," he'd said. "We've got Billy Joe cold on the Nancy Waggoner case. The scratches on his arm nailed that down, but I don't think he played a major role in any of the other killings. He may have been involved in some way, but I don't think he's the dangerous perp we want so badly. Besides, finding this skeleton has put a whole new light on things for me."

Frank had refused to say anything further on the subject, but he urged Ben to get back to him at the first possible moment. The sheriff seemed more uptight than Ben had seen him since the first murder took place. It was evident that the sheriff felt things were becoming more critical by the moment.

Slade got Ben to Memphis early enough so that he easily caught his plane with time to spare. When Ben arrived at the Mobile Municipal Airport, he took a taxi to the Hiram Conegy Mental Health Institute, a private sanitarium. The build-ing was an imposing structure of red brick with white stone trim, some four sto-ries tall. Designed to look like one of the huge manors commonly seen in England, Ben knew that building of the institution must have cost its owners a bundle. The imposing building with its manicured lawns reeked of money. Whoever stayed here, paid plenty for the privilege.

After paying the cab driver, Ben shifted his overnight bag to his other hand. He had decided to come straight to the sanatarium and not take the time to go by his hotel. Ben climbed the long set of wide stone steps that led to a beautifully carved oak door. Its brass handle, kick plate, and hinges probably cost more than a month's pay Ben decided, as he reached for the door handle. The motif of an English manor would have been marred by glass doors and the gold lettering usually found on such buildings.

Ben entered a large lobby no less impressive than the front door. Black marble floors were enhanced by a scattering of gray and white blocks, which in turn matched the dark gray paneling and white woodwork. White marble statues on tall black pedestals looked down on him as he walked across the cold, hard expanse of the entrance. A bit too ostentatious for Ben's liking, especially since the exterior of the building gave no hint of its inner Romanesque decor. He'd bet his last penny that the theme didn't include the utile part of the building.

The directory of offices was posted on a black marble stele, that was more reminiscent of a gravestone than the decorator's intent to reproduce an ancient Roman object. Ben focused on the list of names on the brass plate sunk into the slanted black surface. Sheriff Morgan had said the director would wait for Ben in his office. It was now eight o' clock and beginning to get dark. He hoped the man was still here. Ben scanned the directory and found the office he was looking for. He took the elevator to the top floor, then walked down a long hall that was padded to silence with plush carpeting.

Ben studied each door until he came to the one with the words, "Williard Smythe, Director," lettered in gold. He tapped lightly, then turned the knob. The door opened into an expensively furnished reception area, done in grays and blues with polished chrome accents. No one sat at the modern plexiglass desk complex that dominated the center of the rear wall. Ben bent down to put his overnight bag next to the door.

"Hello," Ben called out. "Detective Ben Edwards here."

"Come in, come in." The male voice came from beyond a partly opened door behind the reception desk.

A very small man followed the voice, one who barely came up to Ben's belt buckle. There was a large smile on his normal-sized face, and as he approached, he held out a miniature hand to shake Ben's. The strength of the man's grip came as a surprise. "I'm Willard Smythe, Detective Edwards," he said, his strong voice as unexpected as the grip. "I hope I can be of some help to you, since you've made a rather long trip."

Smythe was impeccably attired in an Armani suit of silk tweed, a white dress shirt, and a tie of wine and gray silk. His Gucci loafers finished the man's expensive habit. Above the beautiful tie, Ben could see the sharp intelligence in the brown eyes looking up at him. He suspected the little man's wide smile and friendly attitude were fronts for an unfavorable assessment of Ben's own Docker khakis and Land's End sport jacket. Smythe turned and led Ben into the room beyond the reception area. It proved to be a large office with furniture that would fit a normal-sized man's needs.

Ben was wondering how the director coped with the desk, which was a huge walnut affair, when Smythe walked swiftly behind it and disappeared, except for the top of his head. The man's head bobbed along to the middle of the desk, then it, too, vanished. A humming sound began, and Ben watched in fascination as Smythe rose from behind his desk like an Aztec priest ascending his pyramid dais from the rear. Apparently a hydraulic lift raised the chair to compensate for the little man's stature.

The humming stopped, and Smythe leaned forward to prop his abbreviated forearms on the desk and lace his stubby fingers together under his chin. "I understand from what Sheriff Morgan told me that you are interested in visiting with Mrs. Edna Parkington," Smythe said. "Am I correct?"

"Yes. I'd like to ask her one or two questions if that can be arranged."

"Mrs. Parkington has been a client of ours for almost a year now," Smythe told Ben. "She came to us through her niece's efforts. A lovely person, her niece. We try to accommodate the families' wishes whenever we're able."

Ben thought the director looked rather smug over his charitable attitude toward the niece, who, if she was the one Ben had in mind, certainly was lovely. Better than looks, the niece had her father's money, and probably her aunt's too, with which to grease the small palm of Herr Director Smythe. Ben was betting that there was nothing wrong with Mrs. Parkington's mental faculties, and that a deal had been struck between this man and the beautiful Ms. Anderson. He might be able to confirm that much and more, if he could talk to the aunt.

"Could you describe the niece for me?" Ben asked.

"You are also interested in Ms. Anderson?" Smythe was not smiling now.

"Not especially," Ben said casually. "We would like to know something about Mrs. Parkington. If that includes information on her niece, then we'd like to hear that too."

"We, being the law officers back in Arkansas?" Smythe raised his eyebrows.

"Exactly." Ben didn't like the man's dismissive tone when he had said, 'Arkansas.' "Mrs. Parkington has information we believe can help solve a case we're working on. We would appreciate any cooperation you can provide us."

Ben knew he couldn't tell the man that Mrs. Parkington might be able to identify the killer of seven men. Thanks to Smythe, he now knew for certain that Rosalind Anderson was alive, and evidently from what the director said, was acting as administrator for her aunt's affairs. This made it even more urgent that he talk to the elderly woman.

Smythe didn't give Ben a description of the niece, or any other information for that matter. Instead, his behavior had become noticeably hostile. "I have a call in for Ms. Anderson," he said, "which I placed just after Sheriff Morgan called me. It seems she's out of town right now, but her answering service will notify her of my call."

Ben's hopes fell. Rosalind would order Smythe not to let anyone talk to her aunt. He knew he'd have to hurry. Knowing what the answer would be, Ben asked, "May I talk with Mrs. Parkington tonight?"

"Certainly not, Detective." Smythe was fully suspicious of Ben's motives now. "It's late, and all our guests are ready for bed before eight o' clock. If your sheriff had been more open with me about the reason for your visit, I might have been able to get permission before you arrived. If I hear from Ms. Anderson tonight, you may see Mrs. Parkington in the morning."

It was all Ben could do to keep his frustration from boiling into anger. He knew he had to think of something before Rosalind called and blew the whole thing for him. The sheriff wanted to know if Rosalind was alive and functional, and Ben had just learned she was, but Frank also wanted to know what Hank Anderson looked like as an adult. For that, Ben needed to talk to the aunt. She might even have a photograph of her niece and nephew as adults.

The humming began again, and Smythe sank behind his desk. After he'd completely disappeared, the top of his head popped back into view as it had before, and a second later, Smythe was ushering Ben out of his office, through the reception room, and into the hall. He had never been given the boot more efficiently. Maybe the man's size had something to do with it, because Ben felt no inclination to resist. It would be like arguing with a child, he decided, as he bent over to pick up his bag.

With a barely polite goodnight, and a promise to call Ben's hotel room the next morning, Smythe closed the door firmly. Ben heard the click of a lock before he turned to walk back to the elevator. He imagined that the director would be dialing Rosalind's number again before he left the building. He would have to hurry if he hoped to locate the aunt.

Ben passed up the elevators and walked to the lighted exit sign at the end of the hallway. The door beneath it opened to his push and he found himself in a stairwell with steps leading down to the next floor. He descended as quietly as he could, but every sound was magnified through the funnel of open space the stairs provided.

When he reached the third floor level, Ben very slowly pushed open its door until he could see the hallway. It had the same layout as the one he'd just left. The light was very dim at his end of the hall, so he pushed the door open a little wider to get a better view. There were doors on each side of the hall, but all of them in his line of vision were closed. Most of those had glass in their upper halves, with printing on them, indicating they were either offices or storage rooms. If they held patients, at least a few of the doors would be open and there would be people making sounds of coughing, talking, movement, the things that would indicate the rooms were occupied. There was only silence. All of the office workers would have long gone home hours ago.

Ben took the stairs down to the second floor and again pushed open a door. Here, a bright light in the middle of the long hall marked the nurses' station. Ben could see two attendants dressed in white uniforms behind a semi-circular counter. One of them was a man who looked burley enough to hold his own in a fight. Ben had no desire to start one.

He drew back into the stairwell to consider his next move. Unless he looked into every room, he'd have no way of knowing which one belonged to Mrs. Parkington. Even if the doors had the patients' names on them, he'd still had to avoid being seen by the nurses. Ben pushed the door open to a mere slit to get another look at the layout. Directly across from him was a fire alarm. For a brief moment he thought of breaking the glass, but then realized that if he started a panic, the confusion would make it less likely that he would locate Mrs. Parkington, assuming, of course, that she was even on this floor. She might well be on the one below.

Ben was feeling more tense by the second, knowing that he was losing precious time. Smythe may have already reached Rosalind Anderson, and she could give orders he was not to go near Mrs. Parkington. The director might even place a guard at the aunt's door. Ben knew he had to locate Mrs. Parkington as quickly as possible, ask the necessary questions, and get out.

He looked down the hallway again and saw that there was no one at the nurses' station. Setting his bag down in one corner of the stair landing, Ben waited a few seconds to see if anyone would reappear. When no one did, he eased open the door and stepped out into the darkened hallway. Across from where he stood was a room with a square card in a small metal frame fastened to the door. With another glance to make certain the coast was clear, he slipped over to the door.

Elwood Jones, the card read. He quickly moved to the next door, then the next and still no one showed up at the nurses station. Ben figured they were either taking a break or sorting out medicines, or whatever night nurses do. Ben hoped it would keep them busy long enough to find the room he wanted. He went from door to door on both sides of the hall, quickly checking names on the small cards.

He was almost level with the nurses station when he heard a laugh, and then a woman's voice. "One of us better get back there," she said. "If old Hawkins catches all of us away from our station at one time, we'll be job hunting in the morning."

"As if she didn't stay in her office all the time so she won't have to do any of the work," another woman replied.

Ben could tell as the voice grew louder that the nurse was rapidly nearing the hallway where he was standing. He would have to make a move immediately or get caught. The nurse might even try to get physical with him.

CHAPTER 46

▼

Ben ducked into the nearest door. It proved to be the room of a very old man who was so thin he barely made a shape under the covers. He lay with his head thrown back, and mouth wide open. A loud wheezing sound issued from his lungs, as he fought to breathe. Ben wondered why they didn't have him on oxygen, or whatever would help him breathe easier.

Feeling like a peeping tom, Ben turned back to the door to assess the situation. He could see the nurses' desk plainly from where he stood. The male nurse was nowhere in sight. A middle-aged woman bent over, what Ben supposed to be paper work, though it could just as easily be a crossword puzzle. She had one elbow propped on the counter and her hand on her forehead, so that her view of the hallway was effectively cut off.

Ben decided he had to risk going past her to reach the other half of the hallway before someone else showed up. He moved silently past the nurses' station without the woman being aware of his presence. Wiping sweat from his brow with the back of his hand, Ben glanced at the name tag on the first door. Mrs. Parkington.

His heart leapt in relief as he quickly opened the door and stepped inside. This time when Ben looked toward the bed, the patient was looking back at him. The woman opened her mouth wide and Ben tensed, expecting her to yell for help. Instead, she placed one hand over her mouth to cover her yawn. Again, Ben felt sweat break out all over his body. He had put himself into what could be a serious situation. What he was doing was unprofessional, if not illegal, and if he were caught, both Sheriff Morgan and the Mobile police would be after his hide. He took a step toward the bed and said, "Mrs. Edna Parkington?"

"Are you my doctor, young man?" Her voice was soft. "You don't look like the one who came in to see me this morning."

Mrs. Parkington appeared to be in her late seventies, but her skin was clear and smooth, her hair thick and healthy looking, her eyes clear and direct. No trace of confusion clouded them as would be expected in a person who suffered from some form of senility. Ben could see the remnant of the beautiful woman she once had been shining through the patina of old age.

He moved closer to the bed before he spoke. "No, Ma'am, I'm not. I'm Detective Ben Edwards from Ashley Springs, Arkansas. I'd like to talk to you for just a few minutes, if that's all right with you."

"I think I'd enjoy talking to you, young man. There's not much opportunity for real conversation in this place. Most of what I hear are questions and declarative sentences." She waved toward a chair that sat near her bed. "Please, have a seat."

For the first time, Ben saw that the room was attractively furnished. Not at all like the purely institutional one with the old man in it. Except for the hospital bed, Mrs. Parkington's room looked much like the ones found in a well-appointed home. The furniture was dark mahogany, and the chair she offered had beige needlepoint upholstery. Ben knew a little about interior decoration, so he recognized them as valuable antique pieces. He wondered if the bombe' chest and gooseneck rocker, along with a Tiffany lamp and Waterford crystal vase, were from Mrs. Parkington's home. It was an expensive setting for a presumably mentally incapacitated patient, but then he knew money could buy a lot of things in a place like this.

Ben sat down in the chair she offered him. Leaning forward, he said, "Mrs. Parkington, I need to ask you about your nephew, Henry Anderson, Jr."

"I'd rather not talk about him," she said quickly.

"Please, ma'am," Ben hoped to stave off a flat refusal before he stated his reason. "I need to know some things about the Anderson family that only you can tell me. It's connected to a case we're working on, and I would very much appreciate your help."

Edna Parkington seemed to shrivel a little. She pushed down into the bed and pulled the covers a little higher. "I don't care to discuss my sister, Olivia, either. I don't want to think about the things that happened to her." Her voice rose several decibels.

"No, no," Ben hurried to reassure her. "We won't talk about your sister, then. I certainly don't want to cause you any trouble. I just want to help clear up some matters back home." Ben glanced uneasily at the door. He hoped her protest hadn't reached one of the attendant's ears. "You see," he explained hurriedly, "we are pretty sure your nephew is in Ashley Springs. He calls himself Billy Joe Smith, and we just need you to tell us a few things about him and his sister, Rosalind."

Mrs. Parkington straightened up in the bed and looked him in the eye. "I can tell you with certainty that my nephew is not this Billy Joe, whoever that is, or any other person you may have in mind. Nor is he in Ashley Springs."

Ben looked at her more closely. The woman might be old, and she might be afraid, but she seemed very sure of her facts. Her voice held the confidence of one who knew what she was talking about.

"Can you tell me why you're so certain of that?" he asked.

"Henry, Jr. is dead." There was no equivocation in her voice.

Ben tensed. If the nephew was dead, then Billy Joe was not Henry, therefore, the killer was not safely behind bars. Amy and Nancy could be in more danger than he or the sheriff had first thought.

"Do you have any proof of your nephew's death, Mrs. Parkington, like how he died and when? I need to verify that if I may."

"Nothing like a death certificate, if that's what you mean," she said. "But you can see him dead, just as I have seen him for the past twenty years."

Ben felt a sharp disappointment. If Mrs. Parkington imagined that she was seeing her dead nephew, then in spite of appearances otherwise, she was unstable, and Ben could believe nothing she said.

"My niece is in trouble." There was no question in her voice. "Has she done something else?" She looked at Ben, expectantly.

Ben decided to go along with her, to a point, even if the poor lady was a little off. If the nephew really was dead, they had a whole new ball game. He said, "We only suspect she's done something. That's what I'm here for. To learn more about her, if you're willing to share some information with me."

He saw a grim look change her face from a sweet old lady to one who had carried a burden for a long time. Every line in her face sagged, and Ben thought he saw a deep sorrow, as if Mrs. Parkington were grieving. Then she looked up at him and a determination shining in her eyes.

"Take that painting down from that wall there," she demanded, pointing to the wall where the bombe' chest sat. Ben wondered what she thought the picture had to do with her nephew's death, but decided to placate her.

Ben pointed to the larger of an arrangement of paintings that hung above the chest. "This painting?" he asked. At her nod, Ben took it down and carried it back to her bedside.

"No, no," she said as he moved to place the painting on her lap. "You sit down and hold it under the lamp," she ordered. "Get the light directly on it."

He could tell the painting had been done by a novice. But, in spite of the awkward strokes, the scene was clearly that of a river with trees along its far bank. The focal point, however, seemed to be a large tree on the near bank in the center of the picture. It was dark under the tree, with indications of bushes and grasses growing wild. The more he looked at it; the more it disturbed him. It was a crude, yet powerful rendering of a dark scene, made with thick strokes of dark paint. An expression of anger, perhaps?

"Do you see it?" Mrs. Parkington asked.

"I'm sorry, but I don't understand what it is I'm supposed to see." Ben looked up from the painting to see the look of anticipation on her face.

"Well, of course not," she said. "I should have remembered." Edna Parkington pointed to the chest once more. "Look in the top drawer and get that magnifying glass." Ben obeyed her once more. "Now look under the large tree where you see all those bushes. Look for a faint light spot there and you'll see what I mean."

Ben trained the magnifying glass where he was told and began to make out the object that had been painted there. "Oh, my god," he whispered. Looking at the tiny figure painted into what could be meant by the artist to be a hole, things began to come together in Ben's mind. If not for Mrs. Parkington's revelations, he would never have guessed. Not in a million years. Rosalind was the artist.

"That is the first painting Rosalind did after she came to live with me," Edna said. "I could see she had a serious talent, so I paid for painting lessons for her from her trust fund money. For years I didn't know why she said it was just a matter of time until she would get the other half of her parent's fortune. She knew all along, of course, that her brother was dead, and planned to have him declared legally dead when the time came."

Edna's face looked drawn and white, as she continued. "Rosalind frequently had these fearful spells, when hate seemed to seep from her very pores. It was during one of these episodes that she made me look, just as you are looking now, at that plagued painting. She wanted to torture me with the knowledge that my nephew had died in that awful hole in the ground. Rosalind seemed to think I would do nothing about it, and she was right. I've kept silent for much too long time, damn my cowardly soul!"

Ben felt mildly shocked at Mrs. Parkington's vehemence. It seemed so out of character for her, even in the brief time he'd talked with her. But he could understand how she might feel responsible for her niece's evil ways. He was feeling a growing dread that gathered his stomach into a knot and urged him to immediate action. But Ben knew it was important to listen to everything Mrs. Parkington had to say about her niece, so forced himself to concentrate on what she was saying.

Please, Amy, be careful! Ben thought, as he turned his attention to the elderly woman's tale of horror.

"Then her temper tantrums became worse," Edna said, her voice harsh with emotion. "And one day I found my precious little Hector, my Chihuahua, dead in the middle of my bed. She had split his stomach open with a knife and blood was everywhere." She shuddered at the memory. "A few days later, she hanged her own kitten by his neck with one of her shoe laces. I was terrified of her, and Rosalind knew it. The insanity that lurked in the Anderson genes came out in full force in my brother's-in-law daughter."

"I went to Dr. Menche, a friend of mine, and told him what she had done to the two poor little animals. He helped me get her into an institution for the 'mentally unfit,' I think was the euphemism being used then for criminally insane. We had her admitted under the pretension of protecting Rosalind from herself. Of course, I never believed that she would hurt herself. Rosalind would hurt only those she perceived as not allowing her to have her way. I never told Dr. Menche about Rosalind killing her brother. I should have, but I thought she'd be in that place the rest of her life."

Tears rolled down Mrs. Parkington's face, and Ben wanted to comfort her, but knew that precious time was slipping by and he needed to get to the telephone as quickly as possible. Fear for Amy jangled his nerves, so that it was an effort just to stay put. But he also knew he needed to hear the rest of Mrs. Parkington's story.

"Anyway," she said, "that's where she stayed until almost two years ago when the board of trustees decided to release her after an incompetent psychiatrist declared her cured. The overcrowded facility needed her space, quote, 'for those more dangerous to society,' unquote. Rosalind came home and gradually took over my life.

"I was afraid to sleep at night, for fear she'd kill me. She threatened to do so regularly. Then one day, Rosalind announced that she was committing me to this facility, and that I was to give her power of attorney over my estate. I didn't argue. Any place was better than living in the same house with her." Edna looked at Ben, her eyes wide with remembered fright. He could see her whole body trembling beneath the covers. "Rosalind still intends to kill me, Detective, I just don't know how or when. She'll make it look either accidental or natural, so she won't be blamed, you can be sure of that."

"No, she is not going to kill you, Mrs. Parkington." Ben reached out to pat her hand, trying to give her at least some reassurance. "I am leaving immediately for Arkansas, but first I will call and have the police pick up Rosalind. She won't be able to harm you ever again."

Ben took the painting from the chair where he'd placed it and put it back on its hook. He turned back to the frail woman who was looking at him with hope in her eyes. "Please, for your own safety, promise me that you won't tell anyone on the staff that I've been in here. And that you won't show anyone else what you showed me in that painting."

He could see the deep sadness mirrored in the woman's eyes. He couldn't even imagine the torture of the mental anguish Rosalind had put her through. He became even more antsy to get back home.

"I've been keeping secrets for more years than I care to remember, Mr. Edwards. A few more days can't matter." She bowed her head, as if ashamed. "But if I hadn't been a coward, I might have kept Rosalind in the sanitarium. At one time I had decided to go to Dr. Menche and tell him about her killing Hank, but the good doctor died in the fire that burned his house down late one night. I always thought Rosalind had done that, too, but I just didn't have the strength to fight her any longer."

Again, Ben felt a surging urgency to make his call to Frank. "I have to go now, Ma'am," he said. "But I promise I will do everything in my power to get you out of here after I've taken care of things back home."

"Where will I go?" Anxiety traced the wrinkles on her forehead. "To a nursing home? I think I'd just as soon stay here."

"If you have enough money to pay for staying here, Mrs. Parkington, you have enough to pay a private nurse to stay with you in your own home. I do have to leave now, but I should be back in a few days. Keep strong, as you have been for so many years."

With a final squeeze of her hand, Ben went over to the door and eased it open to check the hallway. It was blessedly empty and the nurses' station was once again unattended. With a final wave to Mrs. Parkington, he slipped out into the hallway, breathing a prayer of thanks for the attendants' slothful ways.

Ben retrieved his bag from the stairwell, and quietly made his way back to the first floor. He headed for the pay phone he'd seen on his way up. It seemed to take forever to punch in the series of numbers requested by the computer-generated voice in his ear, but he finally connected with the Ashley Springs police station. No one knew where Frank was. Ben began to give hurried orders to the deputy who came to the phone at his request. His next call was to the Mobile National Airport.

The reservation clerk said they had a flight leaving for Memphis in one hour and five minutes. Ben made a reservation with his Visa, then called Slade Angstrom, who said he could meet him in Memphis. Slade didn't ask questions, hearing in Ben's voice the stress of a man in a big hurry.

"I'll be leaving Mobile in about an hour," Ben told his friend.

"I'll be waiting for you," Slade promised.

Ben's final call was to Amy's house. He let the phone ring ten times before accepting that she wasn't at home. Since it was after ten o' clock, he'd fully expected her to answer. Feeling even more fear for Amy, he hung up and left the building. He just hoped there would still be a taxi roaming the streets at this time of night.

CHAPTER 47

▼

Sheriff Morgan got to the Waggoner home a little after five o' clock. Amy, Nancy, Martha, and Anita had been playing gin rummy at the dining room table for most of the afternoon. It kept their hands busy and their minds off all the things they didn't want to think about. Frank asked to speak to Nancy privately. The three women, having already planned for that event, had gone outside to sit on the back patio.

They no sooner got settled into their chairs than the phone rang. Anita went in to answer it and immediately called Amy. It was Bob Mayson at Simeon's House Inn. He told Amy that Barney had told him where to find her, and that Tim was being taken by ambulance to the hospital. Tim had begun spitting up blood. It didn't look good, Bob said.

Amy hurriedly called Barney to pick her up, then told the three women what Bob had said. Anita's eyes filled with tears. "She may lose her husband, too," she said, bitterness in her voice. "But at least she knows that Mr. Spencer loves and cares for her."

Amy knew that Anita's hurt was still too fresh, what with the double blow of her husband's murder and learning that Abner spent his last evening on earth in the company of another woman. Anita had a long period of healing, both emotionally and spiritually, ahead of her.

Barney pulled up to the curb and blew his horn, and Amy left Martha to console Anita. While Barney drove the few blocks to the shop, Amy explained what Bob Mayson had said. "No matter where you look, there's trouble," she said, and then she was crying. "I feel as if the world is upside down and is never going to get straightened up, Barn."

"I know you do, Boss. It's been a very rough few weeks here, just about more than a body can take, I'd say. But as soon as they can get this murder business settled, I think you'll find life is as good as ever. We just have to hang in there." He reached over and squeezed Amy's shoulder. "You've got a very lonesome buddy waiting for you."

They drove up to the back of their shop. Hannibal had heard the truck motor and was reared up in one of the windows. They could hear his excited, "woof!" through the shop walls.

"Wait a sec, what are your plans?" Barney said, as Amy got out of the truck and started toward her car.

"I'm going over to the hospital to see what Pinkie needs for me to do. If they transfer Mr. Tim to Little Rock and Pinkie wants me to, I'll go with her. I'll call you as soon as I know."

"If it comes to that, I'll go with you," Barney called to her, as she started to drive away. He heard her, "Okay," before she put up her window.

Amy hurried into the hospital and asked where the Spencers were. She found Pinkie in the hallway outside of intensive care. Her friend explained that the doctors wanted to fly Tim to Little Rock. "They think he needs care they can't provide here. I'm waiting until the doctor can decide if Tim should make the trip this afternoon or wait until morning."

While they waited, Amy told Pinkie what the nursing home had told her about Mrs. Sanchez. "For some reason, her dying right at this time seems unnatural, although I know she was in her eighties." Amy wrinkled her brow. "I keep thinking there's something about the day she died that I should remember, but I can't think what it is."

"After I hung up from talking to you, I was sorry I gave you the information on Mrs. Sanchez," Pinkie admitted. "I don't want you involved in any way with the murders, and I shouldn't have encouraged you by telling you what I did. I'm also sorry about Mrs. Sanchez, but maybe that's for the best."

"If I could just think of what it is that's bothering me about her," Amy shrugged. "Too late for that now. So, change of subject. I'm supposed to go out to Gayle's for dinner this evening, but, I'm not in the mood for making happy talk."

"It'll do you good to be with a person your own age and think of something other than all the terrible things that keep happening. I think you should go and have a good time for a change."

Amy doubted she would have a good time, but she didn't tell Pinky that. It was almost seven o' clock before the Spencers left for Little Rock, Tim by helicopter and Pinkie by car with Bob Merriweather.

As Amy drove back to the shop she felt strongly that she shouldn't go to Gayle's, but had no real reason for feeling that way. She wondered why everything seemed so hard now. She really had no excuse to not go, and she was too tired to think of one.

At the shop Barney was closing doors and shutting windows in preparation for going home, with Hannibal following his every footstep. Amy told him about Tim being at the hospital. They discussed the predicament Pinkie and Tim were in now. Then Amy stood to go. She said, "By the way, I promised Gayle I would have dinner with her tonight, remember? Of course, since it's so late, I'm sure she'll call it off again."

"You don't sound disappointed," he said.

"Actually, I'm not. I like Gayle, but for some reason for the past couple of days, I've been thinking I'd rather not be around her as much. Why is that, I wonder?" Amy was genuinely puzzled at her own feelings.

"I have no idea, but maybe you'd better follow your instinct on this one, or your ESP, or whatever it is. If you feel hesitant there's got to be a reason behind it."

"Right," Amy agreed. "But now I have to call her and apologize."

When she reached Gayle, she explained what had happened with Tim. "I'm afraid I forgot everything else, and now it's so late, you'd probably rather I not come out this evening."

"Yes, I do want you to come," Gayle said, to Amy's chagrin. "And don't worry about being late. This is not a formal affair, you know, so come just as you are. You can have a good meal, we'll talk a while, and then you can go home for a good night's rest."

"Okay," Amy agreed. "Look, I have to run by the house first, so I should be there in thirty or forty minutes."

She put Hannibal in the car with her. He moved over until he could lean against her shoulder as Amy drove toward home. Amy had reached the edge of town when she noticed that the air conditioner had the car freezing cold. She reached over to push the button to a lower setting, only to see it wasn't on. Amy checked the air vent and saw that it was open. The outside air had been very warm when she'd gotten into her car. She felt her stomach draw up in dread. Was it happening again?

The cold increased until she shivered uncontrollably, and Amy suddenly felt very sleepy. Hannibal whined and pushed against her, as if he knew something wasn't right. It was his intervention that kept her alert enough to pull the car to the side of the road, then the daylight disappeared and another world closed in around her.

The next thing she knew, Hannibal was whimpering and Barney was pleading with her. "Amy, Amy!" He was leaning into the car and patting her face."Are you all right? What happened?"

She raised her head from the back of the seat to look around. "Yes, I'm all right, Barn. At least I think I am."

Amy felt muzzy as if she had awoken from a deep sleep. Looking around, she realized she was parked in the middle of the drive in front of Green's Family Restaurant. There were several people waiting in their cars to get out, and more standing nearby, obviously curious about what was happening. She didn't doubt that some of them knew her.

Struggling up in her seat, Amy felt embarrassed and confused. "Just let me get out of their way, Barn." She reached for the key to start her car and was relieved to know that she'd at least had enough sense to turn off her motor.

"I'm driving you home," Barney said.

Amy didn't argue when he opened the door and began to seat himself, as she slid over to make space for him, crowding an anxious Hannibal against the passenger door. "Where is your truck?"

"I'm in a parking space across from you," he said as he drove away. "I'll pick up the Suburban at the house."

"What did I do?" Amy said. "I must have put on quite a show, huh?"

Barney's face was drawn tight with worry. "When I saw you pull your car over onto that driveway, I thought you wanted to tell me something, so I swung into a parking space nearby. But you just sat there. Hannibal had started barking, so I knew he was upset. When I got your door open, you were crying and saying, "Please don't do that! Oh, dear God, please don't!' That's when I called your name and patted your face and you came around." His voice was ragged with fear. "Amy, what is going on here? I have to say, you're scaring the hell out of me."

"I'm scaring the hell out of myself," she admitted. "It was another of those visual premonitions, for lack of a better description. But what if I hadn't pulled over just then? I could have killed somebody."

"Yeah, like yourself, maybe," Barney said. "You have *got* to go to a doctor, or to someone who can help you stop this stuff."

"I agree, Barney. But right now, I have to talk to the sheriff."

Amy picked up her car phone and punched in the sheriff's number. It rang, then gave an interrupting ring, which meant the call was automatically transferring to another number. A voice at the other end announced, "Ashley Springs Police Station, how may I help you?"

Amy identified herself and asked where she could find the sheriff. "I must talk to him immediately," she said.

"I can ring his deputy, Ms. Bordeaux. One moment."

Pete Hammond answered. Quickly she explained the urgency of her speaking to the sheriff. To tell you the truth," Pete said, "we're trying to find him ourselves. We haven't been able to contact him since he left Nancy Waggoner's house. Can I help?"

"No, no," Amy insisted. "I've got to tell him that he's in terrible danger. I'm not sure where it will happen, but someone is going to kill him if he's not warned right away!"

"Now just a minute, Amy." Pete's voice lost it's friendly tone. "If you know something I don't, I expect you'd better come on in here and explain what you're talking about."

"There's no time for that, Pete. Just find him, and then don't let him out of your sight." Amy put her phone back on its bracket on the dash.

By now Barney had pulled into Amy's driveway. He parked near her front door and killed the motor, looking even more worried at what he had heard her tell Pete.

"You've got to stop this right now," he demanded. "I don't know what it's all about, or why you're saying the things you are, but there's got to be a way for you to get out of this nightmare."

"Right now, Barn, what you can do is go help Pete find Frank Morgan. I'd go looking for him myself, but he wouldn't respond very well to me telling him he has to stay with someone. He'd be sure to do the wrong thing then."

She leaned on Barney's shoulder a second, then said, "I'm not in any danger from this, so there's no need for you to be so worried. Please, Barney," she begged, "help them find the sheriff. I'm going straight out to Gayle's, so you don't have to worry about me being by myself. I'll make my excuses to leave right after the meal, then I'll go to the police station. Okay?"

He looked at her silently for a moment and Amy could see his fear for her. "What did you see?" he asked softly. She knew exactly what he meant.

"I saw Sheriff Morgan being killed," she said simply. "I don't know where he was, it was dark, with only enough light for me to see who he was. There was a figure dressed in black leaning over him with a knife raised up to strike. When I saw what was about to happen I asked her not to do it. I nearly fainted with terror when the person turned around as if to look at me, but of course, she couldn't see me. Then she turned back to the sheriff and stuck the knife into his throat. I heard him try to call out, but it was more of a wail, or scream. Then he made this hideous gurgling sound, then nothing. That was when I heard you calling my name."

"Do you realize what you just said, Amy? You said 'she.' My god, girl, you're saying you saw a woman kill the sheriff."

Amy was as shocked as Barney. Up to this moment, after every nightmarish vision she had assumed she'd been watching a man at work. But there had been a certain unsettled feeling after each scene. Something in the shape and movement of the person had been telling her it wasn't a man. For some reason, the idea that the killer was a woman frightened her even more.

She stepped out of the car and started toward the house. Barney and a strangely subdued Hannibal followed her.

"For now," she told the two of them, "I'm going to freshen up, then go to Gayle's as I promised her I would. Barney, I want you to go help find the sheriff, and then not let him out of your sight. You can tell him I said I think the killer is a woman, but I haven't a clue as to who the woman is. When she turned toward me, her face was in a dark shadow so that I couldn't see her features. If the sheriff knows he's looking for a woman, he might have an idea who she is."

"And what if you pass out again?"

"I won't, Barn. I received the warning and that's the end of it for now. I have a certainty that it won't recur at least for a while. There's lots of time between each one."

Hannibal slipped through the door ahead of her, and Barney, without saying any more, turned toward his garage apartment. He did not trust her 'certainty,' and had no intention of letting Amy be on her own. He would wait for her to get a little distance ahead of him, and then follow her. Since he knew exactly where she was going, he saw no problem in keeping up with her. Frank Morgan would just have to look out for himself.

After Amy's car disappeared down the driveway, Barney picked up the Suburban's keys, prepared to follow her. The telephone rang just as he shut his door. Knowing he could catch up with Amy easily, he opened the door and picked up the phone. "Barney Scott speaking."

"Barney, this is Pete. Listen, is Amy still there?"

"Just drove off, Pete. Why?"

"I got this call from Ben Edwards in Mobile, Alabama."

"What is he doing in Mobile?"

"Tell you later. Do you know where Amy was going?"

"Out to Gayle Armbruster's house for dinner. Why are you interested in her whereabouts, Pete?" Barney didn't care for the way the conversation was going.

"Ben said we should pick her up and keep her with us, but she'll be okay at Ms.. Armbruster's, don't you think? He just wanted to be sure that she wasn't by herself. Look, everyone's gone home." Barney figured Pete was referring to Lattison's men. "Ralph Henderson's pulling protection duty at Mrs. Waggoner's, so me and Archie could use an extra hand, what with both Ben and the sheriff out of pocket. Could you come in? We have to pick up someone, and I'd feel better if you came along. I'll get you deputized, and you can serve as back up for the two of us."

"Sounds like a rough one. Who is it that you're supposed to pick up?"

"Rather not tell you on the phone, Barney. I'll fill you in when you get here." The clunk in his ear told Barney that Pete had not waited for his answer.

Barney stood by the phone after he'd put it down, undecided as to what he should do. Pete had never asked for help before, so it must be something special. Barney looked at his watch. He would drive out to Gayle's first to be sure that Amy got there. Then, after he helped Pete, he would go back, park at the end of the driveway, and wait to escort Amy back home. She'd just have to get mad if she wanted to. He locked his door and hurried to the Suburban.

Barney drove swiftly west on Highway 166. Amy must have been going at a pretty good speed, because he never did catch sight of her car. However, when Barney turned into the driveway that led to Armbruster's house, he could see the white of Amy's car parked near the front porch. Not wanting her to see him, Barney put his vehicle in reverse and backed out into the highway, turning toward town.

He couldn't help but be curious about Pete's request for his presence. Barney hoped it wasn't going to be too wild an assignment, and certainly not one that would take up a lot of time, because he wanted to be outside Gayle's house well before Amy was ready to leave. Barney would bet, though, that Amy and Gayle would get to visiting, and Amy would stay a lot longer than she intended. Still, he'd be waiting for her, whenever that was.

CHAPTER 48

▼

Much earlier that day, after Frank had talked to Nancy, he felt disgusted and confused in equal parts. He'd had to admit to himself that he had been wrong all along. He had been so certain that the killer was the Anderson boy, parading as Billy Joe Smith. But his gut told him the skeletal remains Jim found would prove to be those of Henry Anderson, Junior. Frank had looked at the plat of the area around the Anderson house and learned that the river bank where the grave was located, had been part of the Anderson property many years ago. So the boy had never left his home. He had been murdered by his own sister.

Nancy Waggoner said that she'd seen Billy Joe driving the veterinarian's truck away from the old country club up on Bitterweed Mountain, and that there had been a woman in the truck with him. She couldn't identify her. The woman had been wearing a cap, like a captain's cap, Nancy said, so she couldn't really see the woman's features.

Frank believed that Smith was merely a pawn in the deadly game being played out in his area. Smith was not the psycho with an agenda, but the easy dupe for a beautiful woman who needed a fall guy. Somehow, and Frank thought he knew how, she probably had convinced him to kill Bud Purefoy. In the Nancy Waggoner incident, the deep scratches on Billy Joe's arms proved him to be her attacker. The DNA test would nail that down. With just the right kind of encouragement, Billy might even confess to his complicity in Bud's death. In any case, the killer would expect Billy Joe to rat as soon as he realized he could be charged for all of the killings. That meant she would be leaving town very soon.

Frank also believed this 'she' was Gayle Armbruster. She was the right age to be Rosalind Anderson. She lived in her former home, and all the killings had occurred after she had come to town. Rosalind, in that guise, had the perfect opportunity to approach the men because everyone of them in that particular group was vulnerable to a beautiful woman.

Also, Rosalind had plenty of motivation, as Frank saw it. The sick things that happened to her as a child, had apparently changed her into an adult monster. He would bet his professional reputation that the reason for the length of time between crime and revenge was that Rosalind had been in an institution somewhere, unable to reach the men until now. He planned to uncover that fact and a whole lot more once he had her put away. After his trip, Ben should be able to confirm Frank's suspicions.

His mind went back to the skeleton that Jim Arnold had discovered, its knees drawn up in the fetal position. In that small tomb, they had found an old piece of candle lying near the skull, a toy gun, a broken pocket knife, and a sterling silver fork next to a Spode china plate. All of the artifacts were pitiful evidence that the young boy had sought refuge there, perhaps where he thought he'd be safe, not only from his father's brutal treatment, but from a sister he feared.

Why had she killed him? Maybe he had threatened to tell the police the truth, that she had murdered their parents. Or, if he had helped her kill their parents, his conscience had driven him to desire confession. Then maybe he hadn't provoked her, and Rosalind just decided to finish the annihilation of her entire family. These were all guesses on his part, but Frank planned to have more than mere guesses before the evening was over. The time for hesitation and caution was over, as far as he was concerned.

Because of his own connection to the past, Frank hoped that when he confronted Gayle, she would admit to him that she was Rosalind. She might even confess to her role in the deaths of the seven men, including Purefoy. He would Mirandize her, then take her to his office where he would call in Lattison and his men. Frank admitted to himself that he wouldn't tackle this alone if it were Henry Anderson he had to deal with. But Gayle was only a woman, and with the advantage of his size and strength, he could handle anything she threw at him.

Frank told Pete he would be in touch later to see if Ben had called in, but did not tell his deputy where he was going. He thought he stood a better chance of getting Rosalind to confess to him if he approached her alone.

He drove to his office first. There was something niggling at him, and Frank knew from past experience that it meant he needed to pay attention to that feeling. He wanted to check out one more thing before he made his trip out to the

Anderson house. The courthouse was closed for the day, so he unlocked the side door and went into the dark building. The clouds that had built up in the west made the unlit spaces almost as dark as night, but Frank didn't turn on the lobby lights. He meant to be gone before anyone realized he was here.

As he climbed the marble stairs, the echos of his high-heeled cowboy boots striking the hard surface of the steps made it sound as if more than one person was on the stairs. He caught himself looking over his shoulder to make certain he was alone. Frank felt ashamed of the relief that washed over him, as he reached the safety of his office and locked the door behind himself

"You're worse than a nervous nanny," Frank lectured himself out loud, as he groped for the lamp on his desk.

In the dim light afforded by the lamp's green shade, he searched his key ring until he found the one he needed. Unlocking the bottom drawer of the file cabinet, he took out a long, slender cardboard box. He placed it on his desk and removed its lid. An old, blood-stained Raggedy Ann doll smiled its embroidered smile at him, as he lifted it from its bed of tissue paper. The memory of Rosalind's doll had teased at Frank's mind until it had convinced him that it had something to say about the present murders. The doll was what he had sent Ben Edwards to pick up in Mount Veda.

He slowly hefted the doll in his hand, noting as he had years ago how heavy it was.

Frank had noticed that fact back then because his sister's child had a doll like this one and always insisted that her Uncle Frank hold her "baby." His niece's doll had been light as a feather compared to the one he now held. Rosalind Anderson had kicked and screamed and fought like a wildcat to hold on to the doll that terrible day when they found her slaughtered parents. Frank now figured she'd had a different reason for not letting the doll out of her arms rather than just wanting to hold on to a favorite toy.

His large fingers fumbled with the snaps, buttons, and hooks until the doll's cloth body lay bare, ready for examination. He turned the doll over on its face and saw what he was looking for, a clumsily sewn slit which ran from the doll's neck, down to its lumpy buttocks. He carefully cut the old threads with his pocket knife, then slipped his fingers into the opening. Rosalind had hidden her diary inside the doll, a small white book with a latch on one side and the words MY DIARY in tarnished gold across the front cover. It was locked. Frank searched the doll for the key, but couldn't find it. Rosalind probably had it around her neck on a chain that day, hidden by the large collar on the dress she'd worn.

He again took out his knife and, with the tip of the blade, carefully twisted open the flimsy lock. Frank then read a few pages toward the back of the book. To his great satisfaction, they confirmed that Rosalind had killed her parents and, that same night, her brother. A scenario played through his mind as he imagined Rosalind luring her brother out into the dark night, walking him to the river bank.

Poor Henry would be scared to go with her, yet even more afraid to defy his sister. Perhaps she'd held the knife against his back and told him to crawl into the godforsaken hole. Frank could almost feel the little boy's terror when he'd realized that everything he'd feared about his sister was true. Rosalind meant to kill him, too.

Out on the river that afternoon, the lawmen had discovered the mouth of the tunnel. It had been piled high with rocks, and when those were removed, there was a thick tree limb that had been shoved into the passage way to the cave. The little boy probably begged all that time for her to let him out, but the cold-blooded monster had gone off and left him to die a lingering death from dehydration and starvation. Frank felt a deep revulsion against the cruelty with which the girl treated an innocent victim.

He put the doll back into its box and slipped the small book into his pocket. Turning out the desk lamp, he felt his way back down the stairs and out into the darkening day, where the faint sound of thunder warned him of a coming storm. He started the county's Suburban and drove out of the parking lot, turning in the direction of the Anderson house.

The sky had darkened even more while he'd been in his office, so that the last light of day was smothered by the thick clouds. Gusts of wind battered at his windows as Frank turned into the Anderson driveway and approached the old two-story house. The large oak trees that lined the driveway were swaying in the strengthening wind and added to the desolate feeling Frank had developed when he'd left the town behind. He had turned off his radio so that his deputies couldn't call him, and the absence of the familiar static and occasional voices made him feel even more alone.

"Get a grip," Frank said aloud, hoping to break the growing feeling that he shouldn't have come without back up. He reminded himself again that he was at least twice her size and handling her should be no problem. He had to admit though, that Rosalind hadn't done all she'd done by relying solely on brute strength. Frank wouldn't give her the chance to get close to him until he cuffed her.

Dark shadows, cast by the cloudy sky that was only slightly lighter than the ground, met and coalesced underneath the trees that surrounded the Anderson house. Vision was poor except for the areas lit by his vehicle's headlights. As Frank had pulled up in front of the house, but before he had switched off his lights, he saw that the front door was open.

Gayle stood there, waiting for him. He walked toward the steps and an involuntary shiver ran down Frank's spine, causing goose bumps to pop out on his arms. A flash of lightning, followed by a loud clap of thunder told him the storm was moving closer, and added to his sense of growing unease.

"Good evening, Sheriff." Gayle said, as he came up the porch steps. "Is something wrong?"

"Good evening, Ms.. Armbruster." Frank reached down and patted his gun holster, as if for reassurance. Her eyes followed the movement. "No," he said, "nothing's wrong. I just need to talk to you for a few minutes."

She stepped back for him to enter. "Of course, please, come in." She turned to lead him into the living room. The dim light from one lamp didn't remove the darkness cast by the heavy furniture in the rather small room. She gestured for him to have a seat, but Frank chose to stand. Gayle perched on one arm of the sofa, looking perfectly at ease.

"Have you ever lived in Ashley Springs before you came here a few months ago?" he asked bluntly, wanting to get done with this very sticky situation.

Gayle seemed unperturbed by his question. "No, I haven't. Why do you ask?"

"You've never lived in this house before?" Frank insisted.

"I told you I have not. I saw this house and thought it perfect for me, so here I am. Why do you ask if I've lived here before?"

Frank didn't like her calm manner. He'd hoped for more of a reaction to his question. "There was a young girl who lived in this house over twenty years ago," he said, watching Gayle carefully. "She left here at a young age, but it would be natural for her to want to come back, to lay to rest any ghosts of the past that might still haunt her. I thought that person could be you."

"That girl wouldn't, in your mind, have some connection with the recent murders, would she?" Gayle stood up and moved toward the front door, causing him to turn toward her new position.

Frank tensed at her words. He kept his eyes on her, prepared for any sudden moves on her part. Something in her face had changed. The dim light kept him from seeing her eyes clearly, but for a moment he could have sworn he saw a spark of red in her enlarged pupils. Again, he felt the rill of goose bumps on his arms as a slight shiver made its way down his spine. He should have brought one of his deputies with him.

C H A P T E R   49

▼

It was almost dark by the time Amy reached Gayle's house. The storm front rumbled at a distance, and stabs of lightning lit the sky intermittently, making the trees and bushes surreal in the strobe-lit world. Her imagination made her shudder as she thought of the dark history attached to the Anderson house. It had been the house of a wealthy family, designed to express that wealth, very large and built in the complex style so popular in the early 1900's.

There were twin turrets and various levels of roofing, each with multiple gables. Intricate carvings trimmed the eaves of each section. Mullioned windows reflected the flashes of lightning that were moving dangerously close. The whole scene reminded Amy of the haunted house she'd seen in replays of *Psycho* on the television. It had loomed over the Bates Motel, dark, mysterious, and threatening. In that movie and others of its genre, there was always a storm to increase the sense of violence to come.

A feeling of dread gripped her as she ran up the steps and onto the shelter of the porch. Amy knew she was letting her imagination run wild, but she couldn't resist looking around to see if she was alone. She nearly jumped out of her skin when Gayle opened the door before she could knock.

"Just in time," Gayle said, as the sky opened up and rain began to pour down in heavy sheets. She closed the door and the downpour became a muted roar on the porch roof.

She looked elegant in black jeans, a black tank top with rhinestones around the scoop neck, and black patent Ros Hommerson sandals. Amy wished she'd taken an extra minute to change out of her own rumpled green linen trousers and matching top. She gave a mental shrug at her vanity and followed Gayle. She was here, Amy reminded herself, only to fulfill an obligation, and how she was dressed was of the least importance.

Gayle led her into the living room which opened into a formal dining room. Both rooms were papered with an elegant cabbage rose pattern on a background of dark green. The blue flowers complemented the hallway's forest green stripes on a light blue background. The woodwork, stained deep walnut, seemed to drink up the light. The overstuffed couch and two matching chairs even had anti-macassars on their arms and backs.

All of it was beautiful, but too gloomy for Amy's taste, even though it was well done and very impressive. Amy knew that the renovation took a lot of energy and time, not to mention money, and Gayle was only leasing the house. And now she planned to leave. To Amy this didn't make sense.

"I'm sure the rest of the house is just as striking," she said in an attempt to be polite.

"Later you'll have the opportunity to make that judgement for yourself," Gayle said, smiling, "but right now, I've got some Chinese food that needs my attention." She led the way to the end of the hallway and through a swinging door to the left.

The kitchen continued the decorative scheme of the twenties with its high wooden cabinets and glass doors with metal latch knobs. On the walls, Gayle had used a navy blue wallpaper with a very small red and yellow print, and an egg yolk yellow for the woodwork. Touches of deep red were used in canisters, a rooster-shaped cookie jar, curtains, and hand towels. Amy was a bit overwhelmed with so many strong colors in such a small space. Amy wouldn't have thought of Gayle's taste running to roosters, either.

Amy reminded herself that she really didn't know the woman all that well, although it seemed that they had been acquainted longer than three weeks.

The wonderful smell that pervaded the kitchen distracted her from those thoughts and reminded Amy that she hadn't eaten in several hours. Gayle opened the bottle of wine Amy had brought with her and filled two wine flutes she'd placed on the counter.

"Here's to us," Gayle said, as she tapped the rim of her glass against Amy's. Her hands had a slight tremble that made Amy wonder why she was so tense.

"So you're leaving us, Gayle." Amy said, after having a sip of wine. "And just when you've gotten this house in such beautiful shape and beginning to make your own place in the community. We'll all miss you, but I understand about your concern for your aunt."

Amy blinked her eyes. She was seeing a blurring of the air around Gayle, a faint aura-like shadow. She took another sip of her wine, hoping that it was just her tiredness that was affecting her eyes. Amy blinked a couple of times, then looked back at Gayle

The blur had taken the form of a faint, but dark cloud hovering over Amy's hostess, and she felt a strong urge to simply pick up her car keys and leave. But she was determined that an overly active imagination, brought on by a stressful day not send her into another of those dreaded visions. She tried to focus on what Gayle was saying.

"Well, you know, family first and all that." Gayle was standing at the stove with her back to Amy now, stirring the vegetables in a large wok. She sounded a bit flippant about her aunt's illness, but maybe that's the way she dealt with life changes. Or maybe there was no aunt, the thought repeated itself in Amy's mind.

"Yes, I do know," she said. "If anything happened to Leigh, I would do what-ever it took to make things better for her."

Amy felt the resistance in the air between them. Apparently Gayle didn't want to talk about her upcoming move. The shadow that hovered over Gayle was gone now. Amy felt a flood of relief. She had to keep a better grip on her imagination if she was going to enjoy the good meal Gayle was preparing.

This is the last time I have to be in her company, she thought. *Lord, help me to stay on an even keel here.*

"You have a beautiful collection of furniture," she said, in an effort to stay mentally present. "I noticed all the pieces match. Where did you manage to find so many early twentieth century sets?"

"Most of it was already in the house," Gayle said, as she continued stirring the mixture in the wok. "There are a lot of scratches and blemishes on most of it, but considering that the house was rented out for twenty years, it's a wonder every-thing is in as good shape as it is. I found the lamps and small tables, along with a few chairs, in the attic. I had fun dragging them out and finding places for each piece."

Following Gayle's instructions, Amy filled glasses with ice water, placed the wine bottle in an ice bucket next to Gayle's place at the table, and prepared their individual salads from a large bowl of greens.

"I hope you don't mind eating in the kitchen," Gayle said.

Earlier, Amy had pushed open the swinging door between the kitchen and the dining room for another peek. Although the dining room was beautiful, it seemed especially gloomy looking. She much preferred eating in the kitchen.

"I eat all my meals in my kitchen," she said. "Of course, that's where Hannibal eats, so he keeps me company."

"I'm sure he makes a wonderful companion." Amy thought she actually heard a wistful note in Gayle's voice. "I once thought I'd like to have a dog."

"What changed your mind?"

"I was living with a person who didn't like dogs. Cats were okay, but not dogs." She abruptly changed the subject. "I think I have everything ready now." Gayle poured more wine into their glasses, then put the vegetable and chicken mixture into two small casserole dishes with lids. She did the same with the fried rice, then placed two sets of chop sticks by their plates.

"Let's eat," Gayle said, as she waved toward the chair where she had placed two of the bowls. Amy didn't argue. She was surprised at how hungry she felt.

"This is wonderful," Amy said, after she'd gotten her first taste. "You are a very good cook, Gayle. As you know, there are no places around here where you can get really wonderful Chinese food, so I have to drive down to Little Rock occasionally to get my fix." Amy laughed. "Maybe I should learn to cook my own as you have."

Quiet settled around the women as they worked on diminishing portions of the rice, chicken, and vegetables. Outside, the storm had lessened until only an occasional rumble of distant thunder broke the silence.

Amy wondered if Barney and the other men had found Sheriff Morgan yet. She pulled her mind away from the dread those thoughts gave her. Instead, she thought of the day she had spent with Ben, and how Hannibal had sat in the back seat of Ben's car with his head between them "A penny?" Gayle said. "From your smile, you must be thinking of something pleasant. Can you share it with me?"

"I was thinking about something Hannibal did."

"You love that dog, don't you?"

"How could I not love him?" Amy laughed. "He'd be immensely pleased if he knew he was being talked about so much, but he's a charmer, just like some men I know."

"Any man in particular?" Gayle looked interested.

Again, Amy laughed. "You're almost as good at asking questions as someone else I know. Would you pass those delicious egg rolls, please?" She had no intention of sharing with Gayle the special feeling she was developing for Ben. Amy was only now admitting it to herself.

She chattered on for several minutes about her plans to build an adult-size doll house in one corner of her shop in which to display the china dolls that she planned to order. When Amy finished the last egg roll, she pushed back her plate. For the last several minutes she'd had a growing sense of urgency to end the evening with Gayle and to get back to her own world.

Gayle had simply stared at her the whole time she talked about the doll house. In fact, Amy sensed that her hostess had become tense again. It was a different tension from that Amy felt during their exchange about Gayle's moving away. Amy couldn't put her finger on it, but it was as if Gayle were waiting for something. She kept glancing at the door that led into the hallway. Amy felt an especially strong urge to leave here and return to the safety of her own world.

"This has been a wonderful meal, Gayle," she said, pushing back her chair and rising. "No restaurant could have done better."

"Good. That means that you're ready for dessert."

Over Amy's protests, Gayle took from the refrigerator two crystal compotes filled with fluffy, lemon mousse, topped with a twist of lime. Gayle placed one in front of her. "Light as the brush of a butterfly's wing," she said.

Amy reluctantly resumed her seat. It was obvious that Gayle had gone to a lot of trouble to prepare the dessert, and it would only take a few more minutes to show her appreciation.

"With such a poetic description, how can I resist?"

To pass the next several minutes, Amy told Gayle about the time she had spent with the Waggoners and how difficult it had been to watch their grief.

"I'm sure it's been very hard for them," Gayle agreed. "It's so generous of you to give your time like that. Most people wouldn't bother."

"Sometimes it's easier to help someone than it is to sit back and do nothing."

"I should do more volunteer work, myself," Gayle said. "But there's always something else I need to do. Now it's too late."

They both jumped when they heard a loud thump on the ceiling of the kitchen. It sounded as if a very heavy object had dropped on the floor above.

CHAPTER 50

▼

"Gayle," Amy felt the sting of alarm. "Is someone else here?"

"Only my cat," she said. "Sorry, I didn't think about her being up there. She loves to play, and she's always knocking things over. She's good company though, so I allow for her shenanigans. Sorry she gave us such a start."

"You didn't mention her when we were talking about pets," Amy remarked. "What kind of cat is she?"

"As I said," Gayle didn't seem pleased with Amy's reminder, "I forgot she was up there. She's mostly Siamese, but she thinks she's human."

Another thud came from above, this one not as heavy as the first. Gayle frowned. "It sounds as if she's decided to trash my room." She laid her napkin beside her plate and scooted back her chair. "Excuse me while I go check things out. If I leave her closed up too long, she can get just plain destructive. I won't be a minute."

Amy started to say she would leave, but before she could speak, her hostess was gone.

The house became very quiet with Gayle's departure. The storm had moved so far away, there wasn't even that distant noise to break the silence. Amy felt edgy. Maybe she'd leave and call Gayle back to apologize after she got home. But that seemed too rude. Besides, she knew this was probably the last time she would see Gayle, so she'd wait a few more minutes and say a proper thank-you and good-bye.

She wondered again about the sheriff. Had they found him, and was he all right? With all the killing that had gone on, Amy was afraid even the sheriff could become a victim. He was in her vision of him this afternoon, and she prayed that this time her mental pictures were completely mistaken.

Shaking her head to rid herself of such gloomy thoughts, Amy poured herself another glass of wine. It was one more than she usually allowed herself, but she knew it would have a calming effect on her, and she needed calming right now. The urge to leave this house was growing stronger by the second. It wasn't just because Amy wanted to look for the sheriff, but another feeling was pressing her to leave. A sense of dread was growing as the minutes ticked by, and Gayle did not return. Everything was very quiet overhead.

Amy wondered what Gayle was doing to convince her cat to behave. The animal must be pretty stubborn for it to take this long. She also wondered why Gayle didn't just let the cat come downstairs. None of her business, she told herself. She much preferred the company of dogs, particularly a dog like Hannibal.

Too nervous to stay still any longer, Amy took her glass and wandered over to the dining room door. She decided to tour the two front rooms while waiting for her hostess. The light from the lone lamp in the living room was too dim to banish the shadows that grouped in corners and hid behind furniture. Amy liked light, and thought Gayle could add greatly to her home's attractiveness if she would put lamps on every table. Amy thought about turning on the overhead light, so she could see the sparkling beauty of the chandelier above the dining table. But changing Gayle's lighting arrangement would be rude on her part. However, her hostess didn't mind leaving a guest alone for a long time.

"Why should I worry about manners, anyhow?" she muttered. "Obviously Gayle isn't."

As Amy passed the lovely mahogany sideboard with the gorgeous gold-leaf framed mirror above it, her eye was caught by a glass dish on the end of the sideboard. It looked like one of the rarest of depression glass pieces, a cornucopia with a deeply fluted edge. Even in the dim light, the lovely piece glowed with the hallmark of rainbow colors in its deep maroon glass.

The objects that Gayle had chosen to put into the dish seemed a little strange. Where Amy would have opted for something like hand blown glass fruit, Gayle had filled the dish with a mish-mosh of odd items, things most people kept in a drawer and out of sight.

Amy gave in to her strong sense of curiosity and took out some of the items for a better look. There was a man's tarnished silver ID bracelet. She couldn't make out the whole name, but the last name looked like Schneider. There was a gold bar tie pin with what appeared to be a real diamond in its center. Amy bent over to look further up into the dish. A small wooden handle was sticking up from among the several other articles.

Amy reached in and pulled on the handle. It proved to be a wooden egg used long ago for darning socks, just like the one Grace Thurmond had. It even had a crack in the side of the handle like Grace's.

A terrible thought began to form in her mind, but before Amy could fully recognize its portent, she heard an anguished voice rise in a wordless howl, then end as abruptly as it began. The hair on the back of Amy's neck stirred in response to the terror she heard in that cry. She raised her head to look into the mirror. The kitchen door was reflected behind her and in the dim light it seemed to move, but it did not open.

The quiet in the house deepened, holding a menacing quality that sent a chill down Amy's spine. The numerous shadows created by the dim lighting shifted, seeming to take on a life of their own. Amy opened her mouth to call out, but closed it quickly with the realization that someone other than Gayle and herself could be in the house. The outcry had held bass tones, like a man's.

"God, help me," Amy prayed, as she cautiously made her way through the living room. Gayle was either in trouble, or she was the one who had caused that scream of fear and pain.

If Amy could call nine-one-one, a deputy would be here in just a few minutes. She walked quietly to the door that opened into the hall. There was no phone on the table there, nor was there a phone on the wall. The office, she thought. Gayle would have one in her office. Quickly, Amy ran down the hall and turned on the light in the small room.

At first glance, there was no phone in sight. Not believing anyone could have an office without one, Amy scrabbled around in the papers that covered the desk top. Nothing. She went behind the desk to see if one might be sitting on the floor, but again, no phone.

"What is this, Gayle?" Amy said aloud, in her frustration. "Whoever heard of a person not having a phone! Where is the blasted thing?"

Amy gave up on the office and hurried up to the sitting room across the hall from the living room. A quick search there left her empty handed, as well. Then the phone was upstairs, she decided, that was the only place left. A clutter of thoughts ran through Amy's mind. The strongest of them told her to get out of the house, and instinctively she turned toward the front door.

But what if that *had* been Gayle screaming? By the time Amy could get to town and get back here with help, Gayle could be seriously hurt, or worse. Forget the phone, Amy knew she had to at least make an attempt to locate the woman.

Refusing to think any farther on Gayle's possible connection with the scream, Amy turned back toward the stairs and slowly made her way up them until she could see into the upper hallway. As in the one below, the lighting was poor. One overhead frosted globe shone with a yellow light that barely reached the stairway where she stood. Hesitantly, she continued moving until she was standing on the top step.

It was so dark past the dim light that someone could be at the end of the hall and, unless they moved, Amy wouldn't see them. By now she was so tense Amy felt as if she were smothering. Forcing a deep breath, she walked slowly down the hallway.

Surely if there was anyone up here, they would make themselves known. But the thick silence continued, unbroken by anything other than her own uneven breathing. Amy could even hear her heartbeat in her ears as she fought against her fear. Looking down the length of the hall, she thought there were four doors, two on each side, but the light was too dim to see them clearly. As she moved away from the stairs, she could also see a door at the very end. She thought it could be a bathroom.

If Gayle was being held against her will, she would be behind one of those doors. But who would do that? Who else was in the house?

Amy reached up to wipe the sweat from her forehead, then took hold of the knob of the nearest door. She turned it as quietly as she could, then eased the door open a crack to peep through. The weak illumination from the hall light behind her only revealed a small area of the floor's carpeting.

"Gayle," she said softly. There was no movement and no sound. Feeling inside of the doorframe, she found the light switch and flipped it on. Only a dim light revealed that the room was empty except for furniture that was old and dark. To Amy, it was as if the house had died in the late twenties and had never been revived. The whole place was gloomy and depressing. Amy closed that door and moved to the next one.

The complete silence in the house was like a weight pushing against her ears. Again, every fiber of her being screamed for her to run. The thought occurred to Amy that Gayle may have fled to save her own self and left Amy to cope with whoever was playing hide-and-seek. But surely she wouldn't do that, Amy told herself. Remembering the object she had seen in the dish downstairs, Amy shuddered as she wondered how Gayle had come into possession of Grace Thurmond's wooden darning egg.

Again, refusing to let herself think along those lines, Amy moved to the next door which was close to the end of the hallway. Calling Gayle's name softly again,

Amy switched the room light on. Fear jerked her hand back and she jumped away from the door. Someone was sitting in a chair next to the bed!

Amy ran back toward the stairs, intending to get outside as quickly as she could. But the person in there had not said anything, and, if Amy's hearing was correct, had not moved from that chair. She turned back to listen again, then slowly crept back to the door. Another quick peek and she saw that the person in the chair had not moved. The figure looked familiar to Amy, now that her mind was functioning again.

She pushed the door open an extra inch to get a better look. A man was tied with ropes to the chair, and was positioned so that his back was to the door. She summoned up the courage to move a little farther into the room. The figure still did not move. Amy had taken two more steps into the room when it hit her. It was Sheriff Frank Morgan sitting there.

"Sheriff," she whispered, as she moved around in front of him. Two bloody holes gaped where his eyes once had been. Blood covered the lower half of his face and the front of his shirt.

"Oh, no!" Amy yelled, as she stumbled through the door and yanked it shut behind her, then promptly became violently ill on the hall rug. The scream she'd heard earlier must have come from him. Did Gayle know he was dead? Did she kill him?

Amy now felt certain that the darning egg was Grace Thurmond's, which meant Gayle had stolen it. Had she taken it after she had killed Walter Thurmond? If she had, that would mean that Gayle killed the other men too.

Even with questions pushing at her brain and jumbling her thoughts, Amy knew she had only seconds to get out of the house. She didn't bother with being quiet. If Gayle, or anyone else, were in the house, they had heard her scream and slam that door. It was time to leave.

CHAPTER 51

▼

Amy was within ten feet of the front door when she heard the squeak of the kitchen door opening. She turned and squinted toward the other end of the hallway. It seemed darker than when she and Gayle had gone to the kitchen earlier, then realized that the light was off. Had Gayle been in the kitchen while she was upstairs looking for her? Amy strained to see who stood there, but could only make out a dark figure.

"Gayle, is that you? I was just leaving because I promised Barney I'd be home before now." Amy began feeling behind her for the door knob, not liking her continuing silence. "I really enjoyed my dinner and I'll call you later."

As she spoke, the silent figure drew nearer. It was a woman all right, but not Gayle. The hair was very long, and it was dark, not blonde like Gayle's. There was something almost hypnotic in the silent approach, and Amy found herself unable to move. As the figure reached the living room doorway, and the light fell across her. She was dressed in a black jumpsuit which zipped up the front. Something dark and wet glistened on the front of it. A smile that held no mirth was fixed on her face as the woman slowly came into stronger light.

Recognition hit Amy like a shock wave. "Mary!" Amy gasped. "What are you doing here?" The question, under the circumstances, sounded foolish even to her own ears, but she was having a hard time making sense of what she saw. "I didn't know you and Gayle were friends," she ended, inanely. Instinct told her that she was in immediate danger.

Mary stopped a few feet from her, as if she knew Amy would flee if she came any closer. She spoke in a voice Amy did not recognize.

"Why couldn't you tend to your own business and stay out of mine? You ran around town asking your questions," Mary accused her bitterly. "You even go digging into the past. A past that had nothing to do with you. But you just had to keep looking didn't you? Finding Walter Thurmond's body didn't give you the right to play detective."

Amy couldn't help herself, she was drawn into this ludicrous conversation, even though it delayed her chances of getting out of the house. "How did you know that's what I was doing?"

"I knew everything you did." Mary's mouth was drawn into a sneer. "You thought you were so smart, keeping your secrets. Well, I know most of them, including those visions you had. I also know that you'll have to die. If it hadn't been for Gayle's interference, you would already be dead." Mary moved a little closer.

Common sense began to reassert itself now that Mary had stated her intentions.

Bafflement at her complete personality change, made it hard for Amy to immediately believe what she was seeing. But her mind was accepting the obvious. Mary was completely insane, and meant to kill her.

Amy eased back until she felt the door against her right shoulder. Moving her arm behind her, she clasped the knob. If only she could get outside, she could hide in the woods close to the road until a car came along. Not a good plan, but all she could think of at the moment.

A chuckle from Mary distracted Amy from her thoughts and her attention jerked back to what Mary was saying, even as a growing sense of danger urged her to run.

"You could care less," the woman was saying. "You and everybody else in this stinking little community. Sure, you were nice to me, but only because I played toady to your face. Do you know how much I hate you? Do you have any idea how much I wanted to spit in your eye when you offered to *let* me manage your shop?"

Mary moved closer. "I wanted to scratch your eyes out, did you know that? Of course you didn't. You're like the rest of the people who live here, stupid and self-centered, filled with your own sense of importance. What do you care for the hell some people have to live with? You've got your own comfortable life, and it doesn't matter to you what we have to suffer. No one cares!" Mary screamed, making Amy's heart leap into her throat. "No one gives a tinker's damn, you bitch!"

The impact of Mary's vitriolic tirade again held Amy in motionless shock. As she listened to the strange diatribe, Amy wondered how she had been so incredibly wrong about this woman.

Mary's face twisted into a sneer, as she said, "Well, you've learned too late that I'm more than your equal. You don't go around gossiping about business that's of no concern to you and expect to get away with it. You want to know about the past? I'll tell you what you were so busy trying to find out. The late, great Dr. Anderson sexually abused his own daughter. He even made her brother do bad things to her so he could watch. Like the story so far, honey?"

Amy forgot about the knob behind her. The filth pouring out of Mary's mouth had her total attention. But why would Mary be so rabid over what Dr. Anderson had done to his children all those years ago? Her mind was a whirl of puzzlement and fear.

Mary was now close enough for Amy to see the hatred burning in her eyes. "It wasn't enough that he wrecked forever any hopes I had of being a normal human being, he helped his friend, Thurmond build a second floor on the country club so he could use it as a private lair for him and his friends. He was the 'anonymous' donor listed in the paper. Did you read that part?"

Her eyes glittered with the fury of remembered abuse and her lips were covered with a froth that drizzled down her chin as she continued her litany of hate. "My father used it for parties, with Hank and me as the entertainment committee. He let those filthy old men play sex games with us while he watched. Did you know that the elite of your fine town are no more than rats in a sewer? With all their fancy airs, they're the worst trash on earth. I fixed them, though. They won't be hurting anyone else!"

Amy's mind, slowed by the building terror that was turning her insides to ice, managed to absorb what the madwoman just said. "My god! You're Rosalind Anderson," she blurted.

With a lightning change of mood, Rosalind dropped her head and began sobbing as if her heart would break. She seemed to revert to the child she had been, when she and her brother had suffered at the hands of that group of lascivious men. Amy thought that if the men didn't deserve their gruesome deaths, they certainly deserved the worst the law allowed.

However, reality quickly reasserted itself. Rosalind raised her head. For Amy it was like looking into the eyes of a demon, for there was no human recognition in them, just the pale face of death staring out. Amy felt herself shivering cold. It spread from her chest into her arms and legs, and chill bumps spread over her body. Amy was desperate to distract Rosalind just long enough to give herself a chance to run.

Amy spoke loudly, "Where is Gayle? What have you done with her?"

For some reason, the question seemed to strike Rosalind as funny, although the laugh that came from her was barren of humor. Rosalind swung her arm up to gesture toward the staircase. In her hand was a long, thin-bladed knife. Amy's heart plunged. She was trapped between the mad woman and the door. In order to open the door behind her, Amy would have to step toward Rosalind, leaving no room for her to dodge the blade. She had no choice but to stand there.

"Your concern for Gayle is touching," Rosalind said, sarcastically. "Why don't we run upstairs and check on her?" She placed the tip of the knife blade against Amy's side. "This will slide in so easily you won't even notice how deep it is until it's too late, so don't think you can move faster than I can. I really would like for you to stay alive for a little while longer."

Amy felt a sharp pain in her right side, then the trickle of warm blood down her side as Rosalind added just enough pressure to pierce the skin. Frightened to the point of not being able to think clearly, and shaking from the increasing cold, Amy carefully walked up the stairs.

Rosalind pushed her into the room across the hallway from the one which held the remains of the sheriff. Amy fully expected to see Gayle mutilated and dead as she opened the door to which Rosalind pointed, but to her relief, Gayle was sitting in a chair, looking at the two of them as they entered the room. She was tied and gagged, but at least she was alive.

On seeing Amy, Gayle began making strangling noises in an effort to say something. It was plain to Amy that she was pleading with Rosalind.

"You don't seem too happy, Doll," Rosalind told Gayle, her voice harsh and rasping. She gave Amy a hard shove onto the bed, forcing her to fall forward onto her stomach. Her legs dangled from the edge of the bed, not quite touching the floor.

"I thought you'd be thrilled to see your friend, Amy, again." Rosalind's voice was filled with anger. "After all, you think so highly of her that you're willing to turn your back on me. Well, it didn't work, honey. Your sweet little friend here is going to die right in front of your eyes, then I'll take care of you."

Amy had turned her head so that she was facing Gayle. She saw the tears pouring down the cheeks of the obviously frightened woman. She also saw that Rosalind had taken a thin rope from one of her pockets. Amy knew that once she was tied up, she'd be as helpless as Gayle. She slowly drew her arms up beneath her chest and waited until she saw Rosalind lay her knife down, preparatory to tying her hands. As Rosalind bent over her, she pushed up with all her strength, placing her feet on the floor to give her enough momentum to bang her head underneath Rosalind's chin. The blow sent Rosalind staggering back, breaking her hold on Amy's wrist.

Momentarily addled by the blow, Amy's reaction was slower than she wanted, but she was on her feet and running before Rosalind recovered her balance. Amy knew she couldn't beat the mad woman to the stairs and get outside in time to hide, so she ran into the room across the hall. Slamming the door behind her, she felt for a key. Thanks to the dim lighting in the rest of the house, her eyes were able to pick up the gleam of the spring lock, and she quickly twisted the metal knob. For good measure, she pushed a nearby chest in front of the door.

She heard Rosalind scream her name as she came out of the other room, and simultaneously hit the door with the force of a battering ram. The door behind which Amy stood reverberated with the strength of the woman's assault. It wouldn't take her long to break open the door at the rate she was slamming against it.

Amy ran across the room to a window which was faintly outlined in the dark and shoved the curtains aside. She grabbed the window's handle and yanked up on it, but the window was stuck firmly in its frame. Behind her, the door thumped against the chest as the flimsy old lock gave way. Desperate to escape, Amy pushed the window upwards with all her might, ripping away two finger-nails in the process. The sash moved just high enough for her to squeeze through.

As Amy backed out of the opening, she skinned her back where the bottom of the window had pushed up her shirt. Praying she wouldn't break her legs, she let go.

"I'll get you, Bitch!" Rosalind screamed above her as Amy tumbled into the tangle of shrubbery below. She fell through the limbs and struck the ground with such a hard thump that she bit her tongue. The blow also knocked the air from her lungs, and she lost a few valuable seconds trying to get her breath.

When Amy managed to pull herself to her feet and stumble out of the shrubs, there was no light to help her see the lay of the land. She did remember seeing trees behind the house when her headlights had swept across them. Amy headed in the direction where she thought the closest and thickest of them would be, stumbling over clumps of weeds and uneven places in the ground.

Rosalind had already gotten downstairs and out the front door. Amy hadn't expected her to be that fast, but she could hear her running around the side of the house, and saw the flickering of a flashlight. She bumped hard into a tree trunk and almost fell, barely managing to stay on her feet. Not only did her forehead smart where she'd met the rough bark, but her head was still throbbing from the blow she'd given Rosalind.

Wanting to get behind cover before the flashlight picked her out, Amy fell to her knees and scrabbled across the yard in the direction of some bushes the approaching light had revealed. She pushed into a thick clump of brush before Rosalind began to sweep the back yard with her flashlight. Afraid to move except when the beam swung away from her hiding place, Amy slowly worked her way farther back into the tall weeds and brush until she reached the heavily wooded area behind her.

Checking to be certain that Rosalind hadn't also reached the brush, Amy stood up and walked as fast as the impeding undergrowth and tree limbs allowed, holding her hands out in front of her to protect her face from the stinging blows of the branches.

A picture of her former friend tied to the straight chair in the upstairs bedroom rose in her mind. How in the world, she wondered, did Gayle get involved with Rosalind? Neither of them had shown any sign of knowing each other on that long ago morning when Amy had introduced them to each other at Mary's house. She gave herself a mental shake. There seemed to be no connection between the madwoman she was fleeing, and the woman she had known as Mary Griffith. Amy could only pray that Barney would come looking for her.

She ran faster, meeting the resisting limbs with even more force. After a few more minutes of slashing her way through the thicket, Amy felt, rather than saw, that she had entered a clearing. No more limbs met her outstretched hands. Her foot struck a bump, and she felt a hard, smooth surface beneath her feet. She reached down and touched the surface of a paved road.

Amy felt weak from the wave of relief that flooded her body. Where there was a paved road, there had to be traffic. She could catch a ride back to town to the police station. For a moment she was undecided as to which way to turn until she saw a glow above the trees to her left. That had to be the town's light reflecting from the low hanging clouds.

She began running as fast as was possible in the unrelenting black of a starless night, hoping a car would come her way very quickly. Amy did not hear footsteps behind her, but suddenly, an arm went around her neck, and she cried out in terror as she was almost lifted off her feet by the strong grip of her assailant. She felt the hot breath on her cheek, as Rosalind whispered hoarsely into her ear, "I didn't give you permission to leave, Bitch."

Amy had a vivid mental picture of Rosalind lifting Gayle's iron beds as if they were made of light wood. She was very strong. The arm around her throat cut off

Amy's breath, and just as she felt herself losing consciousness, Rosalind loosened her grip. Gasping for air, Amy turned toward her attacker, hoping to twist out of the woman's hold. An explosion of pain behind her left ear sent Amy tumbling onto the pavement, and into oblivion. She didn't feel herself being hoisted over Rosalind's shoulder, nor her arms and legs dangling loosely as her captor easily carried her back to the house.

CHAPTER 52

▼

Barney wished he'd never agreed to help. Both Pete and Archie were so disorganized without the sheriff to tell them what to do, that after fifteen minutes of indecision, they were still sitting at the police station. The two deputies had argued on every point and only in the past couple of minutes had decided they would need a search warrant. Pete, who was on the phone with the judge now, repeated, "Yes, Sir," a number of times before he finally hung up.

"I got Judge Golden out of bed," he said, "and he ain't happy. So let's get to his house before the judge changes his mind about signing that warrant."

Barney, who had sat patiently through the nattering and bumbling, as the two had seesawed back and forth on how to handle matters, was disgusted with them both. He had lost all interest in helping them pick up their perp, mainly because he couldn't get Amy off his mind. Barney had seen that she arrived safely at Gayle's before he came to the police station, but his persistent feeling of unease was like an itch he couldn't scratch.

"Pete, you still haven't told me whose house we're going to," Barney said as, the three of them walked out to their two trucks. "Is it someone we'll need help with?"

"Naw," Archie answered for Pete. "You know her, it's that woman, Mary Griffith. You probably know where she lives, out north of here a ways. She won't be no problem, huh Pete?" Archie grinned at the thought that any woman could cause him and Pete any trouble.

Barney had stopped in his tracks. "Wait a damn minute!" he said sharply, causing the other two to halt. "Why are we going to Mary's house?"

Pete lifted his cap and scratched his head. "Ben called and said we were to pick up Ms. Griffith, ASAP, and keep her at the jail until he got back. I don't know why Ben wanted her picked up, but he sure sounded upset enough."

"You know that Mary works for us at the shop, Pete." Barney was outraged at the man's careless handling of an urgent matter. "So why didn't you tell me right away that it was her? You'd better tell me what Ben wants with Mary right now!"

"Honest, Barn, I don't know." Pete seemed surprised at Barney's reaction. "Ben said something like, 'get your hands on her fast before she can hurt anyone else.' He wanted us to pick up any paintings we could find at her house, too. Go figure that one."

"Do you realize it's been over an hour since Ben called you?" Barney was yelling now. "If he said to pick her up, you can bet he's got a damn good reason for it." Barney whirled around to face Archie. The deputy had never seen Barney's temper displayed before. He was thinking that he'd as soon have the sheriff mad at him.

Barney began to give orders. "Archie, you go to the Judge Golden's house and pick up the warrant. Pete, you get in the truck with me. Let's move it."

Neither deputy seemed the least offended that Barney had taken over, but instead, anxious to please him. They both scrambled into the two trucks.

When Barney reached the turnoff to the gravel road leading to Mary's house, he switched off his headlights. He drove very slowly, not wanting to make any more noise than necessary. It would be best to not give Mary advance warning of their presence.

However, they had not gone too far before the two of them could see that the house showed no lights. It sat among the trees almost hidden from view. Barney braked to a stop, and said, "It doesn't look as if she's home, so she may be having dinner out, or something. We'll stake the place out and see what happens." He nodded toward a clump of trees to the right of the road. "I'll hide the truck behind those trees and walk from there. We need to be sure she's really not here. Take your flashlight and wait by the road for Archie and the search warrant. If Mary hasn't shown up by then, wave him down to keep him from blundering up to the house."

Barney had lost all faith in Archie's ability to assess a situation and act accordingly. "Have him hide his truck too. I'm going around to the back of the house, so both of you come back there. We can see her lights when she drives up."

"Sounds good to me, Barn," Pete said, sounding eager to cooperate.

Barney wished he'd taken over sooner than he had. He was praying his plan was a good one. On such short notice, and being inexperienced in capturing criminals, it was all Barney knew to do. "If Mary shows up before Archie gets here, you run behind her vehicle until she parks. By then I'll be nearby. You take the passenger's side, and I'll take the driver's side. Have your gun ready in case it's needed. Got all that?"

"I surely have, Barn. Hell, the sheriff couldn't plan any better than that."

"We both know better than that," Barney said, as he disappeared into the moonless night, leaving an uneasy Pete alone.

Archie drove up about twenty minutes later. Pete flagged him down and repeated the instructions. Archie drove his truck beneath the clump of trees, parking next to Barney's vehicle.

Together, Archie and Pete walked to the back of the house. Barney gave a low whistle so they could locate him where he had hunkered down, back against a tree, near the back door. Lightning was flickering steadily in the southeast, but did nothing to relieve the blackness that surrounded the three men.

"No sign of her yet, Barn," Archie said unnecessarily. "I'm glad we all got here before she did. I got an idea she could be pretty tough."

"What makes you think that? Not thirty minutes ago you seemed pretty confident we could handle a mere woman." The not knowing why they were hiding here, waiting for a woman he'd worked with for several months made Barney extremely nervous. If Ben wanted her so urgently, then he and Amy had misread Mary completely.

Archie was saying, "I got to remembering how I seen her one day at the lumberyard. She'd bought some treated four-by-fours about ten feet long. Those suckers are heavy! She was loading them onto her truck like they was matchsticks. Boy, you talk about muscle! She must be some kind of weight lifting freak."

Barney said nothing. He was remembering how Mary had always avoided discussing anything personal, and quickly turned conversations away from herself. Quiet, timid, plain-looking, she was the type you didn't notice in a crowd.

He felt his stomach tighten with urgency. Where was Mary? Why hadn't she come home yet? He raised his watch close to his eyes to see its illuminated dial. He was alarmed to see that they had been on stake-out for almost thirty minutes. Barney wondered if Mary knew that they were looking for her. He didn't see how that could be possible, but with all the screw-ups already in the works, he figured anything could happen. Pessimism now reigned supreme in Barney's thinking processes.

Pete and Archie had been carrying on a soft conversation, leaving Barney to his thoughts. For several minutes they had speculated on the whereabouts of Sheriff Morgan. They finally agreed that Frank had gone off on a bender.

According to Pete, the sheriff had done that a lot in his younger days. Now, with the pressure being put on him to find the killer, the two deputies were of the opinion that Frank had probably succumbed to his old habits.

Barney said nothing, but he didn't agree with them. Frank might go on a drunk after the killer was caught, but Barney didn't believe the man was capable of such irresponsibility. When he was a deputy maybe, but as the sheriff, never. That left Barney wondering where Frank Morgan was, as well. Remembering Amy's insistence that the sheriff could be in trouble, Ben became anxious to learn if anyone else had heard from Frank. If he hadn't shown up at the police station by the time Barney called in, there definitely was something wrong.

"Ms. Griffith may not be coming home tonight, boys," he said, interrupting their present discussion of the world series. "I'm going to leave the two of you here while I check on Amy. She and Ms. Armbruster should have finished their dinner by now, and I'd like to be there before Amy leaves. Why don't one of you stand watch here and one of you in the truck? The radio needs to be monitored just in case the sheriff does call."

"Good idea, Barn," Pete said, as he stood up to stretch his legs. "I'll stay here, Archie. You can walk back to the truck with Barney. Do you remember Barney's plan that I told you about?"

"Sure," Archie said. "If Ms. Griffith shows up I get out of the truck, run behind her until she stops, and I come up on the passenger side, right? That way, me and you will have her covered on both sides before she knows what's going on." The deputy seemed proud of himself for remembering.

"Exactly right," Pete said, as if he knew his partner needed a little praise after the bruising they'd both taken from Barney.

As Barney and Archie neared the trucks, they could hear the crackling of the radio and a voice calling for Pete. Archie hurried to his truck and pushed the radio mike button. "This is Archie. What's up?"

The police chief answered. "This is David at the station, Archie. I just got back from Little Rock and heard about your assignment. Have you seen anything of Mary Griffith yet?" Archie told him they hadn't. David said, "I got word she was seen this afternoon driving east on Highway Three-Thirty. Maybe she was leaving town, or maybe she was visiting someone out that way. If she's visiting, do you know who that could be?"

Barney, listening to the conversation, snatched the mike from Archie's hand. "This is Barney, David. She knows Gayle Armbruster, who lives out that way, but I don't know if the two of them are friends. Amy's at Gayle's now, and I'm going out there to escort her home. Listen, do you know why Ben wants Mary arrested?"

"I'm glad you're there, Barney," David came back. "I just talked to Ben, and he's made it back to Memphis. Slade Angstrom is there to pick him up, so he should be here in a couple of hours. He said this Griffith woman is really Rosalind Anderson and probably is the killer we've been looking for. Can you believe that?" Incredulity was clear in David's voice. "I sure hope that woman's not at Armbruster's because Amy could be in trouble. You're going there now?"

Barney didn't bother to answer. Before the chief said anything beyond the fact that Mary Griffith was Rosalind Anderson, Barney had already dropped the mike and was running to his truck. He was dead certain that Mary, or whoever she was, had gone to Gayle's house.

"You stay here in case I'm wrong," he yelled at Archie. "Get back on the horn and tell David to send some men out there. Come on Pete, we've got to get to Armbruster's now!"

In seconds, his truck roared out of the gravel drive and hit the highway with tires squawling as Barney yanked the wheel sharply, turning onto the pavement. He didn't bother to see if Pete was following him. Fear for Amy lay like icy lead in Barney's stomach, as he castigated himself for having left her out there. The thought came to him that Anderson may already have been in the house when Amy got there.

As he pressed the accelerator down to the floor, Barney prayed that Amy's ESP was working for her big time.

CHAPTER 53

▼

As Amy came to, she was first conscious of a splitting headache. It was concentrated on the right side of her head like the migraines she occasionally had. Groggy, and feeling sick at her stomach, she raised her head, intending to push herself up from her bed. Immediately, the ache in her head sharpened, sending jags of pain into her arms and legs. With the pain came memory. She wasn't on her bed, or even in her own house, she was back in Gayle's house, lying on the floor.

She tried to put one hand out to help herself up and realized that her arms were bound behind her back, her ankles tied together. Everything came back to her, including the fear. Mary wasn't Mary, she was Rosalind Anderson, and Rosalind meant to kill her. Now Amy was lying here helpless and at her mercy.

"Oh, dear Lord," she whispered, as she also remembered the horror that had been Sheriff Morgan's face. Her stomach rebelled at the mental picture of the blackened eye sockets and the blood that covered his mouth and shirt front.

Amy eased her head back down on the floor, hoping to relax enough to let her stomach settle, at the same trying not to think about the corpse. Goose bumps prickled along her whole body, making her shudder. Would Rosalind do something like that to her? Where was Gayle? Had Rosalind already killed her?

Despair rose to fill her eyes with tears and choke off her breath. Amy knew that blind panic was not far away, when she'd scream until she could scream no longer, or until she was stopped. She had to get herself under control. If there was any chance for her at all, it depended on her keeping her wits about her.

To help distance her thoughts, Amy studied her surroundings. She was on the floor of a bedroom, but it didn't appear to be either of the two she had been in earlier. A dim light filtered through a transom over the door, which gave her some visibility. She was lying not far from the door, on a bare wooden floor. The other bedroom had carpet, she remembered.

Amy needed to get as far away from the door as she could. The beds she'd seen in the other two rooms had a lot of space underneath, so she might be able to slide under this one and at least be hidden from immediate view. She would do whatever she could to make Rosalind's job of finding her harder. Amy pulled her knees up toward her chest and pushed her hips back along the floor. The pain was bad, but when she tried to move her shoulders back in line with her hips, the savage ache in her head stopped her for a moment. But bad as it was, her fear of Rosalind overcame the need to lie still.

Gritting her teeth, Amy alternated the hip and shoulder movements, managing to scoot back from the door. She had only moved a couple of feet, however, when she hit a barrier behind her. Her hands, and the lower part of her arms, were numb from being tied so tightly, so Amy couldn't tell what had stopped her progress. She only knew it didn't feel hard, like a piece of furniture. Dreading the pain, Amy reversed her movements until she had pulled away from the barrier. Then, with an effort that caused nausea to roil in her stomach, Amy rotated herself until she faced away from the door.

The weight of her body on her tied arms caused flashes of hot pain from her wrists, through her shoulders, to the top of her head. For a second or two, Amy thought she would pass out. Tears welled up behind her closed eyelids as she fought against making any sound. Amy stayed very still and waited for the worst to pass. Taking a deep breath, she forced herself to relax, then opened her eyes.

A scream forced its way past her lips, as she scrambled to push herself back toward the door. Frank Morgan's bloody face was no more than six inches from her own. It looked like an evil Halloween mask, with the bloody holes where his eyes had been. Something black across his mouth gave the appearance of a grotesque smile. Terrified that he would move toward her, Amy pushed herself backward, mindless of the blinding pain in her head.

Just as Amy managed to get a little space between herself and the dead man, she heard the door behind her open. Rosalind had come to kill her! Panic darkened her vision and roared in her ears. She heard a whimpering sound, like a puppy that's afraid of the dark, and realized the noise was her own.

"Shhh, Amy, shhh." The whisper was close to her ear. "Please don't make any more noise."

It was Gayle. She bent close to Amy's ear. "I managed to get loose and now I'll untie you. But first you've got to listen to me. Rosalind went outside to hide your car. She got the keys from your purse."

Amy could feel Gayle's hands working at the knots at her wrists, and her voice was barely above a whisper as she said, "She could come back at any minute. Amy, she means to kill both of us. I acted the fool and let Rosalind know I liked you, so it's my fault you're here."

Amy welcomed the hurt that jabbed up into her shoulders from Gayle's efforts to untie the knots. "Hurry, Gayle, please hurry," she implored. Just then she felt the rope give way and her hands, which she could not feel at all, fell like lead to the floor.

"When Rosalind finds out that I'm loose," Gayle whispered, "she will be furious. She'll probably kill me first. Oh, Amy," Gayle was crying softly. "I've been so afraid of her lately, and nothing I've said or done, pleases her."

Amy felt sick with terror. She knew that Rosalind's jealousy of her held the fury of a wronged lover. That, combined with her murderous vendetta against the men in Ashley Springs, made very poor odds that Amy would survive this night. A terrible urgency to run assaulted her nerves, but, unable to use her poor hands, she had to suffer Gayle's attempts at getting the rope loose from her ankles.

"This is my only chance to make it up to you," Gayle continued. "I misjudged my hold on Rosalind, or I wouldn't have invited you out here tonight. When she said she wanted to be here too, but would stay upstairs out of sight, I actually thought it would work. I knew she wanted to spy on me while you were here, so I didn't object. I *wanted* her to see we were merely casual friends. But then, neither she nor I knew Sheriff Morgan would come here.

"We had him tied up, but when we were eating and heard the thump on the ceiling, I knew something had happened." Gayle's whisper turned into soft sobs. "You see, back when I told Rosalind that I'd join her in getting revenge on those nasty old men, I didn't know it was going to turn into a blood bath like it did."

It's too late for all this, Amy thought, her heart beating triple time. *Just get me loose. Oh, God, help me get loose. Please help me get away!*

Amy could feel Gayle's hot tears dripping on her bare legs, as the woman struggled to untie the tightly knotted ropes. Gayle seemed to feel an urgency to explain herself to Amy, because she continued to talk as she worked. "I could understand Rosalind's reason for killing the men, but not in the kinky way she's done that. But then I found out that she had murdered people not even connected to Thurmond and the others. I realized that, even after she'd executed all of the men who had hurt her so badly, Rosalind would continue to kill because that's what she enjoys."

Amy felt the last of the ropes loosen from her ankles. She managed to sit up and she began to rub her hands. The unpleasant prickling in them was a welcome sensation. It meant the feeling was beginning to come back. Amy was startled when Gayle pushed her back to the floor.

"No," Gayle hissed. "You have to lie down and turn back like she placed you. You can't let her know you're untied. Here, I'll help you."

She grasped Amy's shoulders and her hip to help her roll back over to face the door once again. She loosely wrapped the ropes around Amy's ankles, then rose to leave. She leaned over to whisper, "Just in case Rosalind comes in here before I see her, keep your arms behind you, okay?" Amy felt a thrill of fear grip her stomach at the mere thought of Rosalind coming close to her again.

"When I find her, I'll keep her distracted so you can slip out." Gayle said. "I'm afraid for you to try that until I know exactly where she is. I'll call her name out real loud so you'll know when to leave, okay?"

Amy managed to croak, "Gayle, who are you?"

For a moment Gayle said nothing, and Amy thought she wouldn't answer her question. But then she said, "I am Mary Gayle Griffith." As quickly as she had come in, Gayle left, closing the door softly behind her.

Amy's mind was in a whirl of confusion, trying to get a grip on Gayle being Mary, and Mary being Rosalind. But the most confusing thing to her was how she could have worked day after day beside Rosalind and not even suspect something? Or, had she? Amy remembered the feelings of dread that would wash over her at times when she was alone with 'Mary.' But she had never connected that feeling with the woman, not even after her strange reaction to Amy's saying that she had thought about hiring Gayle.

My Lord! She really hated me at that moment and I didn't have a clue.

She brushed aside those thoughts to concentrate on trying to survive. She had no strength for anything else. Amy strained to hear any sounds below that would indicate Rosalind was back. There was nothing but silence.

Amy's head hurt so badly, it affected her sense of time. How long had it been since Gayle left her? How long before Rosalind would be back from moving the car? Amy felt strongly that she wouldn't get another chance to escape, so right now was the time to make a break for it. She sat up again and waited for her head to settle into a manageable throb before attempting to stand.

She staggered and almost fell back to the floor when she first got to her feet. Holding her arms out to give herself balance, very much aware of Frank Morgan's body behind her, Amy crept across the wooden floor, praying it wouldn't creak and give her away. She listened carefully for any sounds from below, but could hear nothing but the whooshing of blood in her ears. She took a firm hold on the door knob and slowly turned it as far as it would go.

The snick of metal leaving metal let her know to pull the door toward her to make a very narrow crack. As she put one eye close to the opening she'd made, Amy wondered if Gayle, whom she still couldn't think of as Mary, had untied her as a cruel joke. What if she and Rosalind were waiting outside the door like two hungry cats at a mouse hole?

Then another unsettling thought occurred to her. Gayle had said that she was terrified of Rosalind herself, so she might at this very moment be outside, putting distance between where Amy stood and herself. *And what if I hang around up here until Rosalind comes after me again with that knife?* With that thought, Amy knew she didn't have a choice. She had to make a break for it right now.

She widened the crack until she could see the immediate area in front of the door, then inched it open enough so she could look up and down the hallway. There was no one in either direction, for which Amy whispered a prayer of thanks. She listened for a long moment, her hearing hindered again by the sound of her own wildly thumping heart and panicky breathing.

The feeling of urgency to act quickly grew even stronger, and Amy fought off the paralyzing effect of her fear and eased out into the hallway. She left the door behind her open for a quick retreat. If they came upstairs, and Amy realized she was now thinking of Gayle being in cahoots with Rosalind, at least she'd know they weren't waiting for her underneath the bedroom window. She'd take her chances of surviving another fall if she had no other option.

Amy had reached the stairs leading down to the front hallway when she heard Rosalind's voice, harsh and abrasive, and raised in anger. She quickly backed away from the railing. As the voices neared the foot of the stairs, she also heard Gayle speaking, her words carrying clearly to where Amy stood. She held her breath.

"Rosalind," Gayle spoke loudly, as promised. "I'm telling you, you're wrong." There was a pleading quality to Gayle's voice. "I wasn't running out on you. I knew I wouldn't be any help to you in that chair. How many times do I have to tell you, the only interest I had in Ms.. Bordeaux was to find out what she knew about the executions!"

"So it's *Ms..* Bordeaux now?" Amy shivered at the venom in Rosalind's voice. "You know you can't lie to me, so quit sniveling. She's dead, you hear me? That bitch is as good as dead!"

Unbelievably, Amy heard Gayle come to her defense. "She really isn't that kind of person, Rosalind. Amy isn't one of us, she wasn't interested in me except as a friend, and that's all I wanted from her. Please, Rosalind, you've got to believe me." Suddenly, Gayle cried out, as if in pain. "You're hurting me!"

"I'll show you hurt, you liar!" Rosalind yelled. "First you say you're helping me by finding out what she knows, and then you only wanted her as a friend. You won't be lying to me much longer, I can promise you that." Her voice held nothing but pure hatred. "You'll never make a fool of me again."

"No, Rosalind, no!" Gayle's voice trembled with her fear. "I would never betray you. You know I've protected you in every way I can. Don't do this!"

An enormous flash of lightening lit the hall where Amy stood, followed instantly by a crash of thunder which shook the house. The continuing roll and thud of thunder drowned out the sounds of their voices, but Amy thought the two might even now be ascending the stairs. It would only be seconds before Rosalind discovered that she was untied, too. She would kill her right there.

Amy turned and ran past the room that held the sheriff's body, and on to the other end of the hall. She yanked open the door she thought might be a bathroom. She was desperate to get out of Rosalind's view before she came up the stairs. The bathroom might even have a window large enough for her to escape through.

To her surprise and great relief, rather than a bathroom, Amy saw a very narrow staircase leading down into the darkness. Giving no thought to the noise she made on the bare wooden steps, Amy all but fell to the bottom of them. She saw two doors and Amy grabbed the knob of the nearest. Mercy of mercies, it led to the backyard. The rain that fell from the blackened skies felt blessedly cool on her face.

Behind her Amy heard Gayle scream, "Please, Rosalind, don't do this!" Two shots rang out inside the house. For the second time that night, Amy ran for the woods.

She'd only taken a few steps when Amy felt a pair of strong arms grab her around the waist. She screamed and began kicking and clawing to get away. If Rosalind was going to kill her, Amy was determined that this time it wouldn't be without a fight. She jammed her elbow into the body behind her.

CHAPTER 54

$\blacktriangledown$

She heard a grunt, like breath leaving the lungs suddenly, then a familiar voice. "Stop, Amy! It's me, David Spratlin." The police chief's voice was low and filled with urgency. "Easy, easy. You're safe now, settle down."

She battled the urge to burst into tears. So weak from sheer relief, her legs gave way beneath her, Amy thought his voice was the sweetest sound she'd heard in a long time. Chief Spratlin practically carried her to the edge of the woods. There, she felt other arms grab her, and heard Barney's voice.

"Oh, thank God, thank God," he said, as they both sank to the ground, disregarding the puddles of water being formed by the rain. Barney rocked Amy back and forth like she was a baby. She began to cry in earnest, stifling the noise against his shoulder.

"Everything's under control now," Barney reassured her. "David and the county boys have the house surrounded and they'll go in and secure the place as soon as they make sure of the women's location. We heard gunshots. Did they shoot at you?"

"I-I think Mary, or rather, Rosalind, shot Gayle," she said, remembering Gayle's plea just before the sound of the gunshot. Amy drew a shuddering breath. "I heard Rosalind scream that she didn't mean to, after the gun went off." Then the picture of Frank's dead body hit her. "Barn, they killed Sheriff Morgan. They took his eyes out." She began crying again.

Barney held her even closer. "You've had a bad time, so just let it all out."

They heard another gunshot, then the yells of the police and deputies. Amy and Barney stayed where they were while lights flashed, voices shouted, and doors slammed inside the house. Several minutes passed, then David Spratlin called out for Barney. He told Amy to stay where she was, but she wasn't about to let him leave her alone in the dark. Together, drenched to the skin, they walked around the house and onto the shelter of the front porch.

"Rosalind Anderson is dead," David said. "She shot herself just as the men opened the door. Mary Gayle was shot a couple of times, once in the chest and once in the stomach, but is still alive. I'm sending her to the hospital." David's voice choked up, as if tears were close. "Frank is dead. Those two bitches butchered him, too."

In the silence that followed David's last statement, they heard the approaching wail of an ambulance.

"Ms. Amy," David said briskly, in control again, "We'll need you to make a statement and then answer a few questions. You are our number one witness here, so what you have to say is really important."

For the first time, Barney got a look at Amy in the light coming from the door David was holding open. He felt blood surge to his head in fear and anger. Amy's face was chalk white, and there was blood covering the side of her head and neck.

"Can't you see she's hurt!" he yelled at David. "Amy, why didn't you tell me you were hurt?" Barney put his arms back around her and led her down the steps and to his truck parked just off the front drive. "I'm taking her to the hospital, David. Not you nor anyone else is going to talk to her until Amy and the doctor says it's okay."

"Don't you want to wait for the ambulance, Barney? Another one is on the way and she can ride in it."

"Are you crazy?" Amy all but screamed. "You want me to stay here so I can answer questions and wait for ambulances? You have no idea what I've been through here." She burst into tears again, as her legs buckled under her.

Barney picked up the nearly unconscious Amy in his arms. "I repeat, she doesn't do anything until she's ready, and a doctor gives his okay."

He carried her to his truck, and Amy was barely aware that Barney was treating her like a child. She probably wouldn't have objected, even if she'd been able.

After Dr. Thompson had examined Amy's head wound, and shone a light into both her eyes. He said he thought she only had a slight concussion. But to be certain that the injury was as minor as he thought it was, he wanted her to stay overnight at the hospital. Amy was too worn out to argue. She doubted it would have done much good anyway, since Barney agreed with the doctor.

Barney sat in a chair near her bed, in spite of Amy's repeated pleas that he go home. Nurses came in at regular intervals throughout the night to rouse her and check her responses. He dozed a few times, but mostly he watched Amy as she slept. Barney felt guilty for not having paid attention to her attempts to learn more about the murdered men's pasts. If he had helped her, perhaps the killing would have ended sooner. But greater than the guilt, was his gratitude that she had not become one of the statistics in the Hickorytree County homicide rate.

As he sat through the night, watching this young woman, whose life since her childhood had been intertwined with his, he recalled memories of nights he'd sat up with Leigh during Amy's childhood illnesses, of ball games in parks and at stadiums, picnics and fishing trips, of driving Amy and her first date to her middle school graduation prom, of him and Leigh waving goodbye as she left for college, and then, of walking her down the aisle at her wedding. All of these experiences had created a history of family for himself, Amy, and Leigh. Barney was deeply thankful that he had been included.

At some point on his trip down Memory Lane, he fell asleep.

"Good morning, people."

A plump, middle-aged nurse hurried over to the window and began yanking open the blind. Barney sat up and rubbed at the stubble on his face. Amy opened her eyes, frowning into the strong sunlight.

"How are we feeling this morning?" The nurse put her fingers on Amy's pulse and looked at her watch, not really expecting an answer. "Are you hungry?" Again, she didn't wait for Amy to say anything. "Breakfast should be along in just a few minutes."

Amy didn't feel up to such energetic, impersonal good cheer. Although she had improved a lot since last night, a dull throbbing headache remained. The bright sunlight beaming directly onto her face only aggravated the pain. She answered in as friendly a tone as she could manage. "Yes, I'm fine, thank you, and yes, I am a bit hungry A cup of coffee would be wonderful."

The nurse jotted down Amy's vital signs, told the two of them that Dr. Thompson would make rounds in about thirty minutes, then bustled back out of the room.

"Good morning, Barn." Amy smiled at him. "I know you're tired, but I'm glad you stayed. I felt safe every time the nurses woke me up, and I saw you there. Thank you."

"You don't have to thank me." Barney stood up to stretch. He could hear his joints pop as he bent over to touch his toes. "Old Arthur is wrecking my joints. How does your head feel?"

"I have a small headache that's all. Nothing a good cup of coffee won't fix." She hesitated a moment, then said, "Do you know whether or not Gayle's still alive?"

"I haven't heard anything, but I'd just as soon she wasn't." Barney's face became grim at the reminder of the danger Amy had experienced. "I suppose that sounds harsh, but the woman put herself into a very dangerous position, then endangered innocent people because she was too chicken, or whatever the reason, to get away from Rosalind and tell the authorities what she knew." He sighed and shook his head. "I've never known of such an evil situation, and I've seen plenty."

"I guess we all feel terrible. I know I do. I keep thinking that if I'd just been more alert to both Mary Gayle and Rosalind, I could have prevented a lot of what happened, too." Amy felt a lump of sorrow push against her throat. She refused to give in to it. "Barn, did you know that Gayle was really Mary Gayle Griffith?"

"David told me while you were in the examination room last night." Barney shook his head. "Sure had us fooled, didn't she?"

"Even worse is, the Mary we thought we knew was really Rosalind Anderson. How could she hide all that hate from us? I know I felt uncomfortable with her at times, she acted so private and shy, but never in a hundred years would I have thought her capable of cold-blooded murder!"

Amy shivered at the memory of almost becoming one of Rosalind's victims, herself. "And Gayle was part of the horror. I liked her so much at first, then I began to feel a little uncomfortable in her company. It's as if something was trying to tell me, and I just wouldn't listen. It's all too much for me to absorb."

Barney reached for her hand. It felt cold and small in his. "I don't have any answers, Amy. I don't know how any person could do what Rosalind did, let alone understand how she managed to live what appeared to be a normal life. That's where the psychiatrists come in, I guess. All I know is, they both had us completely boondoggled. Now, change of subject." he said, in a more cheerful tone of voice. "I ran by the house and got you some clothes." He pointed to a pair of jeans and a shirt he'd laid across a chair. "Also, last night while you were being worked on, I called Leigh." He held up his hand as Amy started to protest. "You know Leigh. If I hadn't let her know what had happened the first minute I could, I wouldn't be fit for hanging when she got through with me."

"That's true," Amy admitted with a grin. "What did she say?"

"I have orders to call her this morning to give her an update on your condition. I don't know what time it will be in London, but she said that was unimportant, to call her anyway. Think you'll feel up to talking to her after we get you home?"

"Of course. It will be good to hear her voice." Amy reached up to hug Barney's neck, and he quickly bent down to accommodate her.

"You don't know the thoughts I was having," Amy said, as she released him, "when I faced Rosalind last night and knew she intended to kill me. I wanted to see you, Leigh, and Hannibal so bad, I ached. I understood then, much better than I ever had before, just how very much the three of you mean to me." She leaned back on her pillow and wiped her eyes on the edge of the sheet. "You'd better hand me one of those tissues, please."

"I strolled through the past myself last night while you slept," Barney said, as he handed her a handful of tissues. "I'd say we're all very lucky to have each other."

He brushed his hand through his hair in an attempt to make it lay flat. "I'll run down and get a cup of coffee? I'll be back up before the doctor gets here. Can I get you anything?"

"My breakfast should be here any minute. Meanwhile, I'm heading for the shower." She saw the look on his face. "No, Daddy, I won't get my bandage wet."

"Daddy, my foot," Barney said, a big grin on his face, as he walked to the door. "If I were your daddy, you'd never have gotten into all this mess. I would have grounded you from the beginning!"

After he left, Amy gratefully slid out of the bed and headed for the bathroom. She was happy to see that Barney even thought to bring her small bag with her toilet articles. He had put them on the basin counter. After showering and brushing her teeth, she felt much better. Amy had just fluffed up her pillows and settled back into bed when her breakfast tray arrived. She quickly drank the cup of coffee, hoping the caffeine would diminish the lingering headache.

Dr. Thompson came in a few minutes later and removed Amy's bandage to get a look at the injury at the back of her ear. When they had shaved some of her hair away from the injury the night before, Amy had cried, more as an expression of the horror she'd experienced than at the loss of her hair. Barney had quipped that the bald spot was nothing compared to the close shave she'd had that evening. Needless to say, Amy had not been amused.

This morning, Dr. Thompson reassured her that she could pull some of her very thick hair over the smaller bandage he'd just put into place. He said he had signed her release papers, but warned Amy that she was to take it easy for the next couple of days.

"Even though you only have a slight concussion," he said, "your body has had as much emotional wear and tear as it needs for a while. So do nothing stressful, like working in that shop of yours. Just relax and let things take care of themselves. And if the headache begins to worsen, call me. It should gradually subside and go away all together in a couple of days."

Barney, who had come in while the doctor was changing her bandage, added his approval to Dr. Thompson's last words. "We'll see that she rests, Doc. The way she scared me last night, I probably won't let her out of my sight for the next year."

When the doctor left, Barney stepped out of the room to let Amy change from the hospital gown into her own clothes. When he came back in, Ben Edwards was with him. Ben went straight to where Amy sat on the side of the bed and took one of her hands in his. His warm brown eyes scanned her face for a moment, as if to assure himself that she was okay.

"I came as soon as I could get away," he said. "Barney tells me that Dr. Thompson wants you to take it easy for a while. I second that idea."

Amy wasn't making any promises. "Tell me about Mary Gayle. Is she still alive?"

"She's refused to have surgery or any other treatment. The doctors said there's a bullet lodged in the wall of her heart. It refracted from a rib, otherwise it would have killed her instantly. The second shell went through her upper abdomen and made a mess of her intestines. She's bleeding internally and needed immediate surgery, but Gayle wouldn't give consent. There is no immediate family to do it for her. She made it very clear she wants to die."

Ben paused a moment, then said. "She wants to talk with you. How do you feel about that?"

"I'm not sure." Amy frowned. "I feel very badly toward her for not letting someone know what Rosalind was doing. That's not something that makes me want to talk to her again."

"But maybe you should," Barney spoke up. "It certainly would help put a period at the end of everything that's happened to you." He smiled. "She saved your life, so I owe her a debt of gratitude."

Amy nodded. "Maybe you're right. I'll think about it."

CHAPTER 55

▼

The next day was cloudy and rain fell intermittently. It lent an autumn look to the air, but since it was only late August, Amy knew there would be many more hot days before cooler weather established itself. She supposed her mood, more than the weather, was the cause of her perception of change.

Amy had a feeling of closure. It was as if one phase of her life had ended and she was waiting for whatever the next phase would be. The horror of the crimes committed by two women she once thought were her friends, had changed the way she perceived people. She knew that forevermore, she would doubt her ability to know a person—to be certain that what she saw was the reality of that person.

She was on her way to the prison ward at the hospital to see Gayle. Both Ben and Barney agreed that the visit would be beneficial to Amy. Another way for her to bring to a close those dreadful weeks. She agreed with them, but most of all, she was grateful to Gayle for saving her life. If not for her, Leigh and Barney might very well be planning her funeral now.

This was the first time Amy had been to the secured section of the hospital. Prisoners from over the county and from the civilian-run Chacqua Prison were kept here for whatever treatment they needed. Dangerous psychiatric patients were temporarily treated here until they could be moved into more secure environments. Gayle qualified for this category.

Amy signed her name on the visitor's log and waited at the barred door while her escort, a tall, heavily built woman in uniform, who briefly introduced herself as Officer Paladine, handed the proper papers through to the guard on the other side. The heavy metal door slid open to allow the two women through, then shut with a clang behind them.

She followed her escort down a long hallway and into an open ward. The odor of disinfectant permeated the air, reminding Amy of the smells she encountered when she volunteered at the nursing home.

Several female patients occupied narrow metal beds down each side of the room. There was a rattling of chains that were fastened to the beds and ended in cuffs on the prisoner's legs. Their arms were free and two of the women raised their index fingers to the female guard. She seemed unmoved by their antics, and Amy caught a slight smile on the guard's face. She realized the woman was enjoying Amy's initiation into the world of prison life.

"You come to see the animals, little girl?" A woman who had to be seventy years old if she was a day, jeered at Amy as she passed by.

"All right, Thelma, behave yourself." The officer spoke mildly.

Amy kept her head down and her eyes on her feet, as she walked between the beds. There was a curtain drawn around the last one to give a semblance of privacy. Even here, death deserved a little dignity. As she stepped around the cloth barrier, she was shocked to see the drastic change in Gayle. Black circles spread from the inside corners of her eyes, all the way to her cheekbones. An involuntary shiver ran over Amy, leaving goose bumps on her arms.

"You've got fifteen minutes, Miss," Paladine said, as she moved several paces away from Gayle's bed, but still inside the curtained area. She folded her arms across her generous chest to wait until the visit was over. Amy was relieved she wouldn't be alone with Gayle.

"I'm glad to see you, Amy." The words came very faintly.

Gayle wore an oxygen mask, and she was connected to an I.V. drip and a heart monitor. But there was no respirator, nor any other piece of complicated machinery that Amy had expected to see. Gayle lifted her hand to remove the oxygen mask. Chains rattled as she moved and Amy saw that, different from the other women, both of Gayle's wrists wore steel bracelets connected to chains just long enough for her to reach her face. There was also a wide leather strap buckled around her lower hips as if extra insurance was needed that the prisoner would remain imprisoned.

From the ghastly illness imprinted in Gayle's features, Amy knew she barely had the strength to continue breathing, which was a very long way from having the energy it would require for her to affect escape.

Gayle's lovely smile reminded Amy of how badly she was fooled by the young woman's masquerade. Feelings were coming back now, and Amy allowed the anger to build inside, using it as an insulation against pity. Ben had told Amy that Gayle wished to die, and Amy thought that from the looks of her, she would soon get that wish.

"Sit here, please," Gayle said, her voice not much above a whisper. "I can't seem to get my breath."

Amy sat gingerly on the very edge of the mattress near the foot of the bed. She wanted to hear what Gayle had to say, but she wanted no physical contact with her. Gayle smiled again as if she understood.

"I'm sorry for what happened to you, Amy." Gayle's voice was not much more than a whisper. "All I ever wanted was to be your friend.'

Amy looked away and remained silent.

"My grandfather got my mother pregnant when she was only thirteen years old. That makes me my own aunt and my mother's sister. Lord knows how many other ways I'm kin to myself." Gayle's attempt to laugh brought on a bad few moments of coughing.

Alarmed, Amy turned to look at the guard, but the large woman only shrugged one shoulder and made no move to help. Amy reached for the oxygen mask and helped Gayle put it back on.

She finally got enough breath back to continue talking. With frequent stops to breathe from the mask, and to fight the pain, Gayle told the pitiful tale of her youth. Some of it was familiar to Amy from what Pinky had told her, but it sounded different when told by the one who had lived through those experiences.

Lester Griffith was a self-taught preacher. An evil man, he used his professed faith in God to rule over Gayle and her mother. He treated them as his slaves and used them as whores. Her mother did nothing to keep him from sexually assaulting Gayle, too terrified to protect her only child.

When she was fourteen, Gayle's life took a turn for what she thought was the better. By then she had developed large breasts and a full figure that was far more mature than the average young teenager. Walter Thurmond, a handsome young man back then, began to pay attention to her whenever she came into his father's Sun Belle grocery store. She knew he was much older than she, but was flattered when he told her she was pretty. One day he asked if she would meet him that night at one of the beer joints near the edge of town. She agreed.

She had slipped out of the house into the dark night, and had walked the three miles into town, and from there all the way across town to the beer joint Walter had chosen. He and several of his friends were waiting for her, Abner Waggoner being one of them.

Gayle foolishly agreed to go for a ride in Walter's brand new Buick roadster. He took her farther out into the country, on a deserted back road where there were no houses, and he and his friends gang-raped her. When they had all had their turn, Walter raped her again.

They left her lying by the side of the road. She managed to get back home without Lester's seeing her. Her hair was a mess, her dress torn and dirty. Gayle realized that she served as merely a few minutes of fun and sexual release for the men. A dumb country hick to be used and thrown away like garbage.

Weeks later, when Gayle knew she was pregnant, she told her mother. Irene spit in her face and told her if she hadn't been whoring around, she wouldn't have gotten pregnant. Irene knew that Lester had been sexually molesting her daughter for years, so Gayle could only wonder at her mother's reasoning. She decided to tell Walter, on the odd chance that he would be willing to help her.

She went into the grocery store, called him aside, and told him that she was pregnant.

His face had paled at first, then turned red with rage. He called her ugly names and said she'd better not come in his store again, or he'd claim she'd stolen something and get her into bad trouble. Walter had looked at her with loathing. "You're not blaming me and my friends for something some old red neck boyfriend of yours did. You're nothing but a no good slut."

Three days later, Walter's father had come to her house. In Lester's presence, he offered her money to have an abortion. "Or," he had said, "you can have that baby. Either way, you keep your mouth shut about my son." He had just admitted that he thought her child was his grandchild and thought nothing of killing it. Mr. Thurmond would not allow his precious son and his elitist friends to take responsibility for what they had done.

Lester had said nothing during the conversation. He held out his hand for the money, then pointed Mr. Thurmond out the door. He took off his wide leather belt and beat Gayle until she lost consciousness, then kicked her repeatedly in the stomach. She lost the baby a few days later.

As soon as Gayle healed from the beating and from losing the baby, she forced her mother to give her some of the money Mr. Thurmond had left. She threatened to tell Lester where Irene hid her whiskey if she didn't. Irene gave her the money.

Gayle bought a bus ticket to Little Rock where she got a job as a waitress. She was fired for dropping a tray of glasses. She walked out to the highway and hitched a ride on the first eighteen-wheeler that stopped. She paid for her travel in crummy motel rooms each night, and only stopped running when she reached Atlanta, Georgia.

A waitress at a truck stop told Gayle about an opening at her sister's flower and plant nursery. "My sister ain't gonna' ask you how old you are, honey," the woman told her.

Gayle walked the five miles to the nursery to apply for that job, and got it. Mr. And Mrs. Rainchild, the owners, not only didn't ask questions, but allowed Gayle to stay rent-free in one of the storage rooms. behind the hot house. She more than paid them back with the long hours she put into the job. But Gayle liked working, it made the time pass faster, and she was glad they didn't try to get close to her. She had things to do and wanted no interference.

Almost a year later, Gayle had saved enough money to buy a round-trip bus ticket to Ashley Springs. She arrived on a Saturday as planned, then spent the day in the city park. For lunch she bought a candy bar and cold drink, leaving her only two dollars to eat on until she could get back to Atlanta.

When the sun had gone down, and the day began to gray, Gayle began her trek to the Blue Lagoon Club, a fancy name for a run-down whore house outside of the city limits. She got there well before eleven o' clock. She settled down under a tree only a few feet from the building's back door.

At exactly eleven, Lester stumbled down the rickety steps and headed for his truck. He always parked it a quarter of a mile down the road, suffering from the illusion that no one knew of his trips to the whore house. He was so drunk that he didn't hear her slip up behind him.

"Hi, Lester," she said, not a foot away from his back. When he swung around to see who had spoken, Gayle plunged an eight-inch butcher knife into his gut. "I hope that hurts as bad as the kicking you gave me, you old bastard." He slumped to the ground without uttering a word. She stayed long enough to be sure he had no pulse.

Gayle put the knife into a plastic bag she'd brought for that purpose. She would make very certain that the murder weapon was never found. She walked rapidly back to the city park where she stayed until daylight. Then she caught the six o'clock bus and left Ashley Springs.

CHAPTER 56

▼

Gayle said she wrote to her mother once, telling Irene where she lived. She never got an answer. Six months after Gayle had killed Lester, she received a letter from a lawyer in Ashley Springs, saying that her mother had committed suicide by hanging herself. From him she learned that she had inherited the farm. The lawyer also said that her mother left a sealed envelope with him addressed to Gayle. She made the trip back to Arkansas to sign papers, make arrangements to lease the farm, and to pick up her letter.

In spite of the unloving history between them, she hoped that her mother would at last say something that confirmed her daughter's right to life. After all the years of being told what a burden and mistake she was, Gayle hoped that her mother had found it in her heart to give her that one last thing of worth.

She left the lawyer's office with the letter and walked to the city park where she sat on a bench to read it. Written on the front of the envelope was the word, "Mary." The note read:

I'm leaving here because there's nothing in this world to keep me. I don't know how you managed it, but I know you murdered my daddy. You've been nothing but a pain and a burden since you were born. Then you took from me the only human being I ever loved. I hope you have a miserable life. Irene.

Tears streamed down Gayle's face, as she quoted her mother's note verbatim. In spite of all that Amy knew of this woman, she felt a deep sorrow for that young girl who was treated so cruelly. Amy took tissues from a box on the stand near the bed and handed them to her. Gayle closed her eyes for a several minutes, looking totally exhausted.

Again Amy looked to Paladin, but the officer continued to ignore her. After what seemed a very long time, Gayle continued her effort. She now had enough money to find a better job and a nicer apartment. In her search through the old farm house, she had found thousands of dollars in cash hidden in cans and boxes in odd places. Her grandfather had apparently saved almost every dollar he'd ever made as a backhoe operator.

But Gayle continued to work at the nursery and live in the rent-free storage room. She felt safe there. She had wrapped the money she'd found in her mother's favorite scarf, then tucked it beneath some old clothing she kept in her suitcase.

Gayle was eighteen when she left Atlanta for New York City. She invested some of her money in a tiny doughnut shop located in a busy neighborhood in Brooklyn. She cleaned out the junky rooms above the store and made them into living quarters for herself. In only five years, Gayle had paid off the shop and doubled her investment.

"Remember I said that you can't go anywhere in the world without running into someone you know?" Gayle asked. Amy nodded that she did. "One day Rosalind came into my shop. We began talking and learned that we were from the same town. That started our friendship."

Rosalind had waited until Gayle closed her shop, so they could further explore their common interests. They began to see each other almost every day. Gayle thought Rosalind was everything she was not and was more than a little "star struck." It was hard for Rosalind to convince Gayle that their lives should have but one focus, revenge on the men who had so badly mistreated the two of them. At first the plans had no reality for Gayle. It was like make-believe, nothing the two of them would actually do. Just something they could fantasize about.

The idea of killing the men was so cleverly introduced, that Gayle hadn't known exactly at what point it became the only form of revenge. Thinking back, she knew it was after she had confessed that she had killed her grandfather. Only much later did she learn that Rosalind had killed her entire family.

"I was so wrong to get involved with her," she whispered. She motioned toward the water pitcher on her bedside table. Amy poured some into a glass and helped her raise her head. She let out a whimper of pain, as she tried to sip the water.

"You've talked far too long, Gayle." Amy said. "I'll come back later."

"Please, Amy, I won't be here later."

The pallor of her face was a dirty gray. The dark circles under her eyes had spread to her temples, and her breath came in shorter and shorter gasps. Amy knew she was speaking the truth. Reluctantly, she sat back down, but this time she moved a little closer.

"I managed to sneak a look at the journal Rosalind kept. Apparently she had a natural aptitude for cutting," Gayle whispered. "She might have made a better surgeon than her father. The mutilations she described in her journal made me sick."

Gayle said that Billy Joe had killed Bud Purefoy. He had done it because he thought that would make Rosalind grateful enough to sleep with him. To her, he was just a stupid jerk who fit into her plan.

"The night you came to dinner, the sheriff showed up too. Rosalind hadn't expected him to make his move so quickly. She forced him upstairs. I left you to plead with her not to kill him, at least not while you were there. You know the rest."

Gayle pushed back into her pillow, and Amy knew she was in great pain. Then she relaxed and seemed to stop breathing. Amy turned to the matron once again. "She needs help. Please call a nurse."

The woman unfolded her large arms and stepped over to the bed to feel Gayle's pulse. "Her heart's still beating. She's just passed out is all. She shouldn't have talked so much."

For the first time, Amy saw that the matron was holding a small tape recorder. The big woman punched a button and Amy could hear it rewinding.

"I missed out on some of what she said at the last when she got to whispering. That's got to be the worst tale I ever heard," the guard said conversationally, as the whirring of the tape stopped. "If she said anything the authorities need to know, then it's all right here." Amy wondered how legal that was.

"Let's go." Paladine turned and started back down the aisle.

Amy turned to see Gayle had opened her eyes. She hesitated, then leaned close to the exhausted woman on the bed.

"Gayle," she said, softly. "I'm sorry for how you were treated as a young person. I know it must have been absolute torture, not having an adult to help you. I wish with all my heart that I had been nicer to you when we were children. But what you and Rosalind did was hideously inhuman, and I'm glad the two of you were stopped."

Gayle opened her eyes, and her smile once again reminded Amy of how beautiful Mary Gayle Griffith had been. "Amy, you look up karma?"

"I did. According to the dictionary, it loosely means fate. But what you did was not fore-ordained, Gayle. You made your own choices, and they were dreadful beyond my understanding. You could have left Rosalind when you knew what her intentions were. Even now, you aren't a helpless victim of fate.

"You can tell God you're deeply sorry for the part you played in those men's deaths and ask His forgiveness. If you truly mean it, He will take you home to Him. I hope you will do that Gayle. Somehow that would make all the horror you helped to generate less potent and less tragic."

"You're probably right," Gayle smiled weakly. "I can't imagine any god who could forgive me. I can't forgive myself." Her eyes drooped, as she whispered, "Don't forget me, my friend."

"I don't think I could, Gayle," Amy said. "I'll ask Father Dolan to come talk to you." She turned and walked swiftly out of the ward. To Amy's relief, the matron had waited for her at the first set of bars.

As Amy left the hospital, a fresh breeze made the leaves dance and tree limbs sway. Most of the clouds had blown away, leaving a clean blue sky above. The welcome warmth of the sun helped to leach the chill from her bones. Amy felt that she'd left behind a tremendous burden, leaving her with a special lift to her heart. The long nightmare was over. The two who had brought so much terror and sorrow to this quiet community would never hurt anyone again.

"Need a ride?" Ben's Explorer was parked at the curb.

"My car is in the parking lot," she said, smiling.

"We'll come back for it later." Ben held out his hand to assist her up into the vehicle.

As Amy settled into the seat beside him, and he continued to hold her hand, she felt as if she'd just entered a safe haven. That told her something about her feelings for Ben. His place in her life was one of the many things she needed to think about.

CHAPTER 57

▼

Amy flopped down in a chair on her lower deck, feeling grim and disgruntled. Gayle had died early that morning. Amy had received a call from the hospital saying they had a piece of paper that said she was responsible for the body.

Puzzled and a whole lot unwilling, she had called the funeral home and made arrangements for them to transfer Gayle's body to their facility. Now she had to figure out what she was supposed to do next. She had placed a call to her lawyer, Joseph Trellis. He was to call her back.

Her cell phone rang at just that moment. Thinking it was Joseph, she answered reluctantly on the third ring.

"I was beginning to think you weren't in." Leigh's cheerful voice sounded in her ear. "How are you, darling?"

"Not feeling particularly well right now." Amy told her aunt how Gayle had made her responsible for her funeral.

"I know that's a shock to you," Leigh agreed, "but when you think about it, Gayle had no family. The last kind act performed for her in this world came from you."

"Maybe, but I thought after yesterday that anything having to with Gayle was behind me. It was so bad having to see her in such agony and to listen to the terrible things that happened to her. I felt a huge relief for her, and for me, that it was all coming to an end."

"Be patient for just a little longer, Amy, and it will be."

"I'm waiting now for a call from Joseph. I'm hoping he can tell me how to go about this so that everything is legal. If Gayle left enough money, I'll use that for the casket. Ugh, I don't even want to think about it."

"I'm sorry you have to, Sweetheart. I wish I could be of some help."

"Joseph will help me, and Barney is on standby. Anita even called to say she would help any way she can. I asked if she felt like going to the shop for a while and she seemed very pleased that I asked."

"Then I'll get off the phone so Joseph can call. I'll talk to you later."

When Joseph did call, it was to say that she should go ahead and make whatever arrangements she needed to. "Lucas Weatherby, the new lawyer in town, became Gayle's lawyer late yesterday afternoon," he said. "She'd asked Father Dolan to recommend a lawyer and he suggested Lucas. As far as legal aspects, you're fine. As for financial, Gayle managed to sign a check, so you're to take whatever money you need from her account at the Sugarloaf State Bank. Lucas said there's enough to cover whatever you deem necessary."

Amy thanked him and put the phone down. It had just dawned on her that she had to find a burial plot for Gayle. She picked up the phone again. When the receptionist at the funeral home answered, Amy asked what did she need to do to buy a plot.

"Oh, you'll have to come in and let me show you what's available," the woman said. "Did you want to bury the deceased in Ashley Springs?"

Amy shuddered at the term "deceased." It sounded so cold and impersonal. "Yes, I'd like one in the city cemetery if possible. I'll be there in a few minutes."

She found a single plot in the back part of the cemetery away from the city street traffic. It was under a very old oak tree and the view was across a creek and into the woods. She went back to the funeral home to sign the papers which made her the owner of a very small piece of real estate. She would wait to cash Gayle's check when she knew what the total amount would be when everything was done. She then hurriedly picked out a casket and ordered a blanket of white roses to cover it.

It was cloudy the day of the funeral, as if the heavens themselves understood the sadness of a young woman's wasted life. Barney and Amy stood on one side of the open grave, while Anita, Nancy, and Brenda stood on the other. Except for Father Dolan, no one else came to say goodbye. The priest read the Twenty-Third Psalm and said a prayer for Gayle's soul. In less than fifteen minutes, they were all making their way back to their cars. Amy thanked Father Dolan for his kindness and Anita and the two girls for their thoughtfulness.

After the others had driven off, Amy said, "I'm going home, Barney. I think I need to weed flowers and just generally get away from it all."

"Yes, you should. I'll call you this evening. Maybe you'll be interested in going out somewhere for dinner."

The phone was ringing when she walked into the house. It was Ben.

"Sorry I couldn't be there this afternoon," he said. "I wanted to be with you during a very unpleasant time. Are you okay?"

"I am now, thank you. There were six of us there counting Father Dolan. That was three more than I expected. Where are you now?"

"I'm sitting in Captain Banachelli's office. He's gone to get a couple of other men. We'll probably be in the war room all night."

Ben had gotten a call from his old boss in St. Louis who insisted that Ben catch the quickest flight out to help him with what he described as a knotty problem. Amy had asked Ben what he supposed the problem was. "It is a particularly nasty crime spree going on in his district. He wants to talk it over to see if we can come up with a strategy that might lead to the capture of the killer. We did a lot of that when I worked for him."

Amy suspected the trip was about more than just a consultation. Ben would probably be offered a job. "I'm sure he will appreciate the help," she said now.

"The Captain just came back in. I think everyone is ready to start the meeting. Stay safe, Amy. I'll call you later."

She felt a tinge of sadness after she hung up. She knew Ben would take the job in St. Louis, then slowly but surely their friendship would dissolve into nothing. She heaved a sigh, then said, "Come on, Hannibal. Let's go weed those flowers."

The big dog got up from his place at Amy's feet and followed her outside.

The next morning, Joseph called to say she needed to come in to talk to him. He wouldn't tell her why, just said that it would be interesting. It was. Gayle had made Amy her sole heir. The huge surprise was the size of her inheritance. She had left behind over a quarter of a million dollars in cash, plus some very successful investments, and the farm land that was a real estate developer's dream.

A stunned Amy looked at Joseph accusingly. "What am I supposed to do with all that?"

"Whatever you want to do with it, is my guess," Joseph said, smiling at Amy's unhappiness. "I know of a lot of people who wouldn't even ask that question."

"A lot of people haven't enough to worry about then. Gayle should have left it to charity." She rose from her chair to leave, then said, "I'm sorry, Joseph. I didn't mean to sound like an ingrate, but I don't feel I've earned the right to have that much money at my disposal." She looked thoughtful for a moment, then added, "I may have an idea or two, though. I'll talk to you after I've finished whatever legal things there are for me to do."

Life really is strange sometimes, Amy thought, as she left the building and walked toward her car. Ideas began to rush through her mind, and she felt an excitement begin to grow as one after another came quickly to the fore.

Amy had already decided she would sell the farmland and add that money to the rest. As she felt for the car keys in her purse, an inspiration bloomed in her mind. Almost fully conceived, she could picture a beautiful center for abused mothers and children. Its program would provide a counseling team, both moral and financial support systems, and a long-range follow-up plan.

Such an organization just might save a few children from being twisted into inept or dangerous adults by their cruel caretakers. The plan would need working on, and it would also need a board of directors that knew appropriate practices for early childhood, but it could be done.

Amy felt as if she had just found something special and unique that, thanks to Gayle, could be more than just a good idea and would add new meaning to her own life. She even thought that the dying woman may have foreseen her coming up with something like this.

Amy smiled. As she got into her car, she said aloud, "Yes, Gayle, I think you knew *exactly* what you were doing."

EPILOGUE

▼

August 25, 2004: These past several weeks have changed me in ways I don't even know. The fact that I was unable to discern the evil right next to me in the shop every day, but yet had premonitions of the deaths, is the most confusing to me. I assumed at the time that God was responsible for me having those visions, even though the face of the killer was never revealed. What disturbs me now is, what if those visions were from a darker authority? That really scares me. I need to take the advice I gave Gayle, then find a way to make my life more meaningful. I take an awful lot for granted. But I also think I may have already started that very thing with the center I and others are planning.

After Ben read Rosalind's journal, he said that everything they had only suspected up to that point proved to be true. Rosalind claimed she'd been killing people since before she got out of the sanatarium. Even in the institution, she had killed a male nurse by pushing a sharpened pencil through his ear, piercing his brain. It was blamed on "some crazy" as Rosalind put it. She also admitted to killing Dr. Menche, who was responsible for her being put into the mental institution. The list was long. Rosalind was an evil killing machine that had no conscience. Thank God she is forever stopped.

Nancy Waggoner is in college at Fayetteville. She's doing great and loves it. Nancy's mother, Anita, is working in my shop. She's so good at everything, that I don't think it will be long before I can leave her in charge. The neatest thing— Barney and Anita have taken a liking for each other. I think they would really be good together. Poor Pinkie will probably not come back to work. She's so broken up over Tim's death.

When Nadine learned of William's criminal behavior, she moved to Memphis where her sister lives. His business has gone downhill, no one speaks to him, and he couldn't be more miserable. What goes around, comes around. Not karma as Gayle believed, but the result of not looking behind you to see where you've been, so you can make corrections for future behavior. I think it's called learning from your mistakes.

Which brings me to Ben. I made a big mistake four years ago when I married Stephen. I learned that two people need to share the same values to make a marriage succeed. Not that Ben and I are anywhere near that point. It's just that I know my feelings for him are growing deeper, and I believe his for me are, too. This may prove to be a moot point anyway. I know he'll accept the position as head of the Department of Detectives, or whatever they call it, because I know that's what he wants. He asked me last night if I'd be interested in living in St. Louis. I told him I didn't think Hannibal could handle all that city traffic. I miss him so much, and he's been gone only a short time.

I already have a buyer for Mary Gayle's property. They didn't even stutter with I named my price. I may have that Center for battered women and abused children a lot sooner than I first thought. Mrs. Parkington, through Ben, learned what my plans are, and insisted I have the Anderson property also. The house burned to its foundation two weeks ago. No foul play is suspected. The fire chief said it was faulty wiring. I'm glad it's gone, and the acreage will make a perfect location for the center I'm planning. Happy children running and playing there will be the perfect antidote for the cruelty and tragedy represented via the Andersons. All's well that ends well, thank the Lord.

August 27, 2004   Leigh has talked me into making the trip to New York with her. From there she wants us to tour Europe. It sounds good to me. I am so ready to get away from the recent memories and start over with my life. Anita can handle the shop with Barney's help, and I've hired two women, both of whom I believe will work out well. I've got some shopping to do for the trip, although I do plan to buy a few things in Paris and London. That sound's so good!

P.S. Ben just called. He asked me to marry him. He said that he would refuse to take the job, even though he's been told it's his (how did I know that?). He offered to fly down tomorrow to put the ring on my finger. He doesn't realize that by *offering* to do that, instead of just doing it, shows me that he still has reservations about us. I told him that I thought the two of us would be giving up things now that would come back to haunt us. I was not willing to risk his future resentment, nor would I want to burden him with mine. I cried, then he cried, then I cried some more. We love each other, but not enough to make such a sacrifice. I hope I can remain strong in my decision for both our sakes. Life is never easy, it seems.

Amy B.

0-595-28370-5